(

BENEATH A PANAMANIAN MOON

BENEATH A PANAMANIAN MOON

DAVID TERRENOIRE

THOMAS DUNNE BOOKS
ST. MARTIN'S MINOTAUR
NEW YORK

THOMAS DUNNE BOOKS.
An imprint of St. Martin's Press.

www.minotaurbooks.com

Library of Congress Cataloging-in-Publication Data

Terrenoire, David.
    Beneath a Panamanian moon / David Terrenoire.—1st ed.
        p.   cm.
    ISBN 0-312-32131-7
    EAN 978-0312-32131-4
    1. Americans—Panama—Fiction. 2. Special operations (Military science)—Fiction. 3. Conspiracies—Fiction. 4. Pianists—Fiction. 5. Resorts—Fiction. 6. Panama—Fiction. 7. Hotels—Fiction. I. Title.

PS3620.E76B46   2005
813'.6—dc22
                                                            2004054944

First Edition: January 2005

10   9   8   7   6   5   4   3   2   1

To Jenny, who is good when times are good, and when times are bad, she's even better.

ACKNOWLEDGMENTS

I want to thank: My draft board, who inadvertently started this adventure. Richard Abate, a great champion, and Peter Wolverton, my patient editor. My mother, who always knew this would happen. Jerry Nutter and Richard Cerilli, who treated me like a writer even when I wasn't writing. Critical readers Melanie Raskin, Jim Palmer, Daun Daemon, Ken Alexander, Connie Riddle, Soren Palmer, and Nick Puryear; early supporters Laurie Harper, Kellie Johnson, Amy Bagwell, John Douglas, Luke Dempsey, and Jay Acton; and all those in my family who helped make this possible. Ladies and gentlemen, we have a book.

BENEATH A PANAMANIAN MOON

CHAPTER ONE

The old man's never more entertaining than when he's pissed, which is most of the time.

"They searched me down to my goddamn socks in Beirut," he said. "Then I got wedged between a fat man and a gum snapper all the way to Munich." He sneezed. "And I think I picked up a bug from a sticky little bastard at Heathrow."

Jackpot.

I watched him in the rearview as he wiped his nose, refolded his handkerchief, and tucked it away. That reminded me to reach across and pull the revolver, snug in its holster, from the glove compartment. I handed it back to the old man. He took a moment to empty the cylinder, work the action, reload, and then clip the piece to his hip.

Smith was one of the last guys on earth to pack a .38. A wheel gun, he called it. Once, when I asked him why, he said he'd never felt comfortable carrying a .45 cocked and locked. "I might shoot off something I'd miss," he said. "Besides, it's not the caliber of the gun, but the caliber of the man behind the gun."

Smith was full of sayings like that, like a fortune cookie with hair.

Settling back into the seat, the old man pulled a flask, took a drink, and then dropped the top on the floor. He disappeared as he snagged the cap, and when his bullet-shaped head reappeared in the mirror, he was as red as a ham.

He caught me. "What's so goddamn funny?"

"Nothing, sir."

"You hand a man a gun and then laugh? Not too smart, Harper."

"No, sir."

He sniffled. "Damn season," he said. "Damn snow. Damn ice. Damn airplanes. Damn government cars." He glared at me in the mirror. "Sweet Christ, boy, turn up the goddamn heat and keep your eyes on the road."

"Yes, sir."

"Cold as a hooker's heart," Smith said. He took another pull from the flask. "I don't know how you stand living here. Like a goddamn Rotary Club, up to its keister in glad-handing boyos with nothing on their minds but money and ass." He sniffled again and coughed.

"Yes, sir."

"You know who I miss?" Without waiting for me to answer he said, "Reagan. The man had style. And the rumor is, his wife gave the best goddamn head in Hollywood. That's impressive, considering the competition, don't you think?" Smith pulled out the handkerchief again, coughed something wet into it, stared at that for a moment, and then tucked it back inside his suit.

"Son, you know what a dialogue is?"

"Yes, sir."

"I say something then you say something back?"

"Yes, sir."

"Just checking. Thought maybe you'd gone to sleep on me up there."

"Watching the road, Mr. Smith."

"Right." Smith settled back into the seat again and we let the rumble of government tires on federal asphalt fill the car.

Smith coughed again and said, "You picked him up? At the airport?"

"Yes, sir. This morning, right on schedule." I had done Smith this favor, knowing that he would try to talk me into something or out of something before the day was through, and I was working up the strength to say no.

"You bug him?"

"I'm retired, sir. You know that."

Smith coughed again. "That doesn't answer my question."

"Yes, sir. I did. One on his person and one in his bag."

"Good boy."

"You didn't say who would be recording."

"That's right. I didn't say."

"But someone is recording him while he's here, right?"

"When I want to be interrogated, Harper, I'll see the wife."

"Yes, sir." I pulled around an SUV the size of a small family farm and gave the driver, a young woman on a cell phone, the evil eye, which she ignored.

"So you saw him, you talked to him?"

"Yes, sir."

"Now, impress me with your powers of observation."

"I'm retired, sir."

"You said that."

"Just so you know. This is just a ride."

"So, you didn't see anything, huh? The guy was just a fucking vapor. Maybe you've gone soft, Harper. Maybe you should think about retiring."

"I am retired."

"Oh, right, you said that."

I'm embarrassed to admit that I wanted to show off for the old man. "He came in from Miami," I said, "which doesn't really tell me much, but it does narrow the airlines and embarkation points. From his accent I'd say he's originally from the Midwest, probably Chicago. His suit's off the rack. He wore a wedding ring, and a West Point class ring, the same year as yours, so I figure you were classmates."

I waited for a word of encouragement. Instead he growled, "It's not about me, boy."

"Yes, sir." Satisfied, I went on. "The Christmas tan means he either spends time under the lights or he's someplace warm."

"Which do you think?" Smith watched me in the mirror as I answered.

"The beach, sir. That's what I think."

"Why?"

"He wears eyeglasses and he had tan lines at his temples. You don't wear glasses on a tanning bed, sir." I gave it a pause. "But that's just a guess. As I said before, I'm retired."

Smith nodded. I let the glow distract me and I drifted across the lane. I jerked the car back, tossing my passenger across the rear seat.

"Goddamn, Harper, you're a fucking menace."

"Sorry, sir. Maybe you should buckle your seat belt."

He growled again.

I pulled into the right lane to let the faster cars zip by. It was past morning rush hour, but the highway was crowded, as it always is around Washington.

"Okay. So, besides the ring and the tan, what else did you see?"

"Well, since you two know each other—"

"He said that?"

"No, sir, I just figured you were classmates at the Point—"

"Anyone can buy a ring, Harper."

"So he wasn't a classmate?"

"I'm telling you not to assume anything or you'll end up wearing your ass for a hat," Smith said.

"Yes, sir."

"Even though you're retired," he said.

I looked up into the rearview and thought I caught a small grin sneak across his lips. "But with all I saw, and you telling me to plant a bug on him, and the line of work you're in, I figure he might be the real thing."

"The real thing?"

"Like you, sir."

"You think I'm the real thing?"

"Yes, sir. I do."

Smith ran a hand over his face. The trip from wherever he'd been had tired him and I could tell he was losing interest in the game, his mind already on the meeting ahead. "Don't believe everything you hear about me, Harper."

"No, sir."

"So what's your conclusion about our visitor?"

"His hands are soft, sir. Someone else does his humping for him. He works someplace warm, he came in from Miami, and looking at the flight schedules into Miami, I'd guess he came in from Honduras, but maybe not. He could have flown in yesterday and spent the night."

"Not bad," Smith grunted. "For someone who's retired." He shook the flask next to his ear, judging from the slosh how much he had left. He hit on the neck again and looked out the window.

The gray Potomac rolled by and across the river the top of the Jefferson Memorial gleamed as white as ice cream. When we crossed Memorial Bridge Smith asked, "What did he say when you didn't take him to the Pentagon?"

"He asked if we were heading into the city, sir. I told him we were."

"Uh-huh," he said, in that noncommittal way that tells me nothing.

I turned onto Pennsylvania Avenue.

"You're too young to remember, but Lafayette Park was once full of hippies telling us Uncle Ho was going to kick our ass."

"Yes, sir." I hoped he wasn't going to talk about Vietnam again. Smith could talk your ear off about his glory days. "And Uncle Ho did kick your ass," I said. "Sir."

Smith burned the back of my neck with his glare. "But Uncle Ho's dead now, isn't he?"

"Last I heard, sir."

Smith laughed. "And how's your new life working out, Harper? You and that piano, I bet you're up to your keister in congressional wives."

"I like my work, sir."

"I bet you do. Well, get it while you can, boy, because when you're as old as I am, the only thing you'll regret is the tail you didn't get. Trust me on that."

"Yes, sir."

"What have we got in the park today? A couple bums," Smith said.

"It's the day before Christmas, sir," I said.

"Really?"

I knew Smith, and I knew he thought of time as just another element of battle, as real and weighted with consequence as hills and weather, but the calendar, except for the turning of seasons, always seemed to catch him by surprise. I often enjoyed reminding him of holidays and anniversaries, just to hear that genuine grunt of astonishment. It made Smith seem fallible.

I pulled up to the brick town house, got out and held the door while Smith unfolded from the rear seat.

"Thank you, Harper. This shouldn't be long."

"I'll wait, sir."

Inside the car, I adjusted the volume on the radio. I heard someone say, "Major Snelling, he's here."

"How's he look?" I recognized the voice of the man I'd picked up at Dulles.

"Like he's eaten snakes for breakfast."

Snelling laughed. The rustling of mic on fabric followed, a door opened, another door, and then his greeting, as big and as unproductive as summer thunder. "Jim, it's damn good to see you. Called the wife yet?"

"I was hoping this would be a pleasure trip," Smith said.

Snelling laughed, too loud and too long.

"So, what's up? Why call me in from the field?" Smith hated aimless chitchat, which made him a great soldier, I guessed, but I couldn't imagine it was a good thing in a spy. But then, he was a different kind of spy.

I heard the smack of papers land on a tabletop. "We have a situation," Snelling said.

There was silence. I assumed Smith was reading whatever Snelling had tossed his way. After a moment Smith said, "I know both of them. This one's good. That Silver Star should have been a Medal of Honor, and would have been under another commanding officer. The other one, I'm glad the son of a bitch is out of the service. He got good men killed for no good reason."

"He's in Panama."

"Really? Great. Nice place for him to die. Maybe something painful."

"He's managing a resort hotel."

"Civilian?"

Snelling laughed. "On the outside. But the place is crawling with mercs."

"So what do we know about the place?"

"We think the hotel is the headquarters for a new private military corporation, a PMC."

"They're popping up all over the globe, offering so much money for the right skills that it's getting tough keeping the special ops guys in uniform. But what's in Panama?"

"They're training bodyguards and security forces for wealthy Latin American families. That's what we know."

"Uh-huh."

"But recently we had a boy come home in a bag."

"From Panama? Jesus Christ, he die from the clap?"

I heard the scrape of a chair. I looked up from the car and saw a man standing in the third-floor window. It was Snelling, looking down. I hoped he didn't recognize me. He said, "It's a mess down there, Jim. You know things are bad in Colombia."

"Yeah, I know."

"With the rebels kidnapping an oil man every goddamn week, the drug war blossoming into a shooting war, and the normal fucked-up politics of the place, we don't need a band of well-armed adrenaline junkies stirring shit up."

"What with all the terrorist threats, the Canal's got to be a real sphincter tuck for the administration."

"Roger that. All it would take is a good C-4 charge against one of the locks and we've got nothing but a big goddamn mud bowl."

"So how does this tie in with the hotel?"

"We don't know. And we'd like to know. Jim, you remember a boy named Winstead?"

"John Winstead? Yeah. I served with him in the Balkans. Boy's a great shot up close, not much for long distances. Perfect for the jungle. Why? He looking for a job?"

"He was the boy in the bag."

There was a very long stretch of silence. When Smith did speak it was barely loud enough to be picked up. "I didn't want to hear that," he said.

"He was killed with his own shotgun. What's that sound like to you?"

"He wouldn't let an enemy get close enough," Smith said. "So I'd look real hard at his friends."

"That's what we thought."

"I liked that boy. What can I do?"

"This whole crew is on a long leash. We need you to find out what's up so we can rein the bastards in. There's chatter on some of the South American lines about something big coming on New Year's, but we don't know what and we don't know where. We think it might be Panama. We'd like to rule these guys out if we can, friend or foe."

"That only gives us eight days. Why not call on some old friends in the area? I'm sure we have a few down there who still have teeth."

"We're working that end," Snelling said, "but we need an independent source. Someone on the ground."

"So you don't trust our old Latin American friends."

"I didn't say that."

"But you want the place shut down?"

"I didn't say that, either. All we want is information. Then maybe with a change in management we can turn this op to our advantage."

I heard Smith light another cigarette. It was his way of stalling, giving himself time to think. "Is Langley behind this?"

"They swear they're not, Jim, and we're inclined to believe them."

"And you want someone from my crew, someone who's outside the normal channels."

"Exactly."

"Do you want someone to gather intelligence," Smith said, "or someone proficient in wet work?"

There was a long pause.

"I need to know," said Smith.

"Intelligence is what we need. We're on the other thing."

"I'm flattered, but why my network?"

"You have someone who's been contacted by this PMC."

A private military corporation was a relatively new example of American entrepreneurial spirit. In places all over the globe, PMCs were marketing themselves as experts in security. Their personnel were drawn, usually through a personal recommendation, from the ranks of former special ops or psy ops military. Back in the day, you could become a mercenary just by answering an ad in a magazine. Now, you needed a solid résumé and references. Corporations had taken over guns for hire.

I had been hit on twice by PMCs, one recently, but the thought of sleeping in mud and eating animals I normally see in zoos held absolutely no interest for me. I'd turned down both without a second thought.

"And this op of mine, what happened when the PMC made its offer?"

"Said he wasn't interested." I heard rustling papers. Snelling said, "This is one of yours?"

Smith was silent for a moment and I knew he was looking at the papers. And then he laughed. "This is priceless," he said. "Just fucking priceless."

A D.C. cop tapped my window and I just about jumped out of my skin. The cop, a look of deep, existential boredom on his face, spun his hand in a lazy loop, telling me either to roll down my window or that he'd mastered a few very small rope tricks. I took a guess and rolled down the window. "Yes, Officer?"

"You can't park here," he said.

"I'm waiting for my boss." I reached into my jacket, slowly, not wanting to spook him, and pulled out my White House credentials. They were phony, of course, but there wasn't a cop in the city that could tell them from the real thing, even side by side.

The cop looked at the ID, and then my face, matching the photo to the flesh. "Who's your boss?"

"I'm sorry, Officer, but that's classified."

Right away I knew it was the wrong thing to say. Some cops actually get off on that secret stuff. They want to think they're strapping on a firearm every morning and stepping into a city peopled with Sidney Greenstreets and Mata Haris. But a lot of cops resent it, too, because it makes them feel locked out of the big game, and it's tough to figure which ones will play along and which ones won't until you pull it on them.

This one had never heard of Sidney Greenstreet. "Sir, if you don't move your vehicle I'm going to have it towed."

I didn't want him calling me in. This particular identity was good but, like congressional integrity, it was a mile wide and an inch deep. So I thanked him, rolled around the block, cursing the traffic. Once back in range I heard Smith say, "What happens if things get rough?"

"Can your boy handle himself?"

Smith snorted. "In a roomful of *chicas,* maybe."

It was suddenly very hot inside the car. I cracked a window.

"Listen, we'll expedite whatever needs to be done," Snelling said. "The administration is committed to democracy in Latin America, but if the president sees anything even remotely resembling a wild-hair freelance militia, even if most of them are all-American, he'll send in the marines to cut some heads."

"Déjà vu, huh, Snelling?"

Snelling muttered something I couldn't make out. Then he said, "I appreciate this, Jim, I do."

"Yeah. Can I go back to work now?"

"Why don't you take a few days, go see Mildred. It's Christmas, Jim."

"I can't, Mack. I don't have time."

"At least let me buy you dinner."

"Thanks, but I've got plans."

After a short silence, Snelling said, "Okay. But keep in touch, Jim, and let me know. I've got one of my own on the ground who can watch your boy's back, just in case. He's not so good at intel, but there's nobody better if things break ugly."

"You think it'll get rough?"

Snelling sighed, long and hard. "That depends on your boy."

(

CHAPTER TWO

A resort hotel in Panama is looking for an employee with a military background and special skills. My guess is they don't mean busboys who can sew, or chambermaids who can yodel. When Smith got back into the car he said, "So, did you hear?"

I said I did.

"Are you ready?"

"Ready for what? Lunch?" I pulled into traffic, heading east.

"To go."

"Go where?"

"Where do you think?"

A cab nearly sideswiped us as I pulled up to the light. "I don't know," I said. "Where?"

"I thought you said you heard?" Smith was starting to get irritated, but not the entertaining kind of irritated.

"I did hear," I said, "just not everything." I told him about the cop, and the time it took to circle the block.

"Well, you missed some important stuff, son."

"I guess I did."

"A PMC is looking for a former soldier, possibly one with special ops training, who also plays the piano well enough to entertain very important people. Do you have any idea how rare a bird you are, Harper?"

I didn't say anything. I could see where this was going. First he'd appeal to my patriotism. Then he'd haul out that mentor bullshit. Then he'd threaten me.

"Why didn't you tell me you were recruited by a PMC?"

"At the risk of repeating myself, sir, I'm retired. I don't do that stuff anymore."

"You still should have told me. But all that's beside the point. You'll contact the PMC today and tell them you've reconsidered."

"But I haven't reconsidered."

"Look, this is no time to be coy. Your country needs you."

I got stuck behind another SUV, which sat through most of a green light before I tapped the horn. "Like before? You mean like when they needed me so much they left me treading water in the Mediterranean?"

"That's water over the bridge," Smith said. "It was a different situation. No boats this time. This time you're going to Panama."

I shook my head, certain I was hearing things. "You're kidding, right, sir? I heard Snelling say he needed someone with special skills. Now, I may have, at one time, had special skills, but I've let them fall away, sir, to the point where I no longer have those skills. In fact, if the truth were known, I am stunningly unskilled."

"You play the piano," Smith said.

"Okay, yes, I play the piano. That is my one skill."

"Lucky for you, that's the one we need."

"Who needs?" I turned onto Massachusetts and dodged a dump truck pulling out of the convention center site.

"The hotel in Panama. They are suddenly in need of a piano player. Their last one was . . ." Smith glanced out his window, mumbling something.

"What?"

Smith sighed, and looked me straight in the mirror. "I said their last piano player was eaten by a shark."

I swerved around two lobbyists.

"Why don't you pull over somewhere, son. I don't want you to run over anyone influential."

I ignored a cab honking behind me and pulled to the curb next to more construction. Gray dust settled over the car. Hard hats stared for a moment, but soon returned to standing around a slab that had been freshly poured over historical dirt.

I turned around so I could see Smith straight on, and said, "It's funny how a mirror can distort things. I thought you said their last piano player was eaten by a shark."

"I did."

"You're not talking metaphorically, as in 'his critics were vicious.'"

"No."

"You're talking about an actual shark, with fins and teeth and the title role in a popular film."

"Yes, a real shark," Smith said. He was exceedingly calm, considering the topic.

"Oh," I said. "Was this an accident?"

"No."

"Uh-huh."

"And they have a party planned for New Year's Eve so, of course, they need a piano player. Because the old one was, well—"

"Eaten," I said.

"Yes. That's where you come in. You have the proper combat arms credentials plus you play piano. Apparently, that is a rare combination."

"We've established that," I said. In all the years I've known Smith, I've never heard him dance around an assignment like this, so I started to sweat a bit, and that made me cranky. "Okay," I said, "I play piano. Yes. But not in Panama. Gracias, but no gracias, Mr. Smith. I'm quite happy here. And, as you may have heard, I'm retired. Now, if you have something in Paris, or New York, that would be different. But Panama, no."

"It's only for a few days," Smith said. "Everything goes right, you do your job, you'll be home in two weeks. It'll be more like a vacation, Harper, a Christmas vacation. Panama is very warm this time of year."

"It's the heat that I'm worried about." I put the car into gear and pulled back into traffic.

"What are you doing?"

"I'm taking you to your hotel. Then I'm getting ready for a gig."

"So you refuse to help your country in a time of need, to work at the pleasure of the president?"

"It'll be a disappointment," I said, "but he'll get over it."

"Consider your future, son, before you make a decision."

"Are you saying I can't say no?"

"Not at all," Smith said. His voice rose half an octave, telling me he was angry. "It's not like we're the mob. We're the goddamn government, boy."

"I'm allergic to sharks, sir. Unless they're broiled and served with lemon butter."

"So you're saying you won't go?"

"That's what I'm saying."

"Fine," he said, in a tone that told me it was anything but fine. He sat back in the seat, looked out the window, and muttered, "Goddamn sunshine patriot. Let a little thing like a shark come between him and his duty."

"Yes, sir."

"Tell me, Harper, who was it helped you become the man you are today? Who believed in you when no one else did?"

"Mr. Rogers, sir."

Smith leaned forward and held on to the front seat, getting as close as he could, his voice in my ear all joshing and pal-like. "I'll tell you what. I'll give you twenty-four hours."

"Thanks, but I don't need twenty-four hours."

"Just in case you change your mind."

"I won't."

He sat back and smiled. "Just in case," he said, "something happens."

The threat just steeled my resolve. There comes a time when a man has to break from his mentor and stand on his own two pedal extremities. Sure, Smith had recruited me and trained me, but he'd also sent me into some very bad places, and after a few years of that, I'd quit. Retired. Turned in my time card.

Since I'd left Smith's service, I'd set myself up in the capital and made all the right connections, a point that just made it all the more ridiculous for me to leave D.C. to poke around some Panamanian banana ranch. I had a life here. In Panama, I could barely order a Cuba libre. With my mind set firmly against the tropics, I went home, showered, and dressed for the only job I was interested in: playing the piano.

I made nine hundred dollars a night playing for parties, dinners, and government get-togethers. I was in so much demand that I owned three tuxedoes—two Versaces and an Armani. Very nice. Not that you have to be wealthy to dress well. Every four years, Washington's pawnshops are packed with formal wear, dry-cleaned to remove the stink of failure.

Smith had not taken my retirement well, and every three or four months he would ask me to freelance, which I usually agreed to do if it was something that didn't take me too far from Washington. But this time I wanted a complete break. I wanted to be free from memorizing party chatter and free from entertaining women whose husbands talked too much.

I took a cab over to State and when I got out I had the feeling someone was watching me, but the hedges looked clear of skulking hit men, and my step soon regained the bounce of the newly liberated. I assumed a little paranoia was natural in someone who'd just stepped in from the cold.

The American ambassador to Honduras was throwing a party and several hundred people were invited, enough to fill the Franklin dining room. I knew Mariposa would be there along with her husband, the Major, and that, if my luck held, I'd be able to deliver on one last assignment. It would be my parting gift to Smith, a consolation prize for his losing a part-time spy.

I liked Mariposa. She was a sweet girl, blinded by romance and trapped in a horrid marriage to a man twenty years her senior. The Major sported a thin mustache, no lips, and a pistol he probably wore with his pajamas. I'd met him twice, didn't like him either time, and I got the feeling he didn't like me much, either.

The glass, black marble, and chrome lobby of the State Department is large enough to hold groups of tourists until they are checked, rechecked, patted down, and passed through metal detectors to their tour guides. But I was a regular, so I stepped into the express lane.

Jameson, the guard, said, "Hell of a shindig tonight, Mr. Harper. Word is, even the president might drop by." I showed him my ID and he checked it against his computer screen and, as he'd done a dozen times before, he asked for my Social Security number. I gave it to him, he nodded, handed back my ID, and waved me through the metal detector. On the other side, Shaneequa wanded me, asked me about my father's health, and then escorted me to the elevator and waited until the doors closed. God help me if I punched the button for any floor other than the one I'd been cleared for. A visitor did that once and half a dozen men with bad attitudes were waiting for him when the doors slid open.

The elevator dropped me off in the hallway that ran from the men's lounge down to the Jefferson reception hall. The men's lounge, for some reason, is decorated in the cowboy decor of Teddy Roosevelt and has been for some time. I passed through displays of pistoleros, chaps, and ten-gallon hats on my way to the lavatory, which was empty, so I bounced a Bob Wills tune off the white tile as I relieved myself.

Still flying high on my newfound freedom, I walked into the Jefferson reception hall, an exceptionally great room in a city full of great rooms. It's a hushed place, even in daylight, with ceilings as high as the National Gallery. A statue of Jefferson dominates one end of the room and the walls are lined with historic paintings, including the original *Spirit of '76*.

One painting in particular always caught my eye and, if I could have, I would have tucked it under my jacket and taken it home. In it, the Capitol Building stands high up on a grass-covered hill. In the foreground a boy is pulling a cow through a gate. It's such a quiet picture of such an easier time that I like to think of myself as that boy, herding bovines in the shadow of the Capitol, as aware of world events as the cow.

The reception hall led to the Franklin dining room where waiters were arranging silver and putting a final polish on the stemware. A string quartet tuned up in the corner as nervous young interns from Protocol scurried about the room double-checking place cards.

The windows from the top floors of the State Department offer a view few citizens get to see, and it is a pity, because it stirs a patriotism in my heart that is genuine and jingo-free. Looking out across the treetops to the Lincoln Memorial, as white as a wedding cake in the spotlights, I felt privileged to be an American.

I loved this city, and it was my love for Washington that made me turn down Smith's assignment. Washington had spoiled me. I was no longer capable of wading through a shark-infested backwater just to play "Auld Lang Syne" in a bug-infested jungle hotel where the guests most likely ate with their hands.

And if I kept rationalizing like this, I'd be free of guilt by New Year's.

Behind me, people began to drift into the reception hall. It was showtime.

I was set up in a cozier room opposite the dining room, where the light from half a dozen fireplaces refracted into rainbows in the low-hanging crystal chandeliers. A Baldwin baby grand was set up next to the Christmas tree in the corner. I sat down and began to play. By the time I was into my Irving Berlin medley, the room was crowded and buzzing with happy holiday conversation. The men wore black tie, and the women wore variations of red, accented with green, or green accented with red. Everyone except Mariposa, who wore an off-white gown, a scandal in tradition-bound Washington, where white after Labor Day was considered a social faux pas on par with dissing Texas. But this ivory-colored gown was the perfect foil for Mariposa's dark skin and black hair. We made eye contact twice. Once, when I played the Honduran national anthem and all other eyes were on the flag, and once when her husband, the Major, left the room with his boss, an overweight general who managed to live extremely well on an army officer's salary.

By nine the crowd was having one last glass of wine before hurrying off to be seen at midnight services. The women of Washington knew how stunning they looked by candlelight and they didn't want to waste an opportunity to be seen twice in the same night in such a pious glow.

Mariposa greeted me and said, "You play so beautifully, Mr. Harper. Thank you."

I gave her a small bow and said, "*Feliz Navidad,* Mrs. Cruz. How are you this evening?"

"I have a slight headache," she said, pressing the back of her wrist to her forehead to demonstrate to everyone, even those at the far end of the room, just how much she was suffering.

"I am so sorry."

"You are too kind," she said. She leaned over the keyboard and whispered, "Meet me in the cloakroom. Five minutes."

I nodded and covered our conversation with a blizzard of high notes that drifted into "Here Comes Santa Claus." She smiled and the lights on the tree sparkled in her eyes.

I looked past her and saw the Major watching us as an army officer in dress blues, his back to us, whispered in his ear. The Major did not look happy. He stared at me and I saw suspicion march across his face and set up camp on his forehead. His mouth quivered and I could guess by the look in his eye that his Christmas wishes involved me, and it wasn't something I'd see on a Hallmark card.

The officer turned, and for the first time I saw his face. It was Smith, and he was filling the Major's ear with news meant to ruin a festive mood.

(

CHAPTER THREE

I think the Major suspects something."

"How could he?" Mariposa said. "With his nose buried so deeply in the General's *culo*."

"Where's the coat-check girl?"

"She went away for a smoke. So we must hurry." Mariposa pulled up the hem of her dress, revealing stockings, a flash of naked thigh, and a pair of jade-green panties.

"Mariposa, please, we've talked about this."

She looked up from her work and in the close darkness her eyes danced. "You know, John, if you said the word, I would kill him, you know that."

I swallowed and shook my head. "Mariposa, I'm flattered, but . . ."

She straightened and smoothed her dress with her hands. "I am a Catholic, John, and I take my vows seriously, so our love must remain tragic and unfulfilled, like your songs, so sad, you know? That is, unless something terrible happened that left me a widow." She held up a small piece of paper and smiled.

"What is that?"

"It is the list of the men my husband will meet tonight in Baltimore. There is something bad happening here, John."

"I don't know if this will help," I said, taking the slip of paper. "But I'll pass it along."

Mariposa placed her hand on my jaw, her nails pressing into the soft flesh of my cheek. "When were you going to tell me, John?"

"Tell you what?"

"That you were leaving for Panama."

As a professional spy, I used to spend hours in front of the mirror practicing my look of bored nonchalance, but Mariposa's question caught me gaping like a fish.

"Did you think I wouldn't know?"

I found my voice and said, "But I'm not. There was some talk, yes . . ."

Mariposa pressed her breasts against my chest and breathed champagne in my face. "Every woman who has ever heard you play and wished she was your instrument—and that is almost every wife in Washington—has heard this rumor. John Harper is leaving the city. The whispers as to why are quite interesting, even for this place. There are the usual pregnancies, one even suggests a mother-daughter doubleheader."

Mariposa was a great fan of the Baltimore Orioles.

She pushed me against the wall and into a distant corner, surrounded by the soft folds of fur and cashmere.

"Mariposa, these rumors are just that. Rumors."

She ran a nail around my ear and said, "What I find interesting, John, is how did you know?"

"Know what?"

"That I would be in Panama for New Year's. Honestly, Mr. Harper, I thought our relationship was one of business." Mariposa's lips were so close to mine that with another coat of lipstick we'd have committed a cardinal sin.

"You're going to be in Panama?" I began to sweat in that over-heated cloakroom. Someone's cell phone went off, the tone dampened by layers of expensive outerwear.

"I am," she said. "My husband is to meet people there." She suddenly froze and put her finger against my lower lip.

"What is it?"

"Sssh," she said, as tense as a deer.

I listened for Wanda, the coat-check woman, telling us she was back, but the voice I heard belonged to a man. And he was agitated, speaking in Spanish, too quickly for me to pick up all but a few words. He was looking for Wanda, that much was clear, and was calling her a cow, an idler, or an economic slump, I wasn't sure which.

It was the Major.

Mariposa and I held our breaths.

After a brief discussion, the Major started pawing through the coats himself, all the while ranting about something that had ruined his Christmas.

"He does not like you," Mariposa whispered.

I caught the words *piano* and *pistola,* words I could translate without Mariposa's help.

General Cruz made soothing sounds, calming his aide. He mentioned Renaldo and Luis, two of the no-neck bodyguards the General traveled with, which didn't do much to improve my holiday spirit.

The Major answered that a husband should clean his own house.

The General, his tone philosophical, said some things about *matrimonio,* and young brides, and then he used the word *piano* again with something that sounded uncomfortably like eviscerate. Mariposa's wide-eyed look of panic translated all I really needed to know.

The cloakroom had four long rows of coats, with Mariposa and I at the very end of the fourth row. That gave me some comfort until Mariposa touched the shoulder of an overcoat and whispered, terror sharpening her voice, "This is my husband's."

The Major found the general's coat and continued looking for his. I heard him moving down the first row, pushing overcoats back and forth on their hangers. At the top of the second row, the Major said something that made General Cruz laugh. I caught something uncomfortable about a *musico's pinga* and hungry dogs. Or, it might have been hungry hair. My Spanish needs work.

Mariposa's eyes, so expressive, nearly vibrated in panic.

The Major searched the third row for his overcoat. The hanger hooks zipped back and forth on the wooden rod as the Major became more agitated. He reached the end of the third row and said in English, "It's always the last place you look, isn't it, sir."

"Indeed."

The Major rounded the top of the third row and headed into the fourth. I pulled Mariposa into the folds of clothing and down to our hands and knees. We waited, face-to-face, barely breathing, as the Major's patent-leather shoes paced back and forth in front of the coats.

He cursed and returned to the third row. We watched as he marched up and down that aisle. With another curse, he came back to the fourth row. That's when I noticed it. There in the aisle was the slip of paper Mariposa had smuggled in to me, still warm, and still incriminating enough to get us both killed.

I watched his shiny black shoes approach and stop a foot from where we were hiding. The Major pushed aside the shoulders of hanging overcoats, one by one, searching for his. I carefully reached out from under the swaying hems and had my fingers on the paper when the Major stepped sideways and placed his sole squarely on his wife's stationery. I slowly pulled my hand back.

The Major, frustrated, started shoving each overcoat away from its neighbor, creating great gaps in our cover. Mariposa and I had to scurry ahead of his search until we hit the wall and could go no further. The coats parted, three feet away, then two, then the Major's shiny black shoes were next to us. I could have reached out and untied them.

"Major Cruz, I am so sorry. I just had to step away for a moment."

The Major made noises of understanding, underlined with a rumble of irritation.

"Please, allow me," the coat-check woman said, and for the first time in what felt like hours, I took a breath. We watched her low-heeled approach. Wanda parted the overcoats and looked down at us with disgust. She removed the Major's overcoat and helped him into it.

The Major gave her a tip, thanked her, and said to the General, "So, Luis and Rodrigo are informed?"

"Yes, and by morning, you and your young wife will be able to enjoy Navidad in peace."

"Thank you, sir."

A moment later Wanda said, "They're gone. You two heathens can come out now."

Mariposa and I scrambled out from under the coats. Mariposa hurried off, leaving me alone to face the wrath of Wanda. I tried offering her a fifty-dollar bill, hoping Grant's face would soften her hard Christmas heart. But she refused the money, crossing her arms and shaking her head with disgust. "And on Christmas Eve, too," she said. "You should be ashamed, Mr. Harper."

"Please, Wanda, take the money."

"I don't want your money." A new light came into her eyes and a smile flickered. "But there is something you can do for me."

I backed away, shaking my head. I was resolved not to get sucked into another one of Wanda's holiday plans. "No. Absolutely not."

"You know what you got to do, Mr. Harper. What you did at Thanksgiving."

I shook my head. "No, Wanda, please, not that. I'm way too tired."

Wanda stood in the doorway and said, "Fine. Be that way. Just don't come asking no favors of Wanda."

"I won't."

"Not ever."

"Don't worry."

"Don't even think about it."

"I promise."

"But you got my number, right?"

"I do, Wanda, but I won't be calling. Have a good Christmas." I edged past her but not quickly enough for me to get by before she grabbed my backside.

"Fine thing on Christmas Eve," I said.

"You don't know what presents Wanda has for you, honey, make you forget all about Saint Nick."

My last set was a short one, with few people left besides the wait staff, and as they picked up glasses and holiday napkins, I packed my music, went down the elevator, and headed north past GWU. As I walked to the Metro station I wondered why my particular stars all seemed to point to Panama, a twisted little country at the ass end of the continent. I knew nothing about Panama except it had a canal and a bad history with the United States. I didn't even own a panama hat. But the damn country kept coming up in

dangerous conversation all day and I didn't like it. I'm not a superstitious man by nature, but I don't purposely walk under ladders.

Mariposa had made me promise to leave town for a few days, at
least until the Major cooled off, so I went back to my apartment to
pack a few things. I would spend the holiday with my father, which
would be novel for both of us. It's not that we don't talk, it's just
that when we do, the conversation never goes anywhere either of us
wants to be.

Still, it was Christmas. Peace, goodwill, and the milk of human
kindness was in the air, and they almost got me killed.

I caught one of the last trains to Crystal City and exactly eleven
minutes later was gliding up the long escalator to ground level, still
wondering why Panama.

Crystal City is a clot of high-rises that are a lot less magical than
their name. Home to hotels, office buildings, and an underground
crammed with trendy shops, Crystal City is a temporary stop for
most. For me, it had been my home for three years. I have a three-
room apartment with no furniture other than a bed and a baby
grand piano. I don't even own a TV, a fact no one can fathom in
this hyperconnected city.

Crystal City stands across from the Pentagon to the north and
Reagan National Airport to the east. Had I looked out my window
September 11, I could have watched that plane come in low over the
Potomac. Apart from the grim possibility of witnessing Armageddon,
Crystal City is about as stimulating as your grandmother's house on
New Year's Eve, unless you thrive on conformity, which many of my
uniformed neighbors naturally do.

I had left a book in my car so I went first into the parking garage.
The garage is in the basement of my building and, like a cavern, is
a constant fifty-four degrees. If the piano business ever fell off I
figured I could grow mushrooms down there to supplement my un-
employment.

I unlocked my car, a used Mazda I bought cheap from a fleeing
Democrat, got my book, a novel about a former FBI profiler who
supposedly lived in my building, and hit the elevator button for the
trip upstairs. The doors opened. A gorilla in Brooks Brothers was
standing inside, his hands clasped in front of him. He cracked his
knuckles and smiled. A gold tooth winked at me.

I begged his pardon and backed away. I looked behind me and there was another man, this one in blue Armani, standing by the last row of cars. He was smiling, too. Everyone was smiling this Christmas Eve except for me and maybe Wanda, the coat-check woman.

I wasn't used to fans following me home and I got the feeling that my autograph was not what they wanted. The first man stepped from the elevator and the doors closed behind him. The second man stepped away from the cars and I heard the snick of a blade opening. It echoed off the concrete and made my chest feel as cold and hollow as the car park.

The first man took three steps toward me and I found myself backed against a new Volvo. The man was big and his muscles strained the fabric of his jacket. He reached for me, his hand the size of my head, but he moved as slow as a sloth, as if he were performing underwater. I rolled along the Volvo's side until I nearly fell into the gap between the front bumper of this car and the rear bumper of the next. A blinking red light on the Volvo's dashboard caught my eye.

The second man, the thin man in Armani, had worked his way to the other side. The knife blade in his fist caught the safety lights. I looked at the first man, then the second, and then I pushed my ass against the Volvo. Instantly the car sprang to life. Its alarm whooped, its horn beeped, and the headlights flashed. The two men stopped, struck stupid by the chaos. I ducked between the two cars, kicking an Infiniti as I passed. It added its horn and alarm to the Volvo's solo.

The two men went sideways and caught up to me between a rented Chevy sedan and a Lincoln Navigator. They rushed in, intent on catching me before the cops arrived. I could see the worry on their faces and the distraction over the alarms. I hoped it would be enough.

I shouldered the Navigator into honking distress as the first man's paw landed on my shoulder. I swung my back to the Chevy and he brought his fist around to meet my face. I watched the knuckles grow to the size of a small planet and then ducked. His hand smashed the driver's-side window of the rental. The second man swung the knife at my ribs and the blade snagged my jacket. I struck out with the hardback, hitting the man's nose. Blood sprayed across his mouth and chin and he dropped the knife. I fell to the concrete and rolled beneath the Navigator, coming up the other side, and sprinted for the gate, hitting every other car along the way until the basement garage was so filled with noise that it was almost impossible to bear.

I hit the gate, hurdled the crossbar, and sprinted across the asphalt and grass toward Crystal Drive. A gray Cadillac pulled to the curb and another man jumped from the passenger side. I faked to the left and the guy went left, then I hit it hard to the right, up over the hood of the Cadillac, and the guy nearly came out of his socks trying to reverse himself. I sprinted across Crystal Drive, dodged a station wagon, my tuxedo tails flapping behind me, my patent-leather shoes beating the pavement, the Italian soles so thin that I could have stepped on a cannoli and gained a pound. As I ran past the Water Park towers I heard the man's footsteps slapping the sidewalk behind me.

I vaulted a boxwood and a low concrete wall just as the Cadillac caught up to me, sliding to a stop on Crystal Drive. The driver got out and I heard the sound of a cough, and then the crack of a supersonic bullet flying past my skull. I ducked right at the rail station and ran down the trail that would take me to the bike path that paralleled the GW Parkway.

The brick trail curved left and right like an inebriated snake, denying the man behind me a clear shot. Then I hit the tunnel that ran beneath the parkway, a seventy-five-meter straight sprint that would give him plenty of time to stop and aim. Which he did.

I heard the pistol cough, heard two cracks as rounds went by my ear. A bullet took out a piece of the asphalt at my feet and then another crack and another tug on my jacket.

I came up the other side, the Metro line over my head, the parkway on my right, and Reagan National, lit up like a Christmas pageant, on my left. I glanced over my shoulder and saw the driver still chasing me, but I'd put an extra fifty yards between us, and even a champion shot would have a hard time hitting a moving target at that distance. He apparently thought so, too, because he stopped, his hands on his knees, and watched me as I sprinted all out into the darkness.

A few minutes later I felt safe enough to stop. I jogged over to a bench near the end of the Reagan National runway where families come and thrill to the northbound jets taking off, so close you could almost reach out and touch the shiny bellies as they roared overhead. But I was the only person there this night, this Christmas Eve, and as I punched in the number on my cell phone, I fingered the bullet hole in the fabric of my tuxedo jacket.

She answered the phone.

"Wanda, I've decided to take you up on your offer."

She didn't sound surprised. "I'm sure the Lord will bless you for it, honey."

"But I need you to pick me up. You know that park off the GW where you can watch the planes?"

"I do."

"Can you come and get me?"

"I'm on my way."

As I waited, my sweat drying in the chill air, I listened to the planes roar overhead, the turbulence making that mysterious swooshy crackling noise that makes kids pee, just a little, in their pants.

Fifteen minutes later an old Pontiac rolled to a stop, the window zipped down, and Wanda said, "Come on, honey, we got people waiting."

I got in.

"I thought maybe you'd change your mind about tonight."

"I am at your service, Wanda."

"You a good man, Mr. Harper, sometimes you just don't know it yourself."

A half hour later I slid onto the worn bench of an old Suzuki upright, a piano that looked as if it had been moved down several flights of stairs with no help other than gravity.

I was in the dayroom of the W.E.B. DuBois Retirement Home in Southeast D.C. Rows of folding chairs were full of little women ranging in color from dark chocolate to coffee and cream. One white face lit up the third row like a single vanilla wafer in a plateful of mocha fudge.

As I played, Wanda's octogenarian mother sat next to me and sang in a thin, warbly soprano. I played "The Little Drummer Boy" so many times that it was weeks before I could shake those rummy-tum-tums out of my hands. And it would be months before I could shake the look on Smith's face out of my head. He was sitting there in the third row, handling the bass and smiling a smile that had little to do with the joy of the Christ child's Nativity.

CHAPTER FOUR

The next morning, I met Smith in the costume shop behind the union's rehearsal hall.

I threaded through a platoon of dancers warming up for a Christmas show at the White House and continued past the marching band that would play on the Ellipse.

Smith was in the costume shop trying on a tux for a dinner that night. I stood in the doorway. The place was hot enough to brown biscuits. Smith turned left and right in front of the mirrors and when he saw me all three of his reflected faces asked the girl searching for ruby studs to "see if you can round up some coffee."

Smith looked as comfortable in that tux as Mussolini must have looked in that tree. His bow tie was undone and hanging around his neck as if he were about to belt out "My Way," and a white carnation pinned to his lapel sagged in the steam heat.

"Sit down, son." Smith pulled his lapels straight and said, "What a jungle fuck." He looked sideways at his triple reflection and asked, "Do you think this is right? The white carnation makes me look like an undertaker, but the red makes me look like a pimp. What do you think?"

"The red, sir. It matches your eyes."

"Now, son, this is no way to begin Christmas."

"You'll excuse me if I'm a little grumpy, sir. I had no place to sleep last night."

"You remember when I got you transferred out of Special Services and into psychological operations?" Apparently Mr. Smith wanted to stroll down memory lane rather than confront my gorilla-filled present. When I didn't answer he said, "Humor me, son."

I nodded. "I remember."

"No one thought you were worth a cup of warm spit. But I knew better. And with time you acquitted yourself. And who taught you how to combine your piano-playing skills with other skills that made your service important to the security of this nation? Who did that?"

"You did, sir, for which I am very grateful, but this Panama thing, you didn't have to—"

Smith stopped me. "A good soldier who plays the piano. You are the only one I could send. And you gave me no choice."

"But the Major's thugs nearly killed me."

"I had faith."

"Faith? That's all that was keeping me from being disemboweled for the holidays? Your faith?"

Smith stripped off the tuxedo jacket. His movements were careful, but casual. "Must be a good life for you here, son."

"Up until last night."

"And it can be again. All I want you to do is to find out a few things."

I blew out a sigh and let the inevitability of the thing settle in for the first time. I was on my way to Panama, and the sooner I could finish the assignment, the sooner I could come back home.

Smith wiped his brow with a handkerchief, popped his collar stud, and said, "Follow me."

We threaded our way through racks of costumes to a tiny, glassed-in space crowded with mannequins and bolts of fabric. Smith pulled out two folding chairs, opened them, and told me to take a seat. The room was so small that our knees nearly touched.

"You're a strange boy, son. But you've got real talent, and I'm not just talking about the piano."

"Thank you, sir."

"But this. I want you to be prepared."

"It's that bad?"

Smith leaned forward, his face inches from mine, and for the first time I saw worry in his eyes, an emotion I thought was alien to the old man. "Have you ever gotten over your aversion to firearms?"

"I just want to live where I don't need one. Like a normal person."

"You almost got killed in St. Thomas because you're afraid of guns."

"I'm not afraid of guns, and I didn't get killed in St. Thomas."

"And in New York a few years ago?"

"If you'll allow me to indulge in a stereotype, sir, piano players don't usually shoot people. In fact, it's often the other way around."

Smith didn't laugh like I'd hoped he would. Instead he rummaged around in a file cabinet and pulled out a bottle of bourbon. He poured three fingers into a glass. "You want one, Harper?"

"No, sir. It's still a little early," I said, glancing at my watch.

"Have a drink, Harper."

There was something in his voice, an unaccustomed softness, even sympathy, that made me reconsider.

Smith reached into the drawer and pulled out another glass. We sat for a long time in the hot office and sipped warm Maker's Mark. I tried not to choke.

Smith poured himself a second and said, "You won't shoot anyone, is that right?"

"It's not that I won't. It's just that I'd rather not."

"But you have."

I closed my eyes and let the pictures pass. "Not to my credit."

"The first one's the hardest," Smith said. "That's the one you remember."

That was a romantic lie. I remembered every one of them. In detail.

Smith put his drink down and folded his hands in his lap. "You know why I recruited you? I mean the first time? Because you have a way of disappearing in a room."

"It's a function of the gig, sir. When you play background for parties, people don't notice you if you're good. It's part of the job."

"And yet you always seemed to watch what was going on, even before we started working together."

"My father taught me to play so that people could see my face."
I gave him a big, showbiz smile.

"Uh-huh." Smith scratched his chest. "And you've always done a
bang-up job for me, no complaints."

"Thank you, sir. Something else my father taught me."

Smith shook his head and said, "Don't bring your family into
this, okay? It only makes it harder."

"Yes, sir."

"All I want you to do in Panama is find out who the guests are at
this resort hotel and why they're there. Nothing else. If things get
bad enough for you to give up your dislike of firearms, I want you to
extract, is that understood?"

"Yes, sir."

"No fooling around."

"No, sir. Not a bit."

Smith pulled out a folder from the same desk drawer that held
the bourbon. "The guests get flown in, a few at a time. The hotel
has a Bell helicopter for commuting and a Huey they use for training security forces. You know, like corporate bodyguards. That's the
story, anyway." He handed me half a dozen eight-by-tens and asked
if I knew what I was looking at.

"Satellite pictures," I said. "Not a commercial satellite." I was
looking down at a cluster of beachfront buildings, their roofs red,
the water blue, the small circles of umbrellas white.

"Notice anything unusual?" Smith handed me a loupe and I
studied the photo.

"No people," I said.

"Why do you think there are no people on a beautiful sunny day
at the beach?"

I looked up from the photo and said, "They know what time the
satellite passes overhead."

Smith nodded and handed me several more photos. These were
pictures of what appeared to be an abandoned city block in the middle of a dense jungle. Only a few of the visible buildings had roofs,
but one photo showed three military trucks.

"What is this?"

Smith shook his head. "That's what we'd like to know."

I handed the photos back to Smith. "Major Cruz will be in Panama for New Year's. Do you think there's some connection?"

Smith nodded again. "I don't think it's a coincidence, if that's what you're asking. Other than that, I don't know. There does seem to be something big planned for New Year's Eve, that much we get from the chatter, but it could just be a big party for a lot of Colombians with money."

"But you don't think so."

"No, and one other thing. The men who make up the hotel staff don't exactly have a degree in hospitality. You know one of them, a Ren Vasquez. He's the one who recommended you in the first place."

"Ren? My God, Ren's a great guy, but not exactly the most stable man on the planet."

"And you've got backup there. He's a man named Ramirez, Phillip Ramirez. Was with the hundred and first. Tried out for Delta, was one of fifteen to finish the course and then turned down a position. Spent a few months in Iraq with special ops, got wounded bad enough for a discharge, and was in Walter Reed for six months, which is where he was recruited by our guys and theirs. I'm assured he's someone you can trust, and he knows you're coming."

I wondered who else knew I was coming and what kind of welcome I'd receive. "You know anything about Panama, Mr. Smith?"

"I went to jungle school there. Caught crabs as big as beavers."

I laughed, because that's what he wanted me to do, and it made him feel better.

"I know this. Since we left the place to the Panamanians, it's pretty much gone to shit. Drug money, the politics of the drug war, the Canal, it's all made the place as squirmy as an earthworm in the sun."

"Yes, sir." I swallowed a knot of bourbon.

He dropped his head and spoke so quietly that I had to lean forward to hear it all. "I want you to promise me you'll be careful."

"I will, sir."

"And Harper?"

"Yes?"

"Wear some sunblock, or you'll fry your ass off."

(

CHAPTER FIVE

Smith promised me I could come home once I'd won the pony. All I needed was a guest list and a better understanding of who they were training and why, and I needed to know before New Year's Eve. But, in spite of the short deadline, Smith let me spend the rest of Christmas with my father, a bit of sentimentality that, coming from Smith, scared me more than mercenaries and unhinged third-world politics.

My father seemed happy to see me, but after he opened my gift, a scarf, we ran out of things to talk about and spent most of the day watching television. Dinner was take-out Chinese. When I told my father I was leaving for Panama, he said, "I was wondering how long it would be before they kicked you out of the nation's capital. What happened, you make a pass at the First Lady?" He wasn't joking. My father never joked about the First Lady.

The next day I was flying into Panamanian airspace, watching the green landscape zip by and thinking December in the tropics might not be so bad after all. I had camouflaged myself in shorts, sandals, a jade-green shirt with orange flowers, and Wayfarer sunglasses. I was ready for anything.

To my surprise, Panama City looked shiny and new from a few thousand feet up. This banana-Miami crowded the curve of a muddy bay and threw up modern skyscrapers the way northern Virginia tossed up Starbucks. The fact that the tall buildings were built on a cocaine foundation didn't make them any less impressive from the air.

Tocumen airport tried its best to live up to the skyline's cosmopolitan promise with native artwork displayed as cultural artifacts along the corridor that ran between the gate and baggage claim. Signs told me that I could find similar artifacts for sale in the gift shop. I would soon find out that everything in Panama is for sale.

At the baggage claim, Panamanian families embraced loudly, Anglo businessmen scurried off to customs, and tourists shouldered their bags and consulted their guidebooks. Among the tourists were two young men who seemed eager to buy dope in a place where all the laws are like Texas. As far as I could tell, I was the only one smuggling in a satchel full of Gershwin.

I waited by the luggage carousel and watched as bag after bag was claimed, the crowd dissipated, and I was alone, watching the belt grind by, empty. Six uniformed and two plainclothes cops watched me with some amusement as it became clear that my three tuxedos, patent-leather shoes, my studs, and my ties were off on their own adventure. It took an hour to file a claim. I didn't know the Spanish word for "luggage" and neither did the clerk. I pointed to one bag that looked similar to mine and she said, "Bueno," and tried to give it to me. She was genuinely surprised when I declined.

My customs agent was eager to spread out everything I owned across her counter. Of the two of us, I think she was more disappointed about my lack of luggage than I was.

"What's this?" she asked.

"That's an MP3 player," I said. "I wear it when I run."

"And this?"

"My laptop," I said.

Disappointed that it wasn't a bomb, she took my passport and went away for a very long time, leaving me alone with a dozen policemen armed with automatic weapons and an annoyed disposition.

When she returned, I stepped outside to the taxi stand. Nothing, not even Washington with summer air so thick you could cut it into seat covers, prepared me for the heat of Panama. And I could feel things—small, bacterial, fungal things—growing on me. I knew that if I set down my carry-on Coach bag it would sprout legs and scurry off into the underbrush.

A cab in neon green, yellow, and red pulled to the curb. I said I wanted to go to "the Chinaman's Drugstore."

He looked at me and said, "You sure?"

I said I was, although I wasn't, and he shrugged, put the car into gear, and took off toward the city.

I amused myself by counting the pictures of the Virgin Mary on the dashboard and wondering what you had to do to rewire Christmas lights for twelve volts.

I tried not to be too concerned about the driver's reaction to the address I'd been given. I'd read the history of Panama on the plane and here I was, a beaming beacon of American middle class knowing that the locals had good reason to dislike all things gringo. For instance, one hundred years ago, when Colombia was reluctant to let us build our big ditch, Teddy Roosevelt carved Panama out of Colombia's backside and set up a malleable dictatorship. The United States claimed a large strip of land on either side of the Canal, and called it the Zone, and ran it like an American colony. The Panamanians soon began to resent the gringos. The Americans ran the Canal, hiring the locals to cut the lawns of their tidy homes and watch their tidy kids go off to their tidy schools. So the Panamanians rioted a few times, just to get the gringos' tight-assed attention. Once, they rioted over the name of a bridge.

When built, the bridge that arched over the Canal was either the Thatcher Ferry Bridge or the Bridge of the Americas, depending on who was talking. In the sixties some students tried to raise the Panamanian flag on the bridge, a riot followed, and several people, all Panamanians, were killed, shot dead by American soldiers. The Americans named the street Fourth of July Boulevard. After the riot, the Panamanians called it the Avenue of Martyrs.

Then there was that whole invasion-and-killing-and-leveling-a-large-part-of-the-city-while-snatching-Noriega thing. Some people still held a grudge about that, more than a decade later. Soreheads.

The driver turned off the wide main boulevard and into a two-lane street dedicated to the consumption of alcohol. From what I could see, many Panamanians were doing their best to keep the local bartenders employed. The store owners and clerks, free for siesta, lounged at small tables and eyed the gringo rolling by in the parrot-colored taxicab.

The driver stopped at a corner wine store, open on two sides and cooled by the ocean breeze blowing across white tile. The driver pointed and said, "This is the Chinaman's Drugstore."

"This is?"

"Yes. This is."

"Okay." I gave him twenty dollars. He didn't offer me change. I got out and waited by the doorway.

A short man in a straw hat, his face round, his eyes red-rimmed, stood next to me. "Hey, *muchacho*. You need a ride?"

"No, I'm waiting for someone."

"You looking to get high?"

"No, no, thanks."

"You want a woman?"

"No."

"You want a man?"

I had to laugh. "No, I'm okay."

"Where you going? I take you anywhere you want to go, five bucks."

"Take me to New York," I said.

He liked that. "I go to New York," he said with a smile, "and I never come home. There are plenty of fine women in New York."

"Yes, fine women."

"Where you going? Come on, I take you there for three bucks, no tip."

I looked at my watch. The luggage ordeal had made me late. Maybe my ride had come and gone. "You know La Boca del Culebra?"

A cloud rolled across the sun and the entrepreneur's disposition darkened. "That's a bad place, amigo. Come on, let me take you to a nice hotel. We got Hilton, we got everything. Nice places, not like La Boca."

"I have a job there," I said.

The little man stiffened. "You? You work there?" Then he laughed. "Oh, you make a joke. Ha ha, very funny man. Come, I take you to a nice hotel."

"What's wrong with La Boca?"

"Yeah, slick, what's wrong with La Boca?"

Neither of us had seen him approach. A tall, tanned man in his late twenties clasped the cab driver's shoulder and squeezed it until his knuckles went white.

The cab driver shook his head. "Nothing, señor. La Boca is a fine place. Very nice. I give it five stars." He slid out from under the new man's grasp and backed away. With a tip of his straw hat, he hurried off.

The tall man looked down at me. He wore a black baseball cap, dark glasses, and dangled an unlit Camel between his lips. "You the piano player?"

"Yeah."

He tilted his head and took me in from my sandals to my Hawaiian shirt. "You always dress like this?"

"Like what?"

"Never mind." He pointed at my satchel. "Is that it?"

"They lost my bag."

"Fucking airlines. Come on, we'll fix you up."

I followed him into the street to a Jeep made about the same time Smith was in his first firefight outside of Da Nang. "Get in," he said.

I did.

The tall man wheeled the Jeep around in a one-eighty, drove up to the Avenue of the Martyrs, and turned left toward the bridge that had united the continents and divided the people forty years before. The Bridge of the Americas spanned the Pacific entrance to the Canal, hundreds of feet above the shipping lanes. Far below, freighters waited their turn through the locks. At the very horizon, a lake plucked from prehistory shimmered in the sun.

For the first time since we started, the driver spoke. "They call me Zorro. Like the movie."

"They call me Harper," I said. "Like the movie."

"There was a movie?"

"With Paul Newman."

"No shit. Is it any good?"

"Yeah. I thought so."

The road was built to withstand the constant rain, but not well, and the seams of hot tar thumped against the tires.

"What's your favorite?" Zorro asked.

"Favorite movie? That's a tough one. I'd guess *Citizen Kane*."

"Never saw it."

"*Dr. Strangelove?*"

"Nope."

"So what do you like?"

"Steven Seagal," Zorro said. He held the cigarette between his lips, drove with his elbows, and cupped a lighter against the wind. "What else?"

"*It Happened One Night.*"

"Nope. How about *Con Air*?"

"Didn't see it. What about *Bringing Up Baby*? Cary Grant and Katharine Hepburn?"

"That in black-and-white?"

"Yeah."

"I don't watch black-and-white. What about the scariest movie you ever saw?"

I thought about that a minute. There was *Psycho,* and *Silence of the Lambs*, and *Sunset Boulevard.* I said, "I don't know, what about you?"

"*All the President's Men,*" he said, and gave me a sideways smile as if he'd been jerking me along. "So really, what do you like? I mean, if you could see any movie you wanted, what would it be?"

There was no hesitation. "*The Big Lebowski.*"

Zorro nearly drove off the road. "I love that movie." He bounced the heel of his hand off the steering wheel, "Yeah!"

We had found common ground. The Dude. I pulled my shirt away from my body and said, "Is it always this hot?"

"Not at night. When it rains you can freeze your ass off."

"Does it rain much?"

"Yeah. A lot."

"I read there was a rainy season."

"Uh-huh. But even in the dry season it rains every day. Once at one o'clock for about an hour, and again at nine." Zorro pulled off the main road and onto a rutted dirt track that ran through the jungle, the vegetation so thick and so close that wet fronds whipped the sides of the Jeep, soaking me to the skin.

"It's the dry season now," Zorro said. "Otherwise it'd be raining."

He twisted the wheel left and right, keeping expertly to the trail that was invisible beyond ten feet of the Jeep's hood. Several times on tight turns, the Jeep went up on two wheels. "These old things flip," Zorro said. "Kelly keeps promising to get us a Hummer."

It was dark under the green canopy and occasionally I saw a flat shadow skitter across the road.

"What the hell's that?"

"Land crab. When they breed they cover the whole fucking highway. They're useless as tits on a nun. Can't drive over 'em 'cause they'll pop the tires, and you sure can't eat 'em."

"What do you do for the hotel?"

"Security."

"Many guests?"

He stared at me longer than was safe considering our speed. The Jeep went up on two wheels again, nearly pitching me into the brush. "Whoa," Zorro said. "That was a rush."

"I play piano," I said, after I'd pried my fingers from the dash.

"I know," he said. "You'll be assigned to Cooper's team. He's another new guy. We're short because of Rosebud."

I didn't think I'd heard correctly over the engine and the sound of my own heart pounding in my ears. "Because of what?"

"Rosebud," he said. "He got eaten by an alligator. He was a friend of mine."

"I'd heard it was a shark."

"Alligator," he said.

"Oh. Sorry."

"It's okay. He was a great guy but couldn't play piano worth a shit."

I wondered if there was a cause-and-effect thing happening here, but I didn't ask.

Zorro drove with his knees while he lit another cigarette. "You any good?"

"Yeah," I said. "I am."

He laughed, but didn't let me in on the joke.

We approached the gates of La Boca and stopped at the guardhouse. A blond man, with shoulders you could screen IMAX on, ambled out and said, "This the new guy?"

"This is him."

The guard, whose flowered shirt and khaki slacks softened the

hard lines of his HK submachine gun, looked me
if I were a new item on the menu and decided, "He
hard."

"You won't say that when he drops a piano on your a
said, and then they both laughed.

The guard looked at his watch, then at the sky. "Best get
butts inside. Flyover's in three."

After we'd driven away I asked, "Who was that?"

"Meat," Zorro said.

"Meat?"

"Yeah. He's the social director."

"What'd he mean by 'flyover'?"

"Satellite," Zorro said, and drove quickly along a street lined
with palm trees. Overhead, an iguana the length of my arm jumped
from one tree to the next. On my right, beyond a hedge, I caught
glimpses of whitecaps and waves, glittering as they curled toward a
shallow beach. We passed a central garden of hibiscus, gardenia,
and bougainvillea.

We passed a tennis court. Men, tanned and dressed in blinding
white, stopped playing and hurried into the shade of an open bar.
Men on a putting green looked skyward and walked toward a shelter beneath the trees.

"We stay in the hotel with the guests. Wait staff and groundskeep-
ers have their own building up beyond the courtyard. The guests'
own security staff, the students, live in separate barracks not far
from here."

"Students?"

"You'll see."

The *bap* of the Jeep's engine startled a flock of parakeets and
they exploded from a treetop. A spider monkey loped across the
road and watched us as we parked in front of the hotel.

This was the resort, a jungle hideaway built for the rich who, dis-
tracted by the demands of World War II, never came. It was a
three-story monument to Deco extravagance with a high, wide veranda surrounding the first floor. I had seen this place before, but
only from above.

"Welcome home," Zorro said. "Now get inside. We've got less
than a minute."

with some clean clothes until the
'ng bag."

in and said, "You want to be inside,

out of the back as Zorro popped
; dust in the sun.

creen doors and into the hotel
..vnt desk, so I took a minute to look
..ed, but there was no hotel register conveniently lying around for me to scan. The movies make this spy work seem
easy. It's not.

Off to the side was the front office. I knocked.

A small fluorescent lamp illuminated a man hunched over a
computer keyboard, pecking out letters one finger at a time. Without looking up he said, "You know where the x is on this thing?"

"Bottom row, to your left."

He looked, found it, and hit it with his forefinger, then checked
the screen to make sure the x hadn't been mislaid somewhere in
the circuitry.

He was another Latino, like Zorro, but rounder, with a boy's
face. His black hair was slicked back and he had a dime in one ear.
His right ear. "Ren?"

He looked up, irritated, but as soon as he saw me his face
brightened. "Harper, my man." Ren jumped up, we did the dap,
fists and knuckles, just like he'd taught me, and then he hugged
me, one armed, pulling me in close to his chest. "Dude, man, you
looking good."

"You, too, Ren. So what's up? Last I heard you were getting your
ass shot at in Iraq."

"Yeah, the hajjis thought they had me up a tree, you know?
Throwing rocks. But I got out of there, man, and one of my old-
time bros got me this gig here where I don't get shot at and I make
a lot more money."

"What the hell are you doing behind a keyboard?" I said, pointing to the computer. Ren had a lot of skills, most of them criminal

in any society not openly engaged in combat, but typing was not one of them.

Ren shrugged. "They figure I can fuck up less in here." Ren sat down again and said, "Let me finish up this letter, okay, and then I'll show you where to bunk."

While Ren searched the keys, I wandered back into the lobby, past two dying palms, and heard the murmur of conversation. I looked into a dining room. A dozen guests sat at tables covered in white linen drinking icy drinks and grazing on cold meats and yellow fruits.

Not unusual in any resort hotel, except that every guest was male and every male was a Latin man between thirty-five and fifty. Was this the secret? Was this what caused the Washington intel community to ponder over satellite pictures and Panamanian autopsies?

Was this a resort for middle-aged gay men?

And then a cute waitress in a short white jacket and swirling black skirt came out of the kitchen and every eye was on her like a bird on a bug and I knew that these men were not gay. These men were in training. And from the testosterone that filled the air, so thick it threatened to warp the veneer off the Baldwin upright in the corner, these men had been in training for some time. It was like football camp or basic training or one of those corporate team-building getaways where bespectacled CFOs bare their male breasts and beat on drums in the firelight.

I walked across the dining room, stopping conversation as I passed, and sat at the piano. I stretched my fingers, aware that every eye in the room was on me. I opened the keyboard, cleared my throat, and began to play "Someone to Watch Over Me," in honor of the surveillance cameras. I was barely into the opening bars before Ren grabbed me by the arm and pulled me into the lobby. There was no applause.

"Dude. You must be crazy," he said. "Don't ever do that."

"I was hired to play the piano. There was a piano. I played."

"Yeah, right, but you don't play if somebody is in there." He dragged me into the office and took a deep breath to calm himself. "You do that again and they'll kill you, man, and that would be bad because I don't know any more piano players. Okay?"

Back inside the office, Ren straightened the collar of my shirt and said, "Now, let's get you in to see the Colonel. He's waiting and he gets unhappy when he has to wait for anything, especially some piano-playing *pendejo*. And you want to keep the Colonel happy," he said. "It's good for everyone."

Ren pointed to one of two office doors behind him. I went through the little wooden gate in the railing and knocked on the door that read "COL. J. PEPE (USA-RET.), MANAGING DIRECTOR."

"Come in."

I opened the door to a small office paneled in polished rosewood, and everything was very neat, very precise, very right-angled, just as I expected it to be. The only sound was the shifting drone of the oscillating fan as it swept the room. The Colonel had his head down, concentrating on fitting tiny batteries into a new digital camera, its instruction sheet unfolded across the desktop. The Colonel's gray hair was cut close and thinning near the crown. I wondered if he knew.

I had read his file and knew about his commands, and how he had been denied promotion and forced into retirement when he shot a reporter.

The Colonel didn't look up, so I looked around the office. On the walls were dozens of photos, almost identical in composition. In each, the Colonel stood smiling, the center of attention in a small group of other smiling officers, some American, some Vietnamese, some Arab, some Latin. In every picture, it was the same stiff pose and the same stiff smile. Like a fashion model who has just one look, but that's the look that gets work. Row after row, uniformed men smiling. A friendly bunch of officers saying, We could shoot you right now.

I waited and I watched as he went back and forth, staring at the tiny print of the instructions and then back to his fumbling fingers.

He had the West Point ring, like Snelling and Smith, and wore a white guayabera, starched, even in the heat. He looked to be in his fifties and tall, even sitting down. A Cuban Monte Cristo sat unlit in the ashtray, its end chewed ragged.

I wondered how the Latino name came with the Anglo face. This guy looked as much like a "Pepe" as I looked like Little Richard.

Without looking up, he said, "Is that how you report for duty, soldier?"

I glanced around the office. He was talking to me. "No, sir," I said, and saluted his thinning hair. "John Harper, civilian, reporting as ordered, Colonel Pepe, sir."

He rotated his face upward as if his head were powered by servos installed in his neck. "Peep," he said.

"I beg your pardon, sir?"

"PEEP," he said again. "PEEP."

I stared at him.

"PEEP!" he repeated. "Not Peppy. Tell me, troop, do I look like a taco-bender to you?"

"No, sir."

"Good." The Colonel went back to his camera and batteries, muttering, "Damn family comes over on the goddamn *Mayflower* and every goddamn asshole with a week's worth of Spanish thinks I'm some kind of border-hopping wetback." He looked up at me and said, "You're our piano player, is that right?"

"Yes, sir."

"Tell me about your service."

"There's not much to tell, sir. I enlisted when I was seventeen. Special Services, the USO—"

"I know what Special Services is."

"Yes, sir. Anyway, I worked the Officers' Club and staff functions."

"You've also spent time at Benning, Huachuca, Bragg. I see some time in New York with the Tenth Mountain—"

"The division band, sir."

"—and there is this list of security clearances, hardly what you would expect for an entertainer."

"I've played for the president, sir. They like to clear people who play at the White House."

He gave me a smile so sharp I could have shaved with it. "Of course. I also saw that you earned some sort of commendation for valor."

I shrugged. "It wasn't a big thing."

"Your superiors thought otherwise."

"Yes, sir."

His face scrunched up and he bobbled his head, pleased. "That's good. First off, you need to know your way around a firearm."

"I'm a little rusty, sir."

"No problem. We'll have one of our men give you a refresher."

"And my ability to play piano, sir?"

"That's for a party we're throwing. Don't worry, there'll be a nice bonus for you." The Colonel smiled again, lots of teeth. "A little surprise, if you will."

"Yes, sir."

"Do you know what we do here, son?"

"No, sir."

"We provide a secure place for influential and well-connected people to relax, away from prying eyes, while we train their security people. Now, considering your résumé, and the fact that you come with high recommendations, I would assume you know something about security."

"Yes, sir, I do."

He gave me the big smile, like in the photos. "Do you consider yourself a badass, Harper?"

"A badass? No, sir. But I did qualify as marksman in basic, sir."

He chuckled. "You ever hear of Colombia, son?"

"Yes, sir."

"Honduras?"

"Yes, sir, I've even played for the ambassador, sir."

"Outstanding." The Colonel studied me, perhaps for the first time. After a long moment, where the only sounds were the shush of the ocean beyond his window, he said, "Oh, and you might want to keep in mind, son, that if you give us any reason to terminate your contract, we do not use lawyers." He went back to his camera and said, "See Kelly. He'll get you squared away."

"Yes, sir."

"And don't listen to anything Kelly says. He won't like you, so get used to it. No appreciation of the finer things. Not a man of culture. He didn't want me to hire you and he'd send you home if he was the boss." The Colonel looked up and smiled. "But he isn't the boss."

"No, sir."

"I'm the boss."

"Yes, sir."

The Colonel stopped smiling. He'd apparently used up his shine quota for the day.

"Now, you're excused. And close the door on your way out."

I went back to see Ren. "Thanks for warning me about his name."

"I like to get you off to a good start, you know. But don't worry; he's not the real boss. Now I'll show you where to sleep, okay? Get your shit."

I followed him across the lobby and up the staircase to the second floor.

"We got a couple other new guys. One, Ramirez, is a Chicano like me. The other's Anglo, like you. Most of the Latinos here are Cubans or PRs. Don't get 'em mixed up, okay?"

Ren still had that dime in his ear. "Okay."

"There's a big difference. All Cubans want to do is kill communists and Democrats, which to them is the same thing. You could trust a Cuban with your sister. Serious, man, because they only get a hard-on for Fidel. But don't take showers with the Ricans. They like the white boys."

"What about Chicanos?"

"Hey, you can trust us with everything but your car, man." Ren laughed and his teeth were perfect.

We walked to the end of the corridor and up a smaller stairway that ran to the top floor. Here, Ren unlocked room 303, pushed open the door, and said, "This is your room. There's a bathroom down the hall."

The air was hot enough to bake a ham.

"It's the low ceiling. Traps the heat," Ren said. "You can open the window, but then the mosquitoes get in."

"What about screens?"

"I'll see if I can find one tomorrow."

"Are all the rooms like this?"

"Just the third floor. For us peons, man. But you got a phone hookup here, so you can plug into the Internet, you know, for the porn."

"Dial-up? I have to use dial-up?"

Ren shrugged. "Hey, it's the third world."

"Where do the guests sleep?"

"Second floor. The rooms there, man, are"—Ren smoothed the air with a gliding palm—"*rico*. And with the guests, the rule is, just so you understand, you never look directly at any of them. Never make eye contact. And you don't say anything unless they ask you something. OK?"

"Yeah," I said, "I got it."

"One more thing. Close the window when you leave your room, 'cause the Panamanians will climb up here and steal all your shit. You got anything nice you want to keep, we got a safe in the office. Fucking people steal your mother's picture just for the frame, no lie."

"Where do the Panamanians sleep?"

"In town."

"Have there ever been, like, regular guests staying here, ones that don't mind being looked at?"

Ren laughed. "Once, some English dude had a guidebook printed like a hundred fucking years ago. He tried to check in but the Colonel chased him away with a shotgun."

"Oh," I said, turning this over.

"I'll get you some sheets and a towel and some clean shit to wear, then maybe I show you around town, huh?"

"Yeah, sure. Hey, Ren?"

"Yeah?"

"I've always wondered, how come you've got a dime in your ear?"

"My father gave it to me," he said.

I waited, but Ren didn't offer anything more than a blank stare, as if he'd explained everything he was going to explain. I didn't push it.

Ren left and I opened the window to the ocean air. I closed the corridor door and unpacked my satchel. I placed my autographed eight-by-ten of Duke Ellington on the dresser and set my laptop on the bed. I took out my MP3 player and unscrewed the back. Inside were several bugs. I pocketed one and taped the others to the bottom of the desk drawer. Hidden inside the earpieces of my sunglasses were three different lock picks and a small torque wrench. Most sets come with seven or more picks, plus the wrench, but I've found that you rarely use more than three. People who carry more than three are either inexperienced or show-offs.

I heard people moving around the other rooms and music from a distant radio blew in on the breeze. There was something else on the breeze, too, but it took me a minute to place it. It was gun oil.

Someone knocked and I said, "Come in."

A thin man with sandy hair that curled in the humidity pushed open the door and said, "You the other FNG?"

"I guess so," I said.

"Welcome to Panama," he said. "My name's Cooper. Call me Coop."

He shifted a volume of Joseph Conrad to his left hand so he could shake with his right.

"You reading *Heart of Darkness*?"

"What else?" Coop walked around the room, picking things up and laying them back down as if he were browsing through a souvenir shop. "Did you fly in?"

"Yes."

"Some view, huh? I mean from the plane." Coop sat on my bed and bounced on the springs.

"Yeah. But what's an FNG?"

"Fucking New Guy," Cooper said. He looked into my shaving kit. "I didn't know what it was, either, until Ren told me. It's a grunt thing."

"Oh."

He picked up my sunglasses and turned them around in the light. "As far as I know, there are three of us. Me, a guy they call Mad Dog, and you. You must be the piano player."

"I am," I said.

"I heard the last piano player got eaten by a snake."

"A shark," I said.

Cooper shrugged. "Just as long as it doesn't eat me." He put on the sunglasses, stood, and crossed back to the dresser where he picked up the MP3 player. "I'm replacing the guy who got shot downtown."

"Is that a euphemism?"

"Whoa, and he uses big words, too." Cooper put on the earphones and punched the button. When he didn't hear anything he scowled and said, "Battery must be dead." He picked up the picture of Ellington and said, "Is this real?"

I carefully took it from him and placed it back on the dresser. "Yes. It's real."

"Cool," he said, and raised his eyebrows in appreciation. "You meet the Colonel?"

"Just now. I think we hit it off."

Cooper took off the earphones, walked over to the window, and sat against the sill. "You'll like the men here. I know some of them from the army," he said. "You know Zorro?"

"He picked me up."

"How about Ice? Meat?"

"No, and what's with the names?"

Cooper laughed. "Apparently, it comes in handy when dealing with the Latins. They put great importance on a nom de guerre." Coop opened my laptop.

I pointed with my chin and said, "You'll tell me when you see something you like."

Coop looked surprised to find himself with my laptop in his lap, as if someone had put it there in his sleep. "Oh, sorry. Just restless, I guess."

"How long have you been here?"

"I got in last week, but like I said, I know some of these guys from Iraq. So what's your specialty? Small arms, demolitions?"

"Gershwin," I said. "Among other things."

Cooper laughed again.

"What do you know about this other guy?"

"They call him Mad Dog. Real deal, I've heard. Been in Iraq, Afghanistan, and other places we're not supposed to know about. I'm sure he has some good qualities; I just haven't seen them yet. So you really do play piano, I mean, not just as a hobby?"

I shook my head. "No, it's not just a hobby."

"Have you met Kelly?"

"Not yet. I understand he's the man around here."

"Yeah, and his wife ran off with a USO singer. That's the story, anyway. Personally, I think he killed them both and buried their bodies in the jungle."

"This just gets better and better," I said.

"And wait until you see his daughter. She was out on the beach today and she is so fine." Cooper bit his bottom lip and slowly moved his head side to side in appreciation of the young Ms. Kelly's brief appearance. "But anyone who gets near that's got a death wish." Cooper laughed again. He laughed easily, and I liked that, but his eyes turned down at the corners, making him look perpetually saddened by his situation, even when he was smiling, and I didn't like the way he was checking out my gear. "Well, listen, nice meeting you and I'll see ya tomorrow. We FNGs have to stick together, right?"

Cooper left and I polished his fingerprints off Ellington's picture. Then I stripped, wrapped a towel around my waist, and went off for a shower, making sure to take my money with me.

I reached the end of the hallway and heard a man counting. Step by step, an extremely drunk, extremely large man placed both feet on each riser and counted, as if he were just now learning to climb stairs.

"Two hundred and forty-six!"

He weaved a bit and closed one eye trying to focus on me. When he raised his head I could see a white scar that ran along his throat, ear to ear. "Two hundred and—"

"Forty-seven," I said.

"That's a lot of steps. I've never seen that many steps in my life. And I seen a lot of steps."

"You must be Mad Dog."

He tried to salute, lost his balance, and stumbled sideways. His forearms were as big as my thighs and covered in tattoos, some good, some jailhouse.

"You," he said, pointing at me, "must be the accordion player." Then he laughed. "You're so little," he said, and held his finger and thumb a quarter inch apart. "Like a little puppy," he said. "C'mere."

"Why?"

"I can't move my legs."

He was still weaving at the top of the stairs, holding himself up by the banister. He draped an arm over my shoulder and I guided him into the corridor.

"Here we are," he sang, "home sweet home." I took the key from his hand, unlocked the door, and dropped him to his bunk.

"I had a little bit to drink."

"I can see that." So this was my backup, the bodyguard who would watch my six while I checked out the clientele.

Mad Dog looked up and said, "Where are your clothes?"

"I was on my way to the shower."

"Let me buy you a drink, you little naked fucker." He was up again, but weaving. A tiny push would do it. So I pushed him.

He fell back onto his bunk and lay there, staring at the ceiling. "Oh, now I'm going to have to kill you." He tried to get up but couldn't lift his bulk from the horizontal. Finally, he gave up and curled himself into a ball. "I'll kill you tomorrow," he said.

Cooper was standing in the corridor, looking in. "I see you met Mad Dog."

"Uh-huh," I said.

"Well, then, I suggest you get some sleep, New Guy, because Mad Dog and I are going to run your ass off in the morning. Ain't that right, Mad Dog?"

Mad Dog mumbled.

"That's an affirmative," Cooper said.

Mad Dog began to snore.

"You think we should cover him up?" I said.

"You his mother?"

"No."

"Then leave him. He'll be okay."

"Okay."

Ren poked his head up from the stairway and said, "Hey, Harper, you wanna go get laid?"

CHAPTER SIX

Cooper begged off, but Zorro came out of his room and mumbled something about mud for his duck, so the three of us climbed into Ren's car and took off for Panama City.

Ren drove a '56 Chevy whose seat belts had rusted through. Ren sat behind the wheel in a chrome and vinyl kitchen chair, Zorro and I sat in back, a ten-gallon jerry can full of gasoline wedged between us. Whenever Ren accelerated, Zorro put his foot against the chair back to keep it from tipping and throwing Ren into the rear with his passengers.

Zorro held the seat upright with his foot and grumbled, "Why don't you bolt this son of a bitch down?"

"Don't need to, man. I got you."

Zorro rolled a joint in the dark. "This place must have been something when the Americans controlled the Canal," he said. "Man, the gringo was king, with servants to do everything; wipe the dog's ass, feed the babies, fuck the old man when the wife didn't want to break a sweat."

Zorro lit the joint, inhaled, and offered it to me. "You get high, man?"

I took the joint and passed it to Ren. "Not any more," I said, as if I'd been through that phase and was now on to something new. The truth was, I had only smoked once before, alone in my apartment, and all I could do was listen to Miles, watch infomercials, and eat everything there was to eat in my apartment including a pint of Godiva ice cream, a bag of Doritos, and an entire container of Tic Tacs I found in the pocket of an old coat. I did feel obligated, as a guest, to offer my opinion that the pot smelled good.

"The Panamanians cure it in rose water. Makes it nice." Zorro rolled another.

"The Panamanians I saw today didn't seem to like us much."

Ren said, "It's no surprise."

Ren passed the joint back to me and I handed it to Zorro. Zorro took it and said, "The old men used to cut the lawns with machetes. On all fours like dogs."

"And they're afraid that, one day, we're going to take the Canal back," Ren said.

"And when that happens, they'll be back on their hands and knees, waiting on the white man." Zorro leaned his head back and smiled a smile as white and wide as the Milky Way.

Ren told him to shut up.

Zorro's head came up and he said, "We coming to it?"

"We're coming to it," Ren said.

"You don't have the hair to go weightless, man."

It was Ren's turn to smile. "You mean airborne?"

"All the way," Zorro said.

"Every day," Ren sang back. And as the glow of city lights filled the horizon, Ren hit the accelerator. The Chevy's speed climbed to seventy and the wall of jungle flew by, rushing from the headlights' beam to the red-tinted darkness behind. The engine noise folded into the wind as we turned into a slow, loping curve. Ahead was a single-lane, hump-backed bridge and we hit it doing eighty. At the top of the bridge, the car left the pavement. Everything inside went weightless—us, the gas can, the kitchen chair, Zorro's joint, everything floated, still and silent, as the Bridge of the Americas, the black sky, and the city lights filled the windshield.

"Jesus Christ," I said, and it came out "Zeeesa Heist" because every cell in my body was suspended in fright.

The car hit pavement, its springs and shocks contracted to the frame, sparks flew, and we rocketed across the Bridge of the Americas.

"Flyin'!" Ren yelled.

"Like the fucking birds!"

By the time we pulled into the city, my heart had begun to beat again. Ren parked behind a three-story apartment building and gave a gang of kids ten bucks to not strip his car. "If I'm lucky I'll have tires when I come back," he said.

The three of us walked through an alley and onto a neon-lit city street.

"Welcome to the happiest place on earth," Ren said. He opened his arms in an embrace that took in all of the people slinking through the night, from bar to hot-sheet hotel, drug deal, and alley-way blow job.

The buildings, two and three stories high, hunched in close to the traffic and shadowed the sidewalks with long porches. Laundry hung like flags of surrender over the railings and women, bored as prisoners, sat and smoked and watched the people in the streets below.

Under the porches the sidewalks were wet with a recent rain and every other storefront was open for nighttime diversions, from drinking and drugs to commercial sex and gambling. There were few tourists. The one group of Anglos I did see were young and foolishly brave, obviously gringo in their frat-boy swagger, inviting trouble from the sullen Panamanian men who lounged in the street.

I followed Ren and Zorro several blocks through a crowded neon neighborhood, past the smoky reminders of my country's colonial presence. Every block had a bar named the Foxhole, Hotel California, or Little Chicago. Anything the owners thought would remind American boys of home, although home never looked like this. Unless, that is, the boy grew up on Bourbon Street.

Most women waited at bars for men to buy them drinks and pay for their attentions. Most men traveled in packs. Some were drunk, and some were on their way, but few of them were happy to be where they were. Men who were alone weren't alone for long. There was always a woman who offered commercial companionship, if only for a few minutes. And everything on the street, from the drunks, the thieves, the hookers, and the homeless, moved to the horn-powered thump of Latin pop.

Ren led us to a small bar called the Silver Key. It had once been a popular place for American GIs and the jukebox itself was a time capsule, stocked with scratched 45s of Hendrix, Cream, Steppenwolf, and the Stones.

The rear wall, behind the jukebox, was painted with a murky mural that was supposed to be the city skyline. It was a night scene, black rectangles against a midnight-blue sky, daubs of yellow for high-rise windows. It looked like a dark and evil place.

The bar ran from just inside the front door to the back wall. Tables and chairs filled the rest of the room. A jukebox was cranked up and Van Morrison belted out one of his big hits. On the chorus, where once drunk soldiers would have sung "G-L-O-R-I-A," there was only Van, and angry people who looked like they'd just missed the last bus home.

A woman with closed eyes, red lips, small hands, and a red satin dress danced by herself. A Panamanian man at the nearest table watched her without enjoyment. When he reached for her, she danced a few steps away, her eyes still closed. He stood up and moved in, not dancing but pressing his belly, and his crotch, against her. She tried to turn away but he grabbed her wrists.

I started to get up but Ren stopped me. With a nod of his head he told me to watch. I did.

The man lifted the girl up and placed her on a chair so that her body was close to his face. The girl opened her eyes and her teeth flashed in the dim light.

The man pushed her dress up, high on her thighs, and buried his face in her crotch. She put her fingers into the tangles of his hair.

The people in the bar watched as the girl's dress rode higher and higher, until the hem of her dress was above her hips and the man's fingers fumbled at the elastic of her underpants.

She pulled the man's head back and his laughter spread across his face, wide and unsuspecting.

In her other hand was a bottle, and as it came up it caught the light like a spark and then it fell back to earth, a meteor falling from the heavens, and bounced off the man's cranium. The man sat down on the floor, grabbed the top of his head, and squeezed his eyes tight against the pain.

Another man, built like a bear, waded through the room, picked up the guy like yesterday's trash and threw him into the street. The girl continued to dance, lost in rock and roll recorded before either of us was born.

When Van Morrison stopped, so did the dancer. She climbed off the chair and pushed her way through to the bar. No one stopped her. She sat next to me and the bartender appeared as if by magic.

"This boy wants to buy me a drink," she said, looking at me with a big smile.

I nodded and said, "Bring me a beer, too."

When the bartender returned, I paid him and said to the girl, "That was a D-flat."

"What? What was a D-flat?"

"The note the bottle made when you hit that guy, the clonk was a D-flat." I hummed the note.

"You some kind of music man?"

"As a matter of fact, I am."

She scanned the bar, not even trying to hide a yawn. "I am a dancer," she said. "I think it is a pure and natural art, requiring nothing but the human body."

"And music," I said.

She looked at me again, her head tilted back, this time looking beyond my skin. "The music can be in your head," she said.

"But you have to hear it first."

She turned toward me and put her hand on my leg, her fingertips rubbing the inside of my thigh. "Would you like me to dance for you?"

"I'm here with my friends."

She took that as a no, shrugged, took her hand away, sipped her expensive drink, and watched the others in the room.

After a few minutes of looking for something more promising, she gave up, grabbed my hand, and said, "Let's get out of here." She pulled me toward the sidewalk and I saw Ren sitting at a table with Zorro and a couple of girls. Ren laughed and waved. The dime in his ear winked in the neon.

On the sidewalk, the girl said, "Come on, let's you and me go over to the hotel. I want you to show me something, gringo boy."

"You want me to show you something?"

"Yes. I want you to show me fifty dollars." She ran her hand up
my chest and caressed my neck. "What do you say?"

"What else would you like to do?"

She looked at me again, curious as to where this was going and
how much more she could charge for it, and said, "You could take
me someplace nice."

"That would be okay."

"Someplace with a piano, you can sing me a song, music man."

"I'd like that."

"Then you'll give me fifty dollars?"

"We'll see how the song goes."

"First," she said, "you have to show me you have money."

I did.

"So, why not just go across the street to the hotel?"

"What, do you object to a little romance?"

The girl laughed again, shaking her head. "Yeah, fine, okay. But
romance costs you more, gringo boy."

"It always does," I said.

I waved for a taxi. A smoking cab pulled to the curb and we
climbed into the back. The girl told the driver, "La Rosita de España." We took off and the girl settled back against me, wrapping
her arms around my chest.

"What's your name?"

"Marilyn," she said. "Like Marilyn Monroe." She seemed to be
having a good time. "Are you from Hollywood?"

"No, Washington. But it's just up the road from Hollywood."

"Hah!" She pulled away and said, "What a fucking liar. I know
where Washington is and Hollywood is in California." She put her
hands together, her two index fingers in the air, and separated
them. "They are like on two different coasts. You think I don't
know this?" She sat back in the seat with a satisfied smile. "I know
all about the United States. I know Ronald Reagan is from Hollywood. And George Bush is from Texas."

"What else do you know about the States?"

"I know Bill Clinton likes fat girls. What about you, you like fat
girls?"

"I played for the president once. President Bush."

She punched my ribs. "Get away. You did not."

"I did. He didn't stay long. And I don't think he ever really heard me because I was on the other side of the room."

"I bet he did hear you, and he ran to get away because you sounded so awful."

"Probably," I said.

"Someday I'll go to the States. I'll go to Hollywood and be a big star, own a house in Malibu and a penthouse in New York, and I will dance and act and maybe learn to sing. Then, when I tire of show business, I will be a pediatrician. What do you think of that?"

"Everyone should have a dream," I said.

"Don't patronize me," she said, "or I'll cut your balls off." She looked serious and then, unable to hold it back, she filled the cab with laughter. "You should have seen your face," she said. I smiled, but the picture of that man in the bar holding his head, his face tight with pain, stayed with me.

The taxi took us toward the ocean and a white hotel lit up like the president's birthday cake. This was La Rosita de España, an old and disapproving dueña to the rest of the city. Our taxi, trailed by its own aura of blue smoke, pulled into the driveway and came to a rattling stop.

The uniformed doorman leaned into the back window and held the door closed as he inspected the passengers. "Perhaps the gentleman has the wrong address," he said. "If you'll allow me, I can direct the driver to another, more suitable casino, sir."

Marilyn shoved open the taxi door, forcing the man to step back. "This is the very famous singer Justin Timberlake, you stupid farmer," she said. "He has come to perform for your privileged guests, tonight only. Step away from the big star from America." She reached back into the car and pulled me outside. "Please come with me, Mr. Timberlake."

Wheeling on the doorman again, she said, "Your manager will hear of this insult." With that she whisked us up the sidewalk, past the royal palms, through the polished double doors, and into the lobby.

The lobby's marble was warmed by acres of buffed mahogany. Beautiful people in beautiful, expensive clothing, drinking beautiful expensive drinks, lounged about, the glitter of gambling and coke in their eyes. They talked about things Marilyn and I were not beautiful or rich enough to understand. They glanced at us and then averted their eyes, hoping we would go away.

On my left was the casino, rumbling with activity. The gamblers stood two deep at the tables, reaching forward to place my entire month's salary on one spin of the roulette wheel. Every seat at the three blackjack tables was filled with serious men betting serious money. It was a busy Friday night and worlds away from the dark squalor of the Silver Key.

Across the lobby was the dining room, an ocean of white linen and long-legged waitresses in starched black-and-white uniforms. Beyond this, in the far corner, was the Prize, a shiny black concert grand, large enough to declare statehood. The bench was empty.

"It is a Steinway," Marilyn whispered with what I thought was appropriate reverence. We started through the doors.

But standing between us and the Steinway was the most elegant bouncer I had ever seen.

"Excuse me, señor and señorita. But you are not properly dressed. May I suggest another establishment that may be a bit more to your liking?"

"How do we have to dress to come in and spend our money on your overpriced Coca-Cola?" asked Marilyn. I doubted this tack would get us any closer to the Steinway.

"Look, all I want to do is play that piano. How much?" I discreetly held out a folded twenty.

"More than that, señor," he said, but took the bill. He also took the next bill. And the next. After sixty dollars had changed hands he bowed and said, "The manager didn't tell me we had a new impresario."

"That's very inconsiderate."

"I will have a word with him in the morning, señor."

Marilyn perched on one of the barstools, her legs crossed, a drink in her hand and a look of aristocratic ennui, like Botox, smoothing her features.

The man put a manicured hand on my shoulder and said, "No rock and roll."

"No, sir."

"Nice dinner music? Otherwise, stomachs get upset, guests go to their rooms, and no one visits the casino. If that happens, I promise you a very unpleasant evening."

"Yes, sir. I understand."

"You have ten minutes," he said, looking at his watch. "Let's see what you've got."

"Yes, sir."

I looked at Marilyn sitting at the bar and she encouraged me with a smile. I walked across the room, slid behind the Steinway, and played "Satin Doll."

The murmur of conversation began to drift away. By the end of the song, the room was still.

This is the moment when the audience will either come with me, or they'll dismiss me as just so much elevator music. *Fasten your seat belts,* I thought. I closed my eyes and jumped into the "Cuban Overture" and its Latin rhythms of 1930s Manhattan. The mistakes I made, I covered, and when I finished, people applauded. Enrique, the bartender, came over with a rum and Coke. "Compliments of the manager," he said with a bow.

For the next few hours I played every romantic ballad I could remember. "It Had to Be You," "How High the Moon," "It Might As Well Be Spring." The bartender brought me another drink.

After "September Song," when the diners were hushed, each contemplating the swiftly moving hands of time, I picked them up with "Somebody Loves Me." After "Lush Life," I took them up to Harlem on the "A Train." My left hand pounded out the rhythm and sent booming counterpoint to the crystal notes spilling from my right. I held my audience and felt that surge of power that's as addictive as heroin. The bartender brought me another drink.

After a botched attempt at a Monk piece, I gave the audience a thousand-watt smile and they laughed, encouraging me to try again. I even sang a few songs. My voice isn't big, but I've heard it described as having an easy charm, and I guess that's accurate. Women find it endearing, and men aren't threatened, which made me perfect for Washington nightlife.

Marilyn sat at the bar and watched me as the cocktail crowd replaced the dinner crowd. They sat at the tables and listened to music written for couples who could chase away the blues of a world war with just the promise of a good-night kiss and the sweet, sweet dream of peace.

If I closed my eyes, I could imagine it was 1943 and everything in the world was in black-and-white.

At the end of the night, when I closed up the Steinway, my audience applauded and then, no longer anchored by old romance, drifted off in the direction of the casino.

At the bar Mr. Montero shook my hand. "I would like to offer you a permanent position, sir. We have trouble keeping musicians like you. The good ones are usually picked up quickly by the cruise ships."

"I'm afraid I can't, sir. I don't think I'll be in town very long."

"Too bad. Perhaps we can give the gentleman a room?"

"Thank you, but I'm already booked at La Boca del Culebra."

Mr. Montero stared at me, displeased, and said, "La Boca?"

"The resort hotel."

The light went out and he said, "I know what La Boca is, señor. It is a place where they train assassins. Now, I must ask you to leave."

He tugged on his ear and two no-necks appeared at his shoulder. "Escort the boy and his whore out of my hotel."

"Whore?" The bouncers hustled us into the lobby. "I'm married to this woman!" As we passed the front desk, I snatched a red rose from a crystal vase. "This woman is the mother of my children!" I hollered, startling the guests. "This is an outrage!"

We were pushed into a waiting cab, and as the taxi pulled into traffic, I handed the rose to Marilyn. "Here," I said. "Flowers and love songs. Didn't I promise you romance?"

Marilyn sat pressed against the far door. Her unhappiness covered her in a blue funk.

"Why so quiet? Didn't you have a good time?"

"Why did you do that?" Her voice was barely a whisper.

"Do what?"

"Bring me here, make me feel good? You didn't have to. You could have just given me money like any other guy."

"I know," I said, "but then I'd be just like any other guy, and I'm not just any other guy."

Marilyn was quiet again, thinking. Then she said, "You really can play music."

"Of course, why would I lie?"

"To impress me."

"How am I doing?"

She smiled. "You got any money left?"

"A little."

"Then I really am impressed." She kissed me.

"Hey!" yelled the cab driver. "No business in my cab, stupid *puta.*"

"Fuck you, pendejo!" A knife appeared in Marilyn's hand and she pressed the point into the flesh just behind his ear. The blade caught the passing streetlights. "You want to call me stupid again?" she said.

The driver said no and Marilyn said, "Say you're sorry."

"I'm sorry," the driver said.

"Now in Spanish."

"*Lo siento,*" the driver said. Satisfied, Marilyn sat back, the knife disappeared, tucked away to whatever hiding place it had come from.

It was close to two when the cab pulled up to the Silver Key. The streets were quiet. The bar was open. I looked in the door but didn't see Ren or Zorro.

"Your friends are probably sleeping here tonight and there are no more buses. Why don't you stay with me? You can catch a bus in the morning if you miss your friends."

The two of us walked, hand in hand, toward Marilyn's room. We stopped and Marilyn touched my cheek. "I like your romance," she said. "You made me feel real special tonight, gringo boy." She took my hand and led me upstairs.

The second-floor corridor looked out onto a central courtyard overgrown with plantains and banana trees. Outside a chipped wooden door, Marilyn stopped, produced a key from her purse, and unlocked the padlock.

"You wait inside," she said and headed down the corridor. I swung the door open and stepped inside.

The room was lit from the street. A thin curtain hung across

French doors that opened onto the balcony. I looked around the room. An iron bed was pressed against the wall. A small table and chair stood in the corner. The tiny tabletop overflowed with make-up, mascara, lipstick, and perfume. Over the table a cracked mirror reflected an American boy out of his element. Wedged into the frame was a picture cut from a magazine. It was a scene from *The Misfits*. Marilyn Monroe and Clark Gable stood smiling next to a pickup truck.

I opened the French doors and went outside, onto the balcony overlooking the street. I leaned against the railing, enjoying the night.

Marilyn came out and stood next to me.

"I'm glad you took me to that hotel," I said. "I had a good time."

"Me, too."

"Would you like to come out and visit me tomorrow at my hotel?"

She looked surprised. "At La Boca?"

"Yes, I have a job for you." I took five twenties out of my wallet and handed them to her. "Is that enough?"

She looked from me to the money and back to me. "That depends, although I have to say, Señor Timberlake, one hundred dollars will get you just about anything you want in Panama."

"Great. We'll spend some time on the beach. I'll take your picture."

She took my hand and said, "I can do that."

"But right now, I should go."

Marilyn backed away, surprised. "You don't want to stay?"

"I shouldn't. Perhaps when we know one another better."

She smiled and said, "More romance, hey, music man?"

"That's right. More romance."

Someone pounded on the door and I nearly jumped over the rail. "Harper! It's me, Ren. You in there?"

I headed for the door, relieved it wasn't a husband Marilyn had neglected to tell me about. "Yeah, Ren, I'm here, hold on." I opened the door and Ren fell into the room.

"Harper! Jesus, man, I been looking all over." I saw that Ren's white shirt was wet, the front soaked and black in the darkness of

Marilyn's room. Immediately, I recognized the smell and stepped back. Ren was gasping for breath. "We gotta go!"

"What happened?"

"We gotta go, man!" I saw that Ren was scared. I was scared, too. The smell came off him in hot copper waves. I was afraid to look under Ren's shirt.

"Ren, oh man, tell me you're all right."

"I been looking all over for you, Harper. Zorro's been stabbed."

I stepped back and ran my hand through my hair, my scalp tingling. "Are you okay?"

"I don't know." Ren sat down on the bed and sobbed. "He's dead, man. Zorro's dead."

Marilyn sat next to him and pulled Ren to her. She held his head against her breasts and rocked him slowly, stroking his hair and humming a song I didn't know. Outside, in the deserted street, it started to rain.

CHAPTER SEVEN

They questioned me for hours. First, two Panama City detectives in stained suits played bad cop/bad cop for a few hours, then they handed me over to a uniformed La Guardia officer who, taking great pride in his profession, found places to hit me that caused incredible pain, but no bruises. Finally, a man from the State Department came in, sat down, and sighed until the sun came up. Together we signed a stack of forms; for a moment I thought we were buying a house together, but in the end he told me not to leave the country. He'd take my passport, just in case, he said. I asked him in case of what, but he sighed again, got up, and left me alone with the original two detectives who made me tell my story all over again.

It didn't take long. Ren had seen me leave with Marilyn and every man in Panama, apparently, knew where Marilyn lived. When Ren couldn't find me in any of the bars he came to her place. From there we went to Ren's car where Zorro was slumped against the door. Zorro's throat had been cut. I think Marilyn closed his eyes, but I'm not sure. My head was buzzing by then, and what happened after that was a blur. I remember the police, and the jail cell, and the interrogation room. But how I got to the cell I didn't remember. What answer I gave that began the beating, I didn't recall that either.

I didn't tell the police about Marilyn. I knew they would be harder on a local than they would be on an American, and I didn't want to think about that.

As Ren told the story, he had seen Zorro drinking with two men around midnight. They weren't Panamanians, but they weren't Anglos, either. Then Zorro left the bar. That was the last Ren saw of him until he found Zorro sitting by the car. Ren tried to get him up, thinking he was just drunk, thinking he had puked on himself. But Zorro had held his liquor. It was a few quarts of his blood that got away.

They let me go but kept Ren for more questioning. A Panamanian man in shiny black shoes gave me a ride back to La Boca. He said he was with the bureau of tourism.

He asked where I was from and how long I'd been in the country and where I had been stationed when I was on active duty. It was the usual expat questionnaire. He said his name was Marquez and I should give him a call if I ever needed anything. He gave me his card.

When we got back to the compound, he let me out in front of the hotel. As I was closing the sedan door he leaned across the seat and said, "This is a beautiful country to visit, señor, but if I were you I would stay close to home for the next few days, you know, to avoid any further unpleasantness. Oh, and please accept my condolences for your friend."

In the outer office, a new guy sat behind the desk. A little guy with a little brown mustache. "You Harper?"

"Yeah."

"I'm Eubanks. Some shit, huh? Kelly wants to see you right away."

"I'd like to get cleaned up," I said.

"He's not happy."

"Okay," I said, "fine." I went to Kelly's office door and knocked.

"Enter!"

I went in and stood, waiting for him to speak. He sat staring at me from behind his desk. The desktop was empty except for a phone, a straightened paper clip, and an army-issue .45. His face was empty of anything I could optimistically interpret as sympathetic. He steepled his fingers and said, "You must be Harper."

"Yes, sir."

"Close the door."

I closed the door. The office was identical to the Colonel's, but without the welcoming pictures. Mr. Kelly was smiling. But it wasn't the kind of smile that made you sleep easily.

"Are you a morning person, Harper?"

"Me, sir? Not as a rule, sir."

"You play the piano," he said. "That keeps you out pretty late, I'll bet."

"Yes, sir."

"I go to bed at ten," he said. "Because I love the mornings. I get up early, put in a little PT, get a good breakfast and a bowel movement. It makes me a happy man." Kelly stood up and came around the desk where his threat filled the room like a steam heater. "This morning upset my schedule," he said.

"I'm sorry, sir."

"I missed my bowel movement."

"I'm very sorry, sir."

"Did you have a pleasant evening, Mr. Harper?"

"No, sir. Not really, sir."

"Approximately sixteen hours in-country and you've already talked to more police than I've seen in thirty years. Must be some kind of record."

"Yes, sir."

"This reflects poorly on your employer."

"Yes, sir."

"Can I expect this kind of behavior to continue? I expected a disciplined soldier who knew how to play the piano but instead I get a musician who once wore a uniform."

"I can explain."

"So, tell me, is this how musicians live? I'd like to know so that perhaps I can adjust everyone else's schedule to fit yours, so as not to disturb you. Is that what you think I should do, Mr. Harper?" On the word "do" he leaned into me, his pecs nearly jumping out of his jersey and shoving me into the wall.

"I'm sorry if I caused any trouble, Mr. Kelly. It was unintentional."

"Oh, no trouble, Mr. Harper. Only one of my men is dead and another is in jail. Not bad for sixteen hours."

"I wish there was something I could do."

Kelly took a slight step back and perched on the edge of the desk, giving me a little space for oxygen.

"There is one thing, Harper. Right now the Colonel needs six men for a job and I find myself mysteriously short of manpower. Golly, I wonder how that happened?" Kelly's eyes bored into me as if he were X-raying my soul and finding a gross malignancy. "Now, I know your contract calls for you to play the piano, but you also have some military experience."

"Yes, sir," I said, "I do."

He let me stand in front of his desk for a long moment before saying, "Harper, about your military record."

"Yes, sir?"

"You seem to have been assigned to highly regarded combat units, and yet there are no records of you doing anything other than music, is that accurate?"

"The army rarely makes mistakes in that regard, sir."

"It must be quite difficult to kill terrorists with a piano."

"Not if you drop it from a great height, sir."

He smiled. "Ah, a sense of humor. Mr. Harper, one thing you need to know is that a sense of humor isn't authorized equipment in this unit."

"Yes, sir."

"I am allowed to make jokes, Harper. You may be the musician, but I am the company's resident comedian."

"Yes, sir."

"And I will make jokes on a regular basis, usually at your expense. Do you understand?"

"Yes, sir."

Kelly walked back around the desk and sat down in the swivel chair. He leaned on his elbows and twisted the paper clip into a tight knot. "Harper. You had a top secret clearance. Now I'm curious, why would a piano player need a top secret clearance?"

"I explained this to the Colonel, sir."

"And now you can explain it to me."

"Yes, sir. I worked at all sorts of functions, sir. Embassies, state receptions, diplomatic luncheons, that sort of thing."

"Ah, yes, that would indeed explain it. But"—he held up a finger thick as a stump—"here's the most perplexing question, the one conundrum that's kept me awake ever since I saw your record cross my desk." He paused, staring into my eyes, hoping to catch the truth as it flickered past. "Given what a fine life you had in Washington, why would you choose to come here?"

"I ran into an unfortunate situation, sir. I needed to leave the city and you needed someone familiar with firearms and Gershwin. We both win."

Kelly stood up, walked to the window, and looked out on the ocean. His back to me, he said, "If it was up to me, you'd be on the first plane home."

"The Colonel said you'd say that."

Kelly turned his head just enough to look at me over his shoulder. "Did he? Did he also tell you he was the boss?"

"Yes, sir, he did."

Kelly turned back to the window and chuckled. "We let him think that. We even occasionally give in to his whims, like his insistence that we have a piano player on staff." Kelly turned around, his hands behind his back, his starched shirt pulled tight across mammoth pecs. "I let the Colonel have his piano player because musicians are, as a rule, harmless."

"Yes, sir."

"And if they prove otherwise, I find delight in breaking them."

"Yes, sir."

"Because music is a waste of human potential," he said. "In fact, when I think of musicians I think of dancing monkeys, prancing around in little costumes, begging for fruit. Is that a fair assessment of your life's ambition, Harper?"

"I would be a fool to disagree, Mr. Kelly."

He laughed again, this time in appreciation. "Indeed. But you will find that I'm a remarkably tolerant man. What kind of music do you play?"

"Popular American music."

"Not rock and roll."

"No, sir, not rock and roll. I like the rhythms but it's not melodically interesting."

"Shut up."

"Jerry Lee Lewis and Little Richard were intriguing—"

"Would you please shut up?"

"And bop had both, rhythm and melody—"

"Shut up!"

"Yes, sir."

"So what is this popular music?"

I could have given him the entire history of Tin Pan Alley, the music that formed the foundation of popular American song, but instead I abbreviated it to: "Ellington, Gershwin, Cole Porter." I wanted to add, "a Negro, a Jew, and a homosexual," just to see how he'd take it, but I didn't. Some things are best left a mystery.

"Jazz," he said, and it had all the appeal of something sticky you accidentally touched in a men's room. "Can you play sacred music?"

"Yes, sir."

"Good, because we need a musician in the chapel." Kelly paced in front of the window. "I wonder," he said, "you not only have the piano-playing abilities the Colonel wants, but you also come to us with solid attaboys from real soldiers. Tell me, how skilled are you with firearms?"

"I prefer Steinway, sir."

"That's unfortunate. Let me see your hands."

I held them out, palms down. Kelly gripped them. He turned them over, examining my palms closely, looking for my future, no doubt. He rubbed his thumbs over my skin and declared, "Too soft. In fact, I think you're soft all over." He put one hand on my chest and shoved with as little effort as I would use to open a door. I flew backward, hit the far wall and fell to the floor, sitting upright, my legs straight out in front of me.

Kelly moved back behind his desk and sat down.

I stood, rubbing my chest. I felt like I'd been struck by a small planet.

"Now, you're here for a very brief time, and if you behave yourself, do what you're told, go only where you are authorized, then perhaps you can return to your soft little life in Washington, without having your hands broken."

"I'd like that, sir."

"In your time here, I would suggest that you not try to fuck me." He smiled that discomforting smile. "You won't try to fuck me, will you, Mr. Harper?"

"Never, sir, no, not ever, not a thought. No fucking in my future, sir, trust me."

"Outstanding. And if you ever bring legal scrutiny to this hotel again, I will pin your testicles to my office door. Do we understand one another?"

"Yes, sir."

"Now get cleaned up. The stink of that whore's perfume is polluting my military air."

I turned toward the door, thankful to get out while I was still alive. My chest throbbed where the man had so casually shoved me.

Ramirez and Cooper were waiting for me in the lobby. They were dressed to run in sweats, even though the morning temperature was in the low eighties with determination to climb even higher. Ramirez was hungover. He perched on the edge of a sofa, his head in his hands. But Cooper looked as though he could run to Canada and back before lunch. He bounced from foot to foot, shaking his hands, eager to go.

"Get your shit, Harper," he said. "We're going to run your ass off."

"Okay," I said.

"Let's go, let's go." Cooper clapped his hands.

Ramirez looked up at Cooper with bloodshot eyes and said, "If you don't stop that, I might have to kill you."

"You have to catch me first," Cooper said, and bounced on the balls of his feet.

"I'll be right back," I said.

"Take your time," Ramirez mumbled. "I might be dead by the time you get back."

I took the steps two at a time, which was about the limit to my running. The truth was, I hated running. I could swim every day, and I worked out with weights, and even did a little kickboxing with a few of the Washington wives, but jogging was as enjoyable as being run over by a bus full of Promise Keepers. I didn't like it.

Sometime in the night, the airlines had delivered my lost bag and there it was, on my bed, its airline tag still attached to the handle. I opened the bag and found the contents all there, but they had been searched. By whom I didn't know, but under the tumble of clothing, among the books and the CDs I'd packed, I found a CD that didn't belong to me. It was a recording of Willie "The Lion" Smith, one of the finest stride players ever. I opened it, put the disk into my player, and put on my headphones. The first cut was "Finger Buster," an aptly named piece. I forwarded to the second cut and heard the hiss of a tape player instead of the muffled pop of a remastered seventy-eight. A man said, "So, which one you think?"

A second man replied, "I am very curious about this one."

"That's an understatement."

"There is some indication of special operations training."

"Yet no certifications."

"And no combat assignments."

"That's the way they'd do it, wouldn't they?" This first man had a New England accent and I recognized my new boss, the Colonel. "Wouldn't they want us to overlook him?"

"How was he recruited?"

"We needed a musician for the party, someone who could also double as security."

"Did he come with references?"

"Yes, a man in the company vouched for his capability and we have letters from several others."

The second man, the younger man, had foreign music in his voice and he lacked the easy familiarity with contractions. "Well, if he is our spy, he will be easy to eliminate . . ." The foreign man let the idea float out there by itself.

"What about this one? The Mexican?"

"He, I think, is very dangerous."

"And Cooper?"

"He is good, but naïve, is what my sources tell me." The younger man laughed and said, "They referred to him as a Boy Scout."

Somewhere, a salsa band started up, forcing the younger man to speak louder. "What about the clerk? What do we do with the clerk?"

"Right. Yes. Vasquez."

"You no longer trust him?"

"Kelly worries about his loyalty."

"But didn't Vasquez recommend the piano player?"

"Yay-uh," the Colonel said. "He did. That's something to watch."

"So you green-light the clerk?"

"Yes, but after Vasquez, no more until the New Year. It was Winstead's death, remember, that we drew this attention."

"That was sloppy, I admit."

"And the other boy with the shark. I don't think anyone believed it was an accident."

"We intended only to drown him, not feed the fish."

"That is a comfort to his family, I'm sure."

"The next will be better, I promise, cleaner," the younger man said. "We will give you, how do the politicians describe it, 'plausible deniability.'"

"The memory of those boys," the Colonel said, his voice barely audible above the band's horn section, "keeps me awake at night."

"It is the overenthusiasm of the men," the younger man said. "You train them to be ruthless too well."

"I see those boys everywhere," the Colonel said, "even in my dreams. That is, when I can sleep."

"Have your new pet, this piano player, play you a lullaby, Señor Pepe. While you sleep, my men will locate and dispose of this spy."

"And if it's the piano player?"

"His music will not protect him, señor."

"I don't know. Maybe he's just here to play the piano," the Colonel said sadly.

"Maybe," the younger man said. "In the meantime, give him to Kelly."

The Colonel laughed.

"You see a joke in this?"

"Give him to Kelly. I just remembered the first time I saw a cow fall into a river of piranha."

The younger man snorted in agreement. They both thought it was funnier than I did.

"But maybe there is no spy," the Colonel said.

"There is a spy. My contacts are never wrong."

"Then why can't they tell us who it is?" The Colonel was frustrated.

"Because this is being played outside of normal channels."

"Goddamn it to hell!" This shout was accompanied by a loud bang, and I pictured the Colonel's fist smacking the table. The Colonel's voice dropped to a whisper. "In the old days we didn't have Americans spying on our operations, not unless it was Hoover, the blackmailing son of a bitch, and his butt boy, Tolson. But today, it's not enough we keep the reporters with their goddamn safari suits and lip gloss contained. Now we have agencies cobbled together by Congress, DOD, Justice, hell, anytime you get three people together for lunch in that town, one of them's goddamn intel."

The Colonel stopped and I wondered why. He had been on such a rant I wondered if maybe he'd popped an artery. Then I heard the waitress ask if they wanted another round and the foreign man said yes.

When she left the foreign man said, "That is one fine beauty there. It is a waste that she is not waiting for me in my bed."

"Can we get back to business?"

"It must be awful to be old," the young man said. His voice was so clear that I knew the microphone must have been planted very close. That meant someone had been watching them, and noticing their habits. This wasn't a chance pickup or surveillance with a shotgun mic.

"Remember, Colonel, your plan depends on everything going smoothly at the New Year's Eve party." The younger man stressed "your plan." "We've laid out all of the clues, everything that would lead them to all the right conclusions. That is the genius of this operation. That is your genius, sir."

"It wasn't my plan alone," the older man said.

"Oh, sir, please. Do not be the modest person." The second man said something else, something neither the microphone nor the Colonel picked up.

"What did you say?"

"I said that we need more money."

"It was just a matter of time. Like Laos."

"Like Laos," agreed the younger man. "So our clients will move more product, we get more money, it is an easy thing, right?"

"I don't want to know about it," the Colonel said. "It all seems so sordid, somehow. But if you think it's right, just do it."

"Before New Year's."

"Yes, before New Year's."

The recording ended and I sat for a moment on the edge of my single bed, suddenly cold. The recording had come from Smith, I knew, but how and when did he get this? And who recorded it? And the bigger question was, How long would it be before the Colonel and this younger man had me fingered? And what about Ramirez? So far he hadn't impressed me with his dedication to covering anything but his bar tab.

A knock interrupted my wallow and Cooper stuck his head in the door. "Come on, man, we have to go." He looked at my shorts and said, "Christ, Harper, you think you're running through the damn country club? Put on some long pants or these jungle bugs will eat you alive."

A few minutes later I stood in the driveway, as ready for the run as I'd ever be. Cooper stretched and Ramirez smoked. Ramirez dropped his cigarette, stepped on it, and without a word started a quick but lumbering jog toward the treeline, hunched over like the Bambino running bases. Cooper followed, and I followed Cooper.

Cooper ran easily, all long-legged strides that were graceful and easy, as if he could do this all day. Where Cooper was a loping giraffe, Ramirez was a rhinoceros, crashing through the brush.

I ran more like a three-legged dog. I could get where I wanted to go, but it wasn't fast and it wasn't pretty and it wasn't anything you wanted to watch for too long except out of a twisted sense of wonder. At first it wasn't too bad. The running trail was clear, and beautiful. Flowers added their fragrance to the path. Monkeys chattered in the trees. Birds offered their song. It was an easy jog through paradise.

An hour later my legs ached, my throat was raw with inhaled pollen, I had a pain between my ribs like molten steel, and the goddamn birds wouldn't stop shrieking. "Christ . . . Jesus," I wheezed. "Can't . . . we . . . stop?"

"The enemy eats those who stop," Ramirez said.

"What enemy?"

"He'll show," he said, "and you better be ready." He and Cooper picked up the pace and I limped after them. After a few miles I'd exhausted my vocabulary of obscenities and was forced to start all

over with variations on the "ass" theme. About the time I'd hit the
Ps, I found them stopped in a small clearing. Both men were sweating, I was happy to see, but neither had succumbed to a coronary.

"I told you he'd catch up," Cooper said.

"Yeah," Ramirez said, "but look at him. He looks like he's about
to pass out."

"He's here, that says something."

"Yeah, it says he's scared of getting lost."

I put my hands on my knees and tried not to throw up. Then I
sat down and figured I'd quietly die here and let the army ants have
me. It was a pleasant thought, my molecules feeding an egg-laying
queen, making babies by the millions. My ribs heaved as I tried to
get enough oxygen to my brain to figure out how to levitate my ass
back home.

"Come on, we got a full day ahead of us and a lot of land to
cover."

"I thought for sure we'd be at the fucking North Pole by now."

"Tierra del Fuego," Cooper said, looking up past the branches
toward the sun. "We've been running south."

"I should have been a dentist," I said.

After resting for a few minutes, we were back on our feet. I was
too tired to push away the vines and branches. I just focused on the
backs of the two men running in front of me. I couldn't let them
get away because I swore that if I ever caught up with them, I
would kill them. Just the thought of it kept me pounding down the
shadows, chasing the two men who were always a few steps in
front of me, always out of reach.

It was shortly before breakfast when we came out of the jungle
and onto the beach, where I fell on my back, knees up, arms out,
ready for my maker to take me home.

"They want us at class at oh nine hundred hours," Cooper said.
"We've got fifteen minutes."

"What class?"

"Security class. They're teaching the security students how to
use antipersonnel mines," Cooper said.

"So they can use them against all the tourists storming the
beach," Ramirez grumbled. "Jesus, if it weren't for the money, I'd
go home and sleep for a few years."

"The money is good," said Cooper. "I just want enough to go back to law school. What about you?"

Ramirez spit in the sand. "I'm spending all mine on hookers and beer."

And the money was good. Damn good for living at the beach. And I was about to run into another good thing about working at La Boca. She was twenty-four, blond, and inexplicably fond of piano players.

CHAPTER EIGHT

I went through the lobby and hit the stairs. I stopped midway and listened. Someone was playing the piano. One. Note. At. A. Time. A woman sang Eartha Kitt's "Santa Baby," but the only words she knew were the title.

"'Santa baby,'" she sang, and played the melody with one finger until the lyrics came back around to "Santa baby" again.

I went into the dining room and there, near the French doors, stood a young woman with hair the color of movie sunlight. She wore a swimsuit bottom and a white button shirt tied just below her breasts. One knee was propped on the piano stool and a flip-flop dangled from her toe.

"There are more words to that song, you know. And if you play three notes at once, you get what's called a chord," I said. "It's all the rage."

She looked up, startled, and she was so beautiful I thought I'd stroked out on the trail and was still lying in the dirt, surrounded by lower primates, hallucinating. And it was okay. In fact, it was better than okay.

"You must be the piano player," she said.

"Word gets around."

"You know how I can tell?"

"How?"

"You're pale. Don't they have sunlight where you come from?"

"Not at night. In December."

She went back to playing each note. "When did you get in?"

"Yesterday."

"So this piano is your responsibility now."

"I'm barely responsible for myself."

She smiled and said, "Do you always smell like that?"

"Like what?"

"Like an alcoholic warthog three days dead in the sun."

"Most days I crawl into the shade." I wiped the sweat from my face with my shirttail and said, "You must be the man's daughter."

She held out her hand. "I am the man's daughter. My name's Kris."

"Hi, I'm—"

"John Harper, I know." She lowered her eyes and her lashes fell against her cheeks. I'm a sucker for that. "I've been looking forward to meeting you. We don't get many music lovers around here. Especially such cute ones."

Flattery. I'm a sucker for that, too. I put on my finest smile.

"Can you really play this thing?"

"A little," I said.

"Could you teach me?"

"It would be a pleasure."

"Right now?" She sat down and slid over on the bench to give me room.

I heard men gathering in the lobby. "I can't right now. But maybe later?"

"I'll be waiting," she said, and I floated up the steps.

I was the last one to class, my hair wet and my clothes damp. When I sat next to Cooper he said, "Who smells like a flower?"

The class was held outside on the edge of a firing range chopped out of the jungle. Cooper, Ramirez, and I were the only Anglos. Sitting on the far side of the bleachers, in their own group, were half a dozen very intense Latinos. One of them quietly translated as the instructor, an Aryan with a ranger haircut, high and tight, stood in the shade and introduced himself.

"Gentlemen, my name is Melvin Short, but most of the staff

here know me as Glory Hog. You might wonder why. So, to save us all time I will explain. It's because of this." He held up a battered *Newsweek* magazine. On the cover was a ranger, his face striped in green and black for combat. It was our instructor, Melvin. "Now, you may call me Mr. Short, or G, or even Hog, but the only person who calls me Melvin is your girlfriend when I bone her, and I do bone her on a regular basis. Is that clear?"

The Latinos did not laugh.

"I'm glad to have new blood to laugh at my material. Welcome aboard, gentlemen. I understand you're familiar with weapons so I may call on you to help me demonstrate for the class, is that all right?"

We nodded. I added a "Yes, sir," out of a habit instilled in me by an insistent young captain and the sole of his boot.

Hog put the *Newsweek* aside, put his hands behind his back, and addressed the Latinos, pausing as the translator repeated each sentence in Spanish. "We will learn only defense here as you have been chosen to protect your bosses at home, not to pursue the bad guy in the field. Considering the brief amount of time you'll be here, that is a good thing because the enemy in the bush is a bad hombre and would eat your heart out." Hog waited for the translation. "Sending you amateurs up against the FARC is like sending Girl Scouts up against the Oakland Raiders in the friggin' Super Bowl."

The translator translated and a few in the audience shifted on their haunches and grumbled. They weren't happy being compared to a bunch of Girl Scouts.

Hog ignored them and picked up a gray tray the size and shape of a small frozen dinner. "This, gentlemen, is a Claymore antipersonnel mine. It is a nasty little item filled with steel balls, seven hundred of them, all about the size of a nine-millimeter bullet. They shred flesh, right down to the bare bloody bone of anything unfortunate enough to be caught in its kill zone. Now, have any of you used Claymores before?"

Ramirez and Cooper raised their hands.

"Anyone else? No? Okay then, pay attention." He gestured into the open firing range. "Most often, you will use Claymores in either an ambush situation in which you place them along the expected route of your enemy, or as a defensive deterrent to an insurgent force around a fixed perimeter. But be aware, gentlemen, that in the hands of a determined enemy, these defensive weapons can also become your worst nightmare. So, watch and learn, people."

The translator whispered the translation and the men nodded their heads, the insult forgotten in their eagerness to see these weapons in action.

The firing range was about three hundred yards deep and twenty-five yards wide. A few rows of coiled barbed wire had been stretched across the field to simulate a defensive position. A single scarecrow, no more than a wooden cross, a gourd head, and an olive-drab shirt stood in the center of the field. On a folding table were wired detonating devices small enough to hold in your hand.

"Ordinarily," said Hog, "you would clear a kill zone all around your position. This range is for demonstration purposes only. Do not, I repeat, do not fight in this narrow a corridor or your enemy will feed your *huevos* to his dogs. Now, are there any questions?"

There were none.

"Okay," said Hog, "I want you all to put on your safety goggles."

We did.

"Now, it's nighttime," Hog said, "and it's as dark as Castro's asshole—"

The translator murmured and the Latin men laughed.

"—you're in your foxhole and you hear this sound." Hog pulled a wire and a can rattled out in the field. "You ascertain the direction of the sound, locate the detonator of the mine in that area, and set it off like this."

Hog picked up a detonator, switched off the safety, and fired one of the mines. The boom was louder than I expected and the scarecrow was knocked backward, stripped of his head, his shirt tattered to rags in one single explosive instant. The men went "Aaaah" like a family watching fireworks on the Fourth of July.

"You!" Hog pointed at me. "Come here."

I stepped off the bleachers and stood in front of the instructor's table.

"Pick up that detonator." Hog pointed to one. I did as I was told.

"This is the safety," he said. "When you want to fire the Clay-more, you switch off the safety and squeeze this." He looked me in the eye, scrutinizing me for any trace of panic or instability. "You okay?"

I said I was.

He clapped me on the shoulder and said, "Outstanding. Now I want you to pretend. Can you pretend, New Guy?"

"Yes, I think so."

"All right. Pretend it's night. Can't see shit. Pitch-black. You got it?"

"Yes."

"Good. You're on guard. You still pretending, New Guy?"

"Uh-huh."

"What do you see?" He held up three fingers in front of my face.

"Where?" I said. "What?"

"Good man." He patted my cheek. Then he waved and a shadow moved out of the treeline. It was a man, camouflaged from head to toe and dressed in a sniper's Gilly suit. If he moved you could see him. If he stopped, he looked like another dusty bump of vegetation in the landscape.

Slowly the shadow worked his way under and through the wire until he was directly in front of the instructor's table. He laid a small canvas satchel at the foot of the table and pulled a handle. As he made his way back through the wire, he stopped at each mine and turned it around, facing us. When all the Claymores were turned, the shadow tied a string to the barbed wire and slowly crept back into the trees.

"You still pretending, New Guy?"

"Yes."

"Now you hear a noise," Hog whispered. Everything was silent. The men in the bleachers leaned forward in anticipation. Even the jungle animals seemed to quiet. Then, all the cans strung to the wire clanked.

"Quick, New Guy! What do you do?" Hog was pressing against me, nose to nose. "The man's coming, he's going to kill you, New Guy. He's going to cut out your mama's heart! Quick, do something!"

"But he turned—"

"He's gonna kill you, New Guy! Quick, take off the safety!"

I did.

"Now what do you do? What did I tell you to do?"

"Fire the mine?"

"Then fire it! Holy shit, New Guy!"

"But the mine's been—"

Hog screamed into my face, "Fire it, fire it, fire it! NOW!"

I pressed the detonator. The boom filled the sunlit morning and everywhere was the shush of little pellets hitting leaves and grass and uniformed men. The Latinos in the bleachers gasped, mouths open wide in terror. Then the canvas satchel popped and sent a thick stream of red smoke swirling into the air around us.

Hog was calm again. "You just wasted your clients, New Guy. Nice work. But don't think you're going home, because that satchel charge just blew you into tiny little pieces about the size of your pecker. Now, get your sorry ass back to the bench." I joined Cooper and Ramirez. They were laughing and brushing sand off their clothing.

"Now, those mines were harmless. But in a real firefight you would all be in a massive world of hurt. The moral, gentlemen, is not to let your guard down. Don't assume that your firepower will save you because it won't." Hog looked at the men on the bleachers. "Can anyone tell the New Guy what he should have done?"

"Stayed home," Ramirez said.

A tall Latino stood up and said, "Use your weapon." He was decked out in twin leather shoulder holsters, each holding a stainless-steel .45 with ivory grips. He drew one and held it high in the air. The sunlight glinted off the barrel. He smiled at all the other men as if to say, "I am the only real killer here. I know how to use my weapon."

"Bueno, Helizondo," said Hog. "Go ahead."

Helizondo laughed and fired his big automatic toward the jungle. He emptied the magazine and looked around at the rest of us, a smile on his face.

"Now that Helizondo is dead," Hog said, "having given away his position with his muzzle flashes, does anyone know what you should do if you hear something out there in the darkness?"

I raised my hand.

"New Guy, I thought you were dead."

"A flesh wound," I said, and Hog laughed.

"So, you want to try again?"

I nodded. "Use a hand grenade," I said.

"Excellent. That's right. Use your hand grenade. Do not fire your weapon at night at any noise or you, like Helizondo, will be dead and so will your comrades because, like an idiot, you have given away your position to the enemy."

Helizondo looked confused as the translator murmured Spanish into his ear. On the word *idiota,* Helizondo straightened as if struck. None of the other Latino men would look at him. Helizondo gathered his dignity, walked over to where I was sitting, and smacked me hard enough to send me backward off the bench. He needed to hit someone for the insult and, since hitting Hog didn't seem like a healthy choice, he chose me because I was the one who had shamed him with the right answer. I understood all this, through the stars that swam around in my head, but understanding and accepting are two very different things.

Before I could get up and defend myself, Ramirez had Helizondo on his back, the muzzle of the man's own .45 in his mouth. Ramirez was whispering in Spanish, too fast for me to understand. He finished by saying, "*Comprende,* motherfucker?", and Helizondo nodded yes, his eyes wide, and Mad Dog Ramirez let him up. Ramirez ejected the magazine, pulled back the slide to clear the chamber, backhanded the magazine into the jungle, and handed the empty pistol to Helizondo, grip first.

"I can see we've run out of time," Hog said, "not to mention patience. So let's take a break." The Latin men stood in their small group and smoked cigarettes and glared at us.

"Thanks, Mad Dog," I said.

"The name's Phil. Only my mother calls me 'Mad Dog.'"

"Thanks, Phil."

"Don't mention it."

CHAPTER NINE

That afternoon, when the entire compound lazed away the hour after lunch waiting for the one o'clock rains to pass, I sat in my room and put together what I knew so far, which wasn't much.

The hotel was training bodyguards and home security. I still didn't know who the guests were, the men who would be the employers of the hotel's graduates, so I'd have to work on that, and the compound in the jungle still needed a look, but even if the guests turned out to be cousins of Saddam Hussein, and the facility was the exact layout of Madonna's Malibu beach house, that still only told me *what* was going on, but not why. And who, besides Phil Ramirez, was on the ground working for Smith? Who had bugged the Colonel's meeting with the foreign man, and could I depend on his help if I found myself wearing my ass for a hat?

The rains stopped and the sun turned the afternoon into a sauna. I was dreaming about air-conditioning and bored, beautiful women when Phil pushed open my door and said, "Frag class. Let's go."

"Me?"

"Hog's giving a class on frags. After you wasted everyone with the Claymores, he wants you there."

"What's to know about a grenade? You pull the pin and throw it."

Phil leaned against the doorjamb, his hands in his pockets. "I know you're not arguing with me."

Phil could have pinched my head off with two fingers, so I said, "Let's go." While I was locking up, I said, "What do you know about Coop?"

"He's okay."

"You served with him?"

"No, but I know guys who have. He's on our side."

That might have been good enough for Phil, but it wasn't good enough for me.

The class was held on the same range as the morning's instruction on Claymore mines. This time the students stood behind a bunker made of earth and wood and watched as Iceman and Hamster demonstrated from a concrete bunker set into the firing line. Hog stood in front of us, his hands behind his back. "Has anyone here ever thrown a live grenade?"

All but two of the Latinos raised their hands. I had tossed exactly one hand grenade in basic training, but I'd tossed it far enough away, and it did explode, so I had my hand up with the rest of the men.

"New Guy, so, unlike the Claymore, this is a skill you've acquired?"

"I wouldn't exactly—"

"Come on down, show us how it's done."

"It was a long time ago," I said.

Hog nodded and said, "Okay, New Guy, fair enough. We don't want you fucking up with a live frag, so we'll give you a quick refresher." He turned to Iceman and Hamster who waited in the bunker. "You men ready?"

Iceman nodded. Hamster, a boy-faced kid with chubby cheeks shifted from foot to foot. "I want to throw this time, Hog, let me throw."

"Fine. Ice, you spot him."

Ice nodded again.

As Hamster went through the motions, Hog explained what was happening. Once again, the translator did his thing.

"You grasp the hand grenade in your right hand," Hog said, "if you're right-handed. Then raise both hands to your chin, elbows out, left index finger inside the pin."

Hamster raised his arms, elbows out.

"You pull the pin."

Hamster pulled the pin.

"You let the spoon go. That's this handle here, and it arms the fuse."

Hamster let the spoon fly.

"Now count to three, and throw."

Hamster counted to three and tossed the grenade like a football. When it was in the air, he and Ice ducked behind the bunker, shielded by three feet of steel-reinforced concrete. Those of us in the class dropped behind the earthworks and waited for the grenade, fifty yards away, to explode with a spray of dirt and a satisfying *crump*.

The men, turned on by the sheer power of a palm-sized piece of mayhem, went, "Oooh."

"Now, New Guy, since you did so well this morning with the Claymores, I want you to take Ice's position and spot me as I throw. Once we take you through it, then it'll be your turn to throw."

"Okay." I stepped into the bunker. Hog waited for me, an olive-drab grenade already in his hand. As I took my place next to Hog, Hamster and Ice stood behind us. I was a little nervous, and I wiped my hands on my pants.

"Don't be scared, New Guy," Hog said. "Your job as spotter is to make sure the grenade clears the bunker. You got that?"

"Uh-huh." I blew out a short breath and wiped my palms again. "You ready?"

I nodded.

Hog repeated his instructions as he went through each step. "Lift the grenade, elbows out. Remember, this isn't any John Wayne bullshit. You're going to throw this from just behind your ear, as if you were a quarterback."

I heard the translator repeat "quarterback."

"You pull the pin." He pulled the pin. I watched him pull the pin.

"You let the spoon fly." I watched the spoon fly.

"This arms the fuse. Now you count one—"

I watched Hog cock his right hand behind his ear.

"—two and shit."

I watched the grenade slip from Hog's right hand, bounce off the dirt, and roll toward Ice and Hamster. Their eyes and mouths gaped in frozen terror. The students behind the earthworks scrambled for cover. I heard a rushing in my ears, like a flood of water over rock. I had no time. The seconds clicked by, the grenade sat in the dirt, and I dropped and covered the grenade with my body.

Lying there with the smell of the earth in my nostrils, the rushing in my ears, seeing Hamster's boot, a speck of red mud on the toe, I felt the hard lump of the grenade in my gut and I thought to myself, "So this is how it ends. My first unselfish act will also be my last. And I'll go out looking at a speck of mud on a stranger's boot." I closed my eyes and tried to think of something better, and for no reason, I saw Kris Kelly's face.

Hog tugged at my shoulder.

I stood up. Silence hung over the range like a blanket. Hamster picked up the grenade. Hog blinked, and brushed dirt from my cheek, which was wet. "I've never seen anything like that," he said, his voice a whisper edged in wonder. "You jumped on that grenade."

"I fell," I said, still unsure if I was whole or halved. "I didn't jump."

"He jumped," Hamster said. "I saw him."

"He jumped on a live grenade," Ice said.

"No, really, I fell."

The men behind the earthworks were all silent.

Hog said, his jaw unhinged, "We've done this to a hundred guys, and no one has ever jumped on the grenade."

"Most guys wet themselves," Hamster said.

"But you jumped on the damn grenade." Hog's face pulled itself out of surprise and into wide-eyed, illuminated appreciation of something he'd never seen before and probably didn't ever expect to see again, like Elvis pumping gas along Route 666. "Goddamn, New Guy," he said, "that was in-fucking-credible."

"He looked like a monkey," Phil hollered, "jumping on a coconut."

The word "monkey" swept through the group, English and Spanish speakers alike. Laughter followed like rain and washed away the remaining tension.

"A fucking monkey man," Hamster said.

Hog gave me a one-armed hug and said, "Monkeyman, you got some damn brass balls, I'll give you that."

The thought drifted through the blind haze of the adrenaline rush. "You mean this was a joke?"

Hog was decent enough to be embarrassed. "It's how we break in the new guys. A hazing, kind of. We never expected anyone to do that," he stammered, his hand wheeling about, searching for words to describe what he had just seen. "To jump, to throw himself . . ." He trailed off.

I stood there in the bunker as, one by one, men walked past and shook my hand and called me "Monkeyman," my new name already polished by their respect. There was still rushing in my ears and my knees trembled. I felt like I might throw up, or let go of my bladder, but I didn't. Instead, I held on to a bright and shining thought of hunting these men down, one by one, and killing them in cruel ways as payback for the strain they had just put on my heart.

CHAPTER TEN

I walked dazed to my room, lay down on my single bed, and stared at the ceiling. In what might have been minutes or hours, Eubanks, the clerk who had replaced Ren, knocked on my door. "Monkey-man," he whispered, "you got company. A girl."

"What?"

"She's in the lobby. Says you told her to come."

I looked at my watch and remembered Marilyn. She had promised to help me today, but that was before Ren had brought us the bad news about Zorro and before I had thrown myself onto a live grenade. I pulled myself together, threw some cold water on my face, and went down to the lobby.

Marilyn was sitting beside a potted palm, reading a paperback, a wide straw hat on the seat next to her. She wore shorts, flip-flops, a bikini top, and sunglasses. At her feet was a woven beach bag big enough to carry twins.

"Marilyn. I'm glad they let you in."

She looked up and smiled. Without the mascara and crimson lipstick she looked like the brightest girl in her freshman class. "I told them I was here to see you and they let me through the gate, no problem. You must be a very important man."

"Oh, yeah, *muy importante*. I'm surprised to see you," I said.

"You asked me to come. Last night." Marilyn whispered. "You gave me the money."

"But after what happened—"

"I'm sorry about your friend. And I am grateful you didn't tell the police about me. But if you want me to go home, I will."

I held up my hands and said, "No, no, please, I want you to stay."

"You look awful," she said.

"It was a long night. And a long day."

"I can come back." She gathered up her hat and bag.

I ran a hand over my face, hoping there would be a new one under there, one that was better-looking. "No. In fact, today is perfect."

She grasped my hand and pulled me to her, kissed my cheek, and whispered in my ear, "I brought the camera, like you told me to."

I nodded and glanced at Eubanks sitting behind the front desk. He was staring at Marilyn standing on her tiptoes, the curve of her backside moons peeking out from beneath her shorts. Caught, he gave me an attaboy smile.

I knew the next satellite flyover wouldn't be for an hour, giving us time to capture candid portraits of all of the horny guests lounging around the patio. I had seen their response to the waitress, and counted on it with Marilyn.

We went out the hotel's front door and around to a quieter part of the beach shaded by overhanging coconut palms. I spread out two towels and took a disposable camera from her bag.

Marilyn stepped out of her shorts. She shook loose her hair and said, "Now what?" She put her hands on her hips and posed in the tiny swimsuit. "Is this okay?"

Marilyn had a gymnast's body, as if she'd spent the past ten years spinning around parallel bars and bouncing past tables full of Eastern European judges. Her skin was the color of café mocha, her bikini the color of bananas, and I was reminded that I'd skipped lunch. "Marilyn, you look good enough to eat. Let's move into the sunlight," I said.

We walked down the beach toward the rear of the hotel. A few of the men, some lounging in the shade of patio umbrellas, some sitting in the sun, watched Marilyn as she scampered along the waterline, kicking rainbows from the surf.

A single male slumbered on the sand, oiled up and as brown as a saddle. I posed Marilyn so that the man's profile was just over her shoulder and said, "Now give me a big smile." She did and I snapped her picture. "Now I want you to stand there," I said, putting her in front of the man, and she did, placing one hand behind her head and the other on the small of her back pushing her breasts toward my camera lens.

"Very sexy," I said, and snapped another picture.

"Now, let me get the patio in the background," I said, and Marilyn bent over, her hands on her knees, and stuck her backside up at the guests, her face up to me.

As soon as I raised the camera, every man on the patio raised a newspaper or magazine. I tried a few more shots but caught only the covers of *People* and *Time*. Marilyn huffed and shook her head. "It's no good. No man wants to see me. I am too brown, not like that." She pointed up the beach and said, "That is what they want."

I saw Kris walking toward us, her blond hair pulled into a pony-tail and her skin pink from the sun. She bent at the waist and, two-handed, lofted a beach towel into the breeze and let it float easily down to the sand.

I said, "Make like Tyra Banks. Let them see just how beautiful a Panamanian woman can be." I snapped a few shots.

Marilyn was reluctant at first, but I pushed her, telling her that next to the gringo girl, pale as a coma patient, she was a jungle flower full of light. "You are a café delight," I said, throwing out metaphors like Mardi Gras beads, "and any man who prefers plain vanilla to chocolate is a philistine."

She giggled, but tossed back her hair. I snapped another shot and moved, winding the camera. Marilyn followed me, smiling, loosening up. She started snapping off poses as quickly as my thumb could advance the film. The patio was behind her and the men were all looking in a single direction, their faces bare, their eyes locked on the reclining *rubia* in the blue two-piece.

I quickly snapped all twenty-four exposures and, Marilyn on my arm, waded back to our shady spot on the beach. Marilyn dropped to her towel, sulking. I put the camera in the bag and stretched out next to her.

"Thanks," I said. "You did great."

Marilyn sat up. "Did you see those greasy old men? And their fat bellies? All staring at that girl?"

"They saw you," I said.

"No they didn't. I could have been naked, my *chucha* in the breeze, and they would not have looked away from her, that girl."

I rolled to my side and put my fingers on Marilyn's shoulder. "You're just as beautiful as that girl."

"Bullshit." Marilyn shrugged my hand away.

"Hey, Monkeyman!"

I shielded my eyes from the glare off the water and saw Hog standing over me. Meat stood a few feet behind him, his rifle in his hands, a very ugly smile spread beneath his mirrored shades.

"You've been taking pictures," Hog said. He shook his head. "I'm going to let that slide because you're new, and because of what happened at the range. But I have to have the camera." He held out his hand.

"But I was just taking pictures to send back home."

Hog waggled his fingers. "Come on, man. Let me have it before Kelly finds out. Pictures are a breach of security. The camera, please."

Marilyn reached into her beach bag and handed me the camera. I handed it to Hog. Hog handed it to Meat, who dropped it into the sand and stepped on it with the heel of his boot. The plastic snapped. Meat picked up the broken body, pulled out the ribbon of film, and threw it all as far as he could into the water. It floated for a moment, the Kodak yellow on the sparkling swell, and then disappeared.

"I won't be able to cover your ass another time," Hog said, "so don't do that again." He shook his head. "You could be in big trouble if Kelly knew."

"I wasn't thinking," I said. "Thanks, Hog, for cutting me some slack."

"I wouldn't have," Meat said.

"That's because you didn't see what he did this morning," Hog said. "The guy's all right." Hog looked at Meat, one corner of his smile turned up, and said, "I remember what you did when Hamster dropped that frag. Should we tell 'em what you did, Meat?"

"Shut up," Meat said, as quick with a witty reply as his name suggested, and turned away.

When they were gone, I lay back and closed my eyes. After a few minutes I said, "Is the camera safe?"

"The camera is safe."

"You did give me the right one."

Marilyn huffed. "Of course I did."

"And what was in that camera he destroyed?"

Marilyn giggled. "Twenty-three pictures of my feet and one of the dog who lives downstairs."

"Very good."

We spent the rest of the afternoon relaxing, until the sand fleas drove us off the beach. I walked Marilyn to the parking lot. She got into a small blue car, its fenders and hood round and fat with 1950s excess, and rolled down her window.

"Where'd you get this thing?"

"It belongs to my neighbor. He lets me borrow it sometimes."

"What is it?"

"A fifty-four Hillman. It's English."

I circled the car. "Does it run all right?"

"No. My neighbor calls it the envy of Sisyphus because he has to push it every day. Do you know who Sisyphus is?"

"Yeah, the guy who pushes the rock up the hill."

Marilyn's eyes twinkled with mischief. "You're pretty smart," she said, "for a musician."

"Is there FedEx here? A way I can send this back to the States and have it arrive tomorrow?"

"Yes, UPS. But not tomorrow. Tomorrow is Sunday."

"Oh, right. Monday, then." I dug into my pocket. "How much do you think it'll cost?"

"Two hundred dollars."

I stopped, my hand still in my pocket.

"I have expenses," Marilyn said.

I pulled my money out and handed it to her. "Here's eighty-five. It's all I've got. You'll have to scrape by on that." I gave Marilyn a business card along with the cash. "Send the camera to that address."

She put everything into her bag, slipped on her sunglasses, and said, "Will I see you tonight?"

"Maybe."

"I'd like that, Monkeyboy."

"Monkey*man*," I said.

"You'll have to prove that," Marilyn said and touched my cheek. The engine started with a rattle like small change in a beggar's cup, and Marilyn drove off in her cartoon car.

CHAPTER ELEVEN

When I returned to my room, it was clear that someone had searched it, careful to put everything back in the right place, but careless about the matchbook corners I'd stuck between the dresser drawers and the frame. There were four drawers and four paper triangles on the floor. The electronic bugs were still taped in their hiding place, but my laptop had been opened and someone had broken my password, I don't know how, and read my e-mail. There was nothing but the usual promises to enlarge my penis and other come-ons that were intended to shake loose my self-esteem and any cash I might have in my pocket.

I logged on to a Viagra site, one of Smith's little jokes, and hit the contact button. Up popped an e-mail form and I typed in:

> I don't give out my credit card number on-line. Watch for money to come by UPS Monday. Don't know how many pills I'll need as the New Year's party has not been confirmed."

I logged off and went to a Web site dedicated to exotic birds. I downloaded a high-res picture of a toucan from the splash page, enlarged a section of his neck, and isolated the map in the feathers' texture. I memorized the map and closed the site.

Find out who is here and what they're up to. Do that and I can go home, Smith promised. He made it sound so easy.

My stomach rumbled, I looked at my watch and saw I was hungry. I showered and changed, thinking a trip into town for a decent meal would be a nice reward for a productive day. I went down the steps, and as I was crossing the darkened ballroom, I heard the piano again.

The rising moonlight poured light through the windows. A lone figure sat at the keyboard, intent on her song.

"Hi, Kris."

"Hi, Monkeyman."

"News travels fast."

"We're bored," she said. She slid to the end of the bench and said, "Come here, and sit next to me."

"What are you playing?"

"A Ben Folds song."

"Ah," I said.

"You don't know who Ben Folds is, do you?"

I admitted I didn't.

"He had a big hit a few years ago."

"Ah," I said again.

"Okay, so I know you don't listen to the radio. Who do you listen to?"

I shrugged and idly played chords that fit under her melody. "James P. Johnson, Bill Evans, Art Tatum, Oscar Peterson, you know. The usual."

She shook her head. "More like the unusual. Have you ever heard of Jimmy Eat World?"

I laughed. "No. And you made that up."

She crossed her heart. "I didn't." She watched my hands. "You have such a nice touch. Will you play something?"

"Sure." I moved to the center of the bench and began to play one of my favorites.

"That's pretty. What's it called?"

"'Our Love Is Here to Stay.'" I particularly like the lyrics. I sang a line for her.

"Nice," she said, "but you don't really believe that stuff."

"I do," I said. "I believe in love so right that it lasts a lifetime.

I believe that each one of us is only half to a whole and that it's our mission on earth to recognize our other half when we meet them."

"You're joking."

"I'm not. And if I didn't believe that, I'd walk into the ocean right now."

"*A Star Is Born,*" she said.

"A classic," I said. "The James Mason version is my favorite. You like movies?"

"I love movies." Kris perked up and said, "Hey, there's an art house in the city." She looked at her watch. "If we hurry, we might be able to catch something good. Last week it was *Double Indemnity.*"

"You forgot your hat," I said, repeating a line that Barbara Stanwyck uses on Fred MacMurray.

Kris clapped her hands. "God! That was such a great scene, and she's standing there in the doorway and you can see she doesn't have his hat."

"And he says, 'Just put it on the chair.'"

"Yes! That was so good! So sexy." She laughed, and the way her hair moved in the moonlight made my heart stop. "So, you up for a movie?"

"I don't know. I was just going into town to get something to eat."

"You missed the last bus," she said. "But I have a car. We can see a movie and get a bite together, what do you say? Come on, I haven't been away from here since before Christmas."

"What about your father?"

"He's off picking up more guests."

"Don't these people do anything but lie in the sun all day?"

Kris shrugged. "They go to the casinos at night, but they're just waiting for the big blowout on New Year's Eve. That's what they're all waiting for." She played a C-major chord, followed by a G. "Are you all right? You look a bit flushed."

"Yeah," I said, "I'm fine."

"Good. I saw you on the beach today with that girl."

I laughed. "I saw you, too. Everybody saw you. I thought the guests were going to drool all over their *Financial Times.*"

"I hope you got some good pictures." Before I could dissect her tone, timing, posture, and expression for any ominous undertone, she said, "I know this terrific place for sushi. I just have to get my keys."

I let her lead me up the stairs to the second floor. She opened the door to a suite of rooms, all with a beautiful view of the courtyard and the water beyond.

"So, you live here with your father?"

"Yeah."

"How long are you staying?"

"I have to go back to school in a few days."

"That's the most depressing news I've heard since I got here."

She said, casually, "You looked like you were having a pretty good time with that girl."

"Sometimes you have to make your own fun."

She did me the huge favor of laughing, and it made me want to make her laugh again. Her skin glowed and I watched as she moved around the room, plunging into and out of the shadows.

"I can't find the fucking keys," she said. "Shit."

She disappeared into an adjoining room and I idly looked around the place. Her suite was so different from my third-floor monk's cell. The ceilings were fourteen feet above cool tile and the windows opened onto a wide balcony. The air hummed with air conditioned air.

I moved about the room, but like most hotel rooms, there weren't many personal items that might tell me more about her. I spotted a photo and a book on an end table. The child in the photo sat in the lap of a weary but attractive woman in her thirties. The child looked like Kris. The woman looked tired. But she had managed a tight-lipped smile for the photographer.

I turned the book over and read the title: *A Peace to End All Peace*.

I heard the jingle of keys and looked up. "I found 'em," Kris said. "Let's go."

I held up the book. "Is this yours?"

"Daddy's, but I just started reading it."

"You know your father hates me."

Kris rolled her eyes. "I'm sure he doesn't. He's a little aloof, that's all." She grasped my hand and pulled me toward the door. "Now let's go or we'll miss the beginning of the movie."

I followed her out to the parking lot. Kris owned a VW Beetle, an old convertible, its top held together by duct tape, its body held together by rust. The paint had faded into a dusty blue and the seats were a goat buffet.

The guard stopped us at the gate.

"Hi, Meat," Kris said. "If Daddy's looking for me, tell him I went to a movie."

Meat stared at me the way a Persian-rug collector might eye an incontinent dog. "With him?" Meat's lip curled back from bright white canines.

"Yeah, with him," she said. "You got a problem with that?"

Meat's shoulders bunched and I could see the muscles in his jaw work. "No, Kris, no problem." And we all knew that there was a big problem and for some reason I figured it would be my problem as soon as Meat and I were alone.

Kris drove through the city like Bonnie Parker outrunning the law. She made quick, unannounced turns and fast sprints between lights. We pulled up across the street from El Leo, a magnificent old theater built in a time when theaters were rightfully called palaces. The marquee was ringed in neon, its name a proud shout into the street in six-foot-high, electrified letters. The movie playing was *Casablanca*.

Kris bought my ticket. "You're my date, remember?" She let me buy the popcorn.

I liked *Casablanca* but I sympathized more with Sam, a piano player caught between two unreasonable people, than I did Bogart. I loved Sam's opening number, "*Shine*," but the lyrics were politically incorrect and I was far too white to sing them anywhere but in the shower.

This was my first time seeing *Casablanca* on the big screen, dubbed from English into Spanish with English subtitles. The actor who dubbed Bogart's voice tried to sound like Bogey, but succeeded in sounding more like the older Bacall. Ingrid Bergman's voice was a Latina Betty Boop, high on helium. But still, when Rick gave up the girl, I looked at Kris and saw the reflected black-and-white flickering across her eyes and in her face I saw the loss, the sacrifice, and the heartbreak laid bare, completely stripped of my generation's new-century cynicism.

Watching Kris's face in that flickering theater made me feel, for the first time, the sadness and nobility of that moment when the plane engines cough, the propellers begin to spin, and Bogart puts Ingrid Bergman on that plane with her husband, Paul Henreid.

The lights came up and Kris dabbed her eyes with her sleeve and I fell in love. It wasn't intentional.

After the movie, we climbed back into the VW and zipped across town, racing the *chiva* buses and taxicabs from one intersection to the next. The city speed was forty-five and everyone ignored it, especially Kris, and the traffic rushed along, bumper-to-bumper, at sixty.

"I'm taking you to this place that makes screwdrivers with fresh-squeezed orange juice," she hollered. "They've also got the best raw bar in Central America."

"I'm completely in your hands," I said.

She flashed a smile as she ran a yellow light and said, "You wish." Then we shot up a wide boulevard, dodging buses and scattering pedestrians like geese.

Kris took me to a dark bar in a fine hotel where the bartender spoke English, Japanese, French, German, and Italian. "The Chinese are very interested in Panama," he said, "so I've been working on my Mandarin, just in case." I made a note of it.

Kris sat close to me, her thigh pressing against mine. Her hair smelled like honeysuckle and popcorn and her breath was fragrant with fresh orange.

We talked about movies and music and mothers. We had lost our mothers, both of us, when we were young.

"I was fourteen," Kris said. "There was an accident."

"I was twelve."

Kris tied her swizzle stick into a knot. "Other people don't get it, do they?"

"No," I said. "I don't think they do."

"How lost you feel."

"And how guilty."

"Right, like it wouldn't have happened if you'd been smarter or prettier."

"Or someone else."

We ordered another drink and the multilingual bartender ran the oranges, each one as big as a softball, through the juicer.

Kris told me about the University of Richmond, where she was a senior, and said, "This is the fifth school I've attended. I keep changing my major. And I probably won't graduate from there, either."

"Why not? How many credits can you have left?"

"Just six, but, I don't know . . ." Kris wrapped her hands around her drink and said, "I don't really fit in there. A lot of rich kids with expensive cars. They think it's cool that I've lived all over the world."

"And you don't?"

"You should know; army posts are the opposite of cool."

The bartender announced last call, in English. We had one more and then walked back to the car. The streets were nearly empty and the smell of garbage and low tide carried on the breeze. I held the driver's door open for Kris and she slipped behind the wheel. "I like you," she said.

"I like you, too," I said, carefully stepping around the emotional land mine.

"You're like this weirdly hip choirboy. You give off the strangest vibes, like you have this big secret you can't ever tell anyone."

I laughed and looked at the clouds skimming high above the halo of city light.

"Well, do you?"

"Do I what?"

"Have a secret you can't tell?"

"Yes," I said.

"Can you tell me?"

I looked at her face. It was open and trusting, eager for me to reveal something about myself that others could never know. "A musician never reveals his secrets."

Her eyes narrowed. "That's a magician."

"We belong to the same union."

"Here I thought we were having a moment." She turned to start the car and I stopped her and I kissed her, and her lips parted and she kissed me back. When we broke, she said, "You're still an asshole."

"I've been told that before."

She shook her head. "It's okay. The fact that you have secrets, I mean. It's kind of sexy," she said. "Like a man of mystery."

"Oh, yeah, that's me."

We listened to a Panamanian station play Latin music all the way home. The nine P.M. rains had swept through, leaving a clear sky, and as we got away from the city, the Milky Way appeared directly above us, a white streak stretched across the universe. When we pulled up to the gate, Meat had apparently gone to bed to dream of stomping me into the mud and Hamster waved us through.

I walked Kris to her door and we kissed good night, and she promised to see me tomorrow and I said it was tomorrow already and she laughed and started to ease the door closed on a whispered good-bye.

The door stopped before it latched. When it opened again, Mr. Kelly was standing behind his daughter, his hand squeezing her forearm. His grasp was so tight that his fingertips were white.

"Do you know what time it is, Mr. Harper?"

"Yes, sir, I do."

He said to Kris, disgust like a fungus fuzzing his words, "Get to bed." He let her go and I could see tears in Kris's eyes, whether from pain or embarrassment I didn't know.

Kelly stepped out and closed the door. We were alone. He loomed over me, his jaw clenched as if he were trying to crack a nut between his molars. "Did anyone give you permission to leave the hotel with my daughter?"

"No, sir." The alcohol I'd had, and the way he'd handled Kris made me careless. I stepped into him, my face in his, and said, "But I thought my virtue was safe accepting her invitation."

Kelly stiffened, not expecting me to stand up to him there, trapped in the hallway. "I don't ever want you speaking to my daughter again. Do you understand me?"

"I think she can choose her own friends," I said. I'm stupid that way because, of course, he hit me. I should have seen it coming, but I was standing so close, and the old man's hands were so quick, that his fist was on its way before I could even blink. Then I was on the floor, looking up at him through a bright light of pain.

"Get out of my sight," Kelly growled, and I did. On all fours, more humiliated than hurt.

I tossed and turned on my single bed. Finally, the adrenaline and shame of being knocked down made me get up, take apart my sunglasses, retrieve my picks, and do what I should have done the night before. I broke into Kelly's office.

It was nothing. No one had bothered to change the lock since the hotel was built and a child could have opened the office door with skills picked up from Scooby-Doo. The file cabinets were harder, but yielded. Pop, and I was in. When I looked through the files, I saw why the security was so casual: There was absolutely nothing of interest. Everything was as boring as the hotel laundry list. I know because I read the hotel laundry list.

So I left a high-gain listening device attached to the underside of Kelly's desk. I made sure the outer office was clear and moved through the dark to the Colonel's door.

This door was dead-bolted, which gave me hope and about sixty seconds of difficulty. The files inside were locked by a steel bar that ran through metal hasps and was secured, top and bottom, with combination locks. I didn't even try. They were way beyond my skill level.

The computer, like the one in Kelly's office, would glow too brightly and attract moths and armed men to the windows, so I let it sleep, knowing I'd be stymied by the password anyway. I'm always disgusted when a movie geek types away for a few seconds, machine-gun quick, and then announces, "I'm in." Yeah, right.

For the Colonel I left my best device, a crystal-controlled telephone transmitter the size of a matchbook. It runs on a single AA battery that will last for two weeks, which I hoped was thirteen days longer than I'd need. That transmitter would pick up both ends of a phone conversation and all conversations in the room. I love technology.

As I was locking up the Colonel's office, headlights swept the lobby. After I was sure I hadn't soiled myself, I crept through the dark dining room, eased out of the rear door and out onto the patio. I found a spot behind a potted gardenia for cover, just above the side entrance. Below me, a three-quarter-ton truck, its bed covered in canvas, pulled up to the drive, cut its headlights, and two men got out.

One man was the Colonel. He was talking to the other man. "We'll get air cover," he was saying, "but the ground initiative is ours."

"The men will do their duty," the other man said. "It is an honor to be chosen to right the wrong of a hundred years."

The new guest's face sported a horizontal white strip across the bridge of his nose. He paused, lit a cigarette, and in the firelight I recognized him as the Gorilla I'd swatted with the hardback on Christmas Eve. He was one of the men the Major had sent to skewer me for talking to Mariposa, and he was a man I'd traveled nearly a thousand miles to avoid.

(

CHAPTER TWELVE

The chapel was a six-pew, white-steepled church that looked as though it had been helicoptered whole out of the Virginia hills and dropped into the rain forest with all its hymnals intact. The Colonel bullied a dozen waiters, landscapers, and busboys into carrying the piano out onto the patio, loading it into the three-quarter-ton truck, and then wrestling it through the narrow chapel doors. In the process, the names of the Father, the Son, and the Holy Virgin Mother were invoked often enough to fill a month of Sundays.

The piano took a few discordant knocks but its soul seemed to be in good shape as I chunked out a few left-hand triads. I stuck to solid majors, minors, and sevenths, no jazz extensions and certainly none of those flatted blue notes that would make the miracle of the wine sound more like last call.

I worried about meeting the Gorilla in the pews but soon realized that all of the Latino guests were either worshiping their inner eyelids from the horizontal prayer position, or had driven into town for mass with the locals. The only people in chapel this morning were Kelly, the Colonel, the Anglo trainers, and Kris, whose shoulders, as revealed by a pale blue sundress, reminded me that there was indeed a kind and generous Creator.

Meat even wore a tie around his keg-sized neck.

I struggled through "A Soldier of the Cross," "At Anchor Laid,"

"Remote from Home," "When the Roll Is Called Up Yonder," and several other martial tunes before the Colonel stepped to the pulpit and talked for an hour about God's army and how we should smite our enemies in His name. Kris sent me holy messages with her eyes while her father gave me looks of damnation and I felt chastised as a sinner, and risen as the redeemed, all in one service. We closed with "Leaning on the Everlasting Arms." The hymn didn't say whether those arms were supplied by Colt or Smith & Wesson.

The rest of the afternoon passed like any other day with the guests lazing about the beach, knocking long putts toward the cup, or playing doubles on the courts. Twice the men ducked inside or under shelter, and just as they spent their days avoiding the overhead satellites, I spent my day hiding from the Gorilla. At five, the men gathered in the bar with the Colonel and Mr. Kelly, for what I assumed was not an evening Bible study, and I cursed my stupidity for not planting a bug in the one private place where all of the men could congregate.

I went outside and around to the rear of the hotel. I tried to look nonchalant beneath the windows of the bar, standing by the blooming hibiscus, pretending to look out over the water, my hands in my pockets, as if I had nothing on my mind besides my spiritual connection to the flora and fauna. Still as a painting, a lone iguana watched me watch him. He opened his mouth and poked his tongue out. As someone said, I get no respect.

Most of the conversation was in Spanish, of course, and between the rush of the breakers, and the roar of my ignorance, I heard nothing of value until one man paused and translated for the Colonel. He said "monkey trap" several times and I moved closer to the window.

"Hey, you, what are you doing there?"

It was Helizondo, one of the many men in Panama who didn't care for me. He had a pistol in his hand, one of his ivory-gripped Colts, and behind him was another Latino security trainee. He was carrying an Uzi. They both aimed their weapons at me.

"I was just watching the waves," I said.

"Then go down to the beach," Helizondo said. "Go away from here." He thrust his pistol like maybe he could throw the bullets at me and save a few pesos on gunpowder.

Taking the hint, and the opportunity, I went into the hotel, up the stairs, and knocked on Kris's door. There was no answer. I was on my way to my room when Eubanks said, "Hey, Monkeyman, you got a call."

It was Marilyn, asking me to dinner. "You wait there and I'll pick you up. Wear something nice."

"How nice?"

"Panama nice."

Which is an oxymoron.

The restaurant was part of the local yacht club and we ate at a table next to the dock. Sailboats and stinkpots rocked easily on the black water as night smothered the Isthmus in humid darkness. The waiter brought us lobster, shrimp, and crab. We ate with our hands, the garlic butter making our fingers slick and fragrant. We smeared our wine glasses and called for more and Marilyn talked of places she'd never seen, and things she would do if she won the lottery, and songs that made her cry.

I asked about her family and she told me her parents had been killed in the Panama invasion.

I made all the awkward apologies that seem so inadequate, and are, when tragedies like this are revealed. I asked how old she was when Operation Just Cause made her an orphan overnight.

"I was five. The sisters at the convent school took me in." Marilyn shrugged. "It was a long time ago."

I did the math in my head and said, "Do you mean you're nineteen?"

"Yes, John, why?"

"You seem older than that, more mature."

Marilyn giggled and said, "So, now I am an old woman, is that what you mean?"

"No, no, I'm surprised, that's all."

Marilyn bit a shrimp in two. "We grow up fast here. It's necessary."

After hosing the butter off our hands and faces, we had a very decent flan and another glass of wine. I must have gotten lost for a moment because Marilyn said, "You seem unhappy. Is there something wrong?"

"I'm sorry, no." I tried a joke—"I was just thinking about the bill for this dinner"—but my delivery wasn't convincing.

Marilyn touched my bruised jaw with her fingertips. "What happened here?"

"A lack of communication," I said. "I should learn to speak the language."

"Panama City is a very dangerous place."

"So I'm finding out."

"In Colón you cannot even walk the streets in the daytime because men will rob you, maybe kill you, for nothing."

"There seems to be a lot of that going around."

Marilyn's fingertips traced my lip. "What can I do to make my piano man happy?"

"You're doing fine." I changed the subject. "Have you ever heard of a monkey trap?"

"Yes." Marilyn shook her head. "But I think it's a fairy tale, you know? Just a story people tell. Why?"

"I heard some people talk about it. I was just curious."

"A monkey trap is this: You hollow out a coconut, fill it with rice or nuts, and bury it in the ground leaving just a small hole exposed, about this big," she said, and formed a small circle with her hands. "Now, you be the monkey."

"Okay."

"You come to the coconut, sniff the treats inside, and you reach into the hole. Go ahead, reach in, little monkey."

I stuck my hand through the circle. "Now what?"

"You grab the treats. Go ahead, make a fist."

I made a fist.

"Now try to pull your hand out."

I couldn't. Marilyn held me tightly by the wrist. "So what, the monkey could just let go," I said, "and get away."

"He could," she said, "but he won't. He wants the treats too much to save himself, even if it means his life." She released my hand.

I rubbed my wrist, surprised by the strength of her grip.

"Who have you heard talking about a monkey trap?"

"Some men around the hotel," I said. "That's all."

Marilyn's face went from serious, to worried, to a forced cheer as quickly as wind moves across water. She said, "Hey! I know what we can do."

"What?"

"We can go see a *bruja*."

"A bruja?"

"Yes, a witch, a psychic, where you get your fortune told. It will be fun."

We drove out of the city, north, beyond the jungles of the Isthmus and into a higher elevation, cooler, and with rolling expanses of grassland cleared for cattle. We were stopped by two bored La Guardia at a military checkpoint, and after they looked over our identification, and I had given each one five dollars, they waved us on. A few miles farther on, Marilyn pulled off the highway and onto a dusty road that ran back through stunted scrub forest. A few hundred yards into the forest we stopped in front of a small adobe house, its front porch strung in Christmas lights and its yard a patch of dust that had been raked at precise right angles. We climbed the steps. Marilyn's hair captured the colors of the Christmas lights. We knocked on the door.

I don't know what I expected. I hadn't pictured a crone, but I hadn't pictured the woman who answered, either.

Marilyn's bruja was an attractive woman in her forties, darker than Marilyn, with curly hair and green eyes that were magnified behind tortoiseshell glasses. She wore a long white dress, open at the collar and cinched at the waist with a black leather belt. A white cat curled around my leg and purred.

"Marilyn, it is a surprise and a pleasure." The woman bent at the waist, hugged Marilyn, and gave her a light kiss on the cheek. "I see you brought an American friend to visit. How nice for both of you. Please, come in." She led us into a tiny living room lit by a single paper-shaded lamp. The bruja settled into a wicker wing chair. Marilyn and I sat next to each other on the sofa.

A toucan, high on a perch, turned his head and sized me up with one marble eye. He was unimpressed with what he saw.

Marilyn introduced me to Miss Turando. "A very wise woman who knows all things."

"Con mucho gusto." Miss Turando let me take her hand. It was cool and dry.

"And why have you and your young friend come to see me, Marilyn?"

"He wants his fortune told. To know about his future."

Miss Turando laughed, her long fingers held against her bosom like a matinee actress in a sham swoon of humility. She leaned forward and placed those fingers on my knee and said, "It is all for fun, Mr. Harper. I am really a nurse at the hospital, but the girls like to pretend I am a *bruja*, so I let them."

"That's kind of you," I said. "And how much do you charge the girls to pretend?"

The smile didn't change, but behind those thick lenses her eyes widened. "I charge only what they think my advice is worth, Mr. Harper, and no more. Now, would you like some tea?"

"I'll be happy to help," Marilyn said, and started to get up.

"No, please, I'll be right back." Miss Turando disappeared into the back of the house. I could hear the tinkle of cups against saucers and she soon returned with a tray. She placed it on the coffee table and poured each of us a cup.

There was also a single glass of water and a white candle.

"Since you both seem to be in a hurry, maybe we should begin." She lit the candle and set it behind the glass so that the flame illuminated the water and flickering shadows danced across the tabletop.

"Have you ever had your fortune told before, Mr. Harper?"

"No, ma'am. This is a first."

Miss Turando smiled and it was oddly comforting. "Just relax, Mr. Harper, and let your thoughts wander where they want to go. Have you been in Panama long, Mr. Harper?"

"Just a few days."

She studied the water and scowled, unhappy with something she saw. Perhaps it was a bad review.

"And are you planning a trip, say, to another part of the country?"

"No, ma'am, I'm not."

She raised her eyebrows, surprised by my answer. "Not even to the far side of the Canal? For a party of some sort? A New Year's Eve party, perhaps?"

"Not that I know of."

"That's good. If you are invited, it would be wise to decline."
I thanked her for her advice.

"You are not a believer, are you, Mr. Harper?"

"Maybe a little skeptical."

"Very wise. Tell me, do you have a dog?"

"No, ma'am, I don't."

"Hmmm. I see a dog. A dog with a man's head in his mouth."
She stared into the shifting currents of the tumbler.

I asked, "Does this dog bite?"

"He will not bite you. Others will not be as fortunate." Miss Turando poured more tea. "There is a young woman." It wasn't a question.

Marilyn smiled and put her hand on my arm.

"Another woman," the bruja said, and Marilyn took her hand
away. "An Anglo woman. American perhaps. Am I right, Mr. Harper?"

"I don't know."

Marilyn whispered, "La rubia."

"Yes, she is blond and you have promised to teach her something, but it is you who will be the student."

Marilyn sank back into the sofa cushions with her arms crossed.
"I bet she teaches you something."

"I'm getting a confusing message here. Someone will be hurt."
Unlike the earlier theatrics, this time she seemed genuinely worried.

"Who?" I asked.

"I don't know." She looked at us, a frown on her face, her large,
magnified eyes darting from me to Marilyn and back again. "I am
frightened for both of you." She paused and took a deep breath.
"Mr. Harper, give me your hands."

She held them in hers and closed her eyes. "I sense music, lots
of music, but"—her eyes opened—"you have too many secrets,
Mr. Harper. I can't tell what is truth and what is fiction."

"That's because he's a spy." Marilyn laughed.

It was a joke to Marilyn, but not to me, and from what I saw in
this bruja's eyes, it wasn't a joke to her, either.

"Please, I'm very tired." Miss Turando stood up. "Please, if you
would be so kind." Her hand was shaking. She stopped us at the

door and seemed almost afraid to be near me. "Mr. Harper," she said, "you would have been wise to stay in the States. Please, please go home as soon as possible. Before the New Year."

"Why? What's supposed to happen? What is so terrible?" I looked from the witch to Marilyn but both faces were pale with fright. If this was a joke, it was a good one.

Miss Turando shook her head and said, "I'm begging you to go. Please." Without another word she closed the door and we heard the bolt slide home.

In the car, Marilyn sat for a long time without starting the engine.

"Are you feeling all right?"

"I don't know," she said, and her voice quavered.

"Hey, it's okay." I tried to touch her hand but she pulled away. "She's just crazy."

"Maybe not so crazy," Marilyn said.

"And there's nothing between me and that girl. Honest." It was a lie, and shameful, and I wanted to take it back even before it had left my mouth.

Without a word, Marilyn started the car, put it into gear, and drove toward the highway.

I looked back at the house with its raked yard and Christmas lights and heard angry dogs barking in the distant hills.

CHAPTER THIRTEEN

Marilyn didn't speak the entire trip. I tried joking about psychic hotlines and why if Miss Turando could see the future she couldn't foresee how much more doctors got paid than nurses, but it just steamed her, and she worked her mouth as if she were about to spit. She pulled up to the hotel's front gate and stopped. She wouldn't look at me.

"If Miss Turando can predict the future, why was she surprised when we showed up? Huh? Tell me that?"

She gave me a look that was a mixture of pity and contempt. "Stop it," she said. "You are just making yourself look foolish. There are things going on here, John, that you don't know anything about."

"This is about the blond girl. You're jealous."

"Just shut your stupid mouth." She twisted the wheel in her hands. "Go on, get out. Now."

I leaned into the open window. "Look, I'd like to thank you for all the help you've given me."

She stared at me for a long time but I couldn't read anything in her eyes. Finally, she said, "Don't ever come to see me again, John Harper. Not ever." Marilyn let out the clutch and took off toward the city, leaving me standing in a circle of light next to Hamster, who was standing guard at the gate.

"Dude," he said, "that was harsh."

"Yeah."

"What did you do?"

"I don't know, Hamster."

"Sometimes it doesn't take much, you know, to make women angry," he said.

"You got that right."

"You two getting it on? Because the word is, you have your eye on Kelly's daughter. Not that I blame you, man, 'cause she's one fine definition of fine."

"No. Marilyn's just someone I met. And there's nothing going on with Miss Kelly, either. I don't think that's a good idea, do you?"

Hamster nodded. "Yeah, right, I guess not. But you wouldn't be the first guy who thought with his little head, bro."

"A wise observation, Hamster."

I walked down the dark road toward the hotel. Lights were on and there were a few people in the bar, but no one stopped me or even looked in my direction. I climbed the stairs and unlocked the door to my room.

There, on my dresser, was my laptop. I opened it and sat on the bed. To anyone tossing my room, and I could tell that someone had tossed it again while I was gone, the computer looked harmless. If you turned it on, the usual window came up and the usual programs ran. But this laptop had been a gift from Smith. This laptop recorded conversations, even when off, that were transmitted by the bugs I'd planted the night before. It couldn't be far away, but two floors, even through this tropical concrete, was close enough.

I listened to Kelly's bug first but, instead of any information about the guests, or what Kelly had planned for New Year's Eve that I could use as my ticket away from this place, all I heard was the stale air of a Sunday afternoon in an empty office.

I switched to the Colonel's frequency and heard the same hush of nothing.

I lay back against the pillow and dozed off, the headphones on, and at some point in the night I was awakened by conversation. At first, still drugged by sleep, I wasn't sure if people were talking in the hallway, or in a dream, and then I realized that the voices were in my ears. The voices were those of the Colonel and the younger man with the accent. They were speaking on the Colonel's phone.

"We are set," the younger man said.

There was a long pause filled with nothing but breathing and the scratch of static. The Colonel said, "I know it must be done."

"Do not think about it. Are we ready for the new year?"

"Yes. The General's yacht is due in port Wednesday morning."

"Good. I will be in touch. Until then, please try and not fuck up any more than you already have. Explaining the loss of one of Major Cruz's men has already taken up too much of my morning," the young man said, and hung up.

The Colonel said to his empty office, "Goddamn little goat fucker."

CHAPTER FOURTEEN

It was three days to New Year's. Three days to find out who was here and what they were up to. What could be easier?

Phil knocked once and pushed open my door. "C'mon, partner, time to run."

"It's got to be Monday," I said. "Monday in hell."

"Isn't there someplace we have to check out?"

"You mean the place in the bush?"

"Yeah. Kelly went into the city for something, which means we've got the morning to ourselves. You're supposed to be the smart one, what do you think?"

"I'm the smart one, huh?"

"That's what I've been told." Phil yawned, letting me see his molars. "So far, I haven't seen it myself."

I didn't bring up that first-night drunk, or that maybe I was as skeptical about my intelligence as anyone. But I did bring up Cooper. "I know I asked you this before, but how well do you know him?"

"I'd trust him with my life," Phil said, "which is more than I can say for you. All I know about you is you're good at picking up women."

"Fair enough."

Cooper was already on the beach, stretching his hamstrings and delts and traps and whatever else he felt a need to stretch. I blinked a few times in the bright dawn, stretching my eyelids for a hard day's labor. Every other muscle in my body hurt too much to move, and what didn't ache burned, itched, or throbbed. I was enduring, as stoically as I could, the scratches, welts, and stings of the natural world, as well as the drubbing I'd been given by Panama's finest and the right cross I'd been too slow to duck. I was beginning to think I wouldn't get out of this place alive.

Cooper looked up from his leg stretches. "What's eating you?"

"I want to run another route today, is that all right?"

Phil was impatient and in a bad mood. "Let's get moving. Another minute of this and I'm going to kill somebody."

"Lead on, Monkeyman," Cooper said.

The three of us took off at an easy pace. I knew the direction I had to go and, with the sun in its spot, and whatever magnetic magic there is in our human skulls that give some of us a sense of direction, I knew we would soon intersect with a path that would take us to a road, across a river, and on to the urban warfare site the satellite had picked up in the jungle. And, of course, I got lost.

After going in the wrong direction for twenty minutes, I stopped and took my bearings again.

Cooper raised an eyebrow, but didn't say anything.

Phil and I argued about where we were, where we were going, and how best to get there. I studied the map in my head, then the sunlight, and then the map again. While Phil was kneeling by a slow-moving stream, a long-legged rodent emerged from the underbrush, stopped, and looked at us. Satisfied we were either harmless or that he could outrun us, the creature sipped water from the stream. He was so close Phil could have swallowed him.

When he was gone, Phil said, "What the fuck was that?"

"It was an agouti," I said, "a member of the guinea pig family."

"An agouti? How did you know that?"

"I read a book, Phil."

"Maybe I'll give that a try," he said.

"I have an idea," I said. "If we're looking for a river, we should be able to find it if we follow this stream."

"That's your idea?"

"Yeah. What do you think?"

Phil looked unimpressed. "What? You read that in a book, too?"

"What's so important about this place you're trying to get to?" Cooper asked.

"I won't know until I get there."

"I hope they have a Starbucks," he said, and started off along the stream. Phil and I followed. It wasn't easy, and there were times we had to detour around a thick tangle of vine, but we kept going in its general direction until it joined a river so muddy it looked thick enough to plow.

"Which way?" Coop said.

I looked up and down stream, trying to match the twists in the river to the bends recorded by the satellite. I took a guess. "This way," I said, and pointed upstream.

We hadn't gone more than a mile when we saw the footbridge, one rope strung across the current, with two other ropes, shoulder high, strung for balance. We crossed over, carefully, the bridge bobbing and swaying under our weight. The river below us was swift and carried trees and bushes torn roughly from an upstream bank.

The path was easy to follow now, and clear. Five- and six-feet wide in places, and well used, it made the next three miles an easy run compared to the struggle of crashing through the foliage alongside the stream. Near the crest of a hill the path widened and spread into what looked like a staging area, with a helicopter LZ among the ruts and the tire tracks of large trucks. Beyond the LZ, streets ran through the first plywood-and-cement buildings of an empty village. The three of us walked down what looked like the main street, wide enough for parades. The buildings on either side were just plywood fronts, like a Hollywood set. The deeper we went, the more detailed the buildings got, with doors and window frames.

"What the hell is this?"

"What's it look like, Coop?"

"It looks like an urban assault course."

Phil bent down and picked up a spent brass casing. "We got live fire." He tossed it to Coop.

"AKs. We don't train with AKs."

"Maybe we don't," I said, "but maybe the students from the hotel do."

"Why would they train with different weapons than the ones we use at the range?"

"I don't know."

Cooper chewed on the inside of his lip, turning the brass casing around in his hand. He looked up and said, "Something doesn't smell right."

It was time to give Cooper a way out. "That's why we're here," I said. "Whatever it is stinks all the way up to Washington."

Cooper looked from me to Phil and back to me again. "Both of you?"

Phil nodded.

"Anyone else at the hotel besides you two?"

"There were. They're both dead," I said. I explained about the satellite photos and the anonymous guests, and how something big was set to go down on New Year's Eve. "I'm supposed to learn who is staying at the hotel, if they're bankrolling something bigger than just training their own personal security forces, and what they're using this place for, a place that even most of the American instructors don't know about. Once I know these things, I can go home," I said. "The question for you is, do you want a piece of this, because if you don't, Phil and I will understand."

Phil said, "That's right, Coop. You can go back to the hotel and nobody will say shit about it."

"No," Cooper said. "I'm good. Just tell me something."

"Yeah?"

"We're the good guys, right?"

Phil pointed a finger at me and said, "He is. I'm not."

Cooper turned it over in his head a few times and said, "Okay, let's see what we've got here."

We split up. Phil went left, Cooper and I went right. The satellites had seen just a small corner of the complex. Most of the streets and structures were hidden beneath triple canopy, impossible to see by air, even by helicopter.

"How'd they know about this place?"

"Infrared shots of night training," I said. "That's when they started asking questions, after seeing the thermals."

"Why can't they use Predators to snap pics of the hotel?"

"They're all in Iraq and Afghanistan. Panama isn't exactly a high priority."

Coop and I walked between the bullet-pocked plywood, made haunted-house creepy by the darkness of the bush and the silence of the jungle around us.

"No wildlife," Coop whispered.

"It's all been chased away by the gunfire," I said, touching a splintered bullet hole.

We turned a corner. Cooper said, "Now this is weird."

There was no question that we were in a simulated city street with alleys and walkways, open plazas, several burned-out cars and a bus, its windows and tires long gone, its shell blackened. Steel silhouettes stood on each corner, on springs, their surfaces dented by live rounds. I touched one. "Whoever this is supposed to be looks mighty dead."

"Mighty dead," Coop said.

Phil came up from our left and our nerves were so stretched that if we'd been armed we might have shot him.

"You guys are jumpy as cats," he said.

"What'd you find?"

"I walked the perimeter. They're using Claymores, RPGs, frags. I even found a launcher for a Stinger."

Cooper stood, his hands on his hips, and turned around in a full circle. That discomforting feeling of having been here before got under his skin and gave him an itch he couldn't scratch. "Déjà vu like a mother. This seem familiar to you, Phil?"

Phil looked around at the dummy structures, with their vacant windows and doors. "Looks like a street," he said and shrugged. "Narrow, like a slum."

Cooper shook his head. "No, not a slum. It could be the old part of the city. What do you think?" Without waiting to hear Phil's answer, Coop walked farther on, trying to match where he was with a place he'd recently been. "This is Casco Viejo, I'm sure of it." He jogged past plywood shattered by live fire, jumped over man-sized divots in the dirt caused by hand grenades, and ran around more burned-out shells of automobiles, their charred steel perforated by bullet holes. Phil and I ran after him, catching him as he stood looking up at a single, large structure at the center of the street.

Here there were doors, kicked in so many times that the impressions of boots were a permanent part of the grain. Inside were complete rooms, and a staircase, the walls shredded by bullet holes and smudged by smoke and tear-gas grenades.

"I don't fucking believe it," Coop said.

"What? What is it?" I asked. "Where are we supposed to be?"

Cooper walked around the open room, the trees overhead speckling the walls with shifting bits of sunlight.

"I was just here. Just two days ago."

"Where? What is this place?"

Cooper stopped, his hands on his hips, staring up at the balcony. "It's the Presidential Palace," Cooper said. "They're training men to storm the Presidential Palace."

CHAPTER FIFTEEN

I did a three-sixty in the open room, taking in the doorways, the staircase, the balcony, every structural detail of the Presidential Palace interior, right down to the plywood reception desk.

"This is stupid," Phil said. "They can't be thinking of taking over the country. They don't have the people."

"How do we know?" Coop said. "We have no idea how many people they've put through this course and then settled into Panama City."

"Sleeper cells," I said. "Terrorists."

"Exactly."

Phil still wasn't convinced. "No one has enough money to overthrow an entire fucking country."

"What if the richest people did it together?"

"The guests at the hotel," Cooper said.

"That's what I'm thinking. I'm also thinking we should boogie on out of here before we get visitors."

We found our way back to the landing zone and started our quick jog back toward the river. All three of us had our own thoughts, our own questions, and the steady physical rhythm of running let us work through them.

"I don't get it," Phil grumbled. "Are they so fucking rich they think they can steal a whole country?"

"I think they're getting drug money, too," I said.

Phil laughed. It sounded more like a bark of disbelief. "Drug money? In Panama?"

"The Colonel mentioned Laos to another man, a young guy with a Cuban accent."

"Cubans," Phil said. "That sounds like spooks."

"And Laos," Coop said. "The Company financed ops in Southeast Asia with drug money. Maybe they're doing the same thing here."

I didn't want to believe it. "No. That's too crazy. The people I work for would know if the CIA were involved."

"Not unless your people are out of the loop," Cooper said. "Is that possible?"

"In Washington, anything is possible except secrets. Someone would know."

"You mean like who killed Kennedy?"

"Phil, don't start."

"Maybe," Phil said, "it's a rogue outfit."

"But why start a revolution in Panama?"

"The Canal," Phil said. "What else has this country got that anyone could possibly want?"

Coop was staying quiet, working through his own questions in his head. As we neared the footbridge Coop stopped, raised his fist in the air, and silently eased into hiding. Phil pulled me off the path into the brush. Coop crawled back to us. "I think there's someone waiting for us across the river."

"You see anyone?"

"No, but it feels hinky," he said. "I'm going to check it out."

"I'm coming with you," Phil said.

Before I could object, they melted into the foliage, as substantial as smoke. *Damn,* I thought, *how did they do that?* After what felt like hours, after I'd exhausted myself straining to hear, see, smell, or intuit anything beyond the usual jungle critters, the two of them reappeared.

"They know we're here. They're setting up an ambush."

"To kill us?"

Phil gave me a look through half-closed eyelids. "No, Harp, I think maybe they want to invite us to a party, what do you think?"

Coop knelt and drew a map in the dirt. "They've strung Clay-mores along the trail here and here, leading up to the bridge."

"Jesus, you're kidding."

Cooper shook his head. "And they've got men here and here along the far bank, armed with AKs."

"What do we do now?"

Phil said, "We can try to run away—"

"And they'll catch us one at a time," Coop said, "later. When we're by ourselves."

"So we're going to take 'em out now," Phil said.

Cooper nodded. "We talked it over."

"Who talked it over?"

"Phil and I."

"You didn't think to ask me what I wanted to do? I'm the smart one."

"We'll let you be smart next time," Phil said. "But right now we have a plan." Phil's thin-lipped grin was an unsettling shadow of the scar that ran across his neck, ear to ear.

I didn't think I was going to like this plan. Then after I heard it, I was sure I didn't like it. "I don't like this," I said. "I think we should reconsider the runaway option."

"Shut up," Phil said. "This is the only way."

"But why do I have to do this?"

"Because," Phil said, "you're the smallest."

"And the one with the least experience," Cooper said.

"And you play piano," Phil said. "To these macho pendejos, that makes you suspect. You're the one they'll go after."

This did nothing to put me at ease, and yet, ten minutes later I was at the rope bridge that crossed the river, hiding in the under-brush and waiting, watching the far riverbank for movement.

Behind me, the explosion of a Claymore split the morning. The air around me convulsed and seven hundred steel balls tore away leaves and bark from the trees.

I screamed and ran from the bushes, holding my head. I raced blindly for the rope bridge, tricky even when you took it slow, but running made it buck and jump like a living thing. The river nar-rowed here considerably, churning up the water and giving the current a dizzying speed beneath my feet.

I was a third of the way across the bridge when a shot zinged past my head, then another, and a voice shouted, "¡Alto!" I did. I al-to'ed so fast the bridge quivered.

Two young men dressed in camo appeared at the far end of the bridge. They carried AK-47s and one aimed his rifle at me while the second stood at the bridge and waved me forward. "Venga," he said. Come. His voice would have carried more authority if it hadn't cracked from a D-flat to a G-sharp.

I started to back up.

"Venga aquí," he said. "Aquí," and pointed to his side of the river. I shook my head. "No. No aquí."

Another man, older, appeared out of the brush and ordered the two younger men to get me. They looked at him as if he must be kidding. I know that look. I had used that look quite a lot myself lately. Obviously, by shouting at them, the older man convinced them that he wasn't joking. The two slung their rifles and started across the bridge toward me.

With each step they took forward, I took a step back.

The older man unholstered his pistol and yelled for me to stop. I took three steps back. The older man shot at me, two times, but at a distance of forty yards, the nearest bullet didn't come any closer than three feet. Which was close enough to make all my hair stand on end and my sphincter pucker up around my jaw. I turned and scurried off the bridge and the two young men scrambled to catch up.

By the time I hit the trail, another man was shooting at me with a rifle, and these shots, fired in three-round bursts, zipped by my head and, like the pistol shots in Crystal City, made my eardrums pulse in a highly unpleasant way. I ran harder. Encouraged by the shots, the young men crossed the bridge. They weren't far behind me. I could hear them thrashing through the brush, Latin hounds on the trail of a frightened Yanqui rabbit.

The trail dog-legged to the left and I went right. I grasped what I needed. The two young men, more confident on dry land, sprinted up the trail. When they crossed in front of my hiding place, I jerked the trip wire. It was no longer tied to a Claymore detonator, but to a young, springy sapling, and as I pulled, the sapling swept across the trail, whipping both men backward and off their feet.

Phil and I jumped them before they could stagger upright. I grabbed a rifle, racked the bolt, and stuck the barrel into the shorter man's eye. They both froze and Phil went to work, ripping their shirts into strips and trussing them up like rodeo calves, their hands and ankles tied together behind them. Gagged, they rolled their eyes, silently pleading for their lives, or at least a more dignified way to die. Phil dragged them whimpering into the bushes.

Cooper came back along the path. "The other two have come out and are looking across the river. It won't be long before one of them tries to cross."

"How many do you think there are?" Phil asked.

"I don't know. Could be a whole company over there in the trees."

Phil thought a minute. "Okay. I don't see how we have much choice. Give Coop your rifle," he told me. I didn't argue.

Quietly, we approached the riverbank. Cooper was right. One of the men was in the middle of the rope bridge. The older man waited on the other side, urging his reluctant comrade forward.

Phil and Cooper came up out of the treeline and aimed the AKs at the man on the bridge and the officer on shore. Phil ordered both of them to cross the bridge. Neither of them moved. The man on the bridge, exposed and alone, was scared. The man on the bank was an officer, too proud to surrender, and brave considering he wasn't the one stuck in the middle of the footbridge.

"Don't make us come over there and get you," Phil shouted.

The officer on the bank pulled a K-Bar knife from his boot. He held it high so that we could see the blade, then he went to work on the bridge.

The man on the bridge saw this, too, and shouted for the man to stop. Quickly, he tried to move back to the far shore before the rope fell away.

"Don't do it!" Cooper yelled.

Phil fired the AK over the man's head but it just inspired the officer to work faster.

First, the right-hand rope went slack and the severed end trailed into the river. The bridge tilted and the man on the bridge held on, suspended from the cat's cradle above the rushing water. The rope at his feet fell away and he was left to hang by one remaining line. The river tugged at his boots.

Phil fired the AK again, closer to the man with the knife, but it was too late. The last rope was cut and the man on the bridge yelped, fell into the muddy water, and was quickly swept downstream. It didn't look like he could swim. I watched the man's head go under. Ten yards farther on, he came up again, coughing and sputtering and slapping the surface. I couldn't watch him drown. I launched myself into the rushing current. It was swift and I swam hard for the middle of the river. The chop and debris made it impossible to see the man, but I did see Phil run along the riverbank, trying to keep up with us.

The river flattened and slowed, and I saw the man's hand flash above the surface. I pulled toward him, kicking across the current.

The river went into a sharp bend and the man was carried into the eddy above the turn, surrounded by circling debris. In a few strokes I was inside the sluggish whirlpool, fighting my way through the trash and snags that pulled at my clothes and tried to drag me under.

The man's eyes were wide with terror. When I grabbed his shirt, he fought me, his arms wheeling, his hands grasping and scratching. I kicked, came up out of the water, and punched the man, as hard as I could, in the jaw. They tell you to do this in lifesaving courses, but they never tell you how difficult it is to knock a man unconscious. I hit him twice more before he went obligingly limp. I rolled him over on his back, put my arm across his chest, and pulled him up to the shore.

At the muddy bank I had to wait for a water snake to glide by before I could drag the man up and into the jungle. The man wasn't breathing, so I tilted his head, cleared his mouth, and started blowing breaths into his lungs. He choked up a fistful of river water and began breathing on his own. That's when I felt the pistol pressed against my head.

"You should have let him drown, Anglo," the man said.

I sat up slowly, afraid to turn around, afraid to speak, afraid to do much more than breathe.

He grabbed my hair and shook me. "Where are my men?"

"Across the river."

He kicked me and jerked me to my feet. "We will make a trade," he said. "We'll see how much the other men value your life."

The man who had fallen into the river was on his elbows, throwing up cold muddy water. The officer called him Santiago and asked if he was all right. Santiago gave him a look that didn't need any translation, but nodded and said he was.

"Bueno." The officer handed Santiago his pistol and told him to watch the river.

His knife at my throat, the officer pushed me down the path. We came to a dirt road and a black SUV. The officer called out for Santiago to come. But Santiago didn't answer. With panic rimming his eyes in white, the officer scanned the trees around him. He pulled me back toward the SUV. As he reached for the door handle, he froze, the blade still at my throat. I couldn't see what was behind me, but I could feel the steel edge of his K-Bar bite into my skin.

Cooper ordered the officer to lower the knife. After what was probably the longest moment of my life, the blade came away from my throat. When I could breathe again, I turned around. The officer was on his knees and Cooper had the barrel of the automatic pistol stuck in the man's ear. Cooper whispered to the man, "Be quiet ¿Comprende?"

The man nodded.

"Bueno." Cooper looked at me and said, "I would have let the bastard drown."

I shook my head. "No you wouldn't."

"I would have at least thought about it."

Fireworks crackled up the road and bullets thunked into the steel of the SUV and tore large, puckered holes out of the window glass.

I dropped and became one with the earth. Shots kicked up wet sand around my face. I rolled out of the road and into the brush. Cooper was behind the SUV, still hanging on to his prisoner. He returned fire with the pistol. "Can you see them?"

I raised my head and the leaves were ripped away by gunfire. I pressed my head into the dirt and hollered, "I see two, but it could be a whole fucking army!"

"I'm coming across."

"No, don't!" But Cooper was up, dragging the officer with one hand while firing with his other. Dirt flew up and the SUV's windows shattered. The Latino officer, afraid, or brave, or just blindly trying to find cover, pulled the other way and for a moment Cooper hung there, caught in the open road. Bullets snatched Coop's shirt and made it dance, tattering the wet fabric like an old flag.

Cooper still had a fistful of the officer's collar. The officer was on one knee in the road and he held up his hands as if shielding his face from the flying dirt. First his index finger and thumb distorted and then exploded. Then his head, from his hairline up, blew away like newspaper in the wind. Cooper and the trees were sprayed with blood and bone. Coop fell, and before I could stop myself, I crawled into the road, grabbed him by the shirt, and dragged him into the trees.

Cooper sat up and touched his body, his eyes shining with disbelief when he saw the blood on his hand.

"Are you shot?"

Coop stared at his hand.

I touched him, touched his ragged shirt, touched his face, touched his hair and legs, until I was sure he wasn't hit.

Urgent voices shouted from up the road.

"Are you okay? Can you run?"

Cooper nodded, still glassy-eyed with shock.

"Then let's run!" I pulled Cooper to his feet and together we sprinted through the bush toward the river. I heard the men behind us, and I braced myself for the bullet that would find me and tear me into pieces like they had torn into the officer. In a single instant a few spinning chunks of copper-jacketed lead had turned him from a man with thoughts, loves, hates, dreams, and obsessions into a wet pile of rags, meat, and bone.

Cooper and I reached the bank and together we went into the river and swam hard for the far side. Bullets zick'd into the water all around us, some skipped off the surface, and others buried themselves in the current. The bank seemed so far away that it was a distant country, and I knew we wouldn't make it.

Phil come out of the treeline and laid down a blanket of fire. The bullets stopped hitting the water long enough for us to make it to the far shore, where Phil was waiting. We scampered up the slippery mud and into the safety of the trees. The sounds of the firefight upriver had slowed to a few sporadic bursts of gunfire.

Coop and I hurried upstream, toward the trail, which I guessed to be several hundred yards away, and hoped to meet up with Phil. When we found him, Phil was kneeling by the bank.

"Are they coming?" Cooper asked him.

"I don't know," Phil said, "but I'm not waiting to find out."

"Where are the prisoners?"

"Fuck 'em," Phil said. "We need to get our asses away from here."

"No," I said.

"Yes," Phil said, and dragged me after Cooper through the bush, downstream, away from the men and the rifle fire, and the officer lying in the road.

We ran as fast as we could through thickets and brambles, piercing thorns and slapping leaves, stinging things and biting things that bug-eyed entomologists would happily catalog in italicized Latin. Slithering things that would have joyfully crawled up my pant leg. But we were moving too fast for nature. We ran, our crashing animal ruckus frightening primates in the trees and propelling flocks of birds into the open air. We ran until our sides hurt and our feet were numb, ran until we could run no longer and we collapsed in a clearing and lay on our backs, huffing daylight and staring up at a small blue patch of sky.

When I could speak I said, "You think we're safe?" My face and neck were whipped raw by wait-a-minute vines and razor grass and the salted sweat dripped into my wounds, keeping me from drifting into a coma.

Cooper said, "No. We're not safe. We've just outrun them."

A spider monkey sat in a tree above us and watched, curious, as the pale apes below collected their scattered thoughts. Phil saw the monkey and said, "What the fuck you looking at?"

The monkey didn't reply.

Phil picked up a hard green piece of fruit and tossed it in the air a few times, getting its heft.

"What's that," I said, "something we can eat?"

"Nah. They're called monkey balls," Phil said. "Some kind of nut or something." Casually, he threw it at the monkey, not aiming, and not hitting anything but leaves, but the monkey shrieked as if he'd been struck, and jumped up and down on his branch.

Phil tossed another monkey ball, this time grazing fur.

The monkey exploded into a schizophrenic tantrum of shrieks, stomps, Tourettic yips, and primate spittle. Enraged beyond all reason, even for a monkey, he defecated into his tiny hand and pitched it at us, showering us with stinking dollops of monkey shit.

As Phil and I scrambled up and out of the monkey's range, Cooper just closed his eyes and said, "I hate this place. I mean I really hate this place."

CHAPTER SIXTEEN

It took four hours, two hitched rides in pickup trucks, and a good soaking in the one o'clock rains to get back to the hotel. Iceman was on the gate and when he saw us straggle up the road he said, "Where you boys been? Man, Kelly's looking everywhere for your sorry asses. He thinks you deserted."

We found Kelly on the hotel veranda. At his feet, spread across a folded sheet, were the parts of an M-60 machine gun, broken down for cleaning. Kelly used a toothbrush, bristles black, to scrub away at the gun's receiver. He saw us, stopped, looked at me and sniffed. "What is that smell, Harper?"

"Monkey shit, sir," I said.

"Appropriate. Go get cleaned up. I need you to run an errand for the Colonel."

Cooper interrupted. He told Kelly our story about stumbling across the urban assault course and the ambush. Kelly would hear of it sooner or later, we knew, and we wanted to give him our version before he had a chance to think of other reasons we might be wandering around the jungle, finding things we shouldn't find.

Kelly listened to the story and then spoke slowly, with a patient smile, as if addressing a learning-challenged class. "Our advanced students are taught hostage rescue, Cooper. If you read a newspaper, you would know that kidnapping in Colombia has become the national sport. That is one reason our little resort here is so popular. It was a stroke of genius for the Colonel to put the idea of a vacation together with the training of personal security. Don't you think? Pure genius."

"What about the men who shot at us?" Phil said.

"Bandits, no doubt. Smugglers, perhaps. This country is never short of violent thugs, Ramirez. You should know that. But I will report this to the local authorities. Now go get yourselves cleaned up before any of the guests see you."

"May I be there?" I said.

"Be where?"

"When you report this to the authorities, sir, just to make sure you get the details correct, sir, and complete."

"I'd like to be there, too," said Coop.

"Yeah, me, too," Phil said.

Kelly looked at each of us, saved an extra moment for me, and then said, "Fair enough. I'll let you know when he arrives and then you can make your statements. In the meantime, make yourselves presentable."

As I was showering I found several leeches stuck to my chest and back. I pulled them off, with shivers of disgust, and watched light-headed as my blood circled the drain at my feet.

By the time I'd dressed, Ren, fresh from interrogation himself, came up and told me that a policeman was waiting in the bar.

"I'm glad to see you, Ren. How'd you do with the cops?"

"They let me go," he said, and touched his swollen lip. "Lack of evidence. It wasn't too bad. A guy from the State Department came down and got me out, you know how it goes."

"Yeah, I do." Ren seemed rather quiet, but I guessed the Panamanian police got Ren to talk enough for two lifetimes.

"When you're done," Ren said, "Kelly wants us to run an errand."

I agreed to meet him later and walked down to the bar. Sitting at a rear table was a small man with a mustache and short hair. He wore a white guayabera shirt and when we approached the table he stood and shook our hands, introducing himself as Lieutenant Consuerte. When we were all seated he said, "I understand you gentlemen had some trouble with bandits this morning."

"I'm not convinced they were bandits," Coop said.

"They were armed with AKs," Phil said.

"And behaved like soldiers," I added.

"Tell me what happened," the Lieutenant said, and pulled a small tape recorder out of a briefcase at his feet. "You don't mind if I record this, do you?"

"No, not at all," Coop said.

We each gave our version of what happened, again leaving out a few details, just in case this man was easily corrupted. Thirty minutes later the Lieutenant turned off the tape recorder, put it back into his briefcase, and stood up. "I'll let you know what we turn up," he said. "But I suspect you stumbled into a band of smugglers, that's all."

"A man was killed," Coop said, barely able to hold back his anger.

The Lieutenant shrugged, his hands up, accepting the hard realities of life. "Such things happen, Señor Cooper. These smugglers do not share our respect for one another. Killings occur every day. Sadly, that is a fact of life in Panama."

The Lieutenant promised he would investigate and get back to us. He left the three of us standing in the hotel lobby. As the Lieutenant climbed into his gray sedan Phil said, "If that guy's a cop, I'm a monsignor."

Cooper watched the sedan drive away and said, "I got a bad vibe. What about you?"

"I don't know about Panama cops, but Washington cops wouldn't be wearing those shoes." They stared at me, waiting. "They're Corfam," I explained. "Great for when the brass comes through, because they keep a high shine, but they're worthless for street work, especially in hot weather, and in case you hadn't noticed, it's fucking hot down here."

"How do you know so much about cop shoes?" Phil said.

"I dated a woman on the force." Cooper and Phil exchanged a glance. "Yeah, so, she was great with handcuffs, is that what you wanted to hear?"

Cooper said, "No details, please."

"And did you see the gun?"

"A twenty-two," Phil said. "That's no cop gun. More like an assassin."

Ren came into the lobby and said, "How 'bout it, Monkeyman, you ready to roll?"

"You go, but watch your back," Phil said. "Coop and I will check out some things while you're gone."

Ren assigned me Zorro's place in the back seat. Sitting in Zorro's seat made me remember that last picture I had of him leaning back against the car door, his life bleeding into his shirt.

Ren looked at me. "By the way, brother, you look like you got kicked down a few flights of stairs."

"Yeah, like you're Ricardo Montalban."

Ren put the car into gear and said, "What the hell, hey? You gotta open yourself up to new things." Ren smiled a Hollywood smile in spite of his swollen lip. "Otherwise, you get old, you know?"

"Ren, I have a feeling neither one of us is going to get old."

We pulled up to the company's gas pumps and filled up Ren's tank, plus the gas can in the back seat.

"This is dangerous, Ren, carrying around a loaded jerry can in the car."

"Man, my gauge is so fucked up I never know if I'm running low. I don't want to get stuck on one of these back fucking roads." Ren ran through the gates and off toward town. After ten minutes my legs ached from holding Ren upright.

"Man, I'm dying back here."

"Here, smoke this. It'll make you feel better."

Like I said, I don't smoke, and I certainly didn't think it was smart to light a blunt while sitting next to a full can of gasoline. "No, thanks."

"Suit yourself." Ren put flame to the end of the joint and puffed. A cloud of smoke was sucked out the window and away in the jet stream.

I let the landscape roll by, the sun white-hot in a scoured blue, the green of the jungle so deep and prehistoric that I expected to see extinct creatures the size of houses come wading through the elephant grass. Ren and I small-talked about people we knew, soldiers mostly, and women. Some we knew, and some we wanted to know better. When I couldn't avoid it any longer I asked, "Why me, Ren? Why'd you recommend me for this job?"

Ren bounced through a pothole the size of Detroit. I held the chair upright and when the crisis had passed, he said, "You were the only guy I knew who played piano."

"That's it?"

"Yeah, and, you know, you always seemed like a stand-up guy."

"But you knew what I was stepping into, right?"

"When I gave 'em your name, I didn't know what kind of shit was going down. *Verdad,* man, the truth. But after Winstead, I knew."

I wanted to ask what Ren had against me, but something else flitted across my mind. "Hey, Ren? This last guy, the piano player, did he have a name?"

"I don't remember. He wasn't here long enough."

I thought about that for a while. At least I had a name. Monkey-man. Eaten by wolves. "So, Ren? This is what I need. I want a list of all the guests who've stayed in the hotel for the past year. Can you get it?"

"Sure, I can get it, but it won't help much. Because that's not what you need. What you need is a list of the students, and I don't have that." He blew on the lit end of the joint, making the coal glow.

"Why do I need the students?"

"Because they're the ones you need."

"But why? What are they going to do?"

"I don't know," he said through another cloud of smoke.

Ren was too high, and already gone. Knowing the answer, I said, "You're getting ready to leave, aren't you, Ren?"

He caught my eye in the rearview mirror. "How'd you know?"

"You and Alonzo dropped the dime."

Ren nodded; his eyes were back on the road but I knew he was seeing Alonzo. I knew because that's what I was seeing, too. It was impossible not to see Alonzo sitting against that car, all that blood thick on his shirt. Impossible.

Ren spoke quietly and I had to strain to hear him over the noise of the wind and the car. "Alonzo knew a guy in Washington, so we said maybe this place was worth a look, that's all. And then Winstead was getting us a layout of a site that Kelly had built in the jungle. That's when we knew something bad was happening, man."

Ren took another hit and flicked the roach out the window. "But they're not going to get me, because I am about to *vámanos* my ass outta here like pronto. I'm getting some money today from a guy who owes me, and after we run this errand, I want you to drop me off in town, okay? By tonight I'll be back in the States eating my mom's cooking."

He reached across the car to the glove compartment, nearly toppling the kitchen chair sideways. The car swerved into the left lane, barely missing a truck full of chickens. Ren pulled out a .45 and threw it in the back seat.

"Hold on to this."

"What for?"

"In case you need it, that's what the fuck for."

"Like that dime in your ear."

"A man never knows."

Ren drove down the Avenue of Martyrs. He turned right, into narrow streets, the traffic slow with bicycles, taxis, buses, trucks, and cars. Ren turned right again, into a dirt street crowded with shacks made of flattened tin and scrap aluminum. We inched in and out of ruts, avoiding kids and dogs playing in the muddy pools of afternoon rain. As we passed by open doors the people watched from the hot darkness inside, their eyes white in the shadows.

"I don't like this, Ren."

Ren stopped the car. "C'mon, man. Just be cool. Put your shirt over that gun. All I want you to do is stand by the door and look like a killer."

"What if someone wants to come in?"

"Then you shoot 'em. Cock and lock, brother man."

I pulled the slide, chambered a round, and locked the hammer. I snicked the safety up with my thumb and tucked the gun into my belt. I thought of Smith and how he worried about shooting off something he'd miss.

Ren wasn't tall, but he had to duck to get in the door. The tin house looked as if it might not make it past the next stiff breeze. I waited outside and tried to look hard. Kids gathered around me, curious about the gringo with his hand in his pants.

"Vamoose," I said, shooing them away with my left hand. "Go away." I looked up and down the street and wondered how I had gotten myself into this. If Smith had shown his saggy white ass in that alley that afternoon, I might have shot him. Maybe not to kill him, but shot him in one of those parts he was so afraid he'd miss.

I waited for what felt like days. Where was Ren? I poked my head in the door, just to see what was taking so long. It was dark, and my eyes hadn't adjusted completely, but I could make out Ren and another man. Then I saw that the other man had a gun. I watched the man turn and point the gun at me. I saw a flash of light, then heard the shot. Even in the tight chamber of the tin house, where the noise was amplified, the calm, analytical part of my brain registered it as small, possibly a .32. The wooden doorframe splintered and everything went from too slow to too fast. Far too fast.

I dropped in the doorway and struggled to free the .45 from my pants. Another shot sprayed dirt in my eyes. I pulled the big automatic clear but I didn't know where to shoot. The room was dark. I was blinded by the muzzle flash and people were moving. I didn't want to hit Ren. All I wanted was to get out of there.

That calm part of my brain, the part that had paid attention to all of my expensive training, told me to lay down suppressing fire. My vision returned enough to see Ren's shape in front of me, kneeling on the dirt floor with a small automatic clutched in both hands. Ren didn't shoot. The man turned and aimed his pistol at Ren's head. Ren still didn't shoot.

I pulled the trigger three times and the boom of the .45 rang the tin hut like a bell. I got to my knees, pulled Ren after me, and, one-handed, fired twice more into the shack. Big holes blew sunlight into the far wall.

"Go, man, go!" Ren was behind me now, up and out of the hut, running for the car. I saw the man's shadow rise up from behind the overturned table. He was a perfect silhouette, just like a range target. I pulled the trigger again and lost him in the lightning.

Ren had the engine started and I jumped headfirst through the open passenger window. I hit the kitchen chair with my shoulder and rolled into the back, onto the floor. The rear window exploded into a thousand sparkles of sidewalk diamonds. I blew my last two rounds into the alley just to discourage anyone from chasing us.

The Chevy jumped forward. The kitchen chair tipped and Ren fell back on top of me and hung there, a turtle unable to right himself, his arms and his feet waving helplessly in the air as the Chevy rolled down the narrow street, sideswiping tin. I hollered, "One of us has to drive," and pushed Ren upright behind the wheel.

I put my head up slowly, and saw the man running, getting closer. He was shooting. Christ, he was shooting at me. A bullet thunked hard into the roof of the car. Thank you, Jesus, he was shooting high.

Ren, finally in control of the careening Chevrolet, blasted through the shanties, hanging on to the wheel, swerving between houses too close, rocking from one side to the next, a gutter ball scattering children like chickens. Ren spun the wheels, adding mud and dog shit to the open misery of these poor people's homes, and five minutes later we were back on the paved city streets. Ren parked outside an open-air bar. He turned off the engine and we both sat in the car, not talking and not really listening to the music from a jukebox down the street. My heart beat like a prisoner inside my chest, demanding a safer home.

"You okay?" I asked, afraid to look and see blood. Please, I didn't want to see any more blood, not for a very long time.

"Yeah, I'm okay."

"What the fuck happened back there?" I said, my voice high on adrenaline. "I can't stop shaking. I'm shaking like a dog shitting cinders!"

"Shitting cinders? What the fuck's that? A dog shitting cinders?" Ren laughed. It was a high, tight laugh that danced away on the salsa.

"I don't know. What? You want to discuss regional idioms now? Is that it? Jesus Christ, we almost get killed and you turn into William fucking Safire?"

"Who?"

"He writes for the *Times*."

"What are you talking about, man? What *Times*?"

"Forget it," I said. I started to feel my limbs and lips again. I put my hand against my forehead. I was cold, near shock.

"Fuck, man," Ren said, "you think you hit him?"

"No. I didn't hit him. Thank God I didn't hit him."

"Whatta you mean? He was trying to kill us. Why didn't you waste him?"

I wanted to ask Ren the same question but I knew the answer. It's not easy pulling the trigger on another man, no matter how they make it look in the movies. "I just wanted it to stop," I said. "That's all. I was scared."

"No shit, man. You got that straight."

"What happened?" I shook pieces of glass out of my hair.

"Dude wouldn't give me my money." Ren held up a tight roll of bills. "But I got this. Looks like even more than he owed me, the stupid asshole."

"You almost got me killed."

"Nah." Ren looked back at me and grinned. "Wasn't even close." Then he took a deep breath and said, "You did okay, Monkeyman. You did okay. I knew you were all right."

When I figured I could hold a drink without spilling it, we went into the bar. I ordered two scotches, on the rocks. Ren ordered the same. We sat and drank them in silence.

Finally, Ren said, "C'mon, man. We still gotta run the Colonel's errand. Then you gotta drop me off, okay?"

"I could take you to the airport," I said.

"No, I can get a ride from one of the hotels."

"What about your stuff? Your clothes?"

"In the trunk, my man, I am ready to fly."

We got in the car and Ren drove to a square of warehouses on the other side of the Old City. The street ran three blocks to a chain-link dead end. Beyond the fence was the sea, and the water glittered, turquoise in the sun, and made the day seem innocent of shootings and squalor and espionage. Most of the warehouses were abandoned, their doors open on empty bays. Rust, the industrial moss, spread across galvanized walls and stained the concrete foundations with runoff. Weeds grew tall and litter piled in drifts against chain link. At the very end of the street, a military truck with no markings, its bed covered in canvas, sat backed against a loading dock. Several men in tan work clothes carried wooden crates out of the truck and into the hot shadows of a warehouse.

A man with a mustache stood near the tailgate, smoking a cigarette and occasionally checking items off on a clipboard. He had a .45 on his belt. I noticed another man near the front of the truck armed with an M-14 rifle.

Ren parked the car, got out and spoke in Spanish to the man with the clipboard. I crawled out of the back and walked up the street, away from the warehouse. The smell of gas in the car was making me sick. Still shaky from Ren's business, I needed a little open air.

A man came out from the warehouse with a cardboard carton the size of a shoebox. He carried it to the car and crawled into the back seat. Ren signed something on the clipboard. He waved at me and headed for the car. The other man got out.

"Hey!"

I turned around and saw Phil hiding in the narrow space between two warehouses, his back against one wall and out of view of the men loading the truck.

"Hey, Harp, don't look this way."

I walked over to the warehouse wall and feigned taking a whiz. When I glanced over my shoulder I could see the man with the rifle watching me.

"What the fuck you doing here?"

"Running an errand for the Colonel. Me and Ren."

"This is not the place to be, Harp."

"I got that feeling." The man was walking toward me now. He said something to the man with the .45.

"Just get in the car and get the fuck out of here."

"Okay. Here comes Ren." I pretended to shake it and zip. I waited for Ren to drive up the street so I could get in. I didn't want to walk any closer to the men with the guns. I'd had enough guns for the day.

Ren drove to the end of the block to turn around. Ren wasn't the best driver, even when straight, so it took a while. I watched from the end of the block as Ren went up on the curb and ran into the chain-link fence. He put the car in reverse, grinding gears and twisting the steering wheel left and right. He had his head hung out the window like a big dog, trying to see around the back end of the Chevy.

"What's he doing?"

"Turning around."

The car came closer. Ren drove between the nose of the truck and the other loading docks. The Chevy rolled slowly toward me.

The two men who had been watching had disappeared and the street was empty. Ren was driving carefully, afraid to tip the chair or run into anything expensive.

When Ren was about twenty yards away, I could feel something bad creep up my throat. For the second time that day, time slowed to a crawl. The heat waves in their shimmer. The rolling litter in a gust of hot wind. Ren's face, split by a stoner's smile. And when the car exploded, I watched the yellow ball of flame erupt and blow out all of the windows. I don't remember being tossed to the ground. I do remember Phil beside me, helping me up. The car exploded a second time and hot twisted chunks of '56 Chevy, big and little, rattled against the warehouse walls like shrapnel. Phil fell on top of me, shielding me with his body.

The men in the warehouse came out and shouted at us over the roar of the fire. Phil jerked me to my feet. I looked at the blazing heap of blackened metal, flames roaring around the frame, black smoke rising quickly into the sky. The doors had been blown open and slammed backward on their hinges. The trunk lid was torn completely off and it lay in the street, a curved sheet of smoking steel. The other thing was something I didn't really want to see, but I did. I saw Ren. He was a torch, a black silhouette inside yellow flames, perched upright on a kitchen chair. His teeth were white.

"C'mon, man, we got to get you out of here." Phil was pulling me between two abandoned buildings. I was still dazed, unable to make one thought connect to another. I saw the man with the rifle take aim.

I tried to shout but I couldn't make a sound come out of my throat. The man fired and the bullet tore a chunk of concrete out of the warehouse foundation. Phil pulled me again and together we ran, me stumbling, my ribs as sharp as razors.

I don't know how far we ran. I just kept my eyes on his back and ran like I did in the jungle. I stumbled across vacant lots and railroad tracks, past boarded-up buildings, down deserted streets, and up foul-smelling alleyways.

When we reached a busy street we stopped running and walked a few feet to the edge of a small park filled with children playing soccer on a concrete field. There were benches under scruffy trees. We sat down, and I tried to catch my breath. Phil was breathing deeply, but easily. I had my elbows on my knees, afraid I was going to throw up.

"Look what I found," Phil said. He held out his fist and turned it over, like a magician about to reveal a little sleight of hand. When Phil opened his palm, a spark of sunlight flashed off a silver disc.

It was a dime. A Roosevelt dime. Nothing unusual. Just a dime.

I went down on all fours and tossed my guts in the street like a dog.

(

CHAPTER SEVENTEEN

When I couldn't be sick anymore, I sat down again and we watched the kids kick the soccer ball from one end of the park to the other.

"You ready to go?"

I said I was.

Phil hailed a taxi at the curb and we climbed inside. There were Christmas lights around the windshield and an illuminated picture of the Virgin Mary on the dash.

"Hey, you guys want to see exhibition?" the cab driver asked, his eyes on us in the rearview.

"No. You know a place called the Chinaman's Drugstore?"

"Sí, señor. But first we go to exhibition, eh?"

"No. The Chinaman's Drugstore. No exhibition," Phil said.

"Okay, but you miss good show." The cab pulled quickly into traffic, forcing a bus to swerve into the oncoming lane.

"What's he talking about?"

"It's a sex show," Phil said. "Juanita and her trained Chihuahua."

"Every night is opening night." The driver grinned.

Phil looked out the window. Anger rolled off him like stream.

"Big time," said the driver. "New show. Get to see donkey fuck gringo."

Phil smacked the back of the seat. "Hey, asshole. You want to see a gringo fuck a cab driver?"

"Okay, okay," the driver said. "Some pipple," he muttered, "got a'solutely no 'preciation of de finer tings."

We rode for a few blocks, Phil building up to say whatever it was he was going to say. After about the fourth block he said, "What the fuck were you doing back there? You think this is a fucking game?"

I said, "I was helping Ren. He was trying to get home."

Phil softened a little. "Yeah, well," he said, "do me a favor. Don't ever help me, okay?"

The city passed by with children at play in the gathering dusk, shopkeepers standing in their doorways, and men watching women watching men. Life hadn't slowed down, even a little. Ren was dead, and soon the black smoke that flattened out over the sunset would be gone, too, blown away by the night wind, and the spinning of the globe, and tomorrow we would be a full day closer to a time when no one remembered Ren, and no one mourned his passing.

"How did you know we were there?"

Phil was thinking about something else, and he ignored me. "We need to see a friend of mine," he said.

The cab dropped us in front of the corner wine store just as the lights came on, illuminating the white-tiled walls and stuffed, dusty fish. The Asian man stood behind the counter, drying his hands on a wine-stained apron.

Phil said, "This is the Chinaman's Drugstore."

"This is where Zorro picked me up," I said. Four days before, but it seemed like a lifetime.

"You need wine," Phil said, "this is the place. I'll even teach you some Spanish. 'Abrio y frio.' That's 'open' and 'cold.' And you ever need me and don't know where I am, you come here and ask for Choppo."

"Who's Choppo?"

"He's coming to pick us up, then I want you to take the car I borrowed back to La Boca."

"No," I said.

"Harp." Phil sighed. "It's time for you to go home. And I mean the States home."

"Not until I know what's going on here. They can't do that to Ren and expect me to back off."

"They didn't expect you to back off. They expected you to be in the back seat of that Chevy," Phil said. "I'm the one who wants you to back off."

"I'm not leaving until I know what's going on."

Phil ran his open hand over his face. He lit a cigarette and blew smoke into the hot afternoon air. "You ever been to Disneyland?"

"No. I don't like amusement parks."

"What kind of person doesn't like Disneyland?" he said. "What are you, a fucking communist?"

"Okay, so what am I missing?"

"Besides a sense of humor?"

I slouched in the corner, arms crossed over my chest. "Fuck you, Phil."

"One summer in high school, I went so often I got to fuck Minnie Mouse. True. It was like a perk, like a special ride for special guests."

I pictured Minnie with her little red skirt pulled up to her ears.

"I loved that big head, man, you could swing from those ears all fucking day. But what I really wanted was a crack at Snow White."

"Why Snow White?"

Phil looked at me and said, "Living with those dwarves, you know she's got pussy that ain't never been touched."

He made me laugh, he did, and then the picture of Ren sitting behind the wheel of his car jumped into my head.

Phil put his hand on my shoulder. "It's done. It don't mean shit."

A 1959 red Cadillac convertible, top down, fins up, pulled to the curb and Phil opened the door. I got into the back seat and Phil sat up front.

The man behind the wheel was easily in his sixties, maybe older, his face lined by a lifetime in the sun. His hair was as black and shiny as the leather seats and his white shirt was open at the collar, revealing a small gold crucifix at his throat.

"¿Choppo, qué pasa?"

"It's been a long time, my friend. I thought you were dead."

"I was. But I came back just to sleep with your woman."

"Lauren will eat you alive. It takes a macho hombre to ride her. Not a Chicano pendejo with a pinga like dis." The man laughed and waggled his little finger.

"I need a favor, Choppo."

"Last time I did you a favor I pissed blood for a week."

"You ever figure out which one of those quecos hit you with a bat?"

"No," he said with a philosophical wave of his hand. "So I had to kill them both. Who's your friend?"

"A piano player."

"Bueno. The world can always use more music." Choppo turned on the radio and a Panamanian folk song boomed from the Cadillac's speakers. As close as I could figure out the lyrics, the song was about a fisherman who shot his wife. That's what passes for a love song in Panama.

In minutes the Cadillac had cruised out of the crowded streets and into the wide, tree-lined boulevards of the old-money neighborhoods. A lot of new wealth, from drugs and international banking, poured into Panama every year and some of it washed up here, on the old estates. And like aging divas, their baroque charms were in need of constant cash and attention. Through the gates of the high walls I glimpsed armies of Panamanian men scurrying across the yards, wrapping up a day of attending to mansions that were as old and corrupt as the country itself.

Choppo stopped the Cadillac and we waited while an armed man nodded and let us pass. Once through the gates we circled a stone fountain and parked in front of the house. Inside, stairways curved around the foyer and up to the second floor. Double doors in the center opened onto a large living room with windows that looked out across the water. Boats, their running lights sparks against the gray, decorated the bay.

Phil and Choppo talked old times and I wandered the room taking in the artwork. Tiny pre-Colombian men with enormous erections were carefully displayed in a long glass case. Above the case was a painting of J.F.K., Martin Luther King, Jr., and Elvis. The three men looked off toward some brighter, less-dead future just out of frame.

The furniture—leather, chrome, and glass—was gathered around a massive ebony table and every seat had a view of the bay and the emptiness beyond.

I wandered over to look at a framed photograph on the far wall. A very young Choppo stood smiling for the camera with another man.

Both men were dressed in army fatigues and both were smoking hand-rolled cigars.

Choppo came up behind me. "You recognize him?"

"It looks like Fidel."

"It is Fidel. He and I were good friends once, before he got involved in politics. Politics will ruin a man faster than a cheating woman."

"I might not have recognized him without the cigar."

"That is not a cigar, amigo."

"Oh."

"It gets boring in the jungle. A little smoke makes it easier to change history, no?"

A young woman came in with a tray. She set the tray on the table and handed each of us a drink before perching herself on the edge of an Eames chair.

Choppo took a seat in the center of the sofa, on stage, and said, "Ah, it is very nice to have you both in my home. Now, what can I do for you, Felipe?"

Phil said, "A friend of ours was blown up today."

Choppo shrugged. "Ah. I see. But grief is an excellent reason to drink. Please."

Phil and I both sipped our drinks. It was straight vodka, as cold as the Arctic, and it went down like ice water.

Choppo drank his off in one swallow and settled back on the couch, his arms spread out over the back, a big smile across his face. Even death didn't seem to dent Choppo's good humor. "*Dígame,*" he said.

"I followed a truck from La Boca to the warehouse district," Phil said.

"And what was in the truck, my friend?"

"Weapons. Plastic explosives."

"A nasty cargo."

"I also found bags of *nieve blanca.*"

"It could have been rice flour, as it was with my friend Manuel."

"You know it wasn't."

"Perhaps if you give me the exact location of this warehouse, I could tell you more."

Phil gave him the address. Choppo got up from the sofa and said, "Let me make a phone call, I'll see what I can find out."

When Choppo had gone, the woman opened the patio doors and let the night breeze fill the room. She also let the breeze billow her skirt, and blow through her hair; she was an actress on a very small stage letting us enjoy the silent performance. When it was over, she said to me, "See me before you leave," and walked onto the patio.

I whispered to Phil, "What did you just do?"

"I traded a warehouse full of cocaine for help with the locals. Why? You got something better?"

Choppo returned to the living room and sat down. "I found out some very interesting things. First, the Guardia Nacional is looking for both of you. I told them you were with me and I assured them you had nothing to do with the explosion. They believed me. They know me as a man of integrity in a country where integrity is a rare commodity."

"What about the cocaine?"

Choppo tilted his head and shrugged wearily. "Your innocence has its price."

"And the warehouse will be empty before morning," I said.

"One way or the other." He was too weary to smile, yes, but he could still be amused. "Influence also has its price," he said, "even in Washington."

"Yes, it does," I said.

"It's best not to go through life with your head in the clouds, young man. In Panama, you could trip and fall."

Choppo called for a taxi to pick us up, and while we waited, I went outside where the woman sat casually in a butterfly chair, smoking a cigarette.

"Thank you for your hospitality."

"You're welcome," she said. She looked toward the water. "Would you like to see our view, Mr. Harper?"

I said I would, and followed her into the yard, a thick carpet of Bermuda grass that stretched to a far seawall. We walked out to where the view broadened and we could see beyond the bay where freighters and cruise ships moved leisurely in that space between water and sky, and a black curtain full of lightning drew across the stars.

"You'll help us stop them," she said.

"Stop who?"

"The men at La Boca."

"From doing what? That's what I don't know. What are they try-ing to do?"

She turned her face to me, the distant lightning reflected in her eyes. The wind blew back her hair and I thought she was the most beautiful woman I had ever seen in my life. "They are trying to steal my country," she said.

"But how, how am I going to stop them?"

"I don't know. And I don't think we have much time."

Phil called me from the house.

Her words stirred up a deep green fear, and where I looked for encouragement, all I saw was sharp darkness littered with hard questions. Now, it wasn't enough for me to know who the guests were; now I had to know the students. And it wasn't enough for me to deliver information, now I had to stop an army.

"It's been a pleasure to meet you, Mr. Harper. I had heard so much about you from our mutual friend, Mr. Smith. He was very complimentary, but he did not do your bravery justice." She al-lowed me to take her hand and I was surprised by the strength of her grip.

"So you made the recordings."

She nodded. "And I will continue to help in any way I can," she said, "but I'm being watched and I must be careful."

Phil called me again and said the taxi was here. I told Lauren that I would do my best and she assured me that would be enough. I did not share her confidence.

We took the taxi back to where Phil had parked the car he'd stolen from La Boca, an old beetle-backed Volvo sedan whose paint had dulled from years in the salt air. Panama has a way of tak-ing the shine off everything. We got in and buckled up just as the nine o'clock rain swept over us, turning the streets into fast-moving rivers. Phil turned on the wipers and they whapped away the water in thick waves.

"Hey, Phil?"

"Yeah."

"How'd you get your nickname? Mad Dog?"

Phil took his hand off the wheel and turned his arm over so I could see the tattoo at the soft crook of the elbow. The tattoo was of a bulldog holding a human skull in its jaws.

"See that?"

"Yeah. How come the eyes look like that?"

"I shot off part of the tat with a needle. Makes him look a little crazy, doesn't it?"

"You mean like drugs?"

"Yeah, like drugs."

"You were a junkie?"

"Yeah."

"I don't think I've ever met a junkie before."

"Fucking figures." Phil reached into his shirt pocket and handed me a joint the size of a Cuban Monte Cristo.

"What's this for?"

"It's from Choppo. He said it was a gift for the man who would change history."

CHAPTER EIGHTEEN

The rain stopped by the time Phil dropped me off at the hotel. I crept past the lobby and up to the third floor. The corridor was empty, and I unlocked my door and fell across my bed. When a knock woke me up, it was morning and I was still in my damp clothes, unshaven, with a sore jaw and the stink of burned hair. It was Tuesday, one day before New Year's Eve.

Eubanks, the little clerk, stuck his head in the door and said, "Kelly wants to see you. He got a phone call from the State Department wondering where the fuck you were."

"Okay." I sat up and ran a hand through my hair. Part of it was extra crispy. "How do I look?"

The kid squinted at me. "You know," he said, turning his head this way and that, "nobody's face is symmetrical."

"Thanks." He was about to go when I said, "Eubanks, you like to get high?"

Eubanks raised his eyebrows in appreciation and gave me his best surfer, "Yah."

I pulled the cigar-sized doobie from my shirt pocket and said, "I need a favor."

Eubanks was transfixed. "Sure, dude."

"I need the password to Kelly's computer."

Eubanks blinked. "But that's classified."

"I have a clearance," I said. "Hell, I've played for the president."

Eubanks took the joint, put it into his pocket, and whispered, "It's 'Osama.'"

"Osama?"

"Yeah. Osama. Weird, huh?"

I thanked Eubanks and went downstairs to Kelly's office. The door was open and I found him standing at his window, watching the whitecaps on the black water. "Ah, Harper, our newest star," he said, way too friendly for my comfort. "I was just discussing today's continuing adventure with the State Department. Have a seat."

I sat on the edge of his visitor's chair.

Kelly stayed at the window. "Seems like every place you show up, someone gets killed. Not a good way to keep friends, is it?"

"No, sir."

"Let's talk." Kelly sat on the edge of his desk, trying to look like my uncle, trying to help out this fine young man who just seemed to draw mayhem the way shit draws flies. Kelly steepled his fingers, and held them to his chin, as if he'd just had an epiphany. "You know, Harper, the Panamanian authorities don't like it when North Americans get killed on their watch. It makes them look slack. It tarnishes their machismo. And when they start looking for someone to blame, they particularly like to blame other North Americans. They find solace in the circularity of the thing, and it gives them closure. Do you comprende?"

"Yes, sir."

"Now, the sticky part of all this is, I have to give them someone. So I was thinking of your friend. What do you think?"

"Phil didn't have anything to do with Ren's murder."

"Now, why would you mention Phil Ramirez? I was under the impression he'd been here all day yesterday. Why, the man Cooper swears to it."

I tried backing away, hoping to cover. "I just assumed, when you said friend—"

"Don't lie!" Kelly was up and standing over me, forcing me against the chair.

"I'm not."

"Would you know the truth if you heard it, you little shit?"

"I know the truth when I see it, and Ren was murdered by your men, Kelly, your men at that warehouse. I know because I recognized them."

Again, I was too slow and too stupid to jump out of the way. His fist came across time zones, catching me square at twelve o'clock. I felt the snap more than I heard it, as my nose broke and I went backward, heels up, taking the chair with me, novas exploding inside my skull. When I could see, Kelly was standing over me, his fists ready to hit me again. I got even by bleeding all over his buffed parquet.

"Get up," he said.

I did.

"Unless you want to spend the rest of your life in a Panamanian prison, I suggest you give up your friend. You and I both know he was there. Wasn't he, Harper?"

"Doe. I wuz alode."

This time I stepped out of the way of Kelly's fist. When it went by my ear I turned into his exposed gut and drove my elbow hard into his solar plexus. He rewarded me with a satisfying "oof."

But he recovered too quickly and before I could spin out of reach he closed his forearm around my neck and squeezed. I pushed and we stumbled backward against his desk. The phone, a jar of sharpened pencils, and a stapler crashed to the floor. I clawed at his forearm as my vision collapsed. I was on my way to blacking out, and I knew if I did, I'd never regain consciousness.

In a move of sheer animal desperation, I drove my thumb backward, aiming for his eye. I missed, but hit him hard enough to cripple my thumb and close enough to his eye for him to loosen his grip. When he did, I dropped to the floor and rolled under his desk.

He fell across the top of the desk, reaching for me, his face red as a ripe tomato, and I hit him with the first thing I could pick up. Swinging the Swingline like a hammer, I drove a staple cleanly into Kelly's forehead. His face squinched in pain and shock, and then he came at me again, blind with rage, and I drove another staple between his eyes, this time smacking the stapler with the heel of my hand. He bellowed like a stuck bull and pulled away far enough for me to back against the wall, the desk still between us, and when he reached across the desk to grab me again, I rolled over to the window and sprang to my feet, my fists up, ready for round two. I'd had enough.

Kelly came at me, blocked several of my best jabs with his forearms, and then barreled into my chest with his shoulder, raising me off my feet. I grabbed his head and held on, twisting like a rodeo rider trying to bring down a running calf. We fell to the floor. I tried to roll away but he pounced on me, my back to the floor. He gripped one of the sharpened pencils in his fist and was driving the point toward the center of my eye.

I held his wrist, but he was stronger, much stronger, and as he put his weight behind the graphite tip, it quivered closer to my eyeball. We hung like that, each grunting with exertion. My arms shook, but I refused to die by a number 2 Ticonderoga. It would be too much like my SATs.

Blood from Kelly's forehead dripped onto my face and I began to pray that he'd stroke out before he could kill me. Just as the equilibrium changed and Kelly's weight began to overcome the stamina of my arms, Eubanks knocked on the office door frame. He looked from me to Kelly, saw the murder in Kelly's eyes, the blood on my face, and the pencil. Eubanks gulped.

Kelly was remarkably cool, considering. He looked at Eubanks and said, "Well?"

"Sorry, Mr. Kelly, sir, but there's a Panamanian here, says he's with the Department of Tourism."

"What the hell does he want?"

"He wants to see Mr. Harper, sir."

Kelly straightened and rolled off me. I stood up, my rage evaporating, but not my caution. He had hit me twice by surprise and it wasn't going to happen again.

Kelly pulled the staple from his forehead and said, "This isn't finished, Harper. Not by a long shot."

"Any time, old man."

"Get the fuck out of my sight. You make me want to puke."

I left the office. Eubanks handed me a wet paper towel and I held it to my nose. I pictured my face with a busted beak and thought it might give me a little character. I try to look on the bright side.

Outside, waiting by his car, was Marquez, the man who had talked to me the night Zorro was murdered. "Good afternoon, Señor Harper. Can you come with me?"

We walked into the garden, away from the buildings and anyone who might want to listen in on the conversation.

"Looks like you're running out of friends, señor."

"Yes, sir."

"Are you all right?" He examined my nose the way another man might examine a painting. "That looks like it hurts."

"I'm okay. What's this about?"

"About yesterday afternoon at the warehouses."

"The explosion?"

"Yes, the explosion. For some reason, the police seem to have lost interest in talking to you, an eyewitness. Do you have any idea why that would be?"

"No, sir."

"Is there anything I should know?"

"You know it was no accident, don't you, sir?" My nose was beginning to clear although the paper towel was red with fresh blood.

"Yes."

We walked a little farther down the path, between orange hibiscus and tiger lily blossoms.

"I read a book about Vietnam not long ago," Marquez said. "It was very interesting."

"Yes, sir."

"It detailed the guerrilla war, 'asymmetrical warfare' I believe your Pentagon calls it."

"Yes, sir."

"And the ingenious ways the Viet Cong overcame their technological shortcomings. One of the simplest, so simple a child could do this, was to wrap a rubber band around a grenade, around the safety"—Marquez snapped his fingers—"what do you call that?"

"The spoon," I said.

"Yes, the spoon. They would wrap the rubber band around the spoon, pull the pin, and drop the grenade into the gas tank of a jeep or truck. The gasoline would eat away at the rubber band, the spoon would fly off, and boom, the vehicle would explode. A very simple but effective time bomb."

"But Ren's car didn't have a gas tank opening big enough," I said. "Not like a jeep."

"I wondered about that, too. Then I remembered seeing a can of gasoline in the back seat of his car on the night Señor Alonzo was killed. That would be big enough, would it not?"

I thought about rubber bands and how they get eaten away in gasoline. I thought about sitting next to that can, holding up Ren's kitchen chair. I thought about Ren being a better driver, or that rubber band being a little thicker, or if my stomach was a little stronger and I hadn't wanted fresh air. I thought about how close I had come to not standing in that garden, bleeding all over my shirt, talking to a man from Tourism about Ren's murder.

"Are you feeling well, Señor Harper?"

"Yes, sir. Just thinking."

"You didn't perhaps get a good look at the man who put the thing in the car?"

"I could point him out if I saw him again."

"I will pass that along."

"By the way, did you happen to speak to Lieutenant Consuerte about those smugglers?"

Marquez shook his head slowly, watching me as if I might slip away. "Smugglers?"

"Yes," I said, and told Marquez about the firefight at the river. He studied me as I spoke and I know he was looking for reasons why I would lie. When I was done he said, "This is the first I've heard of this, and I don't know of any Lieutenant Consuerte. Are you absolutely sure of the name?"

"Yes. It means 'with luck,' doesn't it?"

"It does." Marquez looked confused, but I wasn't. "I will ask around. Perhaps he's new to Panama City."

"Perhaps," I said.

Marquez scribbled in a small notebook and when he tucked the notebook back into his jacket pocket I saw the pistol on his hip. He caught my look, gave me an embarrassed smile, and said, "The tourism industry is very competitive."

"Yes, sir, I'll bet it is."

"Please, sir," he said, "if you can do me a favor."

"I will if I can."

"I think someone may be trying to kill you, and that would re-quire a lot of paperwork." He shook his head, the overworked civil

servant, and said, "I wonder if I could persuade you to return home
before they succeed?"

I promised I would try and he ambled off, in no hurry in the
heat, toward the green sedan parked in front of the hotel.

Kelly stood on the veranda and watched him get in the car and
drive away. He looked at me, his face squinting against the sun, until Marquez's car was through the gate. "You're confined to the
compound, Harper, you got that?"

I said I did and we both knew I had no intention of staying
where I was, but we had to do the dance. It was expected.

CHAPTER NINETEEN

Kelly's patience had run out. I knew that. There was no way he would let me off the isthmus alive and that meant I had to stay as far away from him as possible. The first opportunity he got, he'd pinch my head off like a grape.

I like to think of that as motivation.

After reshaping my nose in the mirror, I went down to the second floor and listened at the door. Not a creature was stirring, not even an agouti. I picked the doorknob lock in under thirty seconds, a personal best, and stepped inside. I figured that maybe, just maybe, the student files were somewhere in Kelly's apartment.

There was sunlight pouring in from the balcony, so bright it hurt my eyes. I found Kelly's bedroom, as spartan as his office, and searched his drawers, one by one. In the nightstand I found a Russian Makarov and wondered where he found the uncommon ammunition for the pistol in this part of the world. I looked behind the one picture, a Kmart print of *The Last Supper,* but there was no convenient safe—not that I had any great skill in safecracking. The floors were hardwood and I crawled around on my hands and knees looking for a trapdoor or loose board or maybe a box of handy info filed neatly under the bed. I searched until my face started throbbing and I had to stand up.

Kris's room was a little pinker than her father's, but even her room was as impersonal as a bus station. She had arrived on Christmas Eve, the same day I'd first heard about La Boca, a day devoid of any joy, peace, or goodwill, and hadn't taken the time to unpack. Her things fell out of an open suitcase and were strewn across the floor. I wasn't enough of a pervert to finger through her underthings, although I was enough of a pervert to think about it. There wasn't any hiding place for papers I could see, so I headed toward the kitchen. I was halfway across the living room when I heard someone on the balcony. I froze, held my breath, and hoped that whoever was out there couldn't hear the pounding of my heart.

The balcony doors were open and a hot breeze blew through the apartment. I smelled honeysuckle. I quickly tiptoed to the front door and slowly turned the knob. With a quick glance into the hall, I started out.

"Harper?"

Kris was standing with her back toward the ocean, the breeze fluttering the hem of her shirt.

"Hi, Kris."

"What are you doing?"

"Uh, the door was open."

"And you just came inside?" She tilted her head and looked at me. Her stare reminded me of her father. It was not pleasant.

"Uh, the truth is, I wanted to surprise you."

She crossed the room and examined my eye, her fingertips barely touching the cheek. "Christ, Harper, you're more likely to scare me to death. What the hell happened to your face?"

"I ran into a tree," I said.

"You need to be more careful around trees. Does it hurt?"

"No, but the way you're looking at me does."

She laughed and said, "I'm sorry, but you look like something a bear ate and shit in the woods."

"Thanks for that lovely simile."

We stood for a moment, the topic of my face exhausted and any other logical topic of conversation way out of bounds.

"Hey, I was just about to go swimming. Want to come?"

"If your father found out, he'd kill me."

"Daddy would what?" She waved that thought away as being

completely ridiculous. "Harper, he's like the biggest pushover. You just have to know how to handle him. Besides, he's not here. He's off on one of his 'missions.'"

"Uh-huh," I said. "But I don't think so."

Kris pulled on my arm. "Come on, don't be a jerk. It'll be fun."

A few minutes later we climbed into her car and I said, "Maybe I should hide in the back. You know, for when we go through the gate."

"Don't worry. I know a secret way out of this place."

We drove toward the back of the compound, and down a rutted road that led to a gate in the chain-link fence. Kris got out and opened it, then got back in the car. "I cut the lock off days ago and no one's noticed," she said. "I think we're safe."

The road was so narrow that branches swept both sides of the open car. I ducked to avoid a branch at the same time Kris ducked and we bumped heads. My head, already beaten like a tambourine, felt like the top was going to explode. Kris giggled and rubbed the bump. I didn't stop her.

The trail broke onto a larger dirt road and Kris turned left. We followed the road through the deep green shade of the high-canopy rain forest. Kris turned down another rutted trail and came up a rise that overlooked a quiet lagoon, protected from the waves by a coral reef seventy yards out. She stopped and we got out and looked over the water. Tall palms rattled against a powder-blue sky. I said, "I thought places like this existed only in postcards."

"Postcards don't have sand fleas. Can you swim with your nose like that?"

"I'm not going to swim," I said, "I don't have a suit."

"Neither do I." Kris pulled her hair back into a ponytail and fastened it with a rubber band. "Well, you gonna take off your pants, or what?"

"No, I'll stay up here."

"Whatever." She stripped off her shirt and shorts, ran down to the sand and waded into the water.

There wasn't much point in my standing by the car with my thoughts in my head so I turned my back and peeled off my clothes.

When I turned around, she was treading water, watching me. She smiled and swam off toward the reef. By the time I was in, dog-paddling to keep my busted nose in the air, Kris was thirty yards out, her skin glistening wet, shiny as a seal.

I paddled out toward her. The water was vodka clear and sunlight rippled across the bottom. A small school of fish swept under me, darting one way, then another. I saw a manta, black as a manhole, glide across the bottom. Its edges stirred up tiny sand devils that swirled in the eddy.

Kris touched my shoulder. Her wet hair framed her face and water drops sparkled on her eyelashes. "I just wanted to tell you about the sharks in the lagoon."

"You mean there are sharks here?" I didn't want to be the second piano player eaten by a shark. Nobody wants to be second at anything.

"Sometimes a sand shark, but nothing that's going to eat you. I've only seen one great white and I came out here almost every day last summer."

"Alone?"

Kris smiled. "Yeah, most of the time. Let's swim out by the reef. There's more to see." Kris went under, her feet giving a graceful little kick at the surface that propelled her out toward the white chop.

I went after her. I watched my own shadow glide as gracefully as the manta over the sand. Bits of rock and coral poked through the smooth bottom and everywhere I looked there were fish in brilliant motion. The wall of coral rose up in front of me and I watched a shadow move smoothly next to my own. Kris said, "You having fun?"

"Yeah, I am."

"I'm glad you came. Just be careful of the sea urchins. They burn like fire. And don't get too close to the coral because it'll cut you."

"Okay."

"And you don't want to bleed in the water."

"You really know how to put a guy at ease."

"Just stuff you should know." Then she was gone again, smooth and sleek and shiny. I swam after her, watching her long legs kick, and thought that with all of the fish and coral and bright fronds of sea flora, Kris was easily the prettiest creature in the pool.

A large school of yellow and black fish engulfed us, hundreds of them, thin and fast and ticklish. Kris grabbed my arm. "We need to get out."

"Why?"

"Just get out!" And then she was gone, kicking fast toward the beach.

When I climbed up onto the sand she said, "Those are tiger fish. They only run like that because of sharks."

"But you said—"

"I said they rarely come past the reef. But when they do, they're usually hungry and they push a school of tigers in front of them. It's best to be safe." Kris sat up and pointed. "Look."

I couldn't see anything at first, just the sunlight on the water. Then I saw the delta of the shark fin, cutting through the waves like a bayonet. It was moving fast, following the tiger fish across the open bowl of the lagoon.

"I've had enough swimming for today, how about you?" Kris said.

"It's going to be a long time before I get into the tub."

Kris brushed the sand from between her toes. "So, what do you think? You like it here?"

"Yeah, I mean, apart from the shark."

"I meant Panama."

"I've been in better places."

Kris curled up on her side, resting her head on the back of her hand. "Tell me what you're doing here, or is that some big government secret?"

"I'm a piano player. The Colonel needed a piano player for his big party. That's all."

"Okay. So don't tell me. You have a girlfriend? Back home, I mean."

"No." For the first time, I was ashamed to think that of all the women I'd known in Washington, not one of them was single. "No, no girlfriends."

"Have you ever killed anyone?"

"Not today."

Kris laughed. I liked the sound of it. She rolled over onto her back and watched the clouds. "I'm serious," she said. "Meat thinks you're some kind of secret agent."

"That's not true. Meat does not think."

Kris laughed again. It was even nicer the second time.

"What'd you do in high school? Any sports?"

"I've always played the piano. I had a steady gig at the veterans' home. Oh, and I was a disc jockey for a few months at an oldies station. The hits of the sixties, over and over and over. They call it 'oldies' because it gets so old."

I rolled over to my side so I could see Kris stretched out next to me, her eyes closed, her hands behind her head. Her breasts pointed up at the tinted sky and my eyes followed her flat stomach down to the tangle of reddish-blond hair where beads of salt water glistened in the sun.

"So why didn't you play something else?"

"The station manager. She was the wife of the local real estate tycoon. She had two toy poodles who left turds in the break room and pee in the hall."

"Very nice."

"And she had a voice like a truck rolling over broken typewriters."

Kris laughed again. Her stomach fluttered and her breasts jiggled in a way that inspired a physical response hardwired deep inside the primal roots of my lizard brain.

"So what happened?"

"When?" I was having a hard time keeping my mind on the story.

"Why'd you quit?"

"I played Otis Redding."

"What's wrong with Otis Redding?"

"Nothing. But this woman stuck her face in the control room door and said, in that voice that could grind steel, 'Johneeee, isn't that a little too Negroid for our sound?'"

"She actually said 'Negroid'?"

"Yeah. Pretty progressive, huh? So I apologized and she went away. Then I put on James Brown, 'Say It Loud, I'm Black and I'm Proud.'"

"Right on, brother."

"I was fired."

"Uh-oh."

"So I broke into the studio, barricaded the doors, put on a two-hour tape of NWA and Run DMC, you know, Old School, and climbed out the back window. It took them forty-five minutes to bust in and stop the tape."

"Ever think you'd be stuck in a place like Panama?"

"Never. What about you?"

"Oh, I've grown up with this shit. The Philippines, mostly. Now that's a place that's truly fucked up. You want a recipe for ruining paradise, start with the Spanish, hand off to the Catholic church, and then, when they're through with it, send in the Marines."

I tried to think of a place where that had happened that wasn't fucked up and couldn't. "This place wouldn't be half bad without all the politics," I said.

"That's what my mother said about Washington."

It was my turn to laugh. "I think your mother and I would have gotten along."

"How'd you get here, John, I mean here, at the hotel? Were you in the service?"

"Yeah. I was. Never saw combat. Too busy playing elevator music at the officers' club."

"Why'd you join?"

"My father always said we were obligated to serve our country. But when my brother didn't come home, we lost heart in that patriotic stuff."

"Your brother was killed?"

"His helicopter went down in the first gulf war. I was twelve and I remember it like it was yesterday. Guy comes to the door. I was watching a Pirates game. I heard my mother scream and my father say, over and over, 'No, it's not true, it's someone else's boy. You've made a mistake. It's someone else's boy.'

"I tried hard to be the perfect son after that, to make up for the one they lost, you know? I learned all that music my parents loved. It didn't help, though. My mother died a few years later."

"What happened?"

I swallowed hard, trying to find a reason not to tell her. Finally, I said it out loud, the thing I'd never said to anyone. "She killed herself."

We were quiet for a long time.

"Parents sure can fuck up their kids." Her voice sounded hard, and cold, and I knew we weren't talking about my parents anymore.

"I think it's why they come in twos, just to make sure the kids get good and fucked up."

White clouds sailed over blue water. Palm fronds rattled in the breeze.

"I miss her," Kris whispered. "She was so soft. Like a TV mom. That's how I remember her. Like a TV mom. You remind me of her, in a way."

"Just what every guy wants to hear, I remind you of your mother."

Her laughter was soft and easy and the sunlight colored her skin. "It's just that she liked all the music you like and she believed all the words."

"You don't?"

"It's all horse shit, in my opinion."

"It doesn't have to be."

Kris rolled over on her side and faced me and I saw the bruise on her ribs. It was large, and purple, and the exact size of a fist. I reached toward her. She thought I was reaching for her breast, and she smiled, but when I put my fingers against her ribs her face clouded over and she covered the bruise with her arm.

"How'd that happen?"

"What?"

"There, right there."

"It's nothing."

"It looks like someone hit you."

"It's nothing," Kris said. The light changed in her eyes and she said, "And what's this?"

"What?"

"This," she said, and gripped my penis. Then she kissed me, her leg over me, and then she was on top and I ran my hands over her back, feeling the sand and the smooth warm skin and her heat pressed against me.

She broke away and ran up the beach to the car. "Stay there, I'll be right back."

Like I was going anywhere.

Then Kris was standing over me, as naked as a Polynesian. She carried a blanket and a bag and she spread the blanket on the sand. Then she took a towel out of the bag.

"Stand up," she said. I stood up. Kris brushed the sand from my back. Then she brushed my chest and arms. Then she brushed the sand from my legs, starting at the ankles, working her way up.

She took me by the hand and led me like a lamb to that blanket. She pulled me down to her and I forgot about everything but this girl, her warm skin, the sun-bleached hair on her stomach, and how her muscles fluttered when I kissed her there. She helped me roll on a condom, giggling, and then she opened to me and I forgot everything but that warmth, her hands in my hair, and finally her voice as she scattered the birds with my name.

As we lay on that blanket, her head on my chest, her hand rubbing my stomach, she began to talk, not about anything in particular, but about where she was in her life, and how much she didn't understand, and how at twenty-four things seemed so hard and she had no idea what she wanted to do except fall in love, and even then she couldn't imagine loving anyone who could possibly love her.

"Groucho Marx said, 'I wouldn't belong to any club that would have me as a member.'"

That made her laugh again, which was all I wanted.

"Come on, I have to show you something," she said.

We dressed, gathered up our stuff, and Kris aimed the car up the road, along the coast, until it turned inland. We went through an abandoned site of low, stucco buildings, their red tile roofs crumbling and chain link rusting in the salt air.

"What is this place?"

"It used to be a leper colony. A boy I met last summer said he lost his virginity here."

"I hope that's all he lost."

"Probably put him off sex for a while," she said. "Don't you think?"

"Not any boy I know."

The ten minutes became thirty minutes and we were crossing the bridge that spanned the Canal. At the Avenue of Martyrs Kris turned left, under the shadow of Ancon Hill.

"Kris, where are we going?"

"There's something you have to see."

We entered Balboa, what had been the administrative headquarters for the zone, the strip of Yanqui colonialism that straddled the Canal for nearly a century.

"How much do you know about the Canal?" Kris asked me.

"Not much. Yellow fever, Teddy Roosevelt, that sort of thing."

"You need to see the locks."

"Kris, I've seen them."

"When?"

"In pictures. In school. I don't know."

"You need to see them for real," she said. "The locks and sex are two of the things in life that aren't overrated."

We drove through a town circle straight out of an Andy Hardy movie, had Andy been raised in the tropics. The town radiated from this center with military precision. "This is Balboa," Kris said. "The people who run the Canal still live here. When the first President Bush invaded, rumors are that the American soldiers brought a bunch of Panamanian politicos associated with Noriega, you know, labor leaders and people like that, up to the high school and shot them."

"You're kidding."

"That's what the Panamanians say. Down there's the Balboa Yacht Club. I bet it'll be hopping tomorrow night, as much as a bunch of tightasses can hop without spilling their Cosmopolitans.

"All this"—she waved her hand at the Hollywood ideal of a small town, now faded and tattered by tropical neglect—"used to be a paradise for American workers. Servants to do everything and zero social problems. Never. If you bitched about something in public, they'd deport you. If you didn't have a job, they'd deport you. Leftist politics? They'd deport you. Crumbling marriage? Adios. Criminal tendencies? Later, pal. It was all so neat and controlled and everyone was oh so happy.

"Then Jimmy Carter fucked up and gave it all away. Now most of the zone is abandoned." Right on cue, we passed a ghost town of crumbling barracks, weed-choked parade fields, and an empty PX, the sign faded and barely hanging on by a rusted bolt.

The first set of locks was just ahead and Kris stopped so we could watch a freighter ease inside the long box and a set of massive doors close behind it. "Pretty cool, huh? Those are the Miraflores locks," Kris said. "We're heading up to the next set, Pedro Miguel, to get a better view."

Blue lights flashed behind us and Kris looked in the rearview mirror. "You're not holding, are you?"

"No," I said.

"And I know you're not carrying a gun. I think I would have seen that."

"I'm clean, ma'am."

A uniformed Asian cop, his hand on his pistol grip, approached the car. His partner, another Asian, approached the car from the other side. He was armed with a short AK on a folding stock.

Kris felt me tense and said, "Relax."

The cop touched his cap. "Hi, Kris."

"Hi, Huang."

Huang leaned in and looked at me. "This the piano player?"

"This is him."

"You heading up to Gold Hill?"

"I thought I'd give him the full tour."

Huang nodded, touched his cap again, and said, "There's a party tomorrow night at Fat's house. You're invited." He said to me, "You can sit in with the band if you want."

"Maybe," Kris said. "You guys take it easy, and happy new year."

Huang laughed. "Not for another couple weeks. Year of the monkey," he said.

Kris said, "Later," put the car in gear, rolled away. She watched in the rearview until the security guards did a U-turn and said, "The Canal hired a Chinese security firm. Lowest bid, you know, the glories of capitalism. It's got everybody's tail in a knot. Nice guys, though, even if they are commies."

Kris turned off the main road and onto a narrow track cut through the scrub jungle. We stopped and Kris said, "Grab that blanket. We hoof it from here."

I followed her up a steep hill, through low jungle that nearly covered the trail. Near the top, the jungle gave way to grass and a stiff wind blew away the mosquitoes. On the crest we could see straight down to the Canal a hundred feet below. A quarter mile away the locks were busy with ships lined up on either side, coming or going.

"This is Gold Hill," Kris said, "and those are the Pedro Miguel locks over there. Those little locomotives are called mules, and they pull the ship through."

"Amazing," I said. "That freighter looks too big."

"The locks can handle everything but oil tankers and aircraft carriers. I watched a sub go through once, that was pretty cool. And once, a Chinese ship full of rice ran aground on the other side of the Miraflores. Water got into the holds and they had to pump the rice out to keep it from expanding and busting the ship apart at the seams. That whole field was covered in rice, stinking in the sun, a real feast for the rats, which brought out the snakes, which bit the workers trying to clear the field."

"Kris, why are we up here?"

"Did you ever wonder about the hotel's name? La Culebra Boca?"

"It means the mouth of a snake, right?"

"It's my father's idea of a joke," Kris said, "and it's not even correct Spanish. But Daddy says he can swallow Panama from there."

"Ah," I said, and wondered just how much of Panama Kelly thought he could digest.

"Now look down at those locks. That's why everyone's so worried," Kris said. "Those locks hold back this entire lake. All it would take is one terrorist with one boatfull of explosives, because if the locks go, everything goes. And once you've pulled the plug, it takes a long time to fill up the tub."

"Why tell me this, Kris?"

"Because I think my father has something planned for tomorrow night." She shook her head no, as if she were trying not to believe her own words. "I think he may be planning to blow up one of the locks."

"And you think I can stop him?"

"You're the only hope I've got," she said.

I could see the light in her eyes, and we kissed for a long time. When we parted, she said, "I'm so glad you broke into my apartment."

"I am, too, Kris."

Kris pulled off my shirt and pushed me back on the blanket.

"The bag is in the car," I said.

"I don't care, John."

Eubanks was at Ren's desk going through paperwork.

"Man," he said, "where you been? Everybody wants to buy you a drink."

"Why?"

"Nobody's ever squared off against the old man before. You got some balls, Harper."

"Is Kelly around?" I looked toward his office door, afraid to see a light.

"Nah, he's off playing soldier. By the way, nice look there with the bandage. It really sets off the black around your eyes."

"Thanks. It's the fashion back home."

"Oh, and a woman called for you, said her name was Marilyn. She left her number." He handed me a slip of paper.

"You mind if I use your phone?"

"Doesn't matter to me." Eubanks went back to sorting papers by size and color.

Marilyn answered on the first ring. "Hi," I said.

"Hi." Her voice was barely a whisper. "I wanted to say I am sorry for the other night. I had no right to be angry with you."

"That's okay."

"I wanted to apologize to you. In person."

"You don't have to, Marilyn, it's okay."

"It's not okay. I was very rude to you and I want to make it up. Can you come in to see me?"

"I don't know."

"No monkey business, I promise."

"I've had a long day, Marilyn. Maybe tomorrow."

"And I wanted to give you a message," she said. "You know, from that man."

"Which man?"

"You know, I sent him those pictures of myself, in the bathing suit. He gave me a message to give to you."

The room went cold. Smith had contacted Marilyn?

"I'll just buy you a drink," Marilyn said. "It is considered bad luck in Panama to start off the new year without making apologies for the old. Wait for me at the gate and I'll pick you up."

"Okay. I'll be there."

Meat was back at the front gate. "Hey, what happened to your face, monkey shit?"

"Meat, I am in no mood for this. I'll tell you what, I'll just stand here and you can get all your witticisms out and I promise I'll be offended later, when I have the energy, okay?"

Meat blinked a few times and said, "Yeah, well . . ."

"That's what I thought."

Marilyn pulled up and around in that jangling Hillman. I climbed in.

Meat leaned over and pointed a meaty finger at me. "One of these days Kelly is going to let me kick your ass, and then it'll be crying time, monkey pussy."

"That's my boy. See you later, Meat."

Meat grumbled and said, "Yeah, later, monkey turd."

So Kelly hadn't unleashed the dogs on me yet. That was a relief. He probably wanted the pleasure of skinning me himself.

I asked Marilyn about Smith. She didn't say anything. I asked again. "Marilyn? You said you had a message for me."

Marilyn chewed the end of her thumb. "I know. I lied. I'm so sorry. I just had to see you and you didn't want to come, so I made that up about that man."

I tried to be angry, but couldn't get out more than a squeak. "Marilyn, you can't go around doing this kind of stuff. If the wrong person heard you, you could get hurt, or worse."

"And what about you, Monkeyboy? You can't just go around making girls feel good about you and then act like you don't know them."

"What are you talking about?"

"Oh, shit." Marilyn stopped the car. Stretched across the road was a boa constrictor, its body as big around as Marilyn's thigh. She got out.

"What are you doing?"

"I'm hurrying him along, what does it look like?" She kicked at the snake with her pointed toe. It was a big snake, and apparently in no hurry.

I got out of the car. "Man, that is a big snake," I said.

"If you're afraid, you can get back in the car, big pussy."

"I'm okay," I said, although I was sure the snake would snap back and swallow Marilyn whole, leaving nothing but her fake Jimmy Choos in the road. "Look, we can get around it now," I said, pointing to the tail.

Marilyn left the snake, turned to face me and kissed me. There, standing by the grill of a '54 Hillman, with a snake big enough to eat Grandma at our feet, she planted one on me and put her hand on my crotch.

"Marilyn, I don't think—"

"Get in the car," she said.

I did.

Marilyn drove around the snake and headed toward the high-way. "Harper? Where you come from, girls can be anything," she said. "They can be nurses and teachers and mothers. It's not like that here."

"I know."

She braked hard and the Hillman slid to a stop and stalled, shuddering, on the highway. A truck blew by us, rocking the car, its horn Dopplering down from a B- to an E-flat.

"Marilyn, you'll get us killed out here."

She faced me, gripping my arm, her fingernails in my flesh. "You think you know something but you don't." She looked into my eyes, searching for some sign of wisdom, and I could see her disappoint-ment. She let go and wiped her face. "Now, tell me, who hit you?" She touched the tape across my nose. "Do you have another girl-friend somewhere, huh, gringo boy? Someone not as sweet as me?"

"It was about politics," I said.

"Never argue politics in Panama." She smiled.

"I'm learning," I said.

"Does it hurt?" She touched my cheeks, first the left, then the right. Her fingers lightly touched my eyebrows and moved along my face.

"Not anymore," I lied.

"Good," she said. She restarted the car and headed toward Panama City. " 'Cause I am going to show you something. You think because of New York maybe and Hollywood, you know how to party, but you better hold on, because you've never seen what it means to have a good time like the good time you have in Panama."

"I can't, Marilyn, I have to get back to the hotel."

"Then I guess you walk," she said, and drove off toward the city's glow.

CHAPTER TWENTY

Marilyn led me from bars to crowded bodegas, the whole city in rehearsal for the big blowout of the next night's New Year's Eve party. We passed a street vendor selling incense, T-shirts, and pictures of movie stars. I asked the man if he had a picture of Marilyn Monroe.

"¡Sí! Marilyn Monroe! Big star!" He pulled a black-and-white photo out of the stack. It was a full face shot, Marilyn's lips painted and pouty, her eyes smoky and staring into the camera.

"How much?" I asked the vendor. "¿Cúanto?"

"Thirty dollars," he said. "Big star."

I reached into my pocket and Marilyn said, "No! Give him ten."

"Ten?" the vendor yipped. "This is signed! See? Her name." The signature was scrawled across the bottom. It looked as if the person who had signed it had had to stop every third letter to check the spelling.

"Okay," said Marilyn, grabbing my arm. "Let's go. This man is a liar and a thief."

"Wait," said the vendor. "Twenty."

"Twelve dollars," Marilyn said.

"Fifteen, and I throw in a baseball signed by Joe DiMaggio for your young man." He held out the picture and a dirty scuffed baseball. Joltin' Joe's signature was amazingly similar to Marilyn's.

"Is very romantic," the vendor said, a wistful look in his eye. "They once were big lovers like you and your young man." He turned to me, an easier mark, and pleaded, "I make more friends than money in this business. You, señor, are my friend. You live here. Not like the sailors and tourists who come and go. And it is almost the new year, señor."

"Okay," I said. "Fifteen dollars."

"You are a big crook," Marilyn said to the salesman. "You are lucky my man is so rich he won't notice how shamelessly you rob us."

The man took my money and gave us the picture and the baseball. "You must come back and see me, señor, on a day you are free of this harsh woman. I would give you something out of sympathy."

Marilyn told him to go choke on the *plata*.

"Come on, Marilyn." I wedged the baseball into my back pocket where it made a bulge like a big-league tumor on my ass. Marilyn slid the picture of the blond movie star into her blouse.

"Thank you, my rich Yanqui lover," she said, putting her arms around my neck.

"That's Yanqui Clipper to you, ma'am."

Marilyn led me through the crowds, holding my hand so I wouldn't get swept away. Bands played in every corner bar. Men guzzled rum from bottles and women lifted their feathery skirts and danced in circles, showing off their legs. It was everything I had been warned about in Sunday school and I thought it was great. I danced with strangers and drank from bottles without wiping the neck.

Later, as we walked along a quiet street far from the raucous bars, Marilyn kissed me so hard it hurt. "You would make a great Panamanian," she said.

"Hey, gringo!" Marilyn and I broke apart. We faced six Panamanian men, drunk and sweaty and looking for trouble.

"Hey, Yanqui! Go home and leave our women!" One of the boys grabbed Marilyn's arm and jerked her away from me. The others formed a tight circle and started pushing, bouncing me around the circle.

"Go jerk your pinga, Yanqui. Whatsa matter, you can't get no *chucha* at home?"

One of the boys hit me in the head. Another punched my ribs.

Another gave me a Saturday-morning kung fu kick that knocked me against the wall.

"Come on, *queco!*" One man moved in closer. He taunted me, urging me to fight. *"¡Venga!"* He had a knife in his hand and made wide swings at me. On one pass I grabbed his arm, twisted it, then shoved him into another man. Another came in from my right. He had a box cutter and he slashed at me, the blade coming closer with each swing.

In a blink, the man behind the box cutter crumpled to the pavement. I saw the arc of a tire iron sweep over the heads of the rubbernecking crowd. I knew from the sound that someone would not be dancing in the new year. The crowd scattered. The tire iron swung again and caught one of the men in the ribs. The man whooshed and went down on his knees keening like a rabbit. The other men backed away, their eyes surprised and frightened.

It was Phil, swinging for the fences. One man, braver than the others or just plain stupid, jabbed at Phil with a knife and Phil spun to the side, a matador before the bull, and brought the tire iron down hard on the boy's extended forearm. The knife clattered to the street. The man screamed like a girl and staggered back, holding his shattered arm against his chest.

Marilyn helped me up while Phil held back the crowd. The curious were gone, and in their place were serious men gathering for a new attack. They circled us like wolves in the firelight. The man with the cracked ribs fumbled in his pocket. I saw the white grip of a nickel pistol. Marilyn saw it, too. She calmly stepped into the street and kicked the man in the crotch. He folded in on himself and fell to his knees.

Phil grabbed me by the collar and pulled me into a stairwell. He sailed the tire iron, end over end, into the center of the mob.

The three of us sprinted up the steps. At the top Phil picked up a trash can and threw it down the stairwell, slowing the men surging up from the street.

We were at the top of a hallway that ran straight back to an open corridor. The corridor looked out over a small inner courtyard lit by a single forty-watt bulb. From the edge of the shadows, chained beneath the giant leaves of a banana tree, a dog snapped and snarled and jerked his chain taut as piano wire.

"Up here," said Marilyn. She stood on the wooden railing, swung out on a drainpipe and shinnied her way up. At the top she pulled herself over the eave and into darkness.

"Go," Phil said. "Go!"

The crowd flooded out of the hallway. "¡Aquí!" they shouted. I climbed the drainpipe. Marilyn grabbed my arms and pulled me onto the roof.

I turned to help Phil. I saw his hands appear, then his face. "Damn," he said, with wonder, "I think someone's biting my leg."

Marilyn picked up an empty wine bottle and looked over the roof's edge, past Phil. She aimed, dropped the bottle, and brightened when she hit her target with a satisfying bonk. Phil's legs came up over the side. Another man was behind him. Marilyn kicked him in the ear and he dropped out of sight.

I helped Phil to his feet and the three of us ran. We jumped over the narrow gaps between two buildings and sprinted to the edge. We had reached the end of the block. There was no place left to go.

The man falling two floors down to the snarling dog threw a discouraging pall over the crowd and most of them decided there were things they would rather do than spend the night in the hospital with the gunshot drunks. Only four men pursued us. Four determined men who looked surprisingly sober.

In front of us was gravity and its hard landing on an unforgiving sidewalk. Behind us were four very human men. This was where we would make a stand. Without saying a word, Phil and Marilyn understood. Together we turned to face our attackers.

The four men closed in.

Phil looked at me and smiled. "You ready for some fun?" He pushed up his sleeves. Marilyn produced a blade, from where I did not want to guess. I took a stance that I hoped looked discouraging but the four men advanced, their arms wide, moving in for the big body-slamming finale.

I rubbed my hands against my jeans. My hand found the baseball in my back pocket and I pulled it out. As the men drew closer, I rubbed the ball against my thigh like a pitcher facing an oh-and-three. DiMaggio's signature smeared. I reared back in the windup dance American boys have watched a million times on the tube.

The men hesitated, surprised at this ballet of sport in the middle of a mugging. I followed through, my right arm whipped forward, and I prayed it would hit somewhere near the strike zone.

With the crack of a corked bat, my man bunted the ball with his forehead. His eyes rolled up and he fell out for the inning. The other men stopped. Phil smiled and said, "You just gotta love this shit." He took a step forward and the men stepped back. The fast-ball seemed to have dampened their morale. They came to a swift and silent conclusion. The *puta* had a knife, the big man looked like he was having way too much fun, and the boy, this gringo boy, had just given their *compadre* a concussion with an all-American dustoff. They turned and ran back the way they came. Marilyn called them names and threw stones at their backs.

"Man, that was in-fucking-credible! Crack! I didn't know you played ball."

"I didn't," I said. "I never played baseball in my life." I looked at my hands and they were shaking.

While Marilyn rifled the man's pockets, Phil and I found a fire escape. The three of us climbed down into the dark and half an hour later we were sitting in Marilyn's room, drinking cold beer.

"Don't ever take up nursing," I said, wincing as Marilyn cleaned my wounds with rum.

"Be still, you big baby."

"Man, I've never seen anything like that. David and Goliath, man. You dropped him faster than sweatpants in July."

"You think he'll be okay?"

"Fuck him," said Marilyn. She reached down into her blouse and came up with the picture of Marilyn Monroe and a small fistful of damp and dirty bills. "All he had was twelve dollars."

"Nothing else?" asked Phil.

"Nothing."

"Not even some identification?" Phil said. "I thought I saw a card."

"Oh, you mean this?" Marilyn held out a laminated ID.

Phil took it and turned it over in his hand. "This is interesting, Harp."

"What?"

"He's one of the trainees at La Boca. I recognize him from the Claymore class." Phil sat back in the chair and slowly, uncon-sciously, rubbed his head. "Marilyn?"

"Yes?" Marilyn listened intently, her concentration so focused it could set kindling on fire.

"Do you have someone you can stay with?"

"Yes, I can stay with a friend."

"Then go there, and don't come back here until we know more about this guy and why he was so ready to kill my boy."

Marilyn nodded, then got up and began to pack her things into a shopping bag.

(

CHAPTER TWENTY-ONE

Phil and I rode back to La Boca, Phil wheeling the Volvo in and out of traffic like he was at Daytona.

"Something wrong? You're driving like you're pissed off about something."

"You mean besides people trying to kill us?"

"Yeah, besides that."

"Yeah. I'm pissed off. I'm pissed at you."

"What for?"

Phil dodged a bus, a truck full of chickens, and a Toyota filled with an extended family and their three dogs. "We've got twenty-four hours to find out what the fuck is going on here," he said, "and you're playing house with a girl you don't even know." Phil tried to light a cigarette in the hurricane of the open car but the lighter wouldn't catch. "Take the wheel," he said, and without waiting he ducked into the lee of the dashboard, flicking the Zippo as if our lives depended on it sparking flame. "Fucking windproof, my fucking ass," he said, and tossed both the cigarette and his lighter into the street.

"Okay," I said, "you're right, but Marilyn said she had a message from Smith, that's the only reason I went."

"And the drinking and dancing, that was all part of the mission, right?"

I didn't even try to float an excuse.

"And what's really fucked up is you're putting that girl in some serious shit. Have you thought about that?"

I nodded and said, "Yes. I have."

"What was that?" He cupped his hand to his ear. "What did you say?"

"I said I had. I put her in danger. I know that."

"Do you use women like this a lot?"

I said no, which was a fat lie that stunk up the car.

"I been thinking about this," Phil said. "I mean, look at you. It's not like you're good-looking or anything, and God knows you don't have any money."

"And your point?"

"Did you ever think that Marilyn is using you?"

I laughed. "Right, Marilyn's using me. What for?"

Phil said slowly, "I want you to think about this: That guy from La Boca, the guy who jumped you tonight, how did he and his friends know where to find you?"

"They followed me."

"Bullshit. I think it was Marilyn."

"She wouldn't do that."

"You've known her for how long?"

"Since Friday."

Phil laughed and I felt scalded by my own stupidity. "C'mon, man, did you see the way she palmed that dude's ID, like she didn't want us to see it?"

"She forgot about it, that's all."

"Goddamn, Harper, you're supposed to be the smart one. So you better start being smart or you'll get my ass killed. And if that happens, my mother will come down here and kick your monkey ass all the way to Peru."

I had nothing to say. I was ashamed, and felt like I'd let everyone down. Again.

"Are you done thinking with your little head now? Can we get back to work?"

"Okay, Phil," I said.

"So, where do we go from here?"

"Back to the hotel," I said, "and this time I think we're going to have to break some stuff."

The sheer delight in destruction, the joy in the forward velocity of brutal movement, the happiness of demolition, lit up Phil's face like a kid at Christmas. "That's my boy," he said. "That's my fucking Monkeyman." As we approached the hotel, Phil said, "We'll stash the car and walk in through the bush."

"You know a back way inside the compound?"

"Shit, yeah, I been using it all day. Meat couldn't guard his ass with a company of Marines and a pair of Kevlar pants."

I followed Phil across a sharp field of elephant grass and into the treeline where it was so completely black that I had to keep my hand on Phil's back so I wouldn't get lost and stumble about in the darkness, unable to see my own feet. We reached the perimeter of the firing range and from there it was a short walk to the hotel. The lights were on in the office and in the bar at the far end of the hotel by the beach. The sounds of drinking and laughter mixed with the shush of the surf.

Hamster stopped us halfway through the lobby. "Hey, Monkeyman, we been looking all over for you." After the past few days, I didn't think this was good news but Hamster put his arm around my shoulder and said, "Let the guys buy you a drink, for going a round with Mr. Kelly, the son of a bitch."

Phil said, "Where is Kelly?"

"He's off on some night-training exercise with his handpicked team of Latino assassins," Hamster said, "and the Colonel's off kissing some Panamanian official's chocolate-brown ass. That means we have the whole place to ourselves."

"Where are the guests?"

"Gone," Hamster said. "Home for New Year's. Maybe out fucking little brown *campesinos*. Who gives a rat's ass? The bar is open!"

I let Hamster guide me into the bar, with Phil following close behind. When they saw me, the men cheered, beat me on the back, and argued about who was going to pour me my first drink. I was handed a lit Cuban cigar and Dutch asked if I'd play something while Cooper and Hog pushed the upright into the crowded room. I sat down at the piano and played a little blues run, just

warming up my fingers. They were all there, all the American trainers: Ice, Hog, Hamster, Dutch, Eubanks, Coop, and a new man
they introduced as Thumper.

Thumper, Ice told me, got his name by being a master with a
grenade launcher. Some earn a ridiculous name, others have a ridiculous name thrust upon them. "Tell Thump how you got your name,
Monk, go ahead."

"Because of his ears," said Hamster, and everyone laughed, loos-
ened up by free alcohol.

"Don't listen to them. They don't know." And of course, they did
know. I looked at these men who, in less than twenty-four hours,
could be overthrowing Panama, men who for one reason or another
had joined in a criminal enterprise, and men who had been there
the day that I, in Phil's words, had jumped on a grenade like a
monkey jumping on a coconut, but they sensed a story coming and
Hog gave me the nod, just to see where it would go.

"So you tell us, Monkeyman, tell us how you got that name," he
said.

I played some accompaniment, good background to bullshit,
and told Thumper about a woman I knew in D.C., an ambassador's
wife, who wanted to learn how to play the piano. "One night, the
wife asked me to stay after, so I did."

Ice leaned forward, suddenly interested. I had added sex, a good
part of any story, and thrown in the hot conflict of adultery at the
same time. "After a few drinks she took off her clothes and said,
'Play me, John, play me like a Steinway.'"

"Oh, man," Thumper said, "'like a Steinway,' I like that."

Phil tossed back a shot of the Colonel's sixteen-year-old single
malt and said, "Where's the monkey, man?"

"Yeah, where's the monkey?"

"Here's the monkey," I said. "See, the ambassador had a little
spider monkey that he treated like his little boy. Dressed it up in
little pants, took it to the movies."

"No shit," said Thumper.

"No shit. And that monkey hated everybody but his daddy. He'd
bite you any chance he got. This monkey not only hated strangers,"
I said, "he hated music—"

"All music, Harper, or just yours?" The men laughed, sucked into the story of the man, the music, and the monkey.

"He hated all music, Ice, but the good thing was, that monkey hid when anyone played the piano so I never saw the little banana-snatcher. Except this one night, when we stopped playing the piano—"

"And started playing each other," Hog said.

"When the monkey came out." Ominous chords.

"Oh, no," said Thumper. "Here it is."

"I was naked, standing at attention, so to speak, and this ambassador's wife is smokin' hot, crawling around on the bed, begging like a dog for a bone."

"Beggin' for a bone," said Hamster.

"And the monkey springs out from under the bed and latches on to the one thing that looks most like lunch—"

"No," said Thumper, horrified.

"Yes."

Thumper squealed. "You mean the monkey bit your johnson?"

"And that's how I got my name," I said.

"I don't believe it."

I went back to playing idle melodies. "I've got the scar to prove it," I said.

The bar was silent. Each man who knew the true story passed a look between them, wondering who was going to ask. It came down to Hamster. He shook his head, sad to be the one to tap an unhappy ending onto such a fine tale, and said, "I'm afraid we gotta call you on that."

"It's not like we want to look at your dick," said Hog.

"But we do need some proof," said Cooper.

The men, as a unit, agreed. "We need to see it."

So I unzipped my pants and pulled out the evidence. There it was, a crescent-shaped, bite-sized scar.

"Amazing," said Thumper.

"Yeah," said Ice. "A-fucking-mazing. What do you think, Phil?"

Phil looked at me and said in disgust, "That is some shit."

"Are you saying it's not true?" I tucked the evidence back inside my pants.

"No," Phil said, "I'm just wondering how many times you're going to tell that story just so you can pull out your dick."

The men roared, Hamster held his ribs, and Ice nearly fell off
his bar stool.

Hog gave me the nod, telling me the story was now official history, because as any soldier knows, a good story always beats a true
story.

True story: I was a kid playing with my aunt's dog and I took his
toy. He bit me. To this day I have trouble seeing the punishment fit
the crime, but the dog saw a hard justice in it. It happened so long
ago that, mercifully, I have no memory of the actual bite, but I've
heard the story a thousand times.

My mother would tell company, "I looked down and his little
shorts were all covered in blood. I thought, oh my God, he's a eu-
nuch." Then she'd smile and hug me and say, "But everything
works now, doesn't it, little man?" I hated that story.

"A piano player with a monkey bite on his dick," said Thumper,
pleased.

Hog looked at his watch and said, "I hate to break this up, guys,
but tomorrow's a busy day. Time to hit the rack."

"What are we doing tomorrow?" Phil asked.

"We're off on some sort of sweep through the boonies," Hamster
said. "I don't know about you guys. Kelly said you, Monk, and
Cooper have a special assignment."

"A special assignment, huh? You don't know what it is?"

"Something to do with a big New Year's celebration they have
planned, that's all I know."

"Yeah," Ice said, "so while you're at a party, we'll be humping the
bush for New Year's Eve, ain't that some shit."

As we all climbed the stairs to the third floor, Thumper said, "I
got just one question. What happened to the monkey? I mean, the
one that bit your dick?"

"I made him into a hat," I said. And on the laughter of half a
dozen men who were on the cusp of a revolution, we told each
other good night.

Phil and I agreed to a few hours' sleep and then, when everything was quiet, we would search the hotel for the student files and
whatever else would help us stop the Colonel's big New Year's

bash. I stepped into my room, not turning on the light, preferring to undress in the dark.

When I slipped into bed, the sheets were warm, and when I felt her flesh against me I nearly jumped to the ceiling.

Kris laughed. "I take it you don't often come home to find a woman in your bed."

"Jesus, you almost gave me a heart attack."

"Let's see if I can jump-start that thing," she said, and slipped her head under the covers.

I pulled her up and said, "No, Kris, I don't want you to do that," which was another big fat lie I told that night. "You have to get out of here. If your father catches us—"

"He's out playing soldier," Kris said, and encouraged that part of me that thinks only of the present.

I stopped her again. It was not an easy thing to do. "Kris, please, I can't. I have things I have to do, things I have to do in a few hours, and I need some sleep."

Kris sat up in bed as if I'd struck her. She was stunning in moonlight, even more beautiful than at the beach, and if Phil hadn't just given me a lecture on my responsibilities, I would have given in. "You need to go back to your apartment, Kris. Please."

"It's that girl," she said, as if just catching on. "You were out fucking that girl."

"Which girl?"

Kris got out of bed, found her shorts and pulled them on. "The girl on the beach. The one you used to take pictures of the guests—"

"What are you talking about?"

"Don't deny it." She slipped on her shirt. "It's why I came outside. None of the men were looking at her. Christ, John, I've seen boys with better chests. So I gave you a hand." She slipped on her sandals. "And now you're fucking her."

"I'm not."

"I don't care, John. I just don't want an STD. Did you wear a condom, John?"

"Kris, nothing happened."

"I don't know why I expected you to be different. I just hope you didn't tell her anything secret."

"What?"

"That girl, what's her name? Marilyn. She works for my father, John."

That jerked me up. "What?"

"That girl works for my father." Kris opened the door, and before slipping into the hallway she said, "Well, John, I guess it's you who got fucked for a change. Hope it felt good." And she closed the door on my spiking paranoia.

Phil came back to the hotel and assured us that Meat was asleep at the guardhouse. "Fucking bastard should be shot." He looked at me and said, "You look like someone ran over your dog."

"I'm fine. Now let's do this so I can get the fuck out of this miserable fucking country."

"Cranky," Cooper said.

"Someone didn't get enough sleep," Phil said.

We moved silently through the hotel. I picked up the phone in the office. No tone.

"They're working on the lines," Cooper said.

"Convenient, isn't it?"

We broke into Kelly's office. I turned on his computer and typed the password "Osama."

The files opened.

Cooper was amazed. "How did you do that?"

"By staying away from drugs," I said. I searched everywhere, but just as with his paper files, these held nothing more interesting than how many stuffed quail it took to feed the guests on Thanksgiving.

Phil was getting impatient. "When do we get to break things?"

"Why not start with the Colonel's files? You'll need a crowbar or a bolt cutter."

Phil went off to find an implement of destruction.

Cooper and I went through a few more of the computer files and found a copy of the guest register with the names blacked out.

"This is no help," I said.

"Get up, let me try," Cooper said. "This is a PDF file and sometimes"—he brought up another page, this time with the names legible—"you can do this."

"What did you do?"

"It's in two layers, an image and a text. Sometimes whoever red-acts a file only blacks out the image part and you can still get the text file underneath."

"Wow. You should consider a career as a spy. Now let's see if we can find the names of all the men who have trained here, especially if they still have a Panama address."

"I don't see anything like that," Cooper said, scanning the docu-ments. "You want me to print this out?"

"Later," I said. "I know where it is."

Phil came back and hovered over my shoulder. "I couldn't find a crowbar, but I think we should look downstairs. There's room to hide all sorts of shit down there."

I made Phil wait, not an easy thing to do, while Cooper and I searched for the names of the sleeper cells. Without any more luck, we closed out and turned off the computer.

"At least we have the names of the men who are financing the operation."

"That's something."

"Are you two finished? Can we break shit now?"

We followed Phil to a locked door inside the kitchen. It was a double-plug Yale cylinder lock, nothing too hard. I took out my picks and scrubbed the pins. One by one, I felt them set. I was tired and all I could think about was Kris and Marilyn and my concentration slipped so it took longer than Phil could stand. "Come on, Harp, open the goddamn door or I'm going to kick it in."

"Almost done." The final pin set, the barrel turned, and I opened the door.

"Did they teach you that in music school?" Coop asked.

"I could make a joke about finding the right key, but I'm too tired."

Cooper produced a penlight and we followed its beam down the stairwell.

Small storage rooms, their doors made of wood and wire mesh, lined the corridor and we stopped to inspect each. The first few were stacked with canned goods and restaurant supplies. We heard a rat scurry in a corner and Coop caught it in the beam of his pen-light. Its eyes glowed and its whiskers twitched, checking us out as we checked him out.

At the end of the corridor we found another locked door. This lock was a new one to me, so I used the torque wrench to move the plug clockwise, and then counterclockwise.

"What are you doing?"

"Seeing which way the plug turns. Some turn right and some turn left. If I guess wrong, I'll have to do this twice."

Cooper held the light for me and asked, "How can you tell which way's the right way?"

"If you turn it in the right direction, the pins stop the plug and it feels mushy. The wrong way and it hits a metal tab and feels solid."

"Ah," Coop said.

Phil was so close that I couldn't breathe. "Can I get some room here?"

He backed off with a grumble.

Annoyed, I said, "Phil, do you think you can do this faster?"

"No, but I can kill you with two fingers."

"Point taken."

I worked on the lock for ten minutes that felt like ten hours. My fingers were slick with sweat and I was getting a headache. Scrubbing the pins, the fastest way to pick a lock, wasn't working. I tried vibrating the pick against the pins. This requires a feel for the intensity and frequency of the vibration that will sympathetically work the pick against the driver pin. But my frequency was off. Finally, I gave up and did it the slow way, pin by pin. "Can you turn off that light? Sometimes it's easier."

"Sure," Coop said, and snapped the light off, leaving us in darkness.

Without my sight I could visualize the inside of the lock and I could concentrate on the pins, each one with its own personality, its own resistance, its own weight, much like piano keys. I worked, pin by pin, until the last pin set and I turned the plug with the torque wrench, slowly, and the bolt snicked back.

The door opened onto a large room, twenty by twenty, three walls lined in metal racks, floor to ceiling. Half of the racks were stacked with plastic cases. Cooper removed one and opened it. Inside were shoulder-fired missiles, each one capable of bringing down a jetliner at five thousand meters.

Phil moved to a stack of wooden crates marked in Chinese calligraphy.

I whispered, "What do you think's in the boxes?"

"It ain't soy sauce," Phil said. He found a screwdriver and opened one of the crates. Inside were rifles, snug in wooden cradles.

Cooper focused his light. "AKs."

Phil took one out and worked the action, the butt wedged into his thigh. "Brand-new," he said.

"What about this?" Cooper stood by the door to a walk-in freezer. "Why would they have a freezer in a place the cooks can't get to?"

"Biological weapons?"

"That's what I'm thinking."

"Then open the goddamn thing," Phil said.

"It's locked."

Phil looked at me. "It's a good thing I like you."

The padlock was easy after the dead bolt. In ten seconds the three of us were inside; the cold air felt good after the wet Panama heat. The freezer was empty except for a black plastic body bag on a rolling gurney. It looked like someone was home.

"Whoever it is, he's a big one," Coop said.

Phil gripped the zipper. "Should I?"

"Might as well." I braced myself, not knowing who our surprise guest would be. Phil zipped the bag open and there, lips blue, frost on his eyelashes, and a bandage across his nose, was the Gorilla. "I know him," I said. "He works for a Colombian major stationed in Washington." I told them about the encounter on Christmas Eve inside the Crystal City parking garage. "The last time I saw him he was talking to the Colonel."

Cooper leaned in close. "Shot behind the ear. Small entry."

"Twenty-two," Phil said, "the choice of spooks and assassins the world over."

"But why would they kill this guy when just a few days ago I heard the Colonel talking to him about righting the wrongs of history."

"What'd he mean by that?"

"I think they're trying to give Panama back to Colombia." Phil looked at me like a part of my brain was showing. "To restore

Panama to Colombia the way it was before Teddy Roosevelt took it."

"He did that?"

"Yeah, he did that. That's how we got the Canal."

"If this major is involved," Coop said, "why would Kelly have his man killed? It doesn't make sense."

"And, the bigger question, why would Kelly and the Colonel want to overthrow Panama in the first place? What's in it for them?"

"Power? Money? Both?"

"What the fuck are these guys smokin'? The American government would never let that happen. They'd take control of the Canal in a fucking heartbeat," Phil said.

"Maybe that's the point," I said. "There are a hell of a lot of people in Washington who would love an excuse to come down here, kick a little ass, and set up the zone again. Lots of people." I perched on the gurney and bumped up against the Gorillasicle. I apologized. "Coop, this humping-the-boonies thing, where are the guys going?"

"Darien."

"I'm guessing that's not Darien, Connecticut."

Phil rubbed his hands over his shoulders. "I'm getting out of here. I'm freezing my ass off."

Cooper and I ignored him. Coop said, "It's the Darien Province, on the Colombian border."

Phil, respect in his voice, said, "A very bad place. *Muy malo.* Headhunters there who'll shrink your *cabeza* down to the size of a mango."

"You're kidding."

"They can't finish the Pan-American Highway because they can't pay anyone enough to work there," Coop added. "It's a scary place."

Phil flapped his arms. "You throw in the Colombian druggies and all the private security forces these rich assholes have, and you've got a place that doesn't fit very well on the tourist brochures. Now can we get outta here?"

Cooper rubbed his chin. "But if this revolution is happening here in Panama City, why are they sending the team to Darien?"

"Does the team know about this? Are the guys part of this?"

I hadn't known them for long, but they didn't strike me as murderers. Killers, yes, but not murderers.

Phil had the same thought. "No way. I know these guys. They wouldn't train people for this shit. Meat, maybe, and Hamster. But most of what you see here is exactly what it's supposed to be, a training facility for private security."

"But behind that front are a few guys—"

"Like Meat," I said.

"Yeah, like Meat and Hamster and, I think, Zorro," Phil said, "until he got scared."

"And these few work with Kelly on the assault on the Presidential Palace."

"But why send the team into Darien?" Cooper asked.

"To get them out of the way," Phil said.

I felt a chill and it wasn't from the freezer fan. "No witnesses."

Cooper looked shocked. "You mean Kelly would kill every man on the team, all of them?"

"They didn't lose sleep over Rosebud," I said. "They didn't hesitate to kill Zorro or Ren."

"But tomorrow—"

Phil looked at his watch. "You mean later today."

"—they could be heading into an ambush."

My finger stroked the swelling under my eye the way a tongue explores the empty socket of a pulled tooth. "Is there some way we can ground the Huey? Something we can do to sabotage her?"

Cooper nodded. "Yeah, sure. I guess we could cause a fuel leak without too much work. That'd do it."

"They'd just use the new Black Hawk," Phil said. "Fly the Colombians out and then come back for the team."

"Phil, you know some of these guys from Afghanistan. Who do you trust?"

"Hog," Phil said, without hesitation. "And Ice."

"Do you think they'd mutiny, I mean, would they take control of the chopper and land it somewhere else?"

Phil shook his head. "No, man, not without some hard evidence. I mean, I'm beginning to think we're crazy myself. Look at us, standing in a deep freeze with a dead man."

"Then what if you give them a heads-up? Warn them about a possible ambush?"

"Then I'd feel sorry for the other guys. But not too sorry."

"Okay. Set that up. In the meantime, if I can find the list of the sleeper cells, we can stop this thing before the first shooter climbs into his body armor. And I'd like to know who that other guy is, the guy the Colonel thinks is a goat fucker."

"Can we go now?"

"Yeah, Phil, we can go now."

Cooper pushed the latch, but it didn't turn. "It's stuck."

Phil said, "It's probably just frozen. Let me try." He gripped the latch in both hands and pushed down, putting the weight of his shoulders into it. He strained and the back of his neck darkened. The handle snapped and Phil fell to the floor, cutting a gash deep into his upper arm.

"Now you've done it," I said. Phil looked at me one-eyed, and I shut up.

"Someone's locked it from the other side," Coop said.

I looked at Phil's arm, reopened the body bag and stripped off the dead man's guayabera. I didn't think he'd miss it.

"Ah, shit," Phil said, "Now I'm going to bleed to death in this fucking ice chest."

"No you won't," I said, tearing strips of cloth from the shirt. "We'll freeze long before that happens."

(

CHAPTER TWENTY-TWO

So, what do we do now?" Cooper said.

The ceiling and rear wall were solid reinforced concrete. The other three walls were made of insulated sheet metal. "Take the Gorilla off that gurney," I said.

"You going to use him to batter down the door?"

"I'm glad you can make jokes, Coop."

"I wasn't joking."

"Phil, you're the strongest one here. How's your arm?"

"Okay," Phil said, and flexed.

"Can you break off one of those legs so we can use it to pry loose this sheet metal?"

Phil and Coop took the Gorilla off the gurney and placed him on the floor. Phil looked at the steel legs and said, "I think I can break one off, but it's going to take a while."

"You have an appointment?"

At last, Phil got his wish to break things. Phil took an active, and serendipitous, approach to the destruction, flinging the gurney against the floor until one leg snapped free. When he was done he was sweating.

"Wrap yourself in that body bag," Coop said, "or you'll catch cold."

With the Gorilla on the floor and Phil wrapped in plastic, I beat the jagged end of the leg into a seam until it opened enough to pry it back. Rivets popped. The sheet metal came loose, slowly, and then the leg bent. "I need another one," I said, and Phil went to work on the remaining three legs, hurling and thrashing the gurney around the small space until another piece of aluminum broke free.

Cooper's lips were blue. "W-w-what if someone hears us?"

"Gee, Coop, that'd be awful. They might even let us out."

"I hadn't thought of that. Goddamn, I'm cold."

"Maybe you should get inside that bag with Phil."

I jammed the new leg into the space. More rivets popped. The three of us got our hands inside and pulled the sheet metal away from the studs. Pink insulation filled the interior and I yanked long pieces of it free to get to the outside wall. When I had room, I kicked at the outside panel. It didn't budge. Coop got on his back and kicked with me. The exterior steel still didn't move.

"Let me try," Phil said.

Coop and I stood. Phil got down on his back and kicked with both feet. The wall seemed to move. He kicked again and the panel cracked open.

"Once more, Phil."

He kicked again and a corner of the steel separated away from the concrete floor.

"Can you squeeze through there?" Coop asked.

"Me?"

"You're the smallest one here," Phil said.

Seeing no one but the three of us and the frozen Gorilla, I got down on my back and said, "Okay, you two push on the panel and I'll slide out the bottom. Ready? Push."

Phil and Coop braced their feet against the steel. A gap opened wider and I stuck my head through, sideways, scraping my ear. I felt the sharp edge at my neck and said, "You'll have to push harder. My chest won't clear."

"It won't open any further," Coop said.

"It has to."

"This is as far as it'll go," Phil said.

"Okay, I'm coming back in." But I couldn't. My head wouldn't come in and my shoulders wouldn't go out. I was stuck. "Push harder!"

"We're pushing."

"Not hard enough."

"Goddamn, Harp, we're pushing as hard as we can."

"All right," I said, "I have an idea."

"Another one?"

"Yeah, take the Gorilla there and stick him under the gap like a wedge. He'll keep it from scrunching back on my neck."

"That's your idea?" Phil said. I could tell he didn't think it was a great plan and in that he had plenty of company.

"It's the best I got," I said.

Coop asked Phil if he could hold the steel and Phil said he thought so. I would have preferred a bit more confidence on his part, but I was in no position to quibble. Coop backed off and the steel edged into my neck.

Phil grunted, pushed with his feet, and the steel lifted again, slightly. When it did, Coop pushed the Gorilla next to me. The dead man's face was an unattractive shade of blue and close enough for me to feel the chill radiate off his skin. "You could have closed his eyes," I said. "He's looking right at me."

"It's probably rough on him, too," Coop said.

Slowly, they wedged the cold corpse into the space. Every time Phil pushed, the steel lifted and I got more wiggle room. Eventually, with pushing and wedging and me wriggling like a reptile, the space widened enough for me to slither out. I stood up in the dark, slipped off the padlock, and opened the door.

Coop and Phil spilled out, shivering. "Goddamn," Coop said, blowing on his hands, "I can't feel my feet."

"I don't think I'll ever be warm again," I said.

"Pussies," Phil said.

We looked down at the dead man's head and shoulders sticking out from under the bent sheet of stainless steel. I said, "I think they're going to know someone's been down here."

"You think?" Cooper stamped from the AKs to the freezer door and back again. "Like maybe the guy who locked us in?"

"We can't stay in the hotel," I said, the master of the obvious. "You guys get your shit. Phil, warn Ice about the ambush tomorrow. Coop, pack up my stuff. I'm just going to print out that guest list and I'll meet you at the car."

I locked all the doors and went back through the kitchen. I crossed the lobby, heading for the office, when I was stopped by the sound Smith once described as the barking dog of firearms. It was the unmistakable chunk of a round being chambered into a pump shotgun. My eyes, accustomed to the dark, could make out a big man sitting in the far corner. From deep in the shadows the man said, "It must be Christmas, monkey shit."

CHAPTER TWENTY-THREE

Meat locked me in one of the basement cages. Me, cans of tomato sauce, tins of olive oil, and a rat shared the space until sun brightened the narrow window above my head. I heard the sound of the Huey, a Vietnam-era warhorse as old as Smith's socks, and I stood on a crate of canned beans so I could see outside. The Huey set down on the helicopter pad behind the hotel and the team moved out to meet it.

They checked packs, radio batteries, rifles, and other gear before climbing on board. I tried to holler, but they couldn't hear me over the whap of the rotors. I didn't know if Phil had warned the men or not, or whether he and Coop had even escaped. All I could do was watch and hope that they knew about the danger and were ready. Iceman, Hog, Hamster, Dutch, and Thumper stepped into the helicopter door, one by one, and with a change in pitch, the Huey lifted slowly off the pad, turned, and flew off toward the east on a hot burst of aerodynamic voodoo.

Meat came down the stairs, followed by Kelly and another man, a Latino who made Meat look like an undernourished kid in a magazine ad.

Kelly looked at me through the cage wire, working his jaw. His forehead sported a bandage, which made me feel better. As if reading my mind, he said, "I don't like you, Harper."

"I can live with that, sir."

He smiled. "But not for long."

"What are you going to do with me?"

Kelly paced back and forth in front of my cage. "That is what we've been discussing, Harper. I want to give you to Meat. The boy needs a pet."

Meat lifted his lip and snarled at me through the wire.

"But the Colonel has other plans. You see, he promised to bring a piano player to a party."

"I play piano," I said, "or perhaps you didn't know."

Meat slammed the cage wire and said, "Shut up."

"That'll do, Meat." Kelly stopped and stared at me for a long time. "You've proven to be remarkably resilient, even ingenious, which makes me worry about letting you live any longer than it would take to frog-march you into the bush. But, for the time being, the Colonel is in command and he wants to show off his performing monkey. So I'm sending you to the party, along with Ricardo."

The big Latino smiled, revealing a set of gold teeth.

"He has orders to kill you, slowly if he can, quickly if he must, if you even look like you're about to escape."

"That hardly inspires a great performance, sir."

"It would be wise to play your best, Harper. Ricardo can be an awfully harsh critic."

Meat leaned in close. I could smell the onions on his breath and a splash of cologne. "And when you get home, monkey nuts, then you and I get to play some games I learned."

"He needs practice, don't you, Meat?"

"Yeah." Meat smiled. "The last piano player died way too quick."

(

CHAPTER TWENTY-FOUR

They stuffed me into a tux and pushed me on board a Bell 407, aqua blue with enough amenities to soothe a jet-lagged Saudi prince. The Colonel sat across from me and the family-fun-sized Ricardo sat beside me. When the chopper lifted off I said, "Ricardo, have you ever read *Heart of Darkness?*"

Ricardo stared at me.

"No, probably not."

Strapped into the executive seats, we flew north, following the Canal to the Atlantic Coast. In Panama, we had to fly north to get from the Pacific to the Atlantic. Why? Because the country is seriously twisted, that's why.

The plan was for me to work a small reception for a visiting general. Musicians call these gigs "casuals," which didn't cover the way I was feeling at all. I was to play some tasteful background while important people mingled on this, the last day of the old year. Ricardo would protect the crowd from unruly caterers, pianists, and other troublemakers. This would go on until seven when the VIPs would fly off to Panama City for dinner, gambling, and a New Year's Eve revolution. Not that I was invited. When the party was over, I was to fly back to the hotel where Meat was waiting to show me his mad skills with electricity.

Ricardo wore a rented tux, the jacket barely large enough to hide his MP-5 automatic rifle. I asked Kelly if I could have a pistol, too, and he declined. He said he didn't trust me with a firearm, and I didn't object. I didn't trust me with a firearm around Kelly, either. Accidents can happen.

As the Bell cruised over Gold Hill, where I had been with Kris only a day before, I asked the Colonel who the party was for.

"A General Guzmán, from Colombia."

I swallowed hard and my ears popped. "You mean Omar Guzmán?"

"Don't tell me you know him," the Colonel said.

"I met him in Washington." I tried to make the next question sound very casual, almost an afterthought. "Is his aide, Major Cruz, going to be there?"

"Probably so. Why?"

"No reason. Nice guy," I said. I didn't say that the Major wanted to kill me. Today, the Major would have to stand in line.

The helicopter flew low over the Canal and I watched the water flash by beneath us and I toyed with the notion of jumping out. It would be less painful than whatever Meat had in mind, I was sure. We passed over Gatun Dam, and the locks, and out into the harbor. Long breakwaters held back the turbulence of the Atlantic and kept the inside of the harbor as placid as a koi pond. The sun was bright and the temperature a comfortable seventy-eight degrees with a nice breeze blowing in off the water. Dozens of ships, large and small, private and commercial, waited their turn to traverse the Canal, and from all of the ships and boats at anchor, I picked out what had to be the General's yacht. It was black and gray with a helipad on the aft deck. The pilot received permission to land and set us down as gentle as an egg.

We were shown into the party area just off the aft deck. The room was large enough for a grand piano, but the General didn't wish to appear too ostentatious, so he'd settled for a baby grand, a white Yamaha, quite sufficient for an afternoon of diplomatic party chatter and alcohol consumption.

Ricardo checked out the yacht and the boats at anchor around us. I kept my head down, just another invisible servant. My sunglasses, worn to cover my black eyes, gave me a little cool anonymity.

As I warmed up with a simple one-four-five blues progression, a woman, willow thin and so beautiful she gave strong men whiplash, joined the party with apologies. She was stunning in a white blouse and green silk pants. I thought the emerald earrings and necklace were a bit much for an afternoon party, but Mariposa was never a slave to protocol. And when she turned and looked at me, I saw that Mariposa had changed her eye color to match the emeralds. Nice touch.

At first, she looked right through me. I was of no more importance than the cut flowers in the crystal vase. Then, as her eyes focused, her mouth formed an O and the blood drained from her cheeks. Quickly, she looked to see if her husband had seen what she'd seen.

The Major, in full-dress uniform, was schmoozing a Panamanian colonel, unaware that the uneviscerated piano player from Washington was a mere fifteen feet away, testing the ivories aboard the General's party barge.

Mariposa was giving me high-voltage eye beams. Whether she was saying she wanted to talk, or whether she wanted me to jump overboard, I couldn't tell. I opted for the former, and when Mariposa excused herself and went down the corridor, I gave her a few minutes and then I stood up. Ricardo placed a hand the size of a small pony on my chest.

"El baño," I said. "Servicios, sanitarios. Inodoro. Orinal," I said, grasping my privates.

Ricardo looked at me through narrowed eyes, deciding whether to let me pee or make me suffer. He nodded and jerked his head toward the corridor. As I was leaving he grabbed my shoulder, put two fingers to his eyes and then pointed at me. I got the message.

As I searched for the bathroom, Mariposa popped out of one of the cabins and pulled me inside.

"If the Major catches you here, he will kill you."

"I could slip into one of your dresses, but that's how I got into this trouble."

That earned me a smile. Whether it was because she thought it was funny or she remembered me in better times, I didn't know. I opted for the latter. "How have you been?"

"I've been so worried about you, John." She removed my sunglasses and her newly green eyes darkened. "John, what have they done to your face? You look terrible."

"I ran into something hard."

Mariposa placed her hand on my cheek and said, "You have no idea how awful my life has been since I saw you last."

Apparently, the discussion of my problems was over.

"But I have something for you." She searched through her Louis Vuitton bag and pulled out a CD. "I don't know exactly what this is, but I think it is important."

I took the CD and put it inside my jacket. "What's on it?"

"It's a list of men in Panama. They're in groups of four and there are addresses for each group. I have also added a list of Panamanian officers who have been calling the house recently. And lately, my husband has been referring to General Guzmán as 'el Presidente,' I don't know why. He says it and laughs, like it is this funny joke he and the General have. It is so obnoxious. Oh, and the Major hasn't heard from Renaldo Cardinale since he came to Panama."

"Is that the big guy with the broken nose?"

"Yes. He said it was a racquetball accident. Who plays racquetball on Christmas Eve?"

"I did that. I broke his nose."

"You? You play racquetball? I didn't know that, John."

"No, I mean I hit him."

"But why?"

"It was a literary disagreement."

She looked confused, and then didn't care. "This information I got for you, John, does it help?"

"Mariposa, my sneaky little butterfly, I could kiss you."

"After the Major is dead. Not before." She touched my lips with her fingertip and I knew that I'd never have enough money to be in Mariposa's league. The Major's health had nothing to do with her unwillingness to bed me.

"I have to get back."

"I must also. Since you left Washington he has watched me like a dog watches his supper dish. I can't even go to the bathroom without him knocking at the door every three minutes, asking if something is wrong. Be careful, John. I don't think my husband likes you as much as I do." She turned on the heel of her Manolos and slipped out the door.

A few minutes later I eased into the corridor, put on my sunglasses and hurried back to the piano.

Guests began to arrive by water taxi and private boat. Ricardo checked each guest's invitation, giving me a little room to breathe, and soon the Major was so busy moving about the crowd of important people that there was as much chance he would notice the piano player as he would the waiters who circulated around the deck with drinks and hors d'oeuvres.

Several couples danced on the aft deck, but most stood inside the salon and filled the yacht with Spanish and laughter. I let myself get lost in the music for a few moments. Thoughts of being fried by Meat or shot through the heart by the Major took a back seat to Ellington, Berlin, and Basie. I even played some Jobim and Gilberto just to watch the women's hips sway to the music and see the officers and moneymen of Panama's new revolution think about things other than military conquest and cash.

Mariposa was as cool as her emeralds and never once looked at me. She was surrounded by attentive men lighting her cigarettes, fetching her drinks, cooing what they hoped were amusing words, and I nearly pitied her husband, the fool with delusions of ever holding this woman for long. Soon, even her vows would mean nothing and she'd either leave him to his pistol and pajamas or give in and smother the Major in his sleep.

It was after six when the sun went down. Darkness spread quickly across the harbor, turning it from a drab slick of gray water into a garden of light, each ship doubled in reflection, and even the rusted freighters looked like fairy-tale barges, their rigging strung with white holiday lights. Colón gathered at the shore and even this city, with all of its criminals and desperate slums, looked like a place of infinite romantic possibilities. I wondered how far I could swim in my tux.

Ricardo nodded that I could quit playing. Under his watch I grabbed a bottle of water and took it to the bow of the yacht. Ricardo stood close by, in case I thought of jumping, which I did.

I felt a hand on my shoulder and then felt Mariposa's breath, perfumed by champagne, in my ear. "Come with me, John, hurry. There is something you must see."

I pointed at Ricardo and said, "I can't. He won't let me."

Mariposa said something in Spanish, too fast for me to translate, and Ricardo bowed and let Mariposa take me by the hand.

"What did you say to him?"

"I told him the General wanted to meet the piano player."

"And where are we going?"

"Below, John, there's something you have to see." She led me down the steps, through the main salon and into the master bedroom, the cabin farthest aft, a space larger than my Crystal City apartment and dominated by a gilded, king-sized bed with a leopard-print cover.

"Elvis lives," I said.

"Come in here," Mariposa said.

"Mariposa, if someone sees us—"

She pulled open a closet door and said, "Look in there."

I stepped into a walk-in loaded with more suits and uniforms than I could wear in a lifetime. "So what? So the General likes clothes."

"Here." Mariposa joined me in the closet and, in spite of everything, I caught an erotic charge. Apparently she did, too, because she said, "Put your mind someplace above your belt, John Harper, that is not why we're here. I want you to see this." She pushed back the suits to get some room, then the shoes, all lined up in their cedar shoe trees like stiff little soldiers on parade. Mariposa pointed to a hatch in the floor and said, "Open that, John."

I got on my hands and knees and pulled up the brass **D** ring. It was a maintenance hatch, used to access pipes and wiring that ran below the deck. I poked my head inside, not knowing what to expect—cocaine, weapons, cash—but what I did see made my scalp break into a sweat. As far as my hand could reach, fastened to the deck and stuffed up into the bulkhead, were brick-sized packets of plastic explosive. Red, white, and green wires connected detonators stuck into each brick.

I jerked my head back, letting the blood drain away. I looked again, making sure that my fatigue wasn't making me see things that weren't there. There they were, right where I'd seen them before.

I tried to find the main detonator but couldn't see that far under the deck. I had no idea if it was time-triggered or set off by hand. Neither option made me feel any better.

"How did you find this?"

Mariposa shrugged. "I get bored, and when I get bored, I get curious. What is it, John? Drugs? Why are those wires attached to drugs?"

I grabbed her by the hand and pulled her back into the bedroom. "We have to get off this boat."

"But I can't. The Major."

"Come on." We went back through the main salon, up onto the deck and down the main corridor to the stern, where the small boats and waiting water taxis bobbed on the chop. I told Mariposa, "You hail one of the water taxis, and get as far away from this yacht as possible."

"John, what was that? Why are you doing this?"

"It's explosives, Mari. There's no time to waste. We have to move."

She grabbed my sleeve. "Where are you going?"

"To find the captain. We need to evacuate the boat. You go, you get into one of those water taxis and get away as far and as fast as you can."

Mariposa gave me a quick kiss on the cheek, and a brief hug, her arms around my neck, and when we broke I saw that everyone on the aft deck was staring at us—Ricardo, couples by the rail, waiters, the crew, and, most significantly, the Major. The earth seemed to hold its breath and the only movement was the Major's hand as it went inside his jacket and withdrew a stainless-steel pistol.

"You! I should have known you would follow us here. And now you have the audacity to assault my wife and dishonor me in front of the General's guests."

"Major, this is not what it looks like."

Mariposa said, "We have to get off this boat."

The Major didn't hear either of us. The Major was deaf to everything but the roar of his wounded pride. "This will be the last time you bring a stain to my family name. Prepare yourself!"

He aimed the pistol, one-handed, and the bore seemed to swallow me up.

"Major," I said, as calmly as I could, "there is no time for this. The entire deck beneath us is packed with plastic explosives."

A murmur ran through the crowd.

"It could go off at any time," I said, keeping my voice steady, not wanting to cause a panic. I turned to the circle of party guests. "Please, I need all of you to abandon ship. I need you to do it now."

The guests began to back away.

"Stop!" the Major hollered. And, he being the man with the gun, the group stopped. All but one man. He kept moving. I was afraid to turn my head to see who it was.

"You stay where you are," the Major shouted.

Then I heard Phil say, his voice soothing, "Major, you have to put the gun away."

"I am going to kill him!"

"I don't have any problem with that, Major, but not here. Think of the General's guests. Think of the women."

The Major's pistol did not waver. "Mariposa," he said, "come to me."

Mariposa left me and went to stand beside her husband. She said many things to him, too low for me to hear, and in the surrounding silence it sounded as if she were reciting the rosary and each revealed mystery would bring us closer to Jesus.

"Now, sir," the Major said, "it is time for you to say your prayers."

Another man, a waiter, moved away from the bar where he'd been standing, his dark eyes glittering with purpose. When he reached the center of the deck he held high a blinking detonator, his thumb on the plunger. His hand shook.

Ricardo pulled the MP-5 out from under his jacket and began to circle the waiter.

The waiter pushed the detonator forward as if it were a religious icon, meant for holding back evil in all its forms, even large tuxedoed men with automatic weapons. Ricardo stopped moving.

Cooper stepped from the crowd, his hands up and open, showing the waiter that he had no weapon. The waiter turned to look at Cooper, then around at the rest of us, his eyes huge, and I knew he wasn't seeing anything beyond his own bright panic. Cooper took another step toward him and the waiter raised the detonator high over his head. "Stop," he said, and Coop stopped.

The Major didn't know what to do next, whether to shoot me, or bring his full attention to this waiter. Being a man of action, he decided to deal with the threat to his person before he dealt with the threat to his honor. "You, what do you think you are doing?" The Major pointed his pistol at the waiter. "I order you to put that down."

Ricardo raised his rifle and the click as he removed the safety could be heard across the bay.

The waiter looked very scared now. His underarms were soaked with sweat and his hair was plastered to his forehead. His eyes darted from the Major to Cooper. Coop was moving slowly toward the waiter, his voice soft with calming words I couldn't hear.

I felt Phil at my side. He said, "This doesn't look good, Harp."

"Where did you two come from?"

"I'll tell you later."

"You think there'll be a later?"

"Are you ready?"

"Ready? Ready for what?"

Cooper moved closer to the waiter, his hand out. He was a few feet from the boy. The Major continued to aim his pistol, but the muzzle was shaking. Ricardo stepped closer, tightening the circle.

"We're going over the side," Phil said. And then he tossed me, one-handed, over the rail. I was airborne, and then plunged into darkness. Behind me, the world shook and the concussion ripped through the water like a liquid hammer.

CHAPTER TWENTY-FIVE

I was underwater and didn't know which way was up. I thought I was going the right way, the only way, until I saw bubbles drift past me and I turned and saw the light. The surface glowed with fire.

I turned around and kicked up and into air that was brighter than daylight. Gasoline burned in pools on the surface. Smoking parts of the General's yacht, and bloody pieces of the General's guests, bobbed all around me.

I heard shouts above the fire's blistering howl. I added my own voice to the chaos, calling for Phil, and Cooper, and Mariposa. I swam to each rounded back and turned each one over, searching for a friend, searching for a partner, searching for life in a stranger's eyes.

I found Mariposa. Her right arm had been torn away, and the back of her head was stripped to the bone, blackened by the blast. I knew it was Mariposa by her wedding ring and her eyes, once again brown, the green contacts gone along with the spark.

I found the Major next. He looked surprised, but other than that, I couldn't see any wounds or burns. I pressed my palm to his chest to check for a heartbeat and in horror I watched my hand sink up to the wrist. Blood blossomed across his shirtfront.

"Harp?"

I heard his voice before I saw him. "Here!" I looked among the shapes for a hand, a face, a movement.

"Harp?"

I swam in a circle, searching among the flames and debris for the voice. I saw him, twenty yards away, and swam toward him, dodging bodies, burning oil, and wood. I heard more shouts now, shouts of rescuers, and in the distance, sirens and the whoop of an alarm.

When I reached him he was floating on his back, his face barely above the surface. "Phil? Are you hurt?" I held him up. He was breathing. His eyes were open, but he wasn't looking at anything. "Where are you hurt?"

Phil's lips moved and I put my ear close to his mouth. He said, "Cooper?"

"I can't find him."

"Find him," Phil said.

"I've got to get you to shore," I said.

"Find him!"

I looked up at what was left of the General's yacht. The aft deck was gone; the rear half of the yacht's superstructure, including the wheelhouse, had been ripped away. The foredeck was littered with the dead, and stunned, wounded people pulling themselves along on bloodied hands, wandering blindly, or lying still, calling for help. The water near the bow was full of survivors who had been blown free. Those lucky few were treading water around the floating dead.

"He was too close, Phil. There's no way. He was too close."

Phil floated, my hand under his back, holding him up. He was silent for so long I thought I'd lost him, then he said, "Get me the fuck out of here."

I grabbed his collar and swam for land, which was the breakwater, a thin spit of concrete and rocks stretched hundreds of yards into the harbor. Searchlights from rescue ships swept the oily water, picking up sadness all around.

I pulled Phil onto the sand and let him lie quiet for a long time. Phil said, "I think I'm okay now." He tried to sit up, but couldn't. "Or maybe not," he said. "I think maybe it's my ribs."

"You stay here. I'll go get help."

"No, you'll have to carry me out."

"If your ribs are broken, you could puncture a lung." I shook my head. "No, Phil, I'm going for help."

He gripped my shirt and said, "I want them to think we're dead. If you leave me here and they find me, how long do you think I'll last?"

"Okay, okay." I helped Phil to his feet. He draped his arm over my shoulder and we began the slow, painful trip inland.

The breakwater is not an easy place to walk, even when healthy. It's barely twenty feet wide and constructed of concrete blocks as big as summerhouses, tossed like dice along the gravel. To get back to land we had to climb up and around these blocks, planting each foot carefully. If Phil fell off, I wasn't sure I'd be able to get him back up by myself.

The gravel bed was littered with broken bottles, condoms, and crack vials. "A great place to get high," Phil said. "Remind me to come out here on my day off."

I helped him up the slope of one block and at the top I looked to see how far we had yet to go. It looked like we were walking to the far end of the earth.

Thirty minutes later we were making our way past concrete gun emplacements, abandoned about the time Americans discovered Diz and Bird and bop, a better time for everyone, even musicians. "Where are we?"

"It's France Field," Phil said. "No one's used it since World War Two."

"The last good time America ever had."

"You're a funny guy, Harp. If I laugh any harder, I think it'll kill me."

There was a group of teenagers, all standing, watching the fire in the harbor. When they saw us staggering toward them, wet and bleeding, they parted to let us pass.

"¿Quién tiene un automóvil?" I said.

"Christ, Harper, are you speaking Spanish?"

"Trying," I said.

One boy came forward and took Phil's other side. "Venga," he said, and helped Phil into the back of a Chevy Vega.

"Gracias."

The boy spoke to me, rapidly, and I told him, "Despacio, despacio, por favor."

Phil croaked from the shadows of the Vega. "He's saying he'll take us to the hospital."

"No, no," I said, and gave him an address. The boy hesitated until Phil pulled a roll of wet bills out of his pocket. The boy nodded and got behind the wheel.

Miss Turando helped Phil remove his shirt. He grunted and, for Phil, that meant he was in serious pain.

She listened to Phil's lungs, her fingers gently probing his ribs. Removing the stethoscope, she said, "There's no pneumothorax, which is good. That means the lungs haven't been punctured. I can't be sure without an X ray, of course, but I believe three ribs have been fractured."

"So, you tape them up and he'll be good to go?"

Miss Turando smiled and said, "He's good to go now. We found that a rib belt only inhibited breathing and encouraged pneumonia. Now we advise the patient to breathe deeply and stay as active as possible, given the pain. I believe your friend will pull through just fine."

"Phil, how you doing?"

"I am *so* fine," he said.

"I've given him some Percocet."

We put Phil in Miss Turando's Mercedes and headed back toward La Boca.

"I can't thank you enough for everything you've done," I said.

Miss Turando kept her attention on the road. "I have many visitors, Mr. Harper, and one of them is a Colombian. He's a very superstitious man who tells me things he shouldn't."

Miss Turando looked at me and I saw sorrow in her eyes. "You need to know something, Mr. Harper. When you were here before?"

"With Marilyn."

"Yes. She paid me to tell you to leave the country. She tried to save your life. I know you think otherwise, but she is trying to help you. She cares for you, I know."

Miss Turando dropped us off a mile from the hotel gate. Before she drove away she said, "You'll do the right thing, Mr. Harper."

"How will I know what that is?"

"You'll know," she said.

I thanked her again. When she was gone, Phil, still flying on Percocet, said, "If you hadn't been in a such a hurry, I mighta got some of that. You know what they say about nurses."

"Yeah," I said, "they marry doctors."

Phil was hanging on to me, looking up into the dark trees, and said, "What are we doing here? I thought you had the names of the cells."

I patted the CD in my pocket, the CD Mariposa had given me, and said, "I want the list of the money men, too, and anything that'll help us convince the authorities we're not hallucinating. There's also the name of a goat fucker."

"A goat fucker?"

"That's just what the Colonel called him. He's a partner in all this, and if we don't find out who he is, he'll slip away and neither one of us will be safe, I know that."

"Okay, Harp, from here on in, you're driving. I'm just along for the ride."

I helped Phil through the jungle and around the hotel by way of the firing range. The going was slow and there were several places where Phil stumbled and fell and I had to lift him up.

At the edge of the treeline I stopped to let Phil rest. Not a single light burned in the hotel and it looked as inviting as a prison in the pale light of the quarter moon. We crossed the range, crept through the garden and up into the lobby. I saw the glow of a computer screen in the office. Sitting in front of the screen was Eubanks, his headphones playing loud music, the heavy bass buzzing around the quiet office. I touched his shoulder but Eubanks, the little clerk, wouldn't be hearing any music other than the celestial choir. Eubanks was dead. I felt for a pulse in his neck, and he was warm to the touch. That meant it hadn't been long since someone, obviously not a music lover, had come up behind him and put a .22 bullet just behind his right ear.

I opened Kelly's office and found it empty. Phil went through his desk as I printed out the list of the operation's financial backers. Phil found nothing more interesting than Field Manual 5–13, the army's catalog of homemade booby traps, fun for the whole family. That caused us to search everything with a lot more care.

The Colonel's office was dark, and the door was ajar. Phil pushed it open and I jumped, the shock and surprise so intense I tasted the electrical juice along my jaw. There, sitting at his desk, was the Colonel. He looked sadly surprised that his long career had ended this way. He, too, sported a new .22-caliber hole, this one right in the middle of his forehead.

"They're taking everyone out, down to the last man," Phil said.

Phil needed help up the stairs. He took one at a time, just as he had the night I'd met him.

As we made the slow climb I asked him how he and Coop had found me on the yacht.

"The party was no secret. We bribed the caterer to get me on the staff and Coop found an invitation in a guy's pocket."

"Was the guy alive?"

"Sleeping," Phil said. "So, what do we do now?"

"Get all this to my boss. We need somebody who swings a bigger hammer in this fight."

"What about Kris?"

"Kris is gone, Phil. Kelly put her on a plane for the States this morning. He told me I was a corrupting influence."

"Well, the old man's right about some things," Phil said, and tried to laugh but each jerk of his diaphragm shoved a hot blade of fire between his ribs.

In the dim light I could see his face was wet and I was surprised. He played such a tough guy, I assumed he was immune to physical pain, and way beyond tears. "Are you okay, Phil? You want to sit a while?"

"No," he said, and wiped his cheeks with the back of his fist. "I was just thinking about Coop."

"I know," I said. "What's that you always tell me? It don't mean shit?"

"Yeah, well, this time it does, Harp."

"All we can do is make the fuckers pay," I said.

"Then let's see what Kelly has hidden away in his apartment," Phil said.

"I was thinking the same thing."

At Kelly's door Phil said, "Work your magic, Monkeyman."

"I can't. I lost my picks in the harbor."

"Then we'll have to use my method. Go get a tire iron."

I ran down the steps, eased through the shadows past Eubanks again, and retrieved the tire iron from the parking lot. Back on the second floor, I did as Phil told me.

"Now, stick it here, and separate the door from the frame."

The gap between the door and the frame widened as I leveraged the tire iron. The wood began to crumble and snap.

"A little more," Phil said.

I pushed harder and looked in the space, trying to see how far I had to go for the bolt to clear. I stopped when I saw that there was no bolt. I pulled out the tire iron.

"Why'd you quit?"

I turned the knob and the door swung open. "It wasn't locked."

"Oh."

The living room was dark except for the moonlight through the windows. Again, I was struck by the impersonality of the place. Aside from a book here and the occasional picture, the room could have belonged to anyone or no one.

"You know where the files are?"

"No. But Kris said he had a study and I've been all through this place except there, beyond the kitchen."

We went from the living room and kitchen to a hallway that led to a small office. A desk and filing cabinet had been pushed against the far wall, under the window with a view of the beach. Phil flicked his Zippo and looked at the desk in the firelight. "It's got a lock," he whispered. "We'll have to break it."

"Check first," I said. Phil tugged on the top drawer and it slid open.

"A smart man learns from his mistakes, Phil."

"Fuck you. Here hold this." Phil handed the lighter to me. The two of us hunched over the open drawer. Phil ran his thumb across the tabs of the manila files and said, "Looks like nothing but tax shit and insurance and stuff."

That's when the overhead came on, catching us like deer in the headlights.

"Okay, get up nice and slow." Meat was standing in the doorway aiming that scattergun at us. At me. "Just keep your hands where I can see them." Meat gave us a lot of room. He respected Phil, even wounded, and kept out of his reach. "I saw you fuckers sneaking around the parking lot," he said.

"So, you're the one who killed Eubanks?"

"What? Who killed Eubanks?"

"And the Colonel."

Meat gaped like a landed fish, trying to suck in the reality of the new world. Yes, he was big and stupid and not capable of doing much more than watching the front gate, but he was still a soldier to his bones and the death of a comrade was hard news. And just as I began to feel sympathy for him, Meat reverted to his old, annoying ways.

"Hey," he said, "I bet you killed them."

I shook my head and sighed. "Meat, don't do this."

He raised his shotgun and aimed at my face. "I want you two to lie down, your hands behind your head, while I figure this out." I knew better than to question his ability, or his willingness to kill. I dropped to my knees.

"You, too." He turned the gun on Phil.

Phil grimaced and said, "I'd like to, Meat, I would, but I busted up a few ribs tonight. I can hardly hold my pecker, man. There's no way I can get on the floor."

"Do it!" Meat stepped forward.

"Okay, but don't stick that goddamn thing up my nose." Phil held on to the edge of the desk and lowered himself to his knees.

Meat was breathing so quickly I was afraid he'd hyperventilate and fall on me.

"I got you fuckers so good," he said. "We'll just wait here for Mr. Kelly. He'll know what to do." A thought, you could see it rise up in his face like a gas bubble, popped into Meat's head. "Hey. Where's your friend? Where's Cooper?"

"He's dead," I said, and my throat ached just saying the words.

"Why should I believe you?" Meat hollered, "Cooper! Come out or I'm going to waste your friend."

"He's not here, Meat. He's dead."

Another light came into Meat's eye, this one a light of suspicion, edged with fear. "He's behind me, isn't he?"

I sighed. Stupidity this intense is a thing of wonder, no less amazing than the density of a star. "Meat, there's no one behind you."

He smiled, satisfied that no one could fool him, and said, "It's like the movies. If you said there was somebody behind me, then there wouldn't be, but you said there wasn't, so there is."

"Is what?" Phil said. "I'm starting to get a headache."

"Someone behind me, right?"

"Well, there wasn't before," I said, "but now there is."

"I told you!" Meat wanted to look. He did. His eyes darted back and forth but he was too afraid to turn his head and see. Like so many scared men without imagination, he settled for bravado. He licked his lips, gave a little dry laugh, and said, "If you're back there, Cooper, you might as well shoot me."

The laughter stuck in his throat when he felt the jab in his lower back. He held the shotgun by the stock and raised his hands. "Shit!" He sounded like he'd fumbled a short pass.

Phil took the shotgun and made Meat sit on the floor.

"Thank you, Kris," I said. "But why aren't you on that plane?"

Kris twirled the plant mister on her finger and squirted a cool splotch of water over my heart. "I didn't think Ingrid Bergman should have left Bogart, either, John."

"Who the fuck's John?" Meat said. "And who's Ingrid Bergman?"

Phil advised Meat to shut up and asked Kris to find some duct tape. She did, and soon Meat was trussed to the rolling desk chair, his mouth gagged behind a strip of silver tape.

Kris had her hands on my face, gently soothing the bruises, now an attractive yellow and blue. "What happened?"

"We were on a boat. Someone blew it up."

"How did you get away?"

"Phil and I were blown off the boat."

"We jumped," Phil said, "before the bomb went off."

I told Kris about the waiter with the detonator and the explosives packed under the deck.

"But how did you know when to jump?"

That was something I'd wondered, too. "Yeah, Phil, how did we know when to jump?"

"The waiter closed his eyes. I watched him close his eyes and I knew."

"You remember Cooper, the tall guy?"

"He looked like the president of his fraternity?"

"That's him. He was a friend, and he's dead. And downstairs,

Eubanks and the Colonel are dead, too, murdered by people working for your father."

Kris remained rock steady and her eyes never left mine. "You're sure?"

"I'm sure."

Kris sat on the floor, her legs crossed, the plant sprayer still in her hand. "Why do you think my father's involved?"

"There's a lot of evidence. I'm sorry."

Kris blinked several times, quickly, and she was no longer looking at me, but at whatever was running through her head. She nodded, having come to some private conclusion, and said, "Okay, what happens now?"

"We were looking for any files he might have. Specifically about his partners in this operation, and what might be planned for tonight." I looked at my watch. It was nearly nine o'clock. "If something's planned for midnight, we've only got three hours to stop it."

"Did you check his desk?"

"There's nothing there," I said.

"Right. Okay. Then they're probably in his safe. Under here." She pulled back the rug and removed a square section of the hardwood floor. Below the floor was a green safe with a combination lock.

"I can't open that," I said.

"I can." Kris got on her knees and elbows and twirled the dial, jerked the handle, and pulled the door open. "There you go." She sat back.

As Phil reached in I stopped him and said, "Kris, honey, we may find things about your father you don't want to know."

Kris stared at me as if I were a good but very slow pooch. "There's not much about my father that I don't know, and what I don't know won't surprise me."

"Okay." I let Phil's arm go and, with a grunt of pain, he pulled out an accordion file. Inside were manila folders. He opened one.

"Here's a guy, Cuban CIA. Name's Romero, but goes by the name of Morton. There's everything on this guy—schools, friends, countries he's worked in, everything. But no good picture. Just one with his face hidden behind a camera, the spy snapping the spy."

"Maybe he's the goat fucker," I said. When Kris gave me a look that suggested I'd lost my mind, I explained the Colonel's conversation.

"So you've been bugging the offices."

"I have. It's my job. It's why I'm here."

"I knew you weren't just a piano player," Kris said. "A spy, I've been fucking a spy."

Meat mumbled something behind his gag that sounded like "I knew it."

We sat around the open safe and read quickly through files, all of us adding pieces to the puzzle until a picture emerged. I found the file on the officer who'd been killed the day of the ambush by the river. His name was Ruiz and he was a member of a Colombian paramilitary group.

I sat back on my haunches. "But why kill so many people?"

Kris looked up from one of her father's ledgers. "Will money do?"

"How much money?"

"A lot," she said. "I can't be sure, but I think these numbers are bank accounts, and next to them are amounts." She looked at the two columns of numbers and said, "We're talking more than two hundred million dollars."

"How do you know they're bank accounts?"

Kris laughed. "International finance was just one of my majors. It looks like the only one that's practical. Who knew?"

Meat's eyes were wide open. He was sweating, even in the air-conditioning. "Meat? You know something about this?" I tore the duct tape from his mouth, and after he'd stopped gasping from having his lips waxed, he told me to go fuck myself.

Phil said, "Oh, Meat, don't be like this. You know you want to tell us."

Meat had more suggestions for Phil.

Phil sighed and said, "If it wasn't for these ribs here, Meat, I'd work you over with my fists."

Some of the tension went out of Meat's body.

"So, I guess I'll have to use electricity." Phil pulled a radio off the desk and jerked the power cord from the back, leaving two exposed wires plugged into the wall socket. Phil poured the water from

Kris's plant mister into Meat's lap and Meat blurted, "Okay, I'll tell you what I know, but it's not much."

"I'm not surprised," Kris said, taking the words right out of my mouth.

"The money was to pay for this, all of this—our salaries, the guns, the hotel, all of it was paid for with money from the Colombians."

"That's a lot of money to run a hotel, even one training body-guards."

"Some of it went to bribe officers in the Panamanian army and some government officials," Meat said. He'd lightened up on the attitude and was almost pleading for us to believe him. "I don't know anything else. That's just what Helizondo told me."

Phil held the two exposed wires close to Meat's glistening eye-ball. "Do all the men working here know this?"

Meat rolled his head as far from the wires as possible. "No, just me and a couple other guys."

"Who?"

"Me, that guy Ruiz, Helizondo, Zorro, and another guy, before your time."

"Winstead?"

"Yeah, he was the other guy. He was killed."

"What about the team? Did you know they weren't supposed to come back from Darien?"

Meat couldn't have been more shocked if Phil had hit him with the high voltage. "No, I didn't know."

"Phil warned them about an ambush, but think of that, Meat, out of all those men, do you think Kelly means to keep you, and only you, alive?"

Meat blinked for the first time since Phil had poured water in his lap.

"Kelly and the Colombians are reducing their exposure and that means eliminating everyone, even the Colonel. He's dead, right now, sitting in his office downstairs, a twenty-two-caliber hole right in the middle of his forehead."

After rolling this around, Meat said, "I hadn't thought of it like that." Meat's eyes snapped back to the frayed wires in Phil's hand.

Phil said, "The first time I zapped you I'd blow the lights, and

I'm afraid of the dark." He jerked the cord from the wall and said, "But I could still cut your ears off."

Kris removed another section of files. "This one's got pictures of Panamanian bankers, Guardia officers, government officials. Hell, even a U.S. diplomat. Most of them with their pants down."

"It happens to the best of us," I said.

"I'm taking these for Choppo," Phil said. "I owe him."

I pulled out half a dozen manila files and opened the first one. "Here's the bartender at the Silver Key." Phil opened another. "Here's that old guy who runs the hot-sheet hotel. Must be part of Kelly's local network." Kris opened a third. "John, maybe you'll want to see this."

She handed me the file. The mug shot didn't capture Marilyn's high cheekbones and beautiful, dark eyes because you couldn't see her eyes. They had both been battered closed and her bottom lip was swollen to twice its size.

Her real name was Rosa Sanchez. She was from El Chorillo, the slum neighborhood burned to its foundations in 1989 by Operation Just Cause. Marilyn's parents were collateral damage, caught in the crossfire, just as she'd said.

Kris, Marilyn, and me. This was a war fought by orphans.

Marilyn, or Rosa, was paid one thousand dollars a month, a fortune to a Panamanian girl. From the accounting, this was just a retainer. She got more when she delivered information. There were many entries, all marked with names and sexual activities. The especially deviant had their own cross-referenced file with places and dates written in Kelly's hand.

Of all the entries in Marilyn's list, the only names I recognized were Winstead's and my own.

Phil handed me a report that detailed every moment I was with Marilyn. Where we had gone, who we had seen, what we had talked about. In the second entry, Kelly had written: "Contact not as easily manipulated through sex as previously suggested. Looks to be turning this operative and may require her elimination along with his.

"She warned me," I said.

"Hey, recognize this guy?" Phil held out another photo. It was my high school graduation picture. "He's got quite a file on you, Harper. Traffic tickets, high school records, and an interview with the owner of a radio station who says here that you're, quote, 'a liberal nigger-lover who doesn't deserve to wear a uniform.'"

"I hope her dogs are dead."

Phil handed me another photo. It was the man who had climbed into the back of Ren's car, several minutes before the Chevy had poured black smoke into the clear blue Panamanian sky.

"Looks like they paid him two thousand dollars to kill you and Ren. But the guy died in a bus accident outside of Colón."

"I've seen enough," I said, putting the file back into the folder.

"Looky-looky," said Phil, reaching into the safe and pulling up a gray metal strongbox. "It's locked."

"Did you check?"

"Yes, I checked."

"You got a bobby pin, Kris?"

She ran off and I hollered after her to bring two. When she returned I took one pin and bent it into a tiny L. As a torque wrench, it wouldn't open anything much more sophisticated than a girl's diary, but it was enough for this. I straightened another bobby pin and went to work. Kris whispered, "I guess it's a waste of time locking my bedroom door, huh, Monkeyboy?"

The box popped open. "Whoa, Phil, look at this." Inside were bundles of brand-new cash, held together with plain paper bands. "They're euros, denominations of five hundred, the new choice of smugglers everywhere. They're not very liquid, but they take up less space than American hundred-dollar bills." I counted the stacks. "My God, there's five million in here."

But Phil wasn't looking, he had both arms inside the safe, pulling at something. "I can't get this," he said, and grunted with effort. "My fingers are too fat. You try."

I stretched out on my stomach and put both hands inside the safe. My fingers ran along the edge and I felt it move. "It's a false bottom," I said.

"He's the smart one," Phil said.

I worked my fingertips into the space, got a thin hold, and tugged. The floor came up. I hauled a green duffel bag onto the floor. Its lock was even less of a challenge than the cash box, a sign that Kelly never expected anyone to get this far. When I opened the duffel, stacks of cash spilled out, and Phil whispered, "Holy sweet Mother of God."

These were more bundles of euros, and from the weight of the bag I estimated an easy four million. I said, "I think I'm about to wet myself."

CHAPTER TWENTY-SIX

Phil was taking the money. I knew that. And even though Kris was the only one entitled to it, she shook her head and said, "I don't want it. I just want to get out of here."

"Phil, can you drive?"

He said he could. "Good, I want you to take these files—"

"And the money."

"and the money, to Choppo's. Lauren will get this stuff into the right hands."

"What are you going to do?"

"I have to take care of some business," I said, and walked around behind Meat's chair.

Meat looked as if he were tied to a quickly sinking ship. "Please don't leave me with him."

"Kris, why don't you help Phil with this stuff?"

She hesitated, but only for a moment, and then she helped Phil carry the files and the duffel down to the Colonel's car. When we were alone, I said to Meat, "Was there someone here recently, someone who would have killed Eubanks and the Colonel?"

"Are you going to let me go?"

"If you tell me what you know."

Meat's eyes rolled around in their sockets. "Okay. It was Helizondo. He was the only one here. It had to be him."

"Where did he go?"

Meat hesitated and a ripple of panic shimmered across my skin. "Marilyn," he said. "He went to kill Marilyn."

Helizondo. The man who'd hit me at the range.

I opened the desk drawer and took out Kelly's GI .45. Meat watched as I ejected the magazine, checked to see that it was loaded, slid it back into the pistol's grip, racked the slide, and aimed the big pistol at Meat's head.

"Where did they go? If you know, now's the time to tell me."

Meat was too afraid to speak.

"You tell me and I'll cut you loose."

Kris appeared in the doorway. "Phil's on his way. He's in pretty bad shape, John."

"You should have gone with him."

Kris shook her head. "Oh, no. I'm with you to the end, John Harper."

I knew better than to argue with her.

"So, where are we going?"

"Meat was just about to tell me. Where did Helizondo go, Meat?"

"To the Pinga. That's where he takes them."

"Takes who?"

"Whoever he's supposed to kill."

"Where is this place?"

"I know it," Kris said. "The real name's La Piña, pineapple, but when the GIs were here they called it 'La Pinga' and the name stuck."

"Ah, imperialist wit," I said.

"All men are just pingas with ears, John, you should know that."

"We can argue about that later. Right now, what do you think we should do with Meat?"

Kris shrugged. "Shoot him."

Meat nearly brought the chair off the floor. "You said you'd let me go."

"Yeah, I did." I taped his mouth shut, and while Kris was getting the car, I rolled Meat down the steps, through the kitchen, and into the basement.

"I have just the place for you, Meat. With any luck, someone will find you before you freeze." I rolled him next to the Major's dead Gorilla and closed the door.

As we were driving through the gate, Kris said, "I would have shot him."

"I know. And I might have let you."

We drove into town, across the bridge that had sent Ren and Zorro airborne on that evening a long time ago. We crossed the larger bridge, the bridge where students died in protest over its name and its flag. We drove into the slum where so many Panamanians, both soldier and civilian, were killed when the first President Bush had waded through the place like an angry giant, kicking over homes, scattering families, looking for the dictator Noriega.

Kris pulled up to the Silver Key. I jumped out. "Wait here."

"Don't be long," she said, already attracting looks from men hanging around the bar. "I'm not sure I like the attention."

I sprinted down the block toward La Piña hotel, a place prostitutes took their twenty-minute johns. I slammed through the narrow double doors and bounded up the steps, three at a time.

There was a small counter at the top of the stairs. Behind the counter was an old man with gray hair and skin the color of roasted coffee. I thought he had fallen asleep watching a TV evangelist on a tiny black-and-white portable. Then I saw the line of blood running from behind his ear, down into the collar of his shirt. The big-haired preacher promised eternal life in heaven in return for a little cash on earth. I hoped the old man had paid up.

I ran down the narrow hallway, kicking in doors. The rooms were so small that I didn't see how a guy could get wood without opening a window. Most rooms were empty. In those that weren't, I probably saved a few guys from the clap. In Panama's sex trade, you couldn't sink much lower than La Pinga.

I kicked open another door and saw Marilyn, naked, stretched out on the bed, her hands and feet tied to the bed frame. She had a gag in her mouth and tears in her eyes. I cleared the place in a nanosecond with the big pistol, the room so small I could almost touch all four walls from the doorway. In my hurry, what I didn't check was the room across the hall. When I bent to remove Marilyn's gag, lights went on inside my skull and I fell into the narrow space between the bed and the wall. The pain that shot up my spine soon settled into a hollow behind my right eye. The pain would stay there for a long time, reminding me not to be stupid.

Santiago, the man I had fished from the river, stood over me, showed me his teeth and a long, sharp filet knife. He bent so close I could smell the rum on his breath. "I'm going to gut the puta. You can watch."

I tried standing but he kicked me with the heel of his boot. It felt like he'd shoved that knife into my lung. I fell back again and gasped for breath and each breath hurt like fire.

Santiago looked over Marilyn, head to toe, and smiled. "No. I'll fuck her first, then I'll kill her. Then I'll kill you. It will be like a party, eh?"

He opened his pants and pushed them to his knees. He started for Marilyn, who squealed against the gag. He cut the ropes holding her ankles and climbed awkwardly between her legs, forcing her knees apart. I tried to rise again and he casually swung his arm, hitting me with the butt of his knife.

"And stay there, gringo, until I am finished. Then maybe I fuck you, too. Okay?" He smiled, I saw a gold tooth, and then I watched his eyes roll back into his head. He fell across me, and when I got out from under, I saw Kris, holding a blackjack in her hand.

"A gift from Daddy," she said. "The only thing he ever gave me without strings attached."

"Wow, I haven't seen one of those since Madagascar," I said, taking the blackjack and feeling the heft of the spring-loaded sap.

"What were you doing in Madagascar?"

"Saving lemurs," I said.

Kris cut Marilyn loose with Santiago's filet knife and then reached down and pulled a silenced .22 from Santiago's belt.

"Are you going to shoot him?"

"No," she said. She ejected the magazine and said, "But only because I can't. No bullets."

I wrapped Marilyn in one of the bedsheets and helped her to her feet. She was weeping, her head against my chest. "He kept saying you were dead!" she said.

"It's okay, Marilyn. You're okay."

"I tried to warn you. I paid Miss Turando to tell you to go home."

"I know. It's okay."

Halfway down the hall we heard men pounding up the stairs in front of us.

I pushed Marilyn and Kris into one of the hot-sheet rooms and ducked into another one across the hall. I'm slow, but I can learn.

The men ran past us. I had seen both men before. The first was Helizondo, the humiliated officer from Hog's weapons class and the man who had murdered Eubanks and the Colonel. The second man had been at the warehouse where Ren had gone on his one final errand.

I stepped into the hallway and caught the second man with the blackjack. I didn't hit him hard, but the lead weight, propelled by the steel spring inside the leather, caught him above the ear. The hotel echoed with the soft *whunk,* like smacking a cantaloupe, and Helizondo stopped, frozen by the sound. I let him turn slowly around until he could see the .45 aimed at his heart.

"Hi, Helizondo," I said.

He smiled. "I'm so happy to see you, Harper. So happy that Santiago left you for me."

"Who writes your stuff? Is there some kind of school for bad-guy trash talk?"

"I am not afraid of you."

"No, I suppose not."

He laughed. "They told me you were no killer."

"They were wrong."

"They told me you don't even like guns."

"Well, they were right about that," I said.

"And you aren't a real soldier, not a warrior. You are a boy. You are a soft American boy who watches too much television and drinks too much Pepsi." As he talked his right hand moved slowly toward his belt.

"Don't do that, Helizondo."

He was still smiling. "They call you 'Monkeyman.' The name of a cartoon." His hand was still moving.

"I will shoot you, Helizondo."

"You rely on other people to do your work, *queco,* you rely on women because you are too much of a coward to fight your own fights."

His smile never flickered, I'll give him that. When he brought that .22 up, that little puckered bore like the dead eye of a snake coming up to look at me, and the .45 rocked in my fist, knocking him down, he never once stopped smiling. Not once. Even when the afterlife was creeping up on him in that dark hallway, he smiled into the abyss. He must have known something I didn't.

I stared down at this man and felt a rancid stew of gut-deep shame, nausea, and primal triumph wash through me. I had survived this day and this man, this mother's son, his heart ripped open by my hand, had not. It was I who was standing in that hallway, and not he. Helizondo had been wrong about so much, but fatally wrong about what it means to take a life. Killing has nothing to do with courage and nothing to do with cowardice. It's always about choice. Today, Helizondo had chosen to die.

Kris put her hand on my shoulder and said, "Come on, John, I hear sirens."

"I've been hearing sirens all day. I'm getting used to them."

Kris and I helped Marilyn to the car and put her into the back seat. The sidewalks were filling up with people eager to get drunk and dance in the New Year. Men, alone and in groups of three and four, already in a staggering state of inebriation, called to any woman on the street with suggestions as to how they could make their night, if not their lives, a little better. Kris got behind the wheel and I asked her if she knew how to get to the Chinaman's Drugstore and she looked at me as if I'd lost my mind.

"You want to go there, after dark on New Year's Eve?"

"Yes." I looked into the street and saw a black Lexus with two men in the front seat a block away. "I think someone's following us."

"Not for long," Kris said, and hit the gas. The car shuddered, shook loose from its lethargy like an old dog, and barreled through the crowds.

The Lexus pulled from the curb, hampered by the pedestrians.

Kris turned right, then up a one-way alley the wrong way. At the end of the alley she went left, down a broad boulevard for two blocks, ducked between an apartment building and a dry cleaner, wedged herself in between two rumbling chiva buses, and cut off a taxi driver who blew his mariachi horn and flashed us the universal finger.

"He's still behind us," Kris said.

She wheeled around a nightclub and into the parking lot of the Panama Hilton, nearly plowing into a tourist bus full of casino-crawlers bent on losing a wad of cash before midnight.

We flew out the far end of the lot, through a section of expensive high-rise apartments, past a government plaza, onto the Avenue of the Martyrs, and then back into the narrow streets of El Chorillo, ignoring stop signs and threading the car between lanes of traffic. I don't think I took more than two breaths the whole trip. By the time we pulled up in front of the open-air wine shop, my fingers were stiff from gripping the dashboard.

"Okay, I want you to go to our bar, the one with the fresh-squeezed-orange-juice screwdrivers. Phil and I will meet you there."

Marilyn leaned forward and touched my hair. "John Harper, I will always be grateful for what you did today."

I looked at Marilyn, the sheet wrapped around her, and I saw Rosa Sanchez, caught up in swift political currents. Marilyn and her country had both been steamrollered by ambitious history.

I, on the other hand, had been given a choice. I could have stayed home, played the VFW dances and the Holiday Inn, married Becky Ferguson, and had a son who would disappoint me as much as I'd disappointed my father. But I had said yes, and I had come to Panama. The only thing Rosa Sanchez had chosen was her name.

Kris looked at me closely for the first time. "John, you're bleeding."

I put my hand to my thigh. "I let the bastard shoot me," I said. I remembered the tug on my pants and was afraid to look. My thigh was wet with blood.

"Take down your pants, John."

I struggled out of my jeans in the close confines of the little car.

Kris pulled a first-aid kit from the glove box. "It's a good thing to have at the beach," she said. As I prayed, Kris wiped away the blood. "It's a through-and-through, but you were lucky. Nothing vital was hit." She looked up at me and said, "And before your mind goes into the gutter, I was talking about your femoral artery." She poured hydrogen peroxide on the wound while I nearly pulled the door off its frame. She patched me up with a roll of gauze and adhesive tape. "That'll do until we can get you some stitches."

"Thanks. Do I need to fill out any insurance forms or anything?"

"No, it's all part of my attempt to bring universal health care to the poor." Kris's face was close to mine and I could see the party in the street reflected in her eyes. We were attracting far too much attention. Soon pimps, drug dealers, prostitutes, and thieves would be circling the car, smelling blood. Or worse, we would attract the interest of the police, wondering if the gringo tourists were perhaps lost, or perhaps they weren't, and perhaps they should be questioned and searched and taken in.

I handed Kris the .45. "Do you know how to use that?"

"I'm IPSC qualified, John."

"What the hell's that?"

"It means I know how to use this."

"I think maybe it's time to go," Marilyn said.

"Right, right. Go and I'll catch up to you at the bar."

I walked into the open-air wine shop, already doing brisk business on the last night of the year. Less than two hours to midnight and some people were into buzz maintenance while still more had said fuck it sometime around six and were into a full-bore, hell-raising, puke-inducing drunk.

When my turn came, the Asian man waited behind the counter, in no hurry, going noplace, and stared at me. I didn't know what to say, so I said, "Tu sabe Phil Ramirez?"

"¿Qué?"

This was going nowhere. "Yo quiero un hombre con el perro aquí." I pointed to the inside of my elbow where Phil had his canine tattoo. "Tu sabe?" This was the best I could do with my vocabulary limited to food, firearms, and sexual activity, three things I didn't think would get me far in the conversation.

"¿Qué?" he said, then smiled. "Quieres vino? Abrio y frío?" he said, offering me wine.

"No! No vino." The man looked puzzled. I thought I'd try another name. "¿Tu sabe Choppo?"

"¿Choppo?" That got his attention. He looked left and right then he leaned over the counter and said, "Twenty dollars."

I handed him the money and he disappeared into the back. When he came out he said, "You wait out there."

I went back to the street. Ten minutes went by, and there

among the drunken yahoos, I saw them. They stood out like nuns on the neon sidewalk crowded with whores, drunken gringos, pick-pockets, coke dealers, and teenage thugs. They were two hard, sober men in white shirts and shiny black cop shoes. They were on opposite sides of the street but both were looking straight at me and coming on fast. I turned and saw two more heading from the other end of the street. Somehow I knew they weren't coming for the wine.

The Asian man behind the counter had disappeared into the back of his shop. There was no Phil, no Marilyn, no Kris with her blackjack to get my ass out of trouble this time. There was only the guy who looks back at me from the mirror every morning and, lately, he hadn't been looking too good.

In times like these, a man takes stock. He looks at the obsta-cles in front of him and is forced to honestly evaluate the skills he's been blessed with. In that moment, he either finds these skills lacking, or he finds a way to incorporate his slim talents to his advantage.

So I listened. Aside from the very practical talent of making al-lies in a crisis, I had also been born with a good ear. I tried to pick out from the neighborhood's noise the sound of my salvation. And I heard it: the simple melody, the single-finger tune, the one song that everyone who's ever been within an arm's reach of a piano key-board can play—the innocent sound of "Heart and Soul." It was coming from a bar across the street. I ran through the traffic still not sure what I was going to do, but near a piano was as good a place to be as any.

The bar was small, dark, and crowded with men just in with the USS *Endurance*. They were drinking and laughing and throwing bottles. Someone would shout "Incoming!" and the glass would shatter above the piano player's head. It had no noticeable effect on his rhythm or ability.

He was a big man, holding his head up and playing the melody with one finger. I went to the bar, bought two Balboas and carried them over to the piano.

The piano player had a tattoo of an eagle, globe, and anchor on his right hand. He was a Marine. And so were his friends.

Bars catering to servicemen are strictly segregated. Squids drink with squids, grunts drink with grunts, and marines drink with marines. Anyone else is made to feel brutally unwelcome, and this bar was, at least for the evening, wall-to-wall jarhead.

"Semper fi," I said, and sat next to the leatherneck, who was still plunking out "Heart and Soul" with his index finger. I handed him a beer.

"Semper fi, Marine," he said. He looked very sad and very drunk.

"Incoming!"

I ducked and a bottle shattered against the wall, showering us in glass. Mr. Heart and Soul didn't blink. Casually, I started playing the left-hand harmony. He looked over at me and smiled. "Hey, man, that sounds like fucking A-okay, you know?"

"Thanks," I said, and watched the door. Three of the white-shirted men came in and looked around. One of them saw me and pointed. They started to wade through the drunken Marines.

I made a suggestion. "Hey, partner, you mind if we play something different?"

"It's the only song I know," he said.

"You could sing!"

"I don't know any songs," he said sadly.

"You know this one." I played a few introductory chords and the bar went silent.

"To the corps!" I yelled.

"Fuck the corps!" they yelled back. Thank God, a cooperative audience. My experience had taught me to play to the crowd. They want Gershwin, give 'em Gershwin. They want Bach, give 'em Bach. This crowd cried out for "The Marines' Hymn" and I gave it to them.

"'From the halls of Montezu-u-ma,'" I sang, and one by one, the men stood and sang with me. "'To the shores of Trip-o-li.'" The bar rang with drunken men in full-throated song. The white-shirted Latinos in shiny black shoes pushed their way toward the piano.

"'We will fight our country's ba-a-ttles,'" we North Americans sang together. The men in white shirts were next to me now. One gripped my elbow. "Venga. Come with me," he yelled.

"'On the land, and on the sea.'"

He pulled me away from the piano. The music stopped.

"Hey!" I yelled. "What the fuck you think you're doing?"

The marines stopped singing, confused, and stared at the reason why their music had been interrupted. They didn't like this. Like the fish in the lagoon, and the birds in the sky, they had been together so long they had come to think with a single, collective mind.

"Hey!" I said again. The room was quiet. The Marines looked at the white-shirted men and the men looked nervous.

My piano-playing partner grabbed one man's shirt. "Why don't you hike your little brown hoochie ass down the fuckin' *calle,* huh, Pancho?"

"We are Colombian officers and you will remove your hand from my apparel," the man said, all puffed up.

My piano partner dropped his hand.

"Oh, excuse me," he said. "I thought you were Panamanian. I hate Panamanians. In fact, the only thing I hate more than Panamanians is fucking officers." The punch came from south of the border and caught the Colombian square on the chin. As he crumpled to the floor, the other two officers froze.

I raised my fist in the air and yelled, "These guys think they can whip the U.S. Marines!"

The Marines looked shocked, then angry, then truly, truly happy. One of the men pulled a gun and the entire room fell on him before the barrel could clear his trousers. I looked for a way out.

I have to say, the two conscious Colombians held their own. I saw a couple of Marines fall as I crawled on all fours across the floor. I edged along the wall, trying to avoid the broken glass. A chair splintered over my head. A man came down hard in front of me and I had to crawl over him. I found the door and hit the sidewalk. There was the other white-shirt waiting for me. He grabbed me by the arm.

That's when La Guardia Nacional, the police force that's always there when you need them but especially when you don't, pulled up in the Black Maria. The first patrolman hollered, "¡Alto!" and cracked the white-shirt with his baton. I put my hands up. "Lo siento," I yelled. "I'm sorry." It was the best I could do.

They threw me into the back of the wagon and I was soon joined by the Marines, who were joined by the four Colombian officers. They were pretty ragged, but that didn't stop the Marines from continuing to beat them all the way to the Modello, the Panama City jail. You would have thought their arms would get tired, but then, you probably haven't been drinking with Marines. I recommend it, at least once.

CHAPTER TWENTY-SEVEN

The Panamanian government, as a whole, works with the same expediency as a Stateside DMV. But inside the Modello, criminals are processed like cattle in a slaughterhouse. The beaten Colombians were taken to the clinic to reflect on the awesome power of music and the Corps.

Those of us who could walk were herded down a dark hallway and thrown into El Tanque de Noche, the Night Tank. It was a large cell, thirty by thirty feet, with bars on two sides and cold stone walls along the other two. In this room was the human debris the La Guardia swept off the streets after dark. On New Year's Eve, this cell would soon be SRO with murderers, rapists, pickpockets, underage prostitutes, drug dealers, and foreign civilians caught in the wrong place at the wrong time, usually with their peckers exposed.

Marilyn had told me a story about two Italian sailors, whose hair length had been considered a misdemeanor by the police, snatched off the street, given a more appropriate buzz cut, and escorted back to their ship in an ambulance. A minor international incident followed when the captain of the Italian liner, in high Italian umbrage, refused to allow any Panamanian officials on board. This humiliated the dictator, Omar Torrijos, who was scheduled to ride through the Canal on the luxury liner as a gesture of Panamanian-Italian friendship.

Not one to take insult lightly, General Torrijos impounded the ship until a substantial amount of cash changed hands and public apologies were issued by the Italian government. The people of El Chorillo cheered their hero in a parade that broke out into a riot that killed three Panamanian students. In Panama, it did not take much for events to spin out of control, and when they did, someone, usually a Panamanian, ended up dead.

But in the Modello, things were always in control, even in the Night Tank. Only visible bottles and guns were confiscated, so the men and women had money, cigarettes, drugs, and weapons, the essentials of modern urban life. But even with temptations and opportunities, there were few problems as the residents fell into a workable social contract: All property was communal. If you were big, you got what you wanted. If you were small, you didn't.

All I wanted was out. Not that the simple life of the Night Tank wasn't appealing, and I did need rest, but I had pressing obligations. My watch was gone, but I could tell we were approaching midnight by the increasing levels of intoxication of the new prisoners.

Another American was brought in and he sat next to me. He was a mycologist, he said, traveling throughout Latin America studying the use of psychedelic fungi in indigenous religious ceremonies. His name was Eric. "I've been in graduate school for eight years," he told me. "The best thing I learned was how to write a grant."

"You mean the government pays you to get high with the Indians?"

"Yeah. What do you do?"

"I play piano. Right now I'm studying the blues."

He laughed. "A philosopher."

"Jail does that to you."

Eric dug into his brown Boy Scout pack and pulled out a plastic bag filled with wrinkled, knotty-looking things the size of my thumb. He popped one into his mouth and swallowed. "You want one?"

"No, thanks."

"Hey, it takes your head places where your body can't go."

Eric and I sat for a while watching the other inmates settle in for the night. People curled up on the stone floor and huddled together for warmth.

"This whole part of the world's gotten real scary," said Eric. "Especially Colombia and southern Panama. Before, almost no one in Darien had guns, and now it's like everyone's got one. I try to tell the *campesinos* that nonviolent resistance is the way to go, like Gandhi and Dr. King, but they get their hands on a machine gun and they want to use it. Can't really blame 'em, I guess, considering how long they've been getting fucked over."

"You've seen the people in Darien with machine guns?"

"Nasty-looking things."

Eric was starting to get a faraway look in his eye. He'd be over the rainbow soon.

"Where'd you see these guns? What'd they look like?"

"Geez, I don't know. But I've seen pictures of them. Seems like whenever there's something on TV about war in the third world you see them. Usually being carried by kids."

"You mean AK-47s?"

Eric shrugged. "I don't know. That's not really my thing, you know?"

"Where'd the guns come from, they say?"

"The Indians say they fall from the sky." Eric smiled, already in a more peaceful place. "I heard they're coming in from Cuba."

"Could be."

"Indians say they come from 'the Lamb.'"

"How many of these mushrooms do you have to eat before you see the Lamb?"

Eric laughed again. Laughter was coming easier now than before. "No, no, it's not like that. This is a real guy. Funny, though."

"What's funny?"

"The Indians call him by a French name."

"The Lamb?"

"Yeah. They call him 'Mouton.' That's French for 'lamb.' Strange, huh?"

"No. I don't think it's strange at all."

"Hey, man, you ever really look at your knuckle? See all those creases." He broke into a wide grin. "Like pleated pants."

I left Eric staring at his fingers, his pupils big enough to suck in the world, his head high enough to consider the universe of an atom.

Most of the other prisoners were sleeping. In a far corner, a Marine was negotiating a trade with one of the prostitutes. Eric was passing boundaries without a visa, and I was wondering about Mouton, or Morton, however you said it, arming the rebellious underclass with crates of AKs and making sure Fidel got the credit, if not the cash.

I learned how government works from my time in Washington and it's really quite simple. If you had a job, you worked to make that job bigger. That was your job. So, if Morton's job was to fight terrorism, it would be a smart career move to make sure there were plenty of terrorists to fight. Arming them with Chinese weapons and making it look as though the Canal were in deep shit would certainly make his job secure.

But Morton's real genius was in getting somebody else to pay for the arms that would go to the revolutionaries. And with the DEA, CIA, NSC, NSA, and other USA acronyms willing to deal with every scummy thug on earth before they would walk across the hall and share intel with one another, Morton could play one group off the other and retire early with whatever cash he'd stashed away in the Caymans.

Deep in chasing these thoughts to ground, I didn't see we had visitors until a guard poked me with a rifle.

"That's him, Officer. That's my husband." In the darkness of the corridor I saw Kris pointing her finger at me and shaking her head. "How can you get involved in a bar fight? And why weren't you in the hotel? I swear, I take my eyes off you for a minute and you end up in prison." She looked at the La Guardia officer. "And a very nice prison it is, I'm sure." The officer looked confused at first, then he looked at me and shrugged. "Mujer?"

"Sí," I said. "My wife."

"Lo siento," he said quietly, obviously a man with his own mujer troubles.

He held a finger to his lips for silence, unlocked the door, and I followed him down the dark corridor, Kris at my side.

"What am I supposed to tell my parents?" Kris said. "And Billy and little Susie. I'm sorry, kids, but your daddy can't come to your high school graduation. He's locked up in a foreign prison for the rest of his life. Honestly, sometimes I think you mean to cause this family grief and upset, that it's your purpose in life."

And on she went until the officer led us through several unlocked doors and into an open courtyard. "Ssssh," he hissed. We walked along the outside wall until we came upon a small barred gate set into the stone. The guard opened the gate and turned his back. Kris and I slid through the opening and strolled casually down an alley. I expected someone to stop us but we joined the people on the street without any alarms going off or angry gendarmes taking target practice at the fleeing gringos.

The sidewalks were in full party mode, with half-naked dancing, open bottles passed from stranger to stranger, and music, everywhere music, accented by fireworks that made me jump.

"How'd you know where to find me?"

"Phil."

"How did you find him? Where is he? Is Marilyn all right?"

"I don't know how he found us. He just showed up at the bar and took us to Choppo's. Yes, Marilyn is safe."

"Okay, okay. Just keep moving."

"I'm so tired I can hardly walk."

I put my arm around Kris's waist and said, "Wherever we collapse, at least we collapse together."

"Marilyn warned me you were a romantic."

"You two had a long talk about me, huh?"

"No, we soon moved on to more interesting things, like getting our legs waxed."

"How is she?"

"About the same as the rest of us. Scared and tired. But she's safe in bed at Choppo's house."

"What time is it?"

"Almost midnight."

As she said that, a church clock began to strike twelve. Sirens howled like dogs in the distance. Music stopped and the entire city waited breathless until the final peal. When it struck, people cheered. They kissed strangers and danced with their wives. Bands tore into happy, sweating songs of celebration. Bells all over the city rang in the new year.

"Happy New Year," Kris said.

I kissed her there in the jumping crowd. I kissed her and felt as though the earth had held still for a moment, long enough for us to enjoy this eye in the hurricane that was about to strike.

Then we heard gunshots and explosions.

"I failed," I said. "It's happening. I couldn't stop it."

Kris held both my hands in hers, as if we were praying. "But you did," she said. "Phil got the files to Lauren and Lauren called your friend in Washington. He's on his way here. Those are fireworks being fired out over the bay, John, it's part of the celebration. No one is trying to take over the Canal, at least not tonight."

"Did the police arrest the people in the cells?"

"I don't know, John, but look up."

I did and saw a burst of red, followed by a boom that rocked the asphalt.

Kris kissed me again and said, "Everything you do is all right by me, John Harper."

I pulled Kris into the doorway of a locksmith's shop where I could kiss her again, away from the crowds. When we broke apart, Kris saw a black and puckered shrunken head mounted in the window, under a bell jar.

She held on to my neck and looked at my face, as painful as that must have been for her, and smiled. "Is that the thing for locksmiths, John? Are shrunken heads the standard, I mean, if you're really good, do you display two heads?"

"Don't ask me, I'm new here."

A long, open car slid quietly down the street toward us. Its headlights were off. Revelers crossed the street in front of its grill, but didn't slow its approach. I pulled Kris closer into the doorway. "Get ready to run," I said.

Kris saw him, too. "I should have known better. I was having fun."

We began to walk, the car following us, down toward a central square where we might find some safety in the crowd. As we walked faster, the car rolled faster. As we came to an intersection, the car picked up a burst of speed, cut us off at the corner, and as it drifted past, Phil hollered, "Need a lift?"

Kris and I ran alongside, and I yelled, "Stop!"

"I can't. My brakes are fucked. Jump in."

So we did. When we hit the seat, Phil hit the accelerator and off we went. At the corner we ran a red light and forced a taxi up onto the sidewalk.

"I wish this thing had a standard transmission," Phil said. One-handed, he wheeled around a bus. "Hey, how'd you like the Modello?"

"Two stars."

The Caddy coasted through a stop sign, barely squeezing between two trucks and a group of tourists. From their curses, I would guess German tourists. We started up an incline, and as the Cadillac slowed to a stop, Phil nosed over to the curb and threw the transmission into park. "Get out and look under the car."

"What am I looking for?"

"Brake fluid."

"I'll look." Kris jumped out of the car and got on her hands and knees, looking under the chassis.

"What do you know about cars?"

"I own a Volkswagen Bug," she said. "An old one."

"Good. So look for a copper line. I'm pumping the pedal. See anything?"

"Yeah." Kris sniffed her fingers. "It's brake fluid."

"That's what I thought. Come on, get back in."

Kris jumped back into the car and wiped her hands on her pants.

"We're not going to drive this thing, are we?" I asked, hoping the answer would be no, but knowing the answer would be yes.

"Too far to walk."

Phil floored the Caddy and burned rubber toward Choppo's bay-side mansion. We accelerated and slowed and took turns too fast through residential neighborhoods. Phil ran up on the sidewalk to miss an oncoming bus, jerked back onto the street and sideswiped a light post.

"I told Choppo not to trust me with his car," Phil said. Kris and I looked out over the bright bay reflecting a million lights and a show of fireworks that jumped up into the shallow sky.

The Caddy went up onto the sidewalk again, between the palm trees and the walls of the old mansions, took out a few thousand dollars' worth of landscaping, and came to a stop beside Choppo's gate.

The chrome and black leather living room never looked more like home. Choppo greeted us at the door with cognac and a cloud of reefer smoke and hugged me like a son, and hugged Kris for a considerably longer time. "Happy New Year to you, my heroes. Heroes of Panama!" he shouted and raised his glass.

The cognac smoldered pleasantly in the empty bowl of my stomach.

Lauren came into the room, kissed each of us on the cheek.

The living room was strewn with Kelly's files. A laptop sat on the coffee table next to one cordless and two landline phones. There were half-full cups of black coffee, an overflowing ashtray as big as a hubcap, and lined paper filled with scribbled notes in three different hands. Phil, Choppo, and Lauren had done a lot of work in a few hours, going through files and working their contacts in and out of three different governments.

Lauren led us to the sofa and I collapsed. Kris sat next to me but it wasn't long before she had her shoes off, her feet curled up under her, her head on my chest. "I am so tired," she said.

"How thoughtless," Lauren said. "Let me show you where to sleep. When you awake you will eat and we will celebrate."

"Thank you," Kris said. She pulled on my hand and said, "Come with me."

"I'll be up in a minute," I said.

When Lauren and Kris were out of the room I asked, "Does anyone know where Kelly is?"

Phil shook his head and Choppo looked away.

"I don't like it."

"There is nothing he can do," Choppo said. "He has no friends. He killed them all, every one."

I looked from Choppo to Phil for an answer.

"All of the men who were supposed to be in the sleeper cells, all of the names on the CD you got from your friend on the yacht; there were nearly three hundred of them," Phil said.

"They were murdered within a week of their training at La Boca," Choppo said.

"Murdered? But how? Didn't anyone notice? How can three hundred men just disappear?"

"Because they were expected to disappear, my friend," Choppo said. "They had taken new identities, new occupations, everything. They were invisible when they left La Boca, and how hard is it for an invisible man to disappear?"

"So the coup was supposed to fail."

"It was never supposed to have happened."

"I can't believe the Colonel knew about this."

"The Colonel believed the U.S. would rush back in to take over the Canal, and the zone, just like the good old days."

"But that still leaves the money men, the Boca guests. Where are they?"

Phil rubbed his face with both hands. "We don't know yet, but there are reports—"

"Unconfirmed," Choppo said.

"—of a downed helicopter."

I didn't think I had a drop left in my body, but at the thought of the entire crew crashing into the jungle, a spike of adrenaline zipped up my spine. "A Black Hawk or a Huey?"

"We don't know."

I nearly jumped up, but my leg wouldn't cooperate. "You warned them, right?"

Phil said, "Yeah, I warned them about an ambush. I didn't think the bastards would shoot the helicopter down."

"They shot it down?" Now I was on my feet. "Why didn't you say that? Do we have rescue teams in the air?"

"Sit down before you hurt yourself, Harp." Phil wasn't taking the news any better than I was; he'd just had more time to turn it over and get used to the jagged edge.

"We don't know what happened. We don't even know if it was the Huey or not. It could have been the Bell, we don't know, so don't get yourself all cranked up, Harp. We did the best we could."

"I should have thought about them shooting down the Huey when we found those Stingers. Goddammit!" It was my fault. If those boys went home in a box it was because I hadn't thought it through. "What about the money? Where's the money?"

Phil glanced at me, just a shift of his eyes. No other muscle moved and yet Choppo caught whatever it was, a spike in the karmic current, a change in the magnetic flux, as it blew across his radar.

"You mean the euros? They're right here," Phil said, and pushed the metal strongbox with the toe of his boot.

I tried to cover, but Choppo knew something wasn't right. "Five million isn't much money when you consider he killed over three hundred people to get it."

Choppo shrugged. "More people have been killed for less money."

I changed the subject, but Choppo still looked at us both with bloodshot eyes and knew he wasn't being invited to share all of the pie, just the pie that was in this room. "Kelly has a partner," I said. "A man named Morton."

"We expect he's dead, too," Choppo said. He stretched his fingers wide like a net and said, "Mr. Kelly is eliminating everyone. He has no interest in partners." Choppo closed a fist and said, "He didn't think to take care of those who helped him, and that, my friend, is what will bring him down. What is it Bob Dylan says? 'When you live outside the law you must be honest'?"

I put my elbows on my knees and hung my head. The throbbing bruises were almost a relief compared to the sick feeling I had gnawing away at my stomach. When I thought of all the people who had been murdered, I felt nauseated. And for what? Not justice for what Colombians considered a one-hundred-year-old wrong. Not the misguided patriotism of the Colonel, and his bloody attempt at attracting Washington's attention. It was all about money, and more money than Kelly could spend in a lifetime. I tried to do the math, wondering just how much money each human life was worth, but I was too tired to add past double digits.

"Where's the file of the families in Colombia?" I wanted to take that to Smith myself. "Smith'll make sure that the proper authorities are informed."

Choppo handed me a manila folder. "Take it. You have earned it. And I want you to take this." He threw one of the bound packs of euros, more than half a million dollars, on the coffee table.

I stared at it for a long time. I thought of the house I could buy for my father, and the new life I could buy for Kris, and if she'd have me, for myself, and I said, "No, I'd have bad dreams, Choppo."

Choppo seemed relieved, but not satisfied.

Lauren joined us. "That makes two women you've brought here for safety, Mr. Harper. Can we expect any more?"

I shrugged and said, "It's the life of a musician."

She pointed at my pant leg, stiff with blood. "Should we look at that?"

Phil jumped up. "Christ, I didn't even see that."

"Blinded by the money, huh, amigo," Choppo said.

"Helizondo shot me," I said. "It's okay. Kris patched me up."

Lauren shook her head. "No. Take off your pants. Choppo, get the first-aid and some towels."

For the second time that night, I struggled out of my jeans. "Better bring hot water, too, Choppo."

She unrolled the gauze and said, "This doesn't look good."

"Just what every patient wants to hear."

"The bullet went into the flesh of your thigh in the front, and out the back, causing two wounds, both needing stitches. And I'll have to clean inside the wound." She looked up at me and I could see in her eyes that this procedure would be highly unpleasant for both of us.

"I have some Valium upstairs," she said to Choppo. "And those antibiotics. Get them. Mr. Ramirez, if you would be kind enough to get the cocaine out of that drawer. And bring me that bottle of vodka."

"Is that for me or you?" I said, and laughed. I was the only one.

"I'm drinking the vodka," Lauren said. "The coke is for the wound. You do what you must."

Choppo returned with the Valium. I took three and washed them down with a tumbler of Grey Goose. Lauren knelt between my thighs, in what would ordinarily be an arousing situation, but not when this beautiful woman was concentrating on two bloody holes in my leg. She cleaned the wounds with expensive vodka and sprinkled the cocaine liberally around my thigh.

Choppo, watching over Lauren's shoulder, tsked and said, "Such a waste."

When she folded a piece of gauze into the jaws of a hemostat and soaked both in a bowl of peroxide, I looked away. Phil stood over me. I gripped both of his hands and he said, "Hang on." When Lauren plunged the gauze into the bullet hole, my breath left me and I squeezed as hard as I could. I began to sweat. It seemed to take hours for her to work the gauze around the inside of the wound, but I knew it was only a few seconds. Finally, she was done and I let my muscles relax. Out of the corner of my eye I watched Lauren thread a sewing needle, and I looked up at Phil and said, "Don't let her cross-stitch a flower on my johnson."

"We'll keep it manly. Maybe an eagle," he said.

I didn't look back until she was pulling the last suture through. My jaw ached.

"Help him up to bed," she told Phil and Choppo. "He'll be a little wobbly for a while."

Kris was in the shower when they helped me into the bedroom. Unlike the living room, this room had been spared the Rat Pack decor. Oriental rugs softened the polished hardwood, the plaster walls were decorated with art that was both local and good, and the woodwork had the patina of decades-old varnish. The four-poster bed called to me. Phil and Choppo laid me on the mattress. My body, from my eyes down to my toes, was just one big throb of pain. Now that I'd stopped running I wanted to sleep away the new year.

I heard Kris come out of the bathroom. She was wrapped in a towel, and carried with her the nicest aroma of steam, soap, shampoo, and clean skin.

Phil said, "He's all yours," and left, closing the door behind him.

We were alone. She lay down next to me, on her stomach, and traced my bottom lip with her index finger. "You smell like a wet dog," she said.

"Maybe I should take a bath."

"Can you?"

"Not by myself."

Kris started the water and then helped me take off my shirt, socks, and underwear. Naked, my arm around her shoulder, I limped into the bathroom and slowly settled into the shallow water, my wounded leg propped up on the rim of the tub.

Kris started with my face, then lathered up my hair and rinsed it clean, scrubbed my neck and my stomach. She had me lean forward so she could wash my back, and it felt so good I never wanted her to stop. She washed my feet and ankles, my calves, and worked her way up my thighs. Then she washed my tender mercies, the soap, warm water, and her grip bringing one of my few unwounded parts to attention, just to show its gratitude.

"What's this, John, a scar?"

"Yeah, I was bit by a dog when I was little. Remind me to tell you a better story when I'm conscious."

"I'm surprised I didn't notice it before. It's kind of cute, like a little grin."

"That's because you make him so happy." Fueled by the vodka and Valium I began singing "All of Me."

Kris helped me out of the tub, dried me off, led me to bed and eased me onto my back. "Lauren found some clean clothes for us," she said. "They're right here."

Kris dropped her towel, climbed up next to me, her face against my shoulder, and said, "John?"

"Yes, Kris."

"Tell me everything's going to be all right."

"Everything's going to be all right," I said, and although I'd been kicked from sea to shining sea and didn't believe it myself, not for a second, just saying the words made me feel a little better. A little.

CHAPTER TWENTY-EIGHT

The fireworks crackled in my sleep, followed by the boom of cannon. I opened my eyes and saw Kris pulling on her pants.

"John, get up!"

I started to ask why when I heard the answer. Men were in the house. There were gunshots and shouts. There were boots on the stairs.

"Let's go," Kris said.

Fear fried off all of the remaining alcohol and Valium. I was moving. "You still have the pistol?"

Kris tossed it on the bed. I scooped it up and checked the magazine. "Go," I said. "I'll be right behind you." I racked a round, stepped into the corridor, and pointed the .45 at the top of the stairs. When I saw the first head come around the corner I fired three times. When it came around again I emptied the magazine.

There's something about a .45 and the noise it makes, and the brick-sized bullets it fires, and the fist-sized holes it makes in the masonry, that causes a man to rethink his intentions.

I'd bought us a sliver of breathing room and used it to toss a pair of pants out of the window and climb, as naked as a housewife's backdoor man, down the ivy that clung to the granite wall. Kris was on the lawn. The bay beyond was lit with ships of all kinds going about their peaceful post–New Year's business.

I joined Kris in the darkness of a feathery mimosa and pulled on the clean pants. I had no shirt, no shoes, and couldn't expect service in any convenience store in the country, but at least I wouldn't get arrested. Not for airing my indecency, anyway.

"What now?" Kris said.

I pointed to the wall that separated Choppo's yard from his neighbor's. Inside the house we heard more gunshots and saw the muzzle flashes light up windows as if the house were suddenly full of Hollywood paparazzi.

"Come on, we'll work our way around the front."

"And do what?" Kris said.

"I don't know."

Kris sprinted toward the far wall and I followed, as fast as I could gimp on one good leg. Behind us the French doors burst open. A man shouted for us to stop. Kris made the wall, was up and over, and then it was my turn. I placed my foot on the wall, my hands at the top, but my leg collapsed under me, sending me sprawling on the wet grass. Bullets ripped chunks of stone from the wall and showered me with sand and rock.

Kris came back over the wall and helped me up. The shooter was running toward us. Kris made a stirrup with her hands and hoisted me over the wall and then followed me, the man hard on her heels. I waited. As Kris came up and over, then down onto the grass, her pursuer's head came over the wall. I cracked him with a stone I'd picked up in the garden. The inscription on the stone read PAZ. The man, peaced out, fell back into Choppo's yard.

"Let's go." I grabbed Kris's hand and we ran across the neighbor's lawn, over a gate and out into the dimly lit street. Lights blinked on all across the neighborhood but no one was foolish enough to come outside. Panama City had seen far too much violence for anyone not to know gunfire, even on New Year's Eve, when they heard it.

We ran across the street toward the water, crouched behind a car and watched the front of Choppo's house forty meters away. We could look through the gate and see a sedan, its four doors open, parked by the fountain. A pickup truck, its bed topped with a canvas cover, was parked across the entrance to the driveway.

We watched a man drag Choppo out onto the front lawn and

force him to his knees. The driver of the truck got out and held an assault rifle on him.

When the men went back into the house, I heard Marilyn scream and then I heard gunshots.

Things were quiet until one of the men came out with Phil and Marilyn, both still alive, both of them with their hands cuffed behind them. Phil staggered and one of the men hit him with a rifle butt. I started to get up, but Kris stopped me. The man pushed Phil and Marilyn into the back seat of the sedan, got in, and the car took off, pausing only for the pickup truck to move aside.

Another man came out the front door, in no apparent hurry. We could see only his silhouette against the house lights as he paused and looked out across the bay, as casually as a homeowner taking in the grand view before going to bed. He turned his back to the bay and lit a cigar. His head was enveloped in smoke for a brief moment before the breeze blew it away. Then he strolled across the lawn to where Choppo was on his knees. He said something to him, too low for us to hear. He pulled a pistol from his belt. Without even a breath he shot Choppo and then shot him three more times as he lay in the damp grass. Four shots that made Kris and I jump with each muzzle flash as if the bullets were entering our own bodies, tearing our flesh, pulverizing our bone, ending our lives.

Again, with no hurry, he pulled a satchel out of the truck cab.

"What is that?"

"It's a bomb," I said.

He walked to the front door, pulled a cord that set the satchel smoking, tossed the bag inside and walked out to the truck. Before he got in he hollered into the night, "Harper! You know where to find me. I'll expect you before sunrise."

As the truck pulled away the satchel charge blew out the first-floor windows and the house began to burn.

Kris whispered, "That was my father. I just watched my father kill a man in cold blood."

CHAPTER TWENTY-NINE

I asked Kris if she had her car keys.

Kris shook her head. "They're in the house." By this time, the first floor was ablaze with flames licking the window frames.

"Maybe we could steal a car."

"No," she said. "I know what to do."

She opened the Volkswagen and pulled a screwdriver and a pack of cigarettes out of the glove box.

"I didn't know you smoked."

Kris stopped and stared at me. "Are you going to tell me they're bad for my health, John?"

I shut up and watched as she stripped away the cellophane and paper from the pack, leaving only the foil. In the dim light from the street Kris popped the hood and stuck her head into the engine compartment.

The sirens were getting closer.

A Jaguar, long and sleek, cruised past the house, the flames reflected in the waxed finish. The Jaguar slowed.

"It's Lauren," I said. I stood up and waved. The car raced up beside us and stopped fast.

Lauren said, "Come on. We don't have much time."

"We have to go to La Boca."

"No, there's a safe house." When I didn't move, she said, "Harper, your work is done. You've done more, much more, than anyone expected. Now, get in."

I thought of Marilyn and Phil and how they'd put their lives in danger to help me. I looked at Kris who was kneeling by the rear of her VW. "You go with her," I said to Kris. "I'll take your car."

"And leave you stranded in the street? No way."

"Kris, please, go with Lauren."

Kris took her head out of the back end of the VW and said to Lauren, "Funny, you don't look like Paul Henreid."

"What's she talking about?"

"A movie. *Casablanca*."

Whether Lauren got it or not, she didn't say. But apparently it was enough. She said to Kris, "Can you start that thing?"

Kris said she could. "Good." Lauren handed me a pistol, a .380. "I think you're crazy. Both of you." Lauren let off the brake and said, "I'll tell Smith where he can find you," and took off.

"I think I've got it," Kris said. "Get in and make sure it's not in gear." A second later, the starter motor turned and the engine rattled to life. Kris jumped into the passenger seat and as we pulled away I said, "Where did you learn that?"

"You're not my first boyfriend, John."

"Am I your boyfriend? I like the sound of that."

We crept through the neighborhood with our headlights off. There were lights in every window as Choppo's house brightened the black water of the bay. At one street we pulled to the curb and let police cars and a fire engine fly by, their lights flashing in the trees and their sirens cutting through the peaceful façade of this first morning of a brand-new year.

When we pulled onto the main road, Kris said, "I think I've got a shirt in this beach bag back here."

She reached into the back and helped me slither into a T-shirt. It was as tight as a wet suit and covered the top part of my chest, leaving my navel exposed.

"You look like a Backstreet Boy," Kris said, and laughed, unable, or unwilling, to spare me.

"Is this it? Don't you have a sweatshirt or something in there?"

"Let me look," she said. She pulled out a tropical shirt of flowered rayon. "How's this?"

"Better."

She held the wheel as I peeled off the Backstreet Boy T-shirt and put on the Beach Boy shirt of tropical wonder.

"That's much better," Kris said.

I was once again decent enough to be seen in a certain low society.

"We're going in the back way," Kris said. We crossed the bridge and a few miles in we turned and sped down the single lane that ran through the abandoned leper colony. Once we reached the beach road, the asphalt ended and the little car bucked and rolled in the ruts of washed-out sand. I was driving so fast I was afraid we'd careen off into the brush. I slowed the car and it was as the engine quieted that I heard her sob. I stopped the car and put my hand on her shoulder. I knew this had to come, and when she collapsed against me I held her and sang the first song that came into my head, soft as a lullaby:

> In time the Rockies may tumble,
> Gibraltar may crumble,
> They're only made of clay, but,
> Our love is here to stay.

I let her cry it out as the water sliced up the silver reflections of the quarter moon. The trees and wild places around us filled with creatures mystified by our smells. Eventually, her crying quieted to sniffles, and Kris wiped her face with the backs of her hands, looked up at me again, and said, "I'm sorry about that."

"Don't be."

"I'm okay now."

"You're sure?"

"Yes," she said. "So let's go get them, okay?"

"There was never another thought in my head."

I started the car, this time leaving the headlights off, and we crawled through the jungle, hugging the coast on a road long forgotten by everyone except lovers, surfers, and smugglers.

We parked near the chain-link fence and walked through Kris's gate, keeping to the shadows. My feet found every sharp blade, every thorn, every prickle and sting on the ground. Insects alerted their friends and we became a feast for every six-legged bloodsucking beast with wings. Soon, we were overlooking the hotel compound. We stopped and watched for any light or movement. The hotel was completely dark, but over the rhythmic rush of waves against the sand, I heard something else in the wind.

I pointed to my left and Kris melted into the shadows, a real soldier's daughter. She was gone so quickly I thought maybe she'd been a hallucination.

I listened again for what might have been an animal or what might have been a boot settling into dry leaves. A click, followed by a *tink* of metal, sounds so small they were almost lost in the wind and the whir of insect song.

I'll give him this; Meat knew his craft. He sprang up as if he'd sprouted full-grown from the earth. He aimed a pistol at my head and said, "You know, monkey shit, you really should have shot me when you had the chance." He took the .380 from my hand and tossed it into the jungle.

"But I didn't, Meat. And I don't think you'll shoot me, either."

"Why shouldn't I?"

"Because Kelly wants me alive. That's why he hasn't killed his prisoners."

Meat smiled, and in the moonlight all I could see was teeth in the big shadow of his head. "Maybe, but wait till you see 'em. Hell, I'd rather be dead."

"Where are they?"

"Kelly's got them tied up to a tree in the garden. Now let's go."

"You're going to have to carry me, Meat."

He chuckled, almost too quietly to hear in the breeze.

"It's the only way."

Meat holstered his pistol and said, "Oh, man, I am going to enjoy this." He raised his fists and waded in.

His first two swings went wide, but he caught me in the ribs with a glancing left. I stepped to the side and jabbed him twice in the ear, which only made him mad. He came at me like a linebacker, his arms wide, and I hit him three more times in the stomach. It was like punching a car.

Before he could drop his weight on me, I ducked under his arm and punched him in the kidney.

He turned and stopped. He was still smiling, but he was breathing heavily. I took a step and tried another jab to his throat, but he blocked it. He came in again, as oblivious as a bull to the punches that banged off his forearms. As I flailed away, looking for an opening, he hit me in the chest, knocking the wind out of me and sending me flying backward into the brush. When I tried to stand he hit me again. His fist connected to the side of my head and I was knocked back to the ground in a blast of light. I managed to get my feet under me, but I was having a hard time focusing. There were two of him when one Meat in the world seemed to be plenty. His shape moved to my left and I swung, missing him. He hit me twice in the ribs and I fell to my knees.

"You done?" he said. He was standing over me, his fists up, ready to hit me again if I stood.

I tried to stand anyway, but I saw another flash and I was back on the ground. There was something seriously wrong with the connection between my brain and my extremities because my arms and legs refused to move when I asked them to. But my hearing, outside of a ringing in my ears, was fine. I heard Meat say, "Now you're done."

"I'm done," I said. "Help me up." Meat grabbed my forearm and jerked me to my feet. When he did I took his pistol. But before I could bring it up, he grabbed my hand and squeezed. "Drop it," he said. "Drop it."

It felt as if he were turning every bone in my hand to jelly, which, as a piano player, scared me more than a broken leg. I couldn't pull the trigger. I couldn't let go. All I could do was look into Meat's face and croak, "Look behind you."

Meat's smile spread across his face and he said, "You got some stones, Harper, I gotta admit."

"Really, look behind you."

"Fool me once," he said.

"No, really."

And as Meat grinned, Kris came up behind him and, like a placekicker, planted her foot between his legs.

Meat let go of my hand and went to his knees. Kris hit him with a stick the size of an ax handle and when he didn't go down she hit him again.

Kris looked at Meat lying in the moonlight and said, "I would have shot him."

"I know. You've said that."

"One day you'll listen to me."

CHAPTER THIRTY

Kris and I crept on our hands and knees to the edge of the garden. It was a beautiful spot for torture, filled with jasmine, hibiscus, and wisteria. Even the steady breeze couldn't blow away the blossoms' perfume.

At the far end of the garden was a stand of live oak, thick with branches, and from the horizontal limb of the largest tree, two bodies hung like Billie Holiday's strange fruit and even in the moonlight I could see they had both been beaten without regard.

I started to go for them, to cut them down, but Kris stopped me. She put her finger to my lips and edged along, her hands searching the grass, until she found black wires. She guided my hand to them so that I knew where they were, and what they were. I nodded and we quietly followed them to a pair of Claymore mines, their faces aimed at Phil and Marilyn.

Kris said, "You get them down. I'll disarm these."

"You know how to do that?"

"John, I was taking apart Claymores when you were playing with Legos."

"Okay." I was deep under the cover of gardenia bushes, crawling on my belly, when the garden lights came on, making the whole area as bright as daylight. I was so close to Marilyn that I could have reached out and touched her feet.

"Harper?" Kelly's voice was unconcerned, almost calm. "I know you're here, Harper. Christ, the whole goddamn forest knows you're here. I don't think you're quite cut out for special ops, boy, what do you think?" He paused, waiting for an answer.

I slowly pulled back the pistol's slide and saw there was a bullet in the chamber.

"Come on, Harper, you know that all I want is the money and then you can go. You've put up a hell of a fight and there's no reason why we can't part as respectful enemies. Morton is on his way and he's looking forward to meeting you. He's become quite an admirer of your work, as I have."

I was looking forward to meeting Morton, too, but I wouldn't have considered myself a fan.

"Now come out," Kelly said. "You've got no place to go and I promise I'll help your friends. I'm sure they could use some medical attention."

I knew Kelly was in the only place he could be, behind a hedge cut in a neat ring around a date palm. I could imagine him, the Claymore detonator in his hands, waiting for me to tell him what he wanted to know so he could kill all three of us.

When I didn't answer, he said, "Fine. If that's the way you want to play this out. You can't win, son. I know you can't leave your friends because they'll die if you don't help them."

I couldn't tell if Phil was still alive, but I could see Marilyn, tied by her wrists to the tree, her toes a foot off the ground. Her face was swollen almost beyond recognition and red, solid red, with blood. But she was breathing. I saw a bubble of blood appear at one nostril. It was horrible, but it was encouraging.

Kelly was still talking. "You know what a monkey trap is, don't you, Harper? Well, of course you do. You're the Monkeyman. And you can't let go, can you, boy? You might think you've done something here, but you haven't. You haven't stopped anything because nothing was supposed to happen."

"But I have the money."

I think Kelly was surprised, and it took him a moment. "Yes, Harper. Good. I knew the big Chicano didn't have the money. I knew it. Because if he had, he would have given it to me, that I know. So, now we can talk. You have my money." When I didn't answer he went on. "What do you say we make a deal? Huh? It's almost day-light. Harper, are you listening? I'll split the money with you. That money will buy a lot of whores, son."

I still didn't answer. But in the distance I heard a wrinkle of sound, a brief snatch of something familiar. Kelly heard it, too.

"Hear that? That's the sound of your friends returning."

"You didn't get to kill them like you killed the others," I said. "You failed."

"The night's not done, Harper."

I didn't like the way he said that, with such confidence. "What do you mean? When they land, you're history."

He waited a moment, and I thought he was weighing his op-tions, trying to figure out how to kill me and still get his money be-fore the helicopter touched down. I was wrong.

Kelly said, "When they land, boy, they'll be history. But I'll tell you what. You give me the money and I'll let you save them. How about that? You get to be the big hero."

"You can't kill them all yourself," I said.

The sound of the chopper was constant now, a distant throb, but constant.

"The helipad's wired with enough HE to be heard from Colón to Panama City," Kelly said. "The minute that old Huey sets down, they'll be nothing but chopper parts and a pink mist all over the compound."

"High explosives? You're bluffing."

"Am I?"

The sound of the Huey was louder now and the helicopter would be over the hotel in a few minutes.

"Okay," I said. "I'll tell you where the money is."

"I didn't think you were that smart, Harper. But it's the right thing to do."

From the darkness to my right, Kris said, "And what do I get, Daddy?"

"Kris? Where are you, sweetheart? Why aren't you in Rich-mond?" For the first time, I thought I heard something close to fear in Kelly's voice.

Kris said, "I couldn't leave him, Daddy. I couldn't leave without making things right."

Now there was a real disappointment in Kelly's voice. "Oh, honey. Why would you throw your life away on this nothing, this insect, this musician?"

"Daddy? You know what I want?"

"Tell me, sweetheart."

"I want you to tell me what happened to my mother. Tell me why she left us."

The Huey was a spark in the sky, its running lights on, the quarter moon reflecting off its windscreen.

"What happened was a long time ago, sweetheart, and it doesn't matter now. We have each other, you and me, and we've always had each other, and always will. These boys don't love you the way I do. They can't. They're just after you for sex, you know that, don't you?"

"Tell me about my mother," Kris said.

The Huey's whop was clearly identifiable now, even to civilian ears. It was the rhythm of Vietnam, the beat to a song of heartbreak and loss.

"Your mother was confused, honey. She didn't know what was best. And that's all I'm trying to do here, do what's best. Think of it, Kris. You'll have everything you ever wanted, honey. Now tell Harper to give us our money. Then we can go home, all of us, okay?"

I snicked the safety off Meat's Beretta.

"I heard that, Harper! Don't think you can shoot your way out of this. You're not that good."

He was right, and I knew that better than anyone.

"Throw the gun out here, boy. You can't win this. You've been lucky so far." He laughed, truly amused. "The luckiest son of a bitch I have ever seen in all my life and that is no bullshit. You are one lucky bastard."

"Throw out your gun," I said. "Then I'll throw out mine."

"Is that all you want? Then, fine." A shotgun flew into the middle of the garden, landing near a statue of Pan.

"Throw the other one out, too."

"You're better at this than I expected, Harper." Kelly threw his automatic out of the brush and it landed near the shotgun.

The Huey's lights were near and soon its big insect body would circle in for a landing.

Kelly had given up his guns too quickly. He was counting on the Claymores to kill me.

Phil and Marilyn hung in the tree, blood like enamel capturing light.

"Harper? You still there? Where are you, boy?"

"I'm here."

"You hear me? You hear that chopper?" He sounded desperate, his words pouring out faster as he sensed his window of escape beginning to close. "What if I give you Kris? Whatta you say to that? Huh? You get your friends, and the girl, just like in the movies. All I want is the money. Hell, half the money. There, I'm being completely honest with you, Harper."

"I'm listening."

"Do you love my daughter, Harper?"

"Yes," I said. "I do."

"Kris, what about Harper? Do you love him?"

"Yes, Daddy, I do."

"Then you have my blessings. Give me the money, boy, and I can protect you. Without my help you don't have a chance. The people who paid me that money aren't as forgiving as I am, son, and they have very long arms. You don't know how long. But you have to tell me now. After that Huey lands, it'll be too late."

If I'd known where the money was, and if I'd thought it would really make a difference, I would have given it to him. I knew that. But Phil had taken the money, and even with that cash, I was a dead man.

"Come on, you're running out of time."

The helicopter had begun its descent, the rotors beating their urgent rhythm. I stepped into the glare, counting on Kris to have disarmed the Claymores. Kris walked out and stood next to me. She took my hand.

Kelly came out from his hiding place. The three of us stood there, twenty feet apart. He held up his hand. In it was the detonator. "Now, tell me where the money is, son."

"I can't. I don't know where it is."

"Then I'm really sorry." He put his thumb on the trigger. "Kris," he said, "come here to Daddy."

"No, Daddy. I'm staying with John."

"Is that your choice?"

Kris said it was.

"Have I been that awful a father?"

"You killed her," Kris said. "You murdered her."

"No, no, I didn't," he said. "She ran away."

Kris stood tall, her head high, and it was only the light glistening off her cheeks that told me she was crying. "I know the truth, Daddy. I've always known."

Kris's father sighed and said, "Well, as much as it pains me to leave without that money, I know when to let go."

He clicked the safety off.

"Daddy! Don't do it. I'm begging you not to do this."

The Huey saw us and circled one more time, the wind shaking the palms. We could see faces in the door. They were telling the pilot to land, land now.

"You made your choice, honey," Kelly shouted. "Just like your mother."

"Tell me, Daddy, so I'll know."

"She said she was running away with another man, honey. Now, how could I let that happen? What sort of man would I be?"

"Tell me, Daddy, what sort of man are you now?"

Kelly's smile fell away.

Kris took my arm and we stood there. Waiting.

The Huey began to settle over the treetops, preparing to land.

"You're just like her. Just like your mother," Kelly said. He thumbed the switch on the detonator and as quick as a blink the garden erupted in flame and thunder and Kris's father was washed away in a hard steel rain.

CHAPTER THIRTY-ONE

The Huey's rotors tossed the palms like an incoming hurricane. The whap of its blades beat against my ears.

I said to Kris, "Help me."

She didn't say anything. I looked into her eyes but she didn't see me. I touched her face and said, "Kris, I need you."

She looked at me. Her eyes focused.

"Kris, don't leave me now."

She nodded.

"Can you get them down?"

"I think so," she said.

I touched her cheek and she put her hand over mine. "I have to wave them off." She nodded, and I sprinted toward the helipad. The Huey was at treetop level, its skids fifty feet from the concrete. Ice was in the door, directing the pilot's descent.

Kelly had not been bluffing. A single nylon filament stretched across the concrete pad, attached to detonators on either side. The detonators were rigged to a spring switch that would trigger the explosives when pressure was applied to the wire, or if the wire was cut.

The wind from the chopper blades roared around my ears and blew dirt in my eyes. I could hear Ice hollering but I didn't know if he was yelling at me or the pilot. They were going to land. Blind, unable to think, not knowing if the high explosives would blow from the pressure of the prop wash, I tried to wave them away. The wind tore at my clothes and hair, the noise sucked the air from my lungs, and I could feel the weight of the chopper hovering above me. They hadn't seen me, or they thought I needed help. Either way, they were going to land.

Kris stood twenty feet away, her hair tossing about her face. She looked as if she were walking in her sleep.

I hollered, "Get the shotgun!"

She gaped at me in confusion.

"The gun! Get the gun!"

She ran off. Ice was in the door fifteen feet above my head, telling me to back away. I stood on the concrete and let the wind buffet me like I was so much weightless trash.

Kris ran to me and handed me the shotgun. Ice mouthed "No!" Hamster raised his rifle and aimed at my head.

I lifted the shotgun in two hands, racked a round, and aimed into the sky. "Go away!"

Kris pulled at my arm. "Stop it, they'll shoot you!"

I shrugged her off and aimed the shotgun into the sky again.

Ice shook his head. The wind tore at our clothing. The helicopter's belly hovered over the pad. Hamster held his rifle steady. I watched his finger move to the trigger. I fired once, pumped the action, and fired again.

The helicopter seemed to rock. Hamster leveled the rifle at my head. I stood in the wash and glare of the chopper's lights, not moving from the pad. Tears blurred my vision and I had to wipe them away with the back of my hand.

When I could see again, I watched Ice put his hand on Hamster's rifle. He spoke into his headphones, the rotors changed their pitch, the wind shifted, the oppressive weight of the helicopter tipped and lifted away. Kris stood next to me. The Huey circled us once, high overhead. Kris held my arm and I asked her if Phil and Marilyn were alive.

"Yes," she said. "I got Phil down, but I was afraid to move Marilyn."

I ran back to the garden. Phil was lying on his back. I felt the pulse in his neck and it was strong. Leaving Phil, I climbed up into the tree and untied the rope around Marilyn's wrists. I saw that Kelly had one final surprise. He had run a nylon line from Marilyn's neck to a grenade wedged into a branch above us. I gently removed the grenade, crimped the pin in place, and put it inside my shirt. Safe now, I lowered Marilyn to Kris. Marilyn was limp and I knew she was dead, just by the way she fell across the grass.

The Huey set down in the far parking lot. New helicopters came up over the horizon and began circling the hotel. The sun broke over the treetops and bathed us all in the false promise of a brand-new day.

CHAPTER THIRTY-TWO

The grounds filled with soldiers. A line of cars came speeding up the road from the gate and stopped, disgorging another army of men in civilian clothes, from suits to the white guayabera and black slacks that is the unofficial plainclothes police uniform in Panama. An EMT truck, its lights flashing, stopped and three paramedics got out. Two other men strode toward us. One was Marquez, the other was a bullet-headed North American carrying a small revolver on his hip.

"Holy Mother of God, Harper, what a jumping Jesus jungle fuck this is."

"My friends need help."

Marquez barked an order and in minutes a helicopter landed and the medics loaded Phil and Marilyn inside for a quick flight to the hospital in Panama City. Marilyn was alive, which was the good news. But it was the only good news.

Smith put his arm around Kris. She put her head against him. Smith looked at me and I nodded, yes, I was fine. He helped Kris walk out to the EMT truck.

I sat there alone in the garden and watched as soldiers bent into the bushes and picked up Kris's father, as heavy as only the dead can be, and carried him away. I sat for a long time. The soldiers kept their distance, as if I were bad luck. A bomb squad stood far back from the helipad and debated how best to disarm the explosives. Smith returned to the garden, alone, and sat down next to me. He offered me his flask. I took a drink and I recognized the sweet taste of Maker's Mark bourbon.

I handed the flask back to Smith.

"Kris told me what happened."

I said nothing.

"She turned the Claymores on her father."

"I know."

"Hell, she probably knows more about armaments than both of us put together."

"Be careful what you teach your children, huh, Mr. Smith?"

He smiled, and it was kind, and comforting. "Glad to see you haven't lost your sense of humor."

"Yeah, I'm a funny guy."

"You'd best have that leg looked at."

"I'm fine."

"Your friends are going to be okay. And I think the girl will be all right."

"That's good."

"The government has everything under control."

"I see you haven't lost your sense of humor, either."

Smith handed me a handkerchief and I wiped my face. "We've contacted Kris's grandparents. She'll be going home soon."

"What's going to happen to Marilyn?"

"Marquez promises she'll be taken care of."

"There's another guy named Morton we need to find."

"We caught him coming in the gate. The police have him in custody."

I thought maybe, just maybe, there would be some justice to come after all. "Did I get everything right, sir? I mean, about what happened here?"

"You did good, son. Lauren sent us copies of everything." He had the good grace to pause out of respect. "It looks like Kelly snookered the Colonel and a whole truckload of rich Colombians. The Colombians thought they were getting a country, the Colonel thought he was getting the Canal, but the only ones who were getting anything but screwed were Kelly and this joker Morton."

"What about the yacht?"

"Another fraud," Smith said. "They wanted it to look like the bomb was set for the locks."

"And it got rid of a whole boatload of co-conspirators," I said.

"That, too."

"What about Morton?"

Smith shrugged. "It's hard to say, son."

"What? You mean he might walk away from this?"

"He has friends, Harper, friends who go back to the first Bush administration."

"But he's a murderer."

"Pretty sad situation, isn't it? If it was up to me he wouldn't out-live old man Fidel." Smith sucked on the flask again. "It's a loose end, son. It happens."

Marquez bent down, shook my hand, and thanked me. "The government of Panama will not forget what you did for us."

Smith handed the flask back to me and said, "Take another drink, son, there's something else I have to explain."

"What? Explain what?"

"No one can know about this except for a very select group of people. The Panamanian government isn't crazy about three-hundred men being murdered on their watch. The Colombians certainly don't need any more trouble, and as for our government, they'd rather handle this through back channels. For your own good, of course."

"For my own good, of course."

Smith put his hand on my shoulder. "Things don't always work out like they should."

"Yeah. You can sew that on a fucking sampler."

"Now, son, bitterness won't get you anywhere but drunk. I'm going to take care of you. You can count on that. Hell, I feel kinda responsible for getting you into this in the first place."

"Kinda?"

"But no sense in pointing fingers, you'll just poke someone's eye out. Hell, son, while you were lying around here on the beach, I was up to my keister in pissed-off Arabs."

I gave him my best squint and hoped the heat would set him on fire, but it didn't.

"I've got your new identification papers in my bag. You want to see?"

"No."

"Come on, son." Smith squeezed my shoulder like an old coach with a losing quarterback. "It's the best we could do. John Harper is missing and presumed dead."

"But my father . . ." It made my chest ache to think of my father getting another visit from a man with his hat in his hands.

"I'll go see your dad myself and explain things."

I thought that was good of him until I realized what it meant. "You mean I can't go home?"

"Not home, no, but hell, it's a big country. If you want, I can fix you up with a civilian job someplace. Of course, you'd have to give up the piano."

"What?"

"And with a new name and a new profession, you've got a running start."

"That's all I get? A running start?"

"And if civilian life doesn't work out, you can work for me anytime, anywhere, and that's a promise."

Smith stood up. "Come on. Another chopper's on its way to take us out of this wretched fucking country." He held out his hand. I took it and he helped me up. We walked out of the garden together.

Meat was in cuffs on the veranda. Hamster was in the yard with his hands over his head. They both looked at me once and then looked away. I hoped it was from shame.

Panamanian soldiers stood around the hotel's door and smoked cigarettes. Others were removing the weapons from the basement and loading them into a waiting truck. The bodies were carried out. Eubanks, the Colonel, and the Major's Gorilla, frozen stiff. Even though he'd tried to gut me, I still didn't think he deserved this.

A green government Taurus was parked in front of the hotel. In the back seat was the man Morton, his hands cuffed behind him. He was wearing the collar of a priest. I asked Smith if I could see him. "I just want to look at the son of a bitch," I said.

"Sure, son, you want to spit in the devil's eye, I think you've earned it."

I walked over to the car. The rear window was halfway up. I

leaned in to look at the man who had coauthored so much misery. "Funny, you don't look like a killer," I said.

"And you don't look like a dead man." He shrugged. "But there you are." Morton was so calm it was as if he were being arrested for an overdue library book. "I know who you are," he said, "and you know what I am. I'd say this isn't over."

Then the bastard smiled and something inside me changed.

"There's no place on earth your Mr. Smith can hide you and your Chicano friend. You are, as you soldiers like to say, seriously fucked."

"No, Morton," I said, "I think it's you who's fucked." I took the grenade from my shirt, and enjoyed the frozen shock on Morton's face as he watched me pull the pin. I dropped the grenade into his lap and I counted long enough to capture a quick snapshot of that face, a snapshot I filed away next to those of Mariposa, Cooper, Zorro, and Ren. Then, as he was screaming, I took Smith's suggestion and got a good running start.

CHAPTER THIRTY-THREE

It's the holidays again and I'm playing all the old tunes. Everything but "I'll Be Home for Christmas."

I've kept tabs on Kris. She picked up the piano faster than I would have ever guessed and I had no idea she could sing like that. No idea. The songs she wrote for her first CD are all so smart and warm, and I'm happy that she's doing well. She's even getting her music played on the radio. I read in the *Times* that she moved to North Carolina and I cut the picture out of the Arts and Leisure section. She looks happy in her new home. She looks happy with her new baby.

As for my father, he travels a lot on short notice to tiny, out-of-the-way places. He says that he sees more of me than Mr. Grubner sees of his son, and his boy lives in Cleveland. We still don't have a lot to talk about, but he's not as disappointed in me as he once was.

And Smith still sends me out on assignments, just to keep things interesting.

The first few months after Panama were the hardest. That's when I limped around Europe, playing piano in dives until I got homesick for fresh mango. I found life was easier in the tropics, even though I broke into a sweat every time someone mentioned meat or a man in a white guayabera looked at me twice.

It was summer in Belize and I was playing in one of the hotels out on the cay. I returned to my room about two and found a box someone had shipped to me from Venezuela. Inside the box I found a short note, a photo, and two million dollars in hundred-dollar bills. There was no return address. The note said to use the cash any way I liked. An equal amount had been sent to an intelligent Panamanian woman who had turned a seaside resort into a home for orphaned boys and girls. The photo was of Marilyn surrounded by a dozen skinny little brown children. All of them looked happy to be where they were loved, Marilyn most of all.

I took the money, and took the chance, and bought a bar on a small island with simple rhythms. Cruise ships visit four times a year. Every day it either rains, or it doesn't. Every night I get to drink and play piano.

Last summer I took on a partner, a big guy who just walked in one day, ordered a beer, and never left.

And last week a woman came in drenched from an early evening rain. The place was empty except for me and the toucan.

"You open?" she said.

"Help yourself." I nodded toward the row of bottles.

She poured a glass of Glenlivet, no ice. I finished the song.

"God bless the child who's got his own," she said, and raised her glass.

"Words to live by."

"You're really good. How'd you wash up here?"

"I shot a man in Memphis."

My partner came into the bar with a bucket of oysters he'd won shooting pool with the hotel chef. "You giving away our booze again?"

"She's working it off," I said, "by listening to me play."

"We can't afford that."

"Madam, I'd like to introduce Phil. He's my partner. He's not long on charm but he's very good with money."

She stood up and shook his hand. "It's a pleasure. My name's Kate."

I started a new tune. "And what's your story, Kate?"

"My husband just left me for a receptionist and I'm looking for a job. A life, really, but I'll settle for a job."

I said, "If you can add ice to my drink, we might be able to work something out."

As she filled out her liquid application, Phil held up a padded envelope. "This came for you today."

I figured Smith had sent a new set of faces to memorize. "Just put it on the bar. I'll get to it later."

"It's from North Carolina."

I stopped playing. "Open it."

Phil ripped through the envelope and removed a single CD in a blank case.

"Is there a note?"

Phil looked inside. "Just this. Should I put it on?"

I nodded and held my breath until I heard the first chords. It was just her and the piano. As the last drops of rain blew out into the ocean, her voice filled the bar. The song was "Our Love Is Here to Stay."

Kate said, "That's Kris Kelly. Is this new?"

Phil held up his hand and we let the song finish.

When it was done I said, "She should stick to her own stuff." Phil and Kate pretended not to notice me dab my eyes with the cocktail napkin, and for that I was grateful.

Kate brought my bourbon on the rocks and said, her voice just a whisper in the quiet bar, "My guess is, there's an interesting story in there somewhere."

Phil shucked an oyster and said, "Hey, Harp, I know, why don't you tell her the one about the monkey."

So I did.